AZINCOURT

Agincourt is one of the epic battles of history. Fought by two badly matched armies in atrocious conditions, it resulted in an extraordinary victory, a triumph of the common man over the aristocrat, which has been celebrated ever since.

'If Bernard Cornwell was born to write one book, this is it. No other historical novelist has acquired such a mastery of the minutiae of warfare in centuries past. No one else could hope to take Shakespeare's Henry V, strip it of its rhetoric and tell the unvarnished truth about the Battle of Agincourt'

Daily Telegraph

'Nobody in the world does this stuff better than Cornwell – action set six hundred years ago is as fresh and vital as six days ago, with rough, tough men at war, proving once again that nothing changes – least of all great storytelling'

Lee Child

'His best book yet. No-one understands the experience of the common soldier better than Bernard Cornwell'

Juliet Barker

Bernard Cornwell was born in London, raised in Essex, and now lives mainly in the USA with his wife. In addition to the hugely successful *Sharpe* novels, he is the author of the *Starbuck Chronicles*, the *Warlord* trilogy, the *Grail Quest* series and the *Warrior Chronicles*.

BERNARD CORNWELL

Azincourt

HARPER

Harper
An imprint of HarperCollins*Publishers*
77–85 Fulham Palace Road,
Hammersmith, London W6 8JB

www.harpercollins.co.uk

This paperback edition 2012
1

First published in Great Britain by
HarperCollins*Publishers* 2008

A catalogue record for this book is
available from the British Library

ISBN: 978-0-00-750137-3

Set in Meridien by Palimpsest Book Production Limited,
Grangemouth, Stirlingshire

Printed and bound in Great Britain by
Clays Ltd, St Ives plc

MIX
Paper from
responsible sources
FSC
www.fsc.org
FSC˘ C007454

FSC is a non-profit international organisation established
to promote the responsible management of the world's forests.
Products carrying the FSC label are independently certified
to assure consumers that they come from forests that are managed
to meet the social, economic and ecological needs
of present and future generations.

Find out more about HarperCollins and the environment at
www.harpercollins.co.uk/green

Azincourt
is for my granddaughter,
Esme Cornwell,
with love.

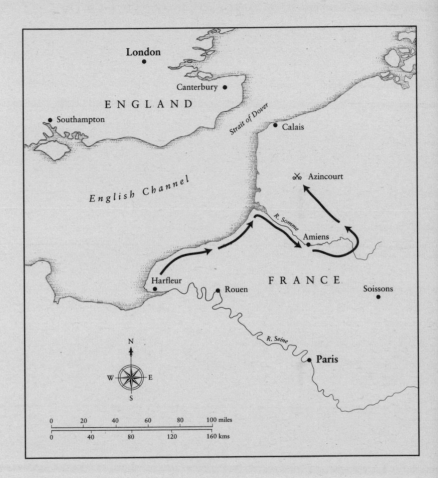

London

Canterbury

ENGLAND

Southampton

Strait of Dover

Calais

English Channel

Azincourt

R. Somme

Amiens

Harfleur

Rouen

FRANCE

Soissons

R. Seine

Paris

N
W   E
S

0   20   40   60   80   100 miles
0   40   80   120   160 kms

Contents

'Agincourt is one of the most instantly and vividly visualized of all epic passages in English history . . . It is a victory of the weak over the strong, of the common soldier over the mounted knight, of resolution over bombast . . . It is also a story of slaughter-yard behaviour and of outright atrocity.'

Sir John Keegan, *The Face of Battle*

'. . . there is a multitude of slain, and a great number of carcasses; and there is none end of their corpses: they stumble upon their corpses.'

Nahum 3.3

Prologue

On a winter's day in 1413, just before Christmas, Nicholas Hook decided to commit murder.

It was a cold day. There had been a hard frost overnight and the midday sun had failed to melt the white from the grass. There was no wind so the whole world was pale, frozen and still when Hook saw Tom Perrill in the sunken lane that led from the high woods to the mill pastures.

Nick Hook, nineteen years old, moved like a ghost. He was a forester and even on a day when the slightest foot-fall could sound like cracking ice he moved silently. Now he went upwind of the sunken lane where Perrill had one of Lord Slayton's draught horses harnessed to the felled trunk of an elm. Perrill was dragging the tree to the mill so he could make new blades for the water wheel. He was alone and that was unusual because Tom Perrill rarely went far from home without his brother or some other companion, and Hook had never seen Tom Perrill this far from the village without his bow slung on his shoulder.

Nick Hook stopped at the edge of the trees in a place where holly bushes hid him. He was one hundred paces from Perrill, who was cursing because the ruts in the lane had frozen hard and the great elm trunk kept catching on the jagged track and the horse was baulking. Perrill had beaten the animal bloody, but the whipping had not helped and Perrill was just standing now, switch in hand, swearing at the unhappy beast.

Hook took an arrow from the bag hanging at his side and checked that it was the one he wanted. It was a broadhead, deep-tanged, with a blade designed to cut through a deer's body, an arrow made to slash open arteries so that the animal would bleed to death if Hook missed the heart, though he rarely did miss. At eighteen years old he had won the three counties' match, beating older archers famed across half England, and at one hundred paces he never missed.

He laid the arrow across the bowstave. He was watching Perrill because he did not need to look at the arrow or the bow. His left thumb trapped the arrow, and his right hand slightly stretched the cord so that it engaged in the small horn-reinforced nock at the arrow's feathered end. He raised the stave, his eyes still on the miller's eldest son.

He hauled back the cord with no apparent effort though most men who were not archers could not have pulled the bowstring halfway. He drew the cord all the way to his right ear.

Perrill had turned to stare across the mill pastures where the river was a winding streak of silver under the winter-bare willows. He was wearing boots, breeches, a jerkin and a deerskin coat and he had no idea that his death was a few heartbeats away.

Hook released. It was a smooth release, the hemp cord leaving his thumb and two fingers without so much as a tremor.

The arrow flew true. Hook tracked the grey feathers, watching as the steel-tipped tapered ash shaft sped towards Perrill's heart. He had sharpened the wedge-shaped blade and knew it would slice through deerskin as if it were cobweb.

Nick Hook hated the Perrill family, just as the Perrills hated the Hooks. The feud went back two generations, to when Tom Perrill's grandfather had killed Hook's grandfather in the village tavern by stabbing him through the eye with a poker. The old Lord Slayton had declared it a fair fight and refused to punish the miller, and ever since the Hooks had tried to get revenge.

They never had. Hook's father had been kicked to death in the yearly football match and no one had ever discovered who had killed him, though everyone knew it must have been the Perrills. The ball had been kicked into the rushes beyond the manor orchard and a dozen men had chased after it, but only eleven came out. The new Lord Slayton had laughed at the idea of calling the death murder. 'If you hanged a man for killing in a game of football,' he had said, 'then you'll hang half England!'

Hook's father had been a shepherd. He left a pregnant widow and two sons, and the widow died within two months of her husband's death as she gave birth to a stillborn daughter. She died on the feast day of Saint Nicholas, which was Nick Hook's thirteenth birthday, and his grandmother said the coincidence proved that Nick was cursed. She tried to lift the curse with her own magic. She stabbed him with an arrow, driving the point deep into his thigh, then told him to kill a deer with the arrow and the curse would go away. Hook had poached one of Lord Slayton's hinds, killing it with the bloodstained arrow, but the curse had remained. The Perrills lived and the feud went on. A fine apple tree in the garden of Hook's grandmother had died, and she insisted it had been old mother Perrill who had blighted the fruit. 'The Perrills always have been putrid turd-sucking bastards,' his grandmother said. She put the evil eye on Tom Perrill and on his younger brother, Robert, but old mother Perrill must have used a counter-spell because neither fell ill. The two goats that Hook kept on the common disappeared, and the village reckoned it had to be wolves, but Hook knew it was the Perrills. He killed their cow in revenge, but it was not the same as killing them. 'It's your job to kill them,' his grandmother insisted to Nick, but he had never found the opportunity. 'May the devil make you spit shit,' she cursed him, 'and then take you to hell.' She threw him from her home when he was sixteen. 'Go and starve, you bastard,' she snarled. She was going mad by then and there was no arguing with her, so Nick Hook left home and might well have starved except that was the year he came first in the six villages' competition, putting arrow after arrow into the distant mark.

Lord Slayton made Nick a forester, which meant he had to keep his lordship's table heavy with venison. 'Better you kill them legally,' Lord Slayton had remarked, 'than be hanged for poaching.'

Now, on Saint Winebald's Day, just before Christmas, Nick Hook watched his arrow fly towards Tom Perrill.

It would kill, he knew it.

The arrow flew true, dipping slightly between the high, frost-bright hedges. Tom Perrill had no idea it was coming. Nick Hook smiled.

Then the arrow fluttered.

A fledging had come loose, its glue and binding must have given way and the arrow veered leftwards to slice down the horse's flank and lodge in its shoulder. The horse whinnied, reared and lunged forward, jerking the great elm trunk loose from the frozen ruts.

Tom Perrill turned and stared up at the high wood, then understood a second arrow could follow the first and so turned again and ran after the horse.

Nick Hook had failed again. He was cursed.

* * *

Lord Slayton slumped in his chair. He was in his forties, a bitter man who had been crippled at Shrewsbury by a sword thrust in the spine and so would never fight another battle. He stared sourly at Nick Hook. 'Where were you on Saint Winebald's Day?'

'When was that, my lord?' Hook asked with apparent innocence.

'Bastard,' Lord Slayton spat, and the steward struck Hook from behind with the bone handle of a horsewhip.

'Don't know which day that was, my lord,' Hook said stubbornly.

'Two days ago,' Sir Martin said. He was Lord Slayton's brother-in-law and priest to the manor and village. He was no more a knight than Hook was, but Lord Slayton insisted he was called 'Sir' Martin in recognition of his high birth.

'Oh!' Hook pretended a sudden enlightenment. 'I was coppicing the ash under Beggar's Hill, my lord.'

'Liar,' Lord Slayton said flatly. William Snoball, steward and chief archer to his lordship, struck Hook again, slashing the whip's butt hard across the back of the forester's skull. Blood trickled down Hook's scalp.

'On my honour, lord,' Hook lied earnestly.

'The honour of the Hook family,' Lord Slayton said drily before looking at Hook's younger brother, Michael, who was seventeen. 'Where were you?'

'I was thatching the church porch, my lord,' Michael said.

'He was,' Sir Martin confirmed. The priest, lanky and gangling in his stained black robe, bestowed a grimace that was supposed to be a smile on Nick Hook's younger brother. Everyone liked Michael. Even the Perrills seemed to exempt him from the hatred they felt for the rest of the Hook tribe. Michael was fair while his brother was dark, and his disposition was sunny while Nick Hook was saturnine.

The Perrill brothers stood next to the Hook brothers.

Thomas and Robert were tall, thin and loose-jointed with deep sunk eyes, long noses and jutting chins. Their resemblance to Sir Martin the priest was unmistakable and the village, with the deference due to a gently-born churchman, accepted the pretence that they were the miller's sons while still treating them with respect. The Perrill family had unspoken privileges because everyone understood that the brothers could call on Sir Martin's help whenever they felt threatened.

And Tom Perrill had not just been threatened, he had almost been killed. The grey-fledged arrow had missed him by a hand's breadth and that arrow now lay on the table in the manor hall. Lord Slayton pointed at the arrow and nodded to his steward who crossed to the table. 'It's not one of ours, my lord,' William Snoball said after examining the arrow.

'The grey feathers, you mean?' Lord Slayton asked.

'No one near here uses grey-goose,' Snoball said reluctantly, with a churlish glance at Nick Hook, 'not for fledging. Not for anything!'

Lord Slayton gazed at Nick Hook. He knew the truth. Everyone in the hall knew the truth, except perhaps Michael who was a trusting soul. 'Whip him,' Sir Martin suggested.

Hook stared at the tapestry hanging beneath the hall's gallery. It showed a hunter thrusting a spear into a boar's guts. A woman, wearing nothing but a wisp of translucent cloth, was watching the hunter, who was dressed in a loincloth and a helmet. The oak beams supporting the gallery had been turned black by a hundred years of smoke.

'Whip him,' the priest said again, 'or cut off his ears.'

Hook lowered his eyes to look at Lord Slayton and wondered, for the thousandth time, whether he was looking at his own father. Hook had the strong-boned Slayton face, the same heavy forehead, the same wide mouth, the same black hair and the same dark eyes. He had the same height, the same bodily strength that had been his lordship's before the rebel sword had twisted in his back and forced him to use the leather-padded crutches leaning on his chair. His lordship returned the gaze, betraying nothing. 'This feud will end,' he finally said, still staring at Hook. 'You understand me? There will be no more killing.' He pointed at Hook. 'If any of the Perrill family dies, Hook, then I will kill you and your brother. Do you understand me?'

'Yes, my lord.'

'And if a Hook dies,' his lordship turned his gaze on Tom Perrill, 'then you and your brother will hang from the oak.'

'Yes, my lord,' Perrill said.

'Murder would need to be proven,' Sir Martin interjected. He spoke suddenly, his voice indignant. The gangling priest often seemed to be living in another world, his thoughts far away, then he would jerk his attention back to wherever he was and his words would blurt out as if catching up with lost time. 'Proven,' he said again, 'proven.'

'No!' Lord Slayton contradicted his brother-in-law, and to emphasise it he slapped the wooden arm of his chair. 'If any one of you four dies I'll hang the rest of you! I don't care! If one of you slips into the mill's leet and drowns I'll call it murder. You understand me? I will not have this feud one moment longer!'

'There'll be no murder, my lord,' Tom Perrill said humbly.

Lord Slayton looked back to Hook, waiting for the same assurance, but Nick Hook said nothing. 'A whipping will teach him obedience, my lord,' Snoball suggested.

'He's been whipped!' Lord Slayton said. 'When was the last time, Hook?'

'Last Michaelmas, my lord.'

'And what did you learn from that?'

'That Master Snoball's arm is weakening, lord,' Hook said.

A stifled snigger made Hook look upwards to see her lady-ship was watching from the shadows of the gallery. She was childless. Her brother, the priest, whelped one bastard after another, while Lady Slayton was bitter and barren. Hook knew she had secretly visited his grandmother in search of a remedy, but for once the old woman's sorcery had failed to produce a baby.

Snoball had growled angrily at Hook's impudence, but Lord Slayton had betrayed his amusement with a sudden grin. 'Out!' he commanded now, 'all of you! Get out, except for you, Hook. You stay.'

Lady Slayton watched as the men left the hall, then turned and vanished into whatever chamber lay beyond the gallery. Her husband stared at Nick Hook without speaking until, at last, he gestured at the grey-feathered arrow on the oak table. 'Where did you get it, Hook?'

'Never seen it before, my lord.'

'You're a liar, Hook. You're a liar, a thief, a rogue and a bastard, and I've no doubt you're a murderer too. Snoball's right. I should whip you till your bones are bare. Or maybe I should just hang you. That would make the world a better place, a Hookless world.'

Hook said nothing. He just looked at Lord Slayton. A log cracked in the fire, showering sparks.

'But you're also the best goddamned archer I've ever seen,' Lord Slayton went on grudgingly. 'Give me the arrow.'

Hook fetched the grey-fledged arrow and gave it to his lordship. 'The fledging came loose in flight?' Lord Slayton asked.

'Looks like it, my lord.'

'You're not an arrow-maker, are you, Hook?'

'Well I make them, lord, but not as well as I should. I can't get the shafts to taper properly.'

'You need a good drawknife for that,' Lord Slayton said,

tugging at the fledging. 'So where did you get the arrow,' he asked, 'from a poacher?'

'I killed one last week, lord,' Hook said carefully.

'You're not supposed to kill them, Hook, you're supposed to bring them to the manor court so I can kill them.'

'Bastard had shot a hind in the Thrush Wood,' Hook explained, 'and he ran away so I put a broadhead in his back and buried him up beyond Cassell's Hill.'

'Who was he?'

'A vagabond, my lord. I reckon he was just wandering through, and he didn't have anything on him except his bow.'

'A bow and a bag filled with grey-fledged arrows,' his lordship said. 'You're lucky the horse didn't die. I'd have hung you for that.'

'Caesar was barely scratched, my lord,' Hook said dismissively, 'nothing but a tear in his hide.'

'And how would you know if you weren't there?'

'I hear things in the village, my lord,' Hook said.

'I hear things too, Hook,' Lord Slayton said, 'and you're to leave the Perrills alone! You hear me? Leave them alone!'

Hook did not believe in much, but he had somehow persuaded himself that the curse that lay on his life would be lifted if only he could kill the Perrills. He was not quite sure what the curse was, unless it was the uncomfortable suspicion that life must hold more than the manor offered. Yet when he thought of escaping Lord Slayton's service he was assailed by a gloomy foreboding that some unseen and incomprehensible disaster awaited him. That was the tenuous shape of the curse and he did not know how to lift it other than by murder, but nevertheless he nodded obediently. 'I hear you, my lord.'

'You hear and you obey,' his lordship said. He tossed the arrow onto the fire where it lay for a moment, then burst into bright flame. A waste of a good broadhead, Hook thought. 'Sir Martin doesn't like you, Hook,' Lord Slayton said in a lower voice. He rolled his eyes upward and Hook understood that his lordship was asking whether his wife was still in the gallery. Hook gave a barely perceptible shake of his head. 'You know why he hates you?' his lordship asked.

'Not sure he likes many people, lord,' Hook answered evasively.

Lord Slayton stared at Hook broodingly. 'And you're right about Will Snoball,' he finally said, 'he's weakening. We all get old, Hook, and I'll be needing a new centenar. You understand me?'

A centenar was the man who commanded a company of archers and William Snoball had held the job for as long as Hook remembered. Snoball was also the manor's steward, and the two offices had made him the richest of all Lord Slayton's men. Hook nodded. 'I understand, lord,' he muttered.

'Sir Martin believes Tom Perrill should be my next centenar. And he fears I'll appoint you, Hook. I can't imagine why he would think that, can you?'

Hook looked into his lordship's face. He was tempted to ask about his mother and how well his lordship had known her, but he resisted. 'No, lord,' he said humbly instead.

'So when you go to London, Hook, tread carefully. Sir Martin will accompany you.'

'London!'

'I have a summons,' Lord Slayton explained. 'I'm required to send my archers to London. Ever been to London?'

'No, my lord.'

'Well, you're going. I don't know why, the summons doesn't say. But my archers are going because the king commands it. And maybe it's war? I don't know. But if it is

12

war, Hook, then I don't want my men killing each other. For God's sake, Hook, don't make me hang you.'

'I'll try not, my lord.'

'Now go. Tell Snoball to come in. Go.'

Hook went.

It was a January day. It was still cold. The sky was low and twilight dark, though it was only mid-morning. At dawn there had been flurries of snow, but it had not settled. There was frost on the thatched roofs and skins of cat ice on the few puddles that had not been trampled into mud. Nick Hook, long-legged and broad-chested and dark-haired and scowling, sat outside the tavern with seven companions, including his brother and the two Perrill brothers. Hook wore knee-high boots with spurs, two pairs of breeches to keep out the cold, a woollen shirt, a padded leather jerkin and a short linen tunic, which was blazoned with Lord Slayton's golden crescent moon and three golden stars. All eight men wore leather belts with pouches, long daggers and swords, and all wore the same livery, though a stranger would need to look hard to discern the moon and stars because the colours had faded and the tunics were dirty.

No one did look hard, because armed men in livery meant trouble. And these eight men were archers. They carried neither bows nor arrow bags, but the breadth of their chests showed these were men who could draw the cord of a war bow a full yard back and make it look easy. They were bowmen, and they were one cause of the fear that pervaded London's streets. The fear was as pungent as the stench of sewage, as prevalent as the smell of woodsmoke. House doors were closed. Even the beggars had vanished, and the few folk who walked the city were among those who had provoked the fear, yet even they chose to pass on the farther side of the street from the eight archers.

'Sweet Jesus Christ,' Nick Hook broke the silence.

'Go to church if you want to say prayers, you bastard,' Tom Perrill said.

'I'll shit in your mother's face first,' Hook snarled.

'Quiet, you two,' William Snoball intervened.

'We shouldn't be here,' Hook growled. 'London's not our place!'

'Well, you are here,' Snoball said, 'so stop bleating.'

The tavern stood on a corner where a narrow street led into a wide market square. The inn's sign, a carved and painted model of a bull, hung from a massive beam that was anchored in the tavern's gable and reached out to a stout post sunk in the marketplace. Other archers were visible around the square, men in different liveries, all fetched to London by their lords, though where those lords were no one knew. Two priests carrying bundles of parchments hurried by on the street's far side. Somewhere deeper in the city a bell started to toll. One of the priests glanced at the archers wearing the moon and stars, then almost tripped as Tom Perrill spat.

'What in Christ's name are we doing here?' Robert Perrill asked.

'Christ is not telling us,' Snoball answered sourly, 'but I am assured we do His work.'

Christ's work consisted of guarding the corner where the street joined the marketplace, and the archers had been ordered to let no man or woman pass them by, either into the market square or out of it. That command did not apply to priests, nor to mounted gentry, but only to the common folk, and those common folk possessed the wisdom to stay indoors. Seven hand-drawn carts had come down the street, pulled by ragged men and loaded with firewood, barrels, stones and long timbers, but the carts had been accompanied by mounted men-at-arms who wore the royal livery and the archers had stayed still and silent while they passed.

14

A plump girl with a scarred face brought a jug of ale from the tavern. She filled the archers' pots and her face showed nothing as Snoball groped beneath her heavy skirts. She waited till he had finished, then held out a hand.

'No, no, darling,' Snoball said, 'I did you a favour so you should reward me.' The girl turned and went indoors. Michael, Hook's younger brother, stared at the table and Tom Perrill sneered at the young man's embarrassment, but said nothing. There was little joy to be had in provoking Michael, who was too good-hearted to take offence.

Hook watched the royal men-at-arms who had stopped the handcarts in the centre of the marketplace where two long stakes were stood upright in two big barrels. The stakes were being fixed in place by packing the barrels with stones and gravel. A man-at-arms tested one of the stakes, trying to tip or dislodge it, but the work had evidently been well done, for he could not shift the tall timber. He jumped down and the labourers began stacking bundles of firewood around the twin barrels.

'Royal firewood,' Snoball said, 'burns brighter.'

'Does it really?' Michael Hook asked. He tended to believe everything he was told and waited eagerly for an answer, but the other archers ignored his question.

'At last,' Tom Perrill said instead, and Hook saw a small crowd emerging from a church at the far side of the marketplace. The crowd was composed of ordinary-looking folk, but it was surrounded by soldiers, monks and priests, and one of those priests now headed towards the tavern called the Bull.

'Here's Sir Martin,' Snoball said, as if his companions would not recognise the priest who, as he drew nearer, grinned. Hook felt a tremor of hatred as he saw the eel-thin Sir Martin with his loping stride, lopsided face and his strange, intense eyes that some thought looked beyond this world to the next, though opinion varied whether Sir Martin gazed at hell or heaven. Hook's grandmother had no doubts. 'He was bitten by the devil's dog,' she liked to say, 'and if he hadn't been born gentry he'd have been hanged by now.'

The archers stood with grudging respect as the priest drew near. 'God's work waits on you, boys,' Sir Martin greeted them. His dark hair was grey at the sides and thin on top. He had not shaved for some days and his long chin was covered in white stubble that reminded Hook of frost. 'We need a ladder,' Sir Martin said, 'and Sir Edward's bringing the ropes. Nice to see the gentry working, isn't it? We need a long ladder. There has to be one somewhere.'

'A ladder,' Will Snoball said, as if he had never heard of such a thing.

'A long one,' Sir Martin said, 'long enough to reach that beam.' He jerked his head at the sign of the bull over their heads. 'Long, long.' He said the last words distractedly, as if he were already forgetting what business he was about.

'Look for a ladder,' Will Snoball told two of the archers, 'a long one.'

'No short ladders for God's work,' Sir Martin said, snapping his attention back to the archers. He rubbed his thin hands together and grimaced at Hook. 'You look ill, Hook,' he added happily, as if hoping Nick Hook were dying.

'The ale tastes funny,' Hook said.

'That's because it's Friday,' the priest said, 'and you should abstain from ale on Wednesdays and Fridays. Your name-saint, the blessed Nicholas, rejected his mother's teats on Wednesdays and Fridays, and there's a lesson in that! There can be no pleasures for you, Hook, on Wednesdays and Fridays. No ale, no joy and no tits, that is your fate for ever. And why, Hook, why?' Sir Martin paused and his long face twisted in a malevolent grin, 'Because you have supped on the sagging tits of evil! I will not have mercy on her children,

16

the scriptures say, because their mother hath played the harlot!'

Tom Perrill sniggered. 'What are we doing, father?' Will Snoball asked tiredly.

'God's work, Master Snoball, God's holy work. Go to it.'

A ladder was found as Sir Edward Derwent crossed the market square with four ropes looped about his broad shoulders. Sir Edward was a man-at-arms and wore the same livery as the archers, though his jupon was cleaner and its colours were brighter. He was a squat, thick-chested man with a face disfigured at the battle of Shrewsbury where a poleaxe had ripped open his helmet, crushed a cheekbone and sliced off an ear. 'Bell ropes,' he explained, tossing the heavy coils onto the ground. 'Need them tied to the beam, and I'm not climbing any ladder.' Sir Edward commanded Lord Slayton's men-at-arms and he was as respected as he was feared. 'Hook, you do it,' Sir Edward ordered.

Hook climbed the ladder and tied the bell ropes to the beam. He used the knot with which he would have looped a hempen cord about a bowstave's nock, though the ropes, being thicker, were much harder to manipulate. When he was done he shinned down the last rope to show that it was tied securely.

'Let's get this done and over,' Sir Edward said sourly, 'and then maybe we can leave this goddamned place. Whose ale is this?'

'Mine, Sir Edward,' Robert Perrill said.

'Mine now,' Sir Edward said, and drained the pot. He was dressed in a mail coat over a leather jerkin, all of it covered with the starry jupon. A sword hung at his waist. There was nothing elaborate about the weapon. The blade, Hook knew, was undecorated, the hilt was plain steel, and the handle was two grips of walnut bolted to the tang. The sword was a tool of Sir Edward's trade, and he had used it to batter down the rebel whose poleaxe had taken half his face.

The small crowd had been herded by soldiers and priests into the centre of the marketplace where most of them knelt and prayed. There were maybe sixty of them, men and women, young and old. 'Can't burn them all,' Sir Martin said regretfully, 'so we're sending most to hell at the rope's end.'

'If they're heretics,' Sir Edward grumbled, 'they should all be burned.'

'If God wished that,' Sir Martin said with some asperity, 'then God would have provided sufficient firewood.'

More people were appearing now. Fear still pervaded the city, but folk somehow sensed that the greatest moment of danger was over, and so they came to the marketplace and Sir Martin ordered the archers to let them pass. 'They should see this for themselves,' the priest explained. There was a sullenness in the gathering crowd, their sympathies plainly aligned with the prisoners and not the guards, though here and there a priest or friar preached an extemporary sermon to justify the day's events. The doomed, the preachers explained, were enemies of Christ. They were weeds among the righteous wheat. They had been given a chance to repent, but had refused that mercy and so must face their eternal fate.

'Who are they anyway?' Hook asked.

'Lollards,' Sir Edward said.

'What's a Lollard?'

'A heretic, you piece of slime,' Snoball said happily, 'and the bastards were supposed to gather here and start a rebellion against our gracious king, but instead they're going to hell.'

'They don't look like rebels,' Hook said. Most of the prisoners were middle-aged, some were old, while a handful was very young. There were women and girls among them.

'Doesn't matter what they look like,' Snoball said, 'they're heretics and they have to die.'

'It's God's will,' Sir Martin snarled.

'But what makes them heretics?' Hook asked.

'Oh, we are curious today,' Sir Martin said sourly.

'I'd like to know that too,' Michael said.

'Because the church says they're heretics,' Sir Martin snapped, then appeared to relent of his tone. 'Do you believe, Michael Hook, that when I raise the host it turns into the most holy and beloved and mystical flesh of our Lord Jesus Christ?'

'Yes, father, of course!'

'Well, they don't believe that,' the priest said, jerking his head at the Lollards kneeling in the mud, 'they believe the bread stays bread, which makes them turds-for-brains piss-shits. And do you believe that our blessed father the Pope is God's vicar on earth?'

'Yes, father,' Michael said.

'Thank Christ for that, or else I'd have to burn you.'

'I thought there were two popes?' Snoball put in.

Sir Martin ignored that. 'Ever seen a sinner burn, Michael Hook?' he asked.

'No, father.'

Sir Martin grinned lasciviously. 'They scream, young Hook, like a boar being gelded. They do scream so!' He turned suddenly and thrust a long bony finger into Nick Hook's chest. 'And you should listen to those screams, Nicholas Hook, for they are the liturgy of hell. And you,' he prodded Hook's chest again, 'are hell-bound.' The priest whirled around, arms suddenly outspread, so that he reminded Hook of a great dark-winged bird. 'Avoid hell, boys!' he called enthusiastically, 'avoid it! No tits on Wednesdays and Fridays, and do God's work diligently every day!'

More ropes had been slung from other signposts about

the marketplace, and now soldiers roughly divided the prisoners into groups that were pushed towards the makeshift gallows. One man began shouting to his friends, telling them to have faith in God and that they would all meet in heaven before this day was over, and he went on shouting till a soldier in royal livery broke his jaw with a mail-shod fist. The broken-jawed man was one of the two selected for the fires and Hook, standing apart from his comrades, watched as the man was hoisted onto the stone- and gravel-filled barrel and tied to the stake. More firewood was piled around his feet.

'Come on, Hook, don't dream,' Snoball grumbled.

The growing crowd was still sullen. There were a few folk who seemed pleased, but most watched resentfully, ignoring the priests who preached at them and turning their backs on a group of brown-robed monks who chanted a song of praise for the day's happy events.

'Hoist the old man up,' Snoball said to Hook. 'We've got ten to kill, so let's get the work done!'

One of the empty handcarts that had brought the firewood was parked beneath the beam and Hook was needed to lift a man onto the cart's bed. The other six prisoners, four men and two women, waited. One of the women clung to her husband, while the second had her back turned and was on her knees, praying. All four prisoners on the cart were men, one of them old enough to be Hook's grandfather. 'I forgive you, son,' the old man said as Hook twisted the thick rope around his neck. 'You're an archer, aren't you?' the Lollard asked and still Hook did not answer. 'I was on the hill at Homildon,' Hook's victim said, looking up at the grey clouds as Hook tightened the rope, 'where I shot a bow for my king. I sent shaft after shaft, boy, deep into the Scots. I drew long and I loosed sharp, and God forgive me, but I was good that day.' He looked into Hook's eyes. 'I was an archer.'

Hook held few things dear beyond his brother and whatever affection he felt for whichever girl was in his arms, yet archers were special. Archers were Hook's heroes. England, for Hook, was not protected by men in shining armour, mounted on trapper-decked horses, but by archers. By ordinary men who built and ploughed and made, and who could draw the yew war bow and send an arrow two hundred paces to strike a mark the size of a man's hand. So Hook looked into the old man's eyes and he saw, not a heretic, but the pride and strength of an archer. He saw himself. He suddenly knew he would like this old man and that realisation checked his hands.

'Nothing you can do about it, boy,' the man said gently. 'I fought for the old king and his son wants me dead, so draw the rope tight, boy, draw it tight. And when I'm gone, boy, do something for me.'

Hook gave the curtest of nods. It could either have been an acknowledgement that he had heard the request, or perhaps it was an agreement to do whatever favour the man might request.

'You see the girl praying?' the old man asked. 'She's my granddaughter. Sarah, she's called, Sarah. Take her away for me. She doesn't deserve heaven yet, so take her away. You're young, boy, you're strong, you can take her away for me.'

How? Hook thought, and he savagely pulled the rope's bitter end so that the loop constricted about the old man's neck, and then he jumped off the cart and half slipped in the mud. Snoball and Robert Perrill, who had tied the other nooses, were already off the cart.

'Simple folk, they are,' Sir Martin was saying, 'just simple folk, but they think they know better than Mother Church, and so a lesson must be taught so that other simple folk don't follow them into error. Have no pity for them, because

21

it's God's mercy we're administering! God's unbounded mercy!'

God's unbounded mercy was administered by pulling the cart sharply out from under the four men's feet. They dropped slightly, then jerked and twisted. Hook watched the old man, seeing the broad barrel chest of an archer. The man was choking as his legs drew up, as they trembled and straightened then drew up again, but even in his dying agony he looked with bulging eyes at Hook as though expecting the younger man to snatch his Sarah out of the marketplace. 'Do we wait for them to die,' Will Snoball asked Sir Edward, 'or pull on their ankles?' Sir Edward seemed not to hear the question. He was distracted again, his eyes unfocused, though he appeared to be staring fixedly at the nearest man tied to the stake. A priest was haranguing the broken-jawed Lollard while a man-at-arms, his face deep shadowed by a helmet, held a flaming torch ready. 'I'll let them swing then, sir,' Snoball said and still got no answer.

'Oh my,' Sir Martin appeared to wake up suddenly and his voice was reverent, the same tone he used in the parish church when he said the mass, 'oh my, oh my, oh my. Oh my, just look at that little beauty.' The priest was gazing at Sarah, who had risen from her knees and was staring with a horrified expression at her grandfather's struggles. 'Oh my, God is good,' the priest said reverently.

Nicholas Hook had often wondered what angels looked like. There was a painting of angels on the wall of the village church, but it was a clumsy picture because the angels had blobs for faces and their robes and wings had become yellowed and streaked by the damp that seeped through the nave's plaster, yet nevertheless Hook understood that angels were creatures of unearthly beauty. He thought their wings must be like a heron's wings, only much larger, and made of feathers that would shine like the sun glowing through the morning mist. He suspected angels had golden hair and long, very clean robes of the whitest linen. He knew they were special creatures, holy beings, but in his dreams they were also beautiful girls that could haunt a boy's thoughts. They were loveliness on gleaming wings, they were angels.

And this Lollard girl was as beautiful as Hook's imagined angels. She had no wings, of course, and her smock was muddied and her face was distorted into a rictus by the horror she watched and by the knowledge that she too must hang, but she was still lovely. She was blue-eyed and fair-haired, had high cheekbones and a skin untouched by the pox. She was a girl to haunt a boy's dreams, or a priest's thoughts for that matter. 'See that gate, Michael Hook?' Sir Martin asked flatly. The priest had looked for the Perrill brothers to do his bidding, but they were out of earshot and so he chose the nearest archer. 'Take her through the gate and keep her in the stable there.'

Nick Hook's younger brother looked puzzled. 'Take her?' he asked.

'Not take her! Not you, you cloth-brained shit-puddling idiot! Just take that girl to the tavern stables! I want to pray with her.'

'Oh! You want to pray!' Michael said, smiling.

'You want to pray with her, father?' Snoball asked with a snide chuckle.

'If she repents,' Sir Martin said piously, 'she can live.' The priest was shivering and Hook did not think it was the cold. 'Christ in His loving mercy allows that,' Sir Martin said, his eyes darting from the girl to Snoball, 'so let us see if we can make her repent? Sir Edward?'

'Father?'

'I shall pray with the girl!' Sir Martin called, and Sir Edward did not answer. He was still gazing at the nearest unlit pyre where the Lollard leader was ignoring the priest's words and looking up at the sky.

'Take her, young Hook,' Sir Martin ordered.

Nick Hook watched his brother take the girl's elbow. Michael was almost as strong as Nick, yet he had a gentleness and a sincerity that reached past the girl's terror. 'Come on, lass,' he said softly, 'the good father wants to pray with you. So let me take you. No one's going to hurt you.'

Snoball sniggered as Michael led the unresisting girl through the yard gate and into the stable where the archers' horses were tethered. The space was cold, dusty and smelt of straw and dung. Nick Hook followed the pair. He told himself he followed so he could protect his brother, but in truth he had been prompted by the dying archer's words, and when he reached the stable door he looked up to see a window in the far gable and suddenly, out of nowhere, a voice sounded in his head. 'Take her away,' the voice said. It was a man's voice, but not one that Nick Hook recognised. 'Take her away,' the voice said again, 'and heaven will be yours.'

'Heaven?' Nick Hook said aloud.

'Nick?' Michael, still holding the girl's elbow, turned to his elder brother, but Nick Hook was gazing at that high bright window.

'Just save the girl,' the voice said, and there was no one in the stable except the brothers and Sarah, but the voice was real, and Hook was shaking. If he could just save the girl. If he could take her away. He had never felt anything like this before. He had always thought himself cursed, hated even by his own name-saint, but suddenly he knew that if he could save this girl then God would love him and God would forgive whatever had made Saint Nicholas hate him. Hook was being offered salvation. It was there, beyond the window, and it promised him a new life. No more of being the cursed Nick Hook. He knew it, yet he did not know how to take it.

'What in God's name are you doing here?' Sir Martin snarled at Hook.

He did not answer. He was staring at the clouds beyond the window. His horse, a grey, stirred and thumped a hoof. Whose voice had he heard?

Sir Martin pushed past Nick Hook to stare at the girl. The priest smiled. 'Hello, little lady,' he said, his voice hoarse, then he turned to Michael. 'Strip her,' he ordered curtly.

'Strip her?' Michael asked, frowning.

'She must appear naked before her God,' the priest explained, 'so our Lord and Saviour can judge her as she truly is. In nakedness is truth. That's what the scripture says, in nakedness is our truth.' Nowhere did the scriptures say that, but Sir Martin had often found the invented quote useful.

'But . . .' Michael was still frowning. Nick's younger brother was notoriously slow in understanding, but even he knew that something was wrong in the winter stable.

'Do it!' the priest snarled at him.

'It's not right,' Michael said stubbornly.

'Oh, for Christ's sake,' Sir Martin said angrily and he pushed Michael out of the way and grabbed the girl's collar. She gave a short, desperate yelp that was not quite a scream, and she tried to pull away. Michael was just watching, horrified, but the echo of a mysterious voice and a vision of heaven were still in Nick Hook's head and so he stepped one quick pace forward and drove his fist into the priest's belly with such strength that Sir Martin folded over with a sound of half pain and half surprise.

'Nick!' Michael said, aghast at what his brother had done.

Hook had taken the girl's elbow and half turned towards that far window. 'Help!' Sir Martin shouted, his voice rasping from breathlessness and pain, 'help!' Hook turned back to silence him, but Michael stepped between him and the priest.

'Nick!' Michael said again, and just then both the Perrill brothers came running.

'He hit me!' Father Martin said, sounding astonished. Tom Perrill grinned, while his younger brother Robert looked as confused as Michael. 'Hold him!' the priest demanded, straightening with a look of pain on his long face, 'just hold the bastard!' His voice was a half-strangled croak as he struggled for breath. 'Take him outside!' he panted, 'and hold him.'

Hook let himself be led into the stable yard. His brother followed and stood unhappily staring at the hanged men just beyond the open gate where a thin cold rain had begun to slant across the sky. Nick Hook was suddenly drained. He had hit a priest, a well-born priest, a man of the gentry, Lord Slayton's own kin. The Perrill brothers were mocking him, but Hook did not hear their words, instead he heard Sarah's smock being torn and heard her scream and heard the scream stifled and he heard the rustling of straw and he heard Sir Martin grunting and Sarah whimpering, and Hook gazed at the low clouds and at the woodsmoke that lay over the city as thick as any cloud and he knew that he was failing God. All his life Nick Hook had been told he was cursed and then, in a place of death, God had asked him to do just one thing and he had failed. He heard a great sigh go up from the marketplace and he guessed that one of the fires had been lit to usher a heretic down to the greater fires of hell, and he feared he would be going to hell himself because he had done nothing to rescue a blue-eyed angel from a black-souled priest, but then he told himself the girl was a heretic and he wondered if it had been the devil who spoke in his head. The girl was gasping now, and the gasps turned to sobs and Hook raised his face to the wind and the spitting rain.

Sir Martin, grinning like a fed stoat, came out of the stable.

He had tucked his robe high about his waist, but now let it fall. 'There,' he said, 'that didn't take long. You want her, Tom?' he spoke to the older Perrill brother, 'she's yours if you want her. Juicy little thing she is, too! Just slit her throat when you're done.'

'Not hang her, father?' Tom Perrill asked.

'Just kill the bitch,' the priest said. 'I'd do it myself, but the church doesn't kill people. We hand them over to the lay power, and that's you, Tom. So go and hump the heretic bitch then open her throat. And you, Robert, you hold Hook. Michael, go away! You've nothing to do with this, go!'

Michael hesitated. 'Go,' Nick Hook told his brother wearily, 'just go.'

Robert Perrill held Hook's arms behind his back. Hook could have pulled away easily enough, but he was still shaken by the voice he had heard and by his stupidity in striking Sir Martin. That was a hanging offence, yet Sir Martin wanted more than just his death and, as Robert Perrill held Hook, Sir Martin began hitting him. The priest was not strong, he did not have the great muscles of an archer, but he possessed spite and he had sharp bony knuckles that he drove viciously into Hook's face. 'You piece of bitch-spawned shit,' Sir Martin spat, and hit again, trying to pulp Hook's eyes. 'You're a dead man, Hook,' the priest shouted. 'I'll have you looking like that!' Sir Martin pointed at the nearest fire. Smoke was thick around the stake, but flames were bright at the pile's base and, through the grey smoke, a figure could be seen straining like a bent bow. 'You bastard!' Sir Martin said, hitting Hook again, 'your mother was an open-legged whore and she shat you like the whore she was.' He hit Hook again and then a flare of fire streaked in the pyre's smoke and a scream sounded in the marketplace like the squeal of a boar being gelded.

'What in God's name is happening?' Sir Edward had heard

the priest's anger and had come into the stable yard to discover its cause.

The priest shuddered. His knuckles were bloody. He had managed to cut Hook's lips and start blood from Hook's nose, but little else. His eyes were wide open, full of anger and indignation, but Hook thought he saw the devil-madness deep inside them. 'Hook hit me,' Sir Martin explained, 'and he's to be killed.'

Sir Edward looked from the snarling priest to the bloodied archer. 'That's for Lord Slayton to decide,' Sir Edward said.

'Then he'll decide to hang him, won't he?' Sir Martin snapped.

'Did you hit Sir Martin?' Sir Edward asked Hook.

Hook just nodded. Was it God who had spoken to him in the stable, he wondered, or the devil?

'He hit me,' Sir Martin said and then, with a sudden spasm, he ripped Hook's jupon clean down its centre, parting the moon from the stars. 'He's not worthy of that badge,' the priest said, throwing the torn surcoat into the mud. 'Find some rope,' he ordered Robert Perrill, 'rope or bowcord, then tie his hands! And take his sword!'

'I'll take it,' Sir Edward said. He pulled Hook's sword that belonged to Lord Slayton from its scabbard. 'Give him to me, Perrill,' he ordered, then drew Hook into the yard's gateway. 'What happened?'

'He was going to rape the girl, Sir Edward,' Hook said, 'he did rape her!'

'Well of course he raped her,' Sir Edward said impatiently, 'it's what the reverend Sir Martin does.'

'And God spoke to me,' Hook blurted out.

'He what?' Sir Edward stared at Hook as if the archer had just claimed that the sky had turned to buttermilk.

'God spoke to me,' Hook said miserably. He did not sound at all convincing.

Sir Edward said nothing. He stared at Hook a brief while longer, then turned to gaze at the marketplace where the burning man had stopped screaming. Instead he hung from the stake and his hair flared sudden and bright. The ropes that held him burned through and the body collapsed in a gout of flame. Two men-at-arms used pitchforks to thrust the sizzling corpse back into the heart of the fire.

'I heard a voice,' Hook said stubbornly.

Sir Edward nodded dismissively, as though acknowledging he had heard Hook's words, but wanted to hear no more. 'Where's your bow?' he asked suddenly, still looking at the burning figure in the smoke.

'In the tavern taproom, Sir Edward, with the others.'

Sir Edward turned to the inn yard's gate where Tom Perrill, grinning and with one hand stained with blood, had just appeared. 'I'm sending you to the taproom,' Sir Edward said quietly, 'and you'll wait there. You'll wait there so we can tie your wrists and take you home and arraign you in the manor court and then hang you from the oak outside the smithy.'

'Yes, Sir Edward,' Hook said in sullen obedience.

'What you will not do,' Sir Edward said, still in a soft voice, but more forcefully, 'is walk out of the tavern's front door. You will not walk into the heart of the city, Hook, and you will not find a street called Cheapside or look for an inn called the Two Cranes. And you will not go into the Two Cranes and enquire after a man called Henry of Calais. Are you listening to me, Hook?'

'Yes, Sir Edward.'

'Henry of Calais is recruiting archers,' Sir Edward said. A man in royal livery was carrying a burning log towards the second pyre where the other Lollard leader was tied to the tall stake. 'They need archers in Picardy,' Sir Edward said, 'and they pay good money.'

'Picardy,' Hook repeated the name dully. He thought it must be a town somewhere else in England.

'Earn yourself some money in Picardy, Hook,' Sir Edward said, 'because God knows you'll need it.'

Hook hesitated. 'I'm an outlaw?' he asked nervously.

'You're a dead man, Hook,' Sir Edward said, 'and dead men are outside the law. You're a dead man because my orders are that you're to wait in the tavern and then be taken back to the judgment of the manor court, and Lord Slayton will have no choice but to hang you. So go and do what I just said.'

But before Hook could obey there was a shout from the next corner. 'Hats off!' men called abruptly, 'hats off!' The shout and a clatter of hooves announced the arrival of a score of horsemen who swept into the wide square where their horses fanned out, pranced, and then stood with breath smoking from their nostrils, and hooves pawing the mud. Men and women were clawing off their hats and kneeling in the mud.

'Down, boy,' Sir Edward said to Hook.

The leading horseman was young, not much older than Hook, but his long-nosed face showed a serene certainty as he swept his cold gaze across the marketplace. His face was narrow, his eyes were dark and his mouth thin-lipped and grim. He was clean-shaven, and the razor seemed to have abraded his skin so that it looked raw-scraped. He rode a black horse that was richly bridled with polished leather and glittering silver. He had black boots, black breeches, a black tunic and a fleece-lined cloak of dark purple cloth. His hat was black velvet and sported a black feather, while at his side hung a black-scabbarded sword. He looked all around the marketplace, then urged the horse forward to watch the one woman and three men who now jerked and twisted from the bell ropes hanging from the Bull's beam. A vagary of wind gusted spark-laden smoke at his stallion, which whinnied and shied away. The rider soothed it by patting its neck with a black-gloved hand, and Hook saw that the man wore jewelled rings over his gloves. 'They were given a chance to repent?' the horseman demanded.

'Many chances, sire,' Sir Martin answered unctuously. The priest had hurried out of the tavern yard and was down on one knee. He made the sign of the cross and his haggard face looked almost saintly, as though he suffered for his Lord God. He could appear that way, his devil-dog-bitten eyes suddenly full of pain and tenderness and compassion.

'Then their deaths,' the young man said harshly, 'are pleasing to God and they are pleasing to me. England will be rid of heresy!' His eyes, brown and intelligent, rested briefly on Nick Hook, who immediately dropped his gaze and stared at the mud until the black-dressed horseman spurred away towards the second fire, which had just been lit. But, in the moment before Hook had looked away, he had seen the scar on the young man's face. It was a battle scar, showing where an arrow had slashed into the corner between nose and eye. It should have killed, yet God had decreed that the man should live.

'You know who that is, Hook?' Sir Edward asked quietly.

Hook did not know for sure, but nor was it hard to guess that he was seeing, for the first time in his life, the Earl of Chester, the Duke of Aquitaine and the Lord of Ireland. He was seeing Henry, by the grace of God, the King of England.

And, according to all who claimed to understand the tangled webs of royal ancestry, the King of France too.

The flames reached the second man and he screamed. Henry, the fifth King of England to carry that name, calmly watched the Lollard's soul go to hell.

'Go, Hook,' Sir Edward said quietly.

'Why, Sir Edward?' Hook asked.

'Because Lord Slayton doesn't want you dead,' Sir Edward said, 'and perhaps God did speak to you, and because we all need His grace. Especially today. So just go.'

And Nicholas Hook, archer and outlaw, went.

PART ONE

Saint Crispin and Saint Crispinian

The River Aisne swirled slow through a wide valley edged with low wooded hills. It was spring and the new leaves were a startling green. Long weeds swayed in the river where it looped around the city of Soissons.

The city had walls, a cathedral and a castle. It was a fortress that guarded the Flanders road, which led north from Paris, and now it was held by the enemies of France. The garrison wore the jagged red cross of Burgundy and above the castle flew the gaudy flag of Burgundy's duke, a flag that quartered the royal arms of France with blue and yellow stripes, all of it badged with a rampant lion.

The rampant lion was at war with the lilies of France, and Nicholas Hook understood none of it. 'You don't need to understand it,' Henry of Calais had told him in London, 'on account of it not being your goddam business. It's the goddam French falling out amongst themselves, that's all you need to know, and one side is paying us money to fight, and I hire archers and I send them to kill whoever they're told to kill. Can you shoot?'

'I can shoot.'

'We'll see, won't we?'

Nicholas Hook could shoot, and so he was in Soissons, beneath the flag with its stripes, lion and lilies. He had no idea where Burgundy was, he knew only that it had a duke called John the Fearless, and that the duke was first cousin to the King of France.

'And he's mad, the French king is,' Henry of Calais had told Hook in England. 'He's mad as a spavined polecat, the stupid bastard thinks he's made of glass. He's frightened that someone will give him a smart tap and he'll break into a thousand pieces. The truth is he's got turnips for brains, he does, and he's fighting against the duke who isn't mad. He's got brains for brains.'

'Why are they fighting?' Hook had asked.

'How in God's name would I know? Or care? What I care about, son, is that the duke's money comes from the bankers. There.' He had slapped some silver on the tavern table. Earlier that day Hook had gone to the Spital Fields beyond London's Bishop's Gate and there he had loosed sixteen arrows at a straw-filled sack hanging from a dead tree a hundred and fifty paces away. He had loosed very fast, scarce time for a man to count to five between each shaft, and twelve of his sixteen arrows had slashed into the sack while the other four had just grazed it. 'You'll do,' Henry of Calais had said grudgingly when he was told of the feat.

The silver went before Hook had left London. He had never been so lonely or so far from his home village and so his coins went on ale, tavern whores and on a pair of tall boots that fell apart long before he reached Soissons. He had seen the sea for the first time on that journey, and he had scarce believed what he saw, and he still sometimes tried to remember what it looked like. He imagined a lake in his head, only a lake that never ended and was angrier than any water he had ever seen before. He had travelled with twelve other archers and they had been met in Calais by a dozen men-at-arms who wore the livery of Burgundy and Hook remembered thinking they must be English because the yellow lilies on their coats were like those he had seen on the king's men in London, but these men-at-arms spoke a strange tongue that neither Hook nor his companions understood. After that they had walked all the way to Soissons because there was no money to buy the horses that every archer expected to receive from his lord in England. Two horse-drawn carts had accompanied their march, the carts loaded with spare bowstaves and thick, rattling sheaves of arrows.

They were a strange group of archers. Some were old men, a few limped from ancient wounds, and most were drunkards.

'I scrape the barrel,' Henry of Calais had told Hook before they had left England, 'but you look fresh, boy. So what did you do wrong?'

'Wrong?'

'You're here, aren't you? Are you outlaw?'

Hook nodded. 'I think so.'

'Think so! You either are or you aren't. So what did you do wrong?'

'I hit a priest.'

'You did?' Henry, a stout man with a bitter, closed face and a bald head, had looked interested for a moment, then shrugged. 'You want to be careful about the church these days, boy. The black crows are in a burning mood. So is the king. Tough little bastard, our Henry. Have you ever seen him?'

'Once,' Hook said.

'See that scar on his face? Took an arrow there, smack in the cheek and it didn't kill him! And ever since he's been convinced that God is his best friend and now he's set on burning God's enemies. Right, tomorrow you're going to help fetch arrows from the Tower, then you'll sail to Calais.'

And so Nicholas Hook, outlaw and archer, had travelled to Soissons where he wore the jagged red cross of Burgundy and walked the high city wall. He was part of an English contingent hired by the Duke of Burgundy and commanded by a supercilious man-at-arms named Sir Roger Pallaire. Hook rarely saw Pallaire, taking his orders instead from a centenar named Smithson who spent his time in a tavern called *L'Oie*, the Goose. 'They all hate us,' Smithson had greeted his newest troops, 'so don't walk the city at night on your own. Not unless you want a knife in your back.'

The garrison was Burgundian, but the citizens of Soissons were loyal to their imbecile king, Charles VI of France. Hook, even after three months in the fortress-city, still did not understand why the Burgundians and the French so loathed each other, for they seemed indistinguishable to him. They spoke the same language and, he was told, the Duke of Burgundy was not only the mad king's cousin, but also father-in-law to the French dauphin. 'Family quarrel, lad,' John Wilkinson told him, 'worst kind of quarrel there is.'

Wilkinson was an old man, of at least forty years, who served as bowyer, fletcher and arrow-maker to the English archers hired by the garrison. He lived in a stable at the Goose where his files, saws, drawknives, chisels and adzes hung neatly on the wall. He had asked Smithson for an assistant and Hook, the youngest newcomer, was chosen. 'And at least you're competent,' Wilkinson offered Hook the grudging compliment, 'it's mostly rubbish that arrives here. Men and weapons, both rubbish. They call themselves archers, but half of them can't hit a barrel at fifty paces. And as for Sir Roger?' The old man spat. 'He's here for the money. Lost everything at home. I hear he has debts of over five hundred pounds! Five hundred pounds! Can you even imagine that?' Wilkinson picked up an arrow and shook his grey head. 'And we have to fight for Sir Richard with this rubbish.'

'The arrows came from the king,' Hook said defensively. He had helped carry the sheaves from the Tower's under-croft.

Wilkinson grinned. 'What the king did, God save his soul, is find some arrows from old King Edward's reign. I know what I'll do, he said to himself, I'll sell these useless arrows to Burgundy!' Wilkinson tossed the arrow to Hook. 'Look at that!'

The arrow, made of ash and longer than Hook's arm, was bent. 'Bent,' Hook said.

'Bent as a bishop! Can't shoot with that! Be shooting around corners!'

It was hot in Wilkinson's stable. The old man had a fire burning in a round brick oven on top of which a cauldron of water steamed. He took the bent arrow from Hook and laid it with a dozen others across the cauldron's top, then carefully placed a thick pad of folded cloth over the ash shafts and weighted the cloth's centre with a stone. 'I steam them, boy,' Wilkinson explained, 'then I weights them, and with any luck I straightens them, and then the fledging falls off because of the steam. Half aren't fledged anyway!'

A brazier burned beneath a second smaller cauldron that stank of hoof glue. Wilkinson used the glue to replace the goose feathers that fledged the arrows. 'And there's no silk,' he grumbled, 'so I'm having to use sinew.' The sinew bound the slit feathers to the arrow's tail, reinforcing the glue. 'But sinew's no good,' Wilkinson complained, 'it dries out, it shrinks and it goes brittle. I've told Sir Roger we need silk thread, but he don't understand. He thinks an arrow is just an arrow, but it isn't.' He tied a knot in the sinew, then turned the arrow to inspect the nock, which would lie on the string when the arrow was shot. The nock was reinforced by a sliver of horn that prevented the bow's cord from split-ting the ash shaft. The horn resisted Wilkinson's attempt to dislodge it and he grunted with reluctant satisfaction before taking another arrow from its leather discs. A pair of the stiff discs, which had indented edges, held two dozen arrows apiece, holding them apart so that the fragile goose-feather fledgings would not get crushed while the arrows were transported. 'Feathers and horn, ash and silk, steel and varnish,' Wilkinson said softly. 'You can have a bow good as you like and an archer to match it, but if you don't have feathers and ash and horn and silk and steel and varnish you might as well spit at your enemy. Ever killed a man, Hook?'

'Yes.'

Wilkinson heard the belligerent tone and grinned. 'Murder? Battle? Have you ever killed a man in battle?'

'No,' Hook confessed.

'Ever killed a man with your bow?'

'One, a poacher.'

'Did he shoot at you?'

'No.'

'Then you're not an archer, are you? Kill a man in battle, Hook, and you can call yourself an archer. How did you kill your last man?'

'I hanged him.'

'And why did you do that?'

'Because he was a heretic,' Hook explained.

Wilkinson pushed a hand through his thinning grey hair. He was thin as a weasel with a lugubrious face and sharp eyes that now stared belligerently at Hook. 'You hanged a heretic?' he asked, 'short of firewood, are they, in England these days? And when was this brave act done?'

'Last winter.'

'A Lollard, was he?' Wilkinson asked, then smirked when Hook nodded. 'So you hanged a man because he disagreed with the church about a morsel of bread? "I'm the living bread come from heaven," says the Lord, and the Lord said nothing about being dead bread on a priest's platter, did He? He didn't say He was mouldy bread, did He? No, He said He was the living bread, son, but no doubt you knew better than Him what you were doing.'

Hook recognised the challenge in the old man's words, but he did not feel capable of meeting it and so he said nothing. He had never cared much for religion or for God, not till he heard the voice in his head, and now he sometimes wondered if he really had heard that voice. He remembered the girl in the stable of the London tavern, and how her eyes had pleaded with him and how he had failed her. He remembered the stench of burning flesh, the smoke dipping low in the small wind to whirl about the lilies and leopards of England's badge. He remembered the face of the young king, scarred and unforgiving.

'This one,' Wilkinson said, picking up an arrow with a warped tip, 'we can make into a proper killer. Something to send a gentry's soul to hell.' He put the arrow on a wooden block and selected a knife that he tested for sharpness against his thumbnail. He sliced off the top six inches of the arrow with one quick cut, then tossed it to Hook. 'Make yourself useful, lad, get the bodkin off.'

The arrow's head was a narrow piece of steel a fraction longer than Hook's middle finger. It was three sided and sharpened to a point. There were no barbs. The bodkin was heavier than most arrowheads because it had been made to pierce armour and, at close range, when shot from one of the great bows that only a man muscled like Hercules could draw, it would slice through the finest plate. It was a knight-killer, and Hook twisted the head until the glue inside the socket gave way and the bodkin came loose.

'You know how they harden those points?' Wilkinson asked.

'No.'

Wilkinson was bending over the stump of the arrow. He was using a fine saw, its blade no longer than his little finger, to make a deep wedge-shaped notch in the cut end. 'What they do,' he said, staring at his work as he spoke, 'is throw bones on the fire when they make the iron. Bones, boy, bones. Dry bones, dead bones. Now why would dead bones in burning charcoal turn iron into steel?'

'I don't know.'

'Nor do I, but it does. Bones and charcoal,' Wilkinson said. He held the notched arrow up, blew some sawdust from the cut, and nodded in satisfaction. 'I knew a fellow in Kent who used human bones. He reckoned the skull of a child made the best steel, and perhaps he was right. The bastard used to dig them up from graveyards, break them into fragments and burn them on his furnace. Babies' skulls and charcoal! Oh, he was a rotten turd of a man, but his arrows could kill. Oh, they could kill. They didn't punch through armour, they whispered through!' Wilkinson had selected a six-inch shaft of oak while he spoke. One end had already been sharpened into a wedge that he fitted into the notched ash of the cut arrow. 'Look at that,' he said proudly, holding up the scarfed joint, 'a perfect fit. I've been doing this too long!' He held out his hand for the bodkin, which he slipped onto the head of the oak. 'I'll glue it all together,' he said, 'and you can kill someone with it.' He admired the arrow. The oak made the head even heavier, so the weight of steel and wood would help punch the arrow through plate armour. 'Believe me, boy,' the old man went on grimly, 'you'll be killing soon.'

'I will?'

Wilkinson gave a brief, humourless laugh. 'The King of France might be mad, but he's not going to let the Duke of Burgundy hold on to Soissons. We're too close to Paris!

The king's men will be here soon enough, and if they get into the town, boy, you go to the castle, and if they get into the castle, you kill yourself. The French don't like the English and they hate English archers, and if they capture you, boy, you'll die screaming.' He looked up at Hook. 'I'm serious, young Hook. Better to cut your own throat than be caught by a Frenchman.'

'If they come we'll fight them off,' Hook said.

'We will, will we?' Wilkinson asked with a harsh laugh. 'Pray that the duke's army comes first, because if the French come, young Hook, we'll be trapped in Soissons like rats in a butter churn.'

And so every morning Hook would stand above the gate and stare at the road that led beside the Aisne towards Compiègne. He spent even more time gazing down into the yard of one of the many houses built outside the wall. It was a dyer's house standing next to the town ditch and every day a girl with red hair would hang the newly coloured cloths to dry on a long line, and sometimes she would look up and wave at Hook or the other archers, who would whistle back at her. One day an older woman saw the girl wave and slapped her hard for being friendly with the hated foreign soldiers, but next day the redhead was again wiggling her rump for her audience's pleasure. And when the girl was not visible Hook watched the road for the glint of sunlight on armour or the sudden appearance of bright banners that would announce the arrival of the duke's army or, worse, the enemy army, but the only soldiers he saw were Burgundians from the city's garrison bringing food back to the city. Sometimes the English archers rode with those foraging parties, but they saw no enemy except the folk whose grain and livestock they stole. The country folk took refuge in the woods when the Burgundians came, but the citizens of Soissons could not hide when the soldiers ransacked their houses for hoarded food. Sire Enguerrand de Bournonville, the Burgundian commander, expected his French enemies to arrive in the early summer and he was planning to endure a long siege, and so he piled grain and salted meat in the cathedral to feed the garrison and townsfolk.

Nick Hook helped pile the food in the cathedral, which soon smelt of grain, though beneath that rich aroma was always the tang of cured leather because Soissons was famous for its cobblers and saddlers and tanners. The tanning pits were south of the town and the stench of the urine in which the hides were steeped made the air foul when the wind blew warm. Hook often wandered the cathedral, staring at the painted walls or at the rich altars decorated with silver, gold, enamel and finely embroidered silks and linens. He had never been inside a cathedral before and the size of it, the shadows far away in the high roof, the silence of the stones, all gave him an uneasy feeling that there must be more to life than a bow, an arrow and the muscles to use them. He did not know what that something was, but the knowledge of it had started in London when an old man, an archer, had spoken to him and when the voice had sounded in his head. One day, feeling awkward, he knelt before a statue of the Virgin Mary and he asked her forgiveness for what he had failed to do in London. He gazed up at her slightly sad face and he thought her eyes, made bright with blue and white paint, were fixed on him and in those eyes he saw reproof. Talk to me, he prayed, but there was no voice in his head. No forgiveness for Sarah's death, he thought. He had failed God. He was cursed.

'Think she can help you?' a sour voice interrupted his prayers. Hook turned and saw John Wilkinson.

'If she can't,' Hook asked, 'who can?'

'Her son?' Wilkinson suggested caustically. The old man looked furtively around him. There were a half-dozen priests saying masses at side altars, but otherwise the only other folk in the cathedral were nuns who were hurrying across the wide nave, shepherded and guarded by priests. 'Poor girls,' Wilkinson said.

'Poor?'

'You think they want to be nuns? Their parents put them here to keep them from trouble. They're bastards of the rich, boy, locked away so they can't have bastards of their own. Come here, I want to show you something.' He did not wait for a response, but stumped towards the cathedral's high altar that reared golden bright beneath the astonishing arches that stood, row above row, in a semicircle at the building's eastern end. Wilkinson knelt beside the altar and dropped his head reverently. 'Take a look in the boxes, boy,' he ordered Hook.

Hook climbed to the altar where silver and gold boxes stood on either side of a gold crucifix. Most of the boxes had crystal faces and, through those distorting windows, Hook saw scraps of leather. 'What are they?' he asked.

'Shoes, boy,' Wilkinson said, his head still bowed and his voice muffled.

'Shoes?'

'You put them on your feet, young Hook, to keep the mud from getting between your toes.'

The leather looked old, dark and shrunken. One reliquary held a shrivelled shoe so small that Hook decided it had to be a piece of child's footwear. 'Why shoes?' he asked.

'You've heard of Saint Crispin and Saint Crispinian?'

'No.'

'Patron saints of cobblers, boy, and of leather-workers. They made those shoes, or so we're told, and they lived here and were probably killed here. Martyred, boy, like that old man you burned in London.'

'He was a . . .'

45

'Heretic, I know. You said. But every martyr was killed because someone stronger disagreed with what he believed. Or what she believed. Christ on His cross, boy, Jesus Himself was crucified for heresy! Why the hell else do you think they nailed Him up? Did you kill women too?'

'I didn't,' Hook said uncomfortably.

'But there were women?' Wilkinson asked, looking at Hook. He saw the answer in Hook's face and grimaced. 'Oh, I'm sure God was delighted with that day's work!' The old man shook his head in disgust before reaching into a purse hanging from his belt. He took out a handful of what Hook presumed were coins and dropped them into the huge copper jar that stood by the altar to receive the tribute of pilgrims. A priest had been watching the two English archers suspiciously, but visibly relaxed when he heard the sound of metal falling onto metal in the big jar. 'Arrowheads,' Wilkinson explained with a grin. 'Old rusted broadheads that are no good any more. Now why don't you kneel and say a prayer to Crispin and Crispinian?'

Hook hesitated. God, he was sure, would have seen Wilkinson drop valueless arrowheads into the jar instead of coins, and the threat of hell's fires suddenly seemed very close and so Hook hurriedly took a coin from his own pouch and dropped it into the copper jar. 'Good lad,' Wilkinson said, 'the bishop will be right glad of that. It'll pay for a sup of his ale, won't it?'

'Why pray to Crispin and Crispinian?' Hook asked Wilkinson.

'Because they're the local saints, boy. That's their job, to listen to prayers from Soissons, so they're the best saints to pray to here.'

So Hook went to his knees and prayed to Saint Crispin and Saint Crispinian that they would beg forgiveness for his sin in London, and he prayed that they would keep him safe in this their town of martyrdom and send him home unscathed to England. The prayer did not feel as powerful as those he had addressed to the mother of Christ, but it made sense, he decided, to pray to the two saints because this was their town and they would surely keep a special watch on those who prayed to them in Soissons.

'I'm done, lad,' Wilkinson announced briskly. He was pushing something into his pocket and Hook, moving to the altar's flank, saw that the frontal's end, where it hung down to the floor, was frayed and ragged because a great square had been crudely cut away. The old man grinned. 'Silk, lad, silk. I need silk thread for arrows, so I just stole it.'

'From God?'

'If God can't afford a few threads of silk, boy, then He's in dire trouble. And you should be glad. You want to kill Frenchmen, young Hook? Pray that I have enough silk thread to tie up your arrows.'

But Hook had no chance to pray because, next day, under the rising sun, the French came.

The garrison had known they were coming. News had reached Soissons of the surrender of Compiègne, another town that had been captured by the Burgundians, and Soissons was now the only fortress that barred the French advance into Flanders where the main Burgundian army lay, and the French army was reported to be coming east along the Aisne.

And then, suddenly, on a bright summer morning, they were there.

Hook watched their arrival from the western ramparts. Horsemen came first. They wore armour and had bright surcoats, and some galloped close to the town as if daring the bowmen on the walls to shoot. Some crossbowmen loosed bolts, but no horseman or horse was hit. 'Save your arrows,' Smithson, the centenar, ordered his English archers.

He flicked a careless finger at Hook's strung bow. 'Don't use it, lad,' he said. 'Don't waste an arrow.' The centenar had come from his tavern, the Goose, and now blinked at the cavorting horsemen, who were shouting inaudibly at the ramparts where men were hanging the Burgundian standard alongside the personal standard of the garrison's commander, the Sire de Bournonville. Some townsfolk had also come to the walls and they too gazed at the newly arrived horsemen. 'Look at the bastards,' Smithson grumbled, gesturing at the townsfolk, 'they'd like to betray us. We should have killed every last one of them. We should have slit their goddam French throats.' He spat. 'Nothing will happen for a day. Might as well drink ale while it's still available.' He stumped away, leaving Hook and a half-dozen other English archers on the wall.

All day the French came. Most were on foot, and those men surrounded Soissons and chopped down trees on the low hills to the south. Tents were erected on the cleared land, and beside the tents were the bright standards of the French nobility, a riot of red, blue, gold and silver flags. Barges came up the river, propelled by giant sweeps, and the barges carried four mangonels, huge machines that could hurl rocks at the city walls. Only one of the massive catapults was brought ashore that day, and Enguerrand de Bournonville, thinking to tip it back into the river, led two hundred mounted men-at-arms on a sally from the western gate, but the French had expected the attack and sent twice as many horsemen to oppose the Burgundians. The two sides reined in, lances upright, and after a while the Burgundians wheeled back, pursued by French jeers. That afternoon smoke began to thicken as the besieging French burned the houses just outside Soissons's walls. Hook watched the red-headed girl carry a bundle towards the new French encampment. None of the fugitives asked to be admitted to the city, instead they went towards the enemy lines. The girl turned in the thickening smoke to wave farewell to the archers. The first enemy crossbowmen appeared in that smoke, each archer protected by a companion holding a thick pavise, a shield large enough to hide a man as he laboriously re-cranked the crossbow after each bolt was loosed. The heavy bolts thumped into the walls or whistled overhead to fall somewhere in the city.

Then, as the sun began to sink towards the monstrous catapult on the river's bank, a trumpet sounded. It called three times, its notes clear and sharp in the smoke-hazed air, and as the last blast faded, so the crossbowmen ceased shooting. There was a sudden surge of sparks as a thatched roof collapsed into a burning house and the smoke whirled thick along the Compiègne road where Hook saw two horsemen appear.

Neither horseman was in armour. Both men, instead, wore bright coloured surcoats, and their only weapons were slender white wands that they held aloft as their horses high-stepped delicately on the rutted road. The Sire de Bournonville must have expected them because the west gate opened and the town's commander rode out with a single companion to meet the approaching riders.

'Heralds,' Jack Dancy said. Dancy was from Herefordshire and was a few years older than Hook. He had volunteered for service under the Burgundian flag because he had been caught stealing at home. 'It was either be hanged there or be killed here,' he had told Hook one night. 'What those heralds are doing,' he said now, 'is telling us to surrender, and let's hope we do.'

'And be captured by the French?' Hook asked.

'No, no. He's a good fellow,' Dancy nodded at de Bournonville, 'he'll make sure we're safe. If we surrender they'll let us march away.'

'Where to?'

'Wherever they want us to be,' Dancy said vaguely.

The heralds, who had been followed at a distance by two standard-bearers and a trumpeter, had met de Bournonville not far from the gate. Hook watched as the men bowed to each other from their saddles. This was the first time he had seen heralds, but he knew they were never to be attacked. A herald was an observer, a man who watched for his lord and reported what he saw, and an enemy's herald was to be treated with respect. Heralds also spoke for their lords, and these men must have spoken for the King of France for one of their flags was the French royal banner, a great square of blue silk on which three gold lilies were emblazoned. The other flag was purple with a white cross and Dancy told him that was the banner of Saint Denis who was France's patron saint, and Hook wondered whether Denis had more influence in heaven than Crispin and Crispinian. Did they argue their cases before God, he wondered, like two pleaders in a manor court? He touched the wooden cross hanging about his neck.

The men spoke for a brief while, then bowed to each other again before the two royal heralds turned their grey horses and rode away. The Sire de Bournonville watched them for a moment, then wheeled his own horse. He galloped back to the city, curbing beside the dyer's burning house from where he shouted up at the wall. He spoke French, of which Hook had learned little, but then added some words in English. 'We fight! We do not give France this citadel! We fight and we will defeat them!'

That ringing announcement was greeted by silence as Burgundian and English alike let the words die away without echoing their commander's defiance. Dancy sighed, but said nothing, and then a crossbow bolt whirred overhead to clatter into a nearby street. De Bournonville had waited for a response from his men on the walls, but, receiving none,

50

spurred through the gate and Hook heard the squeal of its huge hinges, the crash as the timbers closed and the heavy thump as the locking bar was dropped into its brackets.

The sun was hazed now, shining red gold and bright through the diffusing smoke beneath which a party of enemy horsemen rode parallel to the city wall. They were men-at-arms, armoured and helmeted, and one of them, mounted on a great black horse, carried a strange banner that streamed behind him. The banner bore no badge, it was simply a long pennon of the brightest red cloth, a rippling streak of silken blood made almost transparent by the vapour-wrapped sun behind, but the sight of it caused men on the wall to make the sign of the cross.

'The oriflamme,' Dancy said quietly.

'Oriflamme?'

'The French war-banner,' Dancy said. He touched his middle finger to his tongue, then crossed himself again. 'It means no prisoners,' he said bleakly. 'It means they want to kill us all.' He fell backwards.

For a heartbeat Hook did not know what had happened, then he thought Dancy must have tripped and he instinctively held out a hand to pull him up, and it was then he saw the leather-fledged crossbow bolt jutting from Dancy's forehead. There was very little blood. A few droplets had spattered Dancy's face, which otherwise looked peaceful, and Hook went to one knee and stared at the thick-shafted bolt. Less than a hand's breadth protruded, the rest was deep in the Herefordshire man's brain and Dancy had died without a sound, except for the meat-axe noise of the bolt striking home. 'Jack?' Hook asked.

'No good talking to him, Nick,' one of the other archers said, 'he's chatting to the devil now.'

Hook stood and turned. Later he had little memory of what happened or even why it happened. It was not as though Jack Dancy had been a close friend, for Hook had no such friends in Soissons except, perhaps, John Wilkinson. Yet there was a sudden anger in Hook. Dancy was an Englishman, and in Soissons the English felt beleaguered as much by their own side as by the enemy, and now Dancy was dead and so Hook took a varnished arrow from his white linen arrow bag that hung on his right side.

He turned and lowered his bow so that it lay horizontally in front of him and he laid the arrow across the stave and trapped the shaft with his left thumb as he engaged the cord. He swung the long bow upright as his right hand took the arrow's fledged end and drew it back with the cord.

'We're not to shoot,' one of the archers said.

'Don't waste an arrow!' another put in.

The cord was at Hook's right ear. His eyes searched the smoke-shrouded ground outside the town and he saw a crossbowman step from behind a pavise decorated with the symbol of crossed axes.

'You can't shoot as far as they can,' the first archer warned him.

But Hook had learned the bow from childhood. He had strengthened himself until he could pull the cord of the largest war bows, and he had taught himself that a man did not aim with the eye, but with the mind. You saw, and then you willed the arrow, and the hands instinctively twitched to point the bow, and the crossbowman was bringing up his heavy weapon as two bolts seared the evening air close to Hook's head.

He was oblivious. It was like the moment in the green-wood when the deer showed for an instant between the leaves, and the arrow would fly without the archer knowing he had even loosed the string. 'The skill is all between your ears, boy,' a villager had told him years before, 'all between your ears. You don't aim a bow. You think where the arrow will go, and it goes.' Hook released.

'You goddam fool,' an archer said, and Hook watched the white goose feathers flicker in the white-hazed air and saw the arrow fall faster than a stooping hawk. Steel-tipped, silk-bound, ash-shafted, feathered death flying in the evening's quiet.

'Good God,' the first archer said quietly.

The crossbowman did not die as easily as Dancy. Hook's arrow pierced his throat and the man twisted around and the crossbow released itself so that the bolt spun crazily into the sky as the man fell backwards, still twisting as he fell, then he thrashed on the ground, hands scrabbling at his throat where the pain was like liquid fire, and above him the sky was red now, a smoke-hazed blood-red sky lit by fires and glowing with the sun's daily death.

That, Hook, thought, had been a good arrow. Straight-shafted and properly fledged with its feathers all plucked from the same goose-wing. It had flown true. It had gone where he willed it, and he had killed a man in battle. He could, at last, call himself an archer.

On the evening of the siege's second day Hook thought the world had ended.

It was an evening of warm and limpid light. The air was pale-bright and the river slid gently between its flowery banks where willows and alders grew. The French banners hung motionless above their tents. Some smoke still sifted from the burned houses to rise soft into the evening air until it faded high in the cloudless sky. Martins and swallows hunted beside the city's wall, swooping and twisting.

Nicholas Hook leaned on the ramparts. His unstrung bow was propped beside him as his thoughts drifted back to England, to the manor, to the fields behind the long barn where the hay would be almost ready for cutting. There would be hares in the long grass, trout in the stream and larks in the twilight. He thought about the decaying cattle byre in the field called Shortmead, the byre with rotting thatch and a screen of honeysuckle behind which William Snoball's young wife Nell would meet him and make silent, desperate love. He wondered who was coppicing the Three Button wood and, for the thousandth time, how the wood had got its name. The tavern in the village was called the Three Buttons and no one knew why, not even Lord Slayton, who sometimes limped on crutches beneath the tavern's lintel and put silver on the serving hatch to buy all present an ale. Then Hook thought of the Perrills, malevolent and ever-present. He could not go home now, not ever, because he was an outlaw. The Perrills could kill him and it would not be murder, not even manslaughter, because an outlaw was beyond the law's help. He remembered the window in the London stable, and knew God had told him to take the Lollard girl through that window, but he had failed and he thought he must be cut off from the heavenly light beyond that window for ever. Sarah. He often murmured her name aloud as though the repetition could bring forgiveness.

The evening peace vanished in noise.

But first there was light. Dark light, Hook thought later, a stab of dark light, flame-black red light that licked like a hell-serpent's tongue from an earthwork the French had dug close to one of their gaunt catapults. That tongue of wicked fire was visible for an instant before it was obliterated in a thundercloud of dense black smoke that billowed sudden, and then the noise came, an ear-punching blow of sound that shook the heavens to be followed by another crack, almost as loud, as something struck the city wall.

The wall shook. Hook's bow toppled and clattered onto the stones. Birds were screaming as they flew from the flame, smoke and lingering noise. The sun was gone, hidden by the black cloud, and Hook stared and was convinced, at least for a moment, that a crack had opened in the earth and that the fires of hell had vomited their way to the surface.

'Sweet bloody Christ!' an archer said in awe.

'Was wondering when that would happen,' another archer said in disgust. 'A gun,' he explained to the first man, 'have you never seen a gun?'

'Never.'

'You'll see them now,' the second man said grimly.

Hook had never seen a gun either, and he flinched when a second one fired to add its filthy smoke to the summer sky. Next day another four cannons added their fire and the six French guns did far more damage than the four big wooden machines. The catapults were inaccurate and their jagged boulders often missed the ramparts and dropped into the city to crush houses that started burning as their kitchen fires were scattered, but the gun-stones ate steadily at the city wall, which was already in bad repair. It took only two days for the outer face of the wall to crumble into the wide fetid ditch, and then the gunners systematically widened the breach as the Burgundians countered by making a semicircular barricade behind the disintegrating wall.

Each gun fired three times a day, their shots as regular as the bells of a monastery calling men to prayer. The Burgundians had their own gun, which had been mounted on a southern bastion in the expectation that the French would attack from the Paris road, and it took two days to drag the weapon to the western ramparts where it was slung up onto the roof of the gate-tower. Hook was fascinated by its tube, which was twice as long as his bowstave and hooped like an ale-pot. The tube and its bindings were made of dark pitted iron and rested on a squat wooden carriage. The gunners were Dutchmen who spent a long time watching the enemy guns and finally aimed their tube at one of those French cannon and then set about the laborious task of loading their machine. Gunpowder was put into the barrel with a long-handled ladle, then tamped tight with a cloth-wrapped rammer. Soft loam was added next. The loam was puddled in a wide wooden pail, rammed onto the powder, then left to dry as the gunners sat in a circle and played dice. The gun-stone, a boulder chipped into a crude ball, waited beside the tube until the chief gunner, a portly man with a forked beard, decided the loam was dry enough, and only then was the stone pushed down the long hooped barrel. A wooden wedge was shoved after it and hammered into place to keep the shaped boulder tight against the loam and powder. A priest sprinkled holy water on the gun and said a prayer as the Dutchmen used long levers to make a final small adjustment to the tube's aim.

'Stand back, boy,' Sergeant Smithson told Hook. The centenar had deigned to leave the Goose tavern to watch the Dutchmen fire their weapon. A score of other men had also arrived, including the Sire de Bournonville who called encouragement to the gunners. None of the spectators stood close to the gun, but instead watched as if the black tube were a wild beast that could not be trusted. 'Good morning, Sir Roger,' Smithson said, knuckling his forehead towards a tall, arrow-thin man. Sir Roger Pallaire, commander of the English contingent, ignored the greeting. He had a narrow, beak-nosed face with a lantern jaw, dark hair and, in the company of his archers, the expression of a man forced to endure the stench of a latrine.

The portly Dutchman waited till the priest had finished his prayer, then he pushed a stripped quill into a small hole that had been drilled into the gun's breech. He used a copper funnel to fill the quill with powder, squinted one more time down the length of the barrel, then stepped to one side and held out a hand for a long, burning taper. The priest, the only man other than the artillerymen to be close to the weapon, made the sign of the cross and spoke a quick blessing, then the chief gunner touched the flame to the powder-filled quill.

The gun exploded.

Instead of sending its stone ball screaming across to the French siege-works the cannon vanished in a welter of smoke, flying metal and shredded flesh. The five gunners and the priest were killed instantly, turned to blood-red mist and ribboned meat. A man-at-arms screamed and writhed as red-hot metal sliced into his belly. Sir Roger, who had been standing next to the screaming man, stepped fastidiously away and grimaced at the blood that had spattered across the badge on his surcoat. That badge showed three hawks on a green field. 'Tonight, Smithson,' Sir Roger spoke amidst the blood-reeking smoke that writhed about the rampart, 'you will meet me after sundown in Saint Antoine-le-Petit's church. You and your whole company.'

'Yes, sir, yes,' Smithson said faintly, 'of course, Sir Roger.' The sergeant was staring at the ruined cannon. The first ten feet of the shattered barrel lay canted and ripped open, while the breech had been torn into jagged shards of smoking metal. Part of a hoop and a man's hand lay by Hook's feet while the gunners, hired at great expense, were nothing but eviscerated carcasses. The Sire de Bournonville, his jupon spattered with blood and scraps of flesh, made the sign of the cross, while derisive jeers sounded from the French siege lines.

'We must plan for the assault,' Sir Roger said, apparently oblivious to the wet horror a few paces away.

'Very good, Sir Roger,' Smithson said. The centenar scooped a jellied mess from his belt. 'A Dutchman's goddam brains,' he said in disgust, flicking the gob towards Sir Roger who had turned and now strode away.

Sir Roger, with three men-at-arms all wearing his badge

of the three hawks, met the English and Welsh archers of the Soissons garrison in the church of Saint Antoine-le-Petit just after sunset. Sir Roger's surcoat had been washed, though the bloodstains were still faintly visible on the green linen. He stood in front of the altar, lit by guttering rushlights that burned feebly in brackets mounted on the church's pillars, and his face still bore the distant look of a man pained to be in his present company. 'Your job,' he said, without any preamble once the eighty-nine archers had settled on the floor of the nave, 'will be to defend the breach. I cannot tell you when the enemy will assault, but I can assure you it will be soon. I trust you will repel any such assault.'

'Oh we will, Sir Roger,' Smithson put in helpfully, 'rely on it, sir!'

Sir Roger's long face shuddered at the comment. Rumour in the English contingent said that he had borrowed money from Italian bankers in expectation of inheriting an estate from an uncle, but the land had passed to a cousin and Sir Roger had been left owing a fortune to unforgiving Lombards. The only hope of paying the debt was to capture and ransom a rich French knight, which was presumably why he had sold his services to the Duke of Burgundy. 'In the event,' he said, 'that you fail to keep the enemy out of the city, you are to gather here, in this church.' Those words caused a stir as men frowned and looked at each other. If they failed to defend the breach and lost the new defences behind it, then they expected to retreat to the castle.

'Sir Roger?' Smithson ventured hesitantly.

'I had not invited questions,' Sir Roger said.

'Of your goodness, Sir Roger,' Smithson persevered, knuckling his forehead as he spoke, 'but wouldn't we be safer in the castle?'

'You will assemble here, in this church!' Sir Roger said firmly.

'Why not the castle?' an archer near Hook demanded belligerently.

Sir Roger paused, searching the dim nave for whoever had spoken. He could not discover the questioner, but deigned to offer an answer anyway. 'The townspeople,' he finally spoke, 'detest us. If you attempt to reach the castle you will be assaulted in the streets. This place is much closer to the breach, so come here.' He paused again. 'I shall endeavour to arrange a truce for you.'

There was an uncomfortable silence. Sir Roger's explanation made some sense. The archers knew that most folk in Soissons hated them. The townspeople were French, they supported their king and hated the Burgundians, but they hated the English even more, and so it was more than likely that they would assault the archers retreating towards the castle. 'A truce,' Smithson said dubiously.

'The French quarrel is with Burgundy,' Sir Roger said, 'not with us.'

'Will you be joining us here, Sir Roger?' an archer called out.

'Of course,' Sir Roger said. He paused, but no one spoke. 'Fight well,' he said distantly, 'and remember you are Englishmen!'

'Welshmen,' someone intervened.

Sir Roger visibly flinched at that and then, without another word, led his three men-at-arms from the church. A chorus of protests sounded as he left. The church of Saint Antoine-le-Petit was stone-built and defensible, but not nearly so safe as the castle, though it was true the castle was at the other end of the town and Hook wondered how difficult it would bc to reach that refuge if townsfolk were blocking the streets and French men-at-arms were howling through the breached ramparts. He looked up at the painted wall that showed men, women and children tumbling into hell. There were priests

59

and even bishops among the doomed souls who fell in a screaming cascade to a lake of fire where black devils waited with leering grins and triple-barbed eel-spears. 'You'll wish you were in hell if the Frenchies capture you,' Smithson said, noticing where Hook was looking. 'You'll all be begging for the comforts of hell if those French bastards catch you. So remember! We fight at the barricade and then, if it all goes to shit, we come here.'

'Why here?' a man called out.

'Because Sir Roger knows what he's doing,' Smithson said, sounding anything but certain, 'and if you've got sweethearts here,' he went on with a leer, 'make certain the little darlings come with you.' He began thrusting his meaty hips backwards and forwards. 'Don't want our sweethearts left in the streets to be humped by half the French army, do we?'

Next morning, as he did each morning, Hook gazed north across the Aisne to the low wooded hills where the beleaguered garrison hoped to see a Burgundian relief force. None came. The great gun-stones whirred across the ashes of the burned houses and bit into the crumbling wall to start up their clouds of dust that settled on the river to drift seawards like pale grey stains on the water. Hook rose early every morning, before it was light, and went to the cathedral where he knelt and prayed. He had been warned not to walk the streets by himself, but the people of Soissons left him alone, perhaps scared of his height and size, or perhaps because they knew he was the one archer who prayed regularly and so tolerated him. He had abandoned praying to Saint Crispin and Saint Crispinian because he reckoned they cared more about the townsfolk, their own folk, and so he prayed instead to the mother of Christ because his own mother had been called Mary and he begged the blessed virgin for forgiveness because of the girl who had died in London. On one such morning a priest knelt beside him. Hook ignored the man.

'You're the Englishman who prays,' the priest said in English, stumbling over the unfamiliar language. Hook said nothing. 'They wonder why you pray,' the priest went on, jerking his head to indicate the women who knelt before other statues and altars.

Hook's instinct was to go on ignoring the man, but the priest had a friendly face and a kindly voice. 'I'm just praying,' he said, sounding surly.

'Are you praying for yourself?'

'Yes,' Hook admitted. He prayed so that God would forgive him and lift the curse that he was certain blighted his life.

'Then ask something for someone else,' the priest suggested gently. 'God listens to those prayers more readily, I think, and if you pray for someone else then He will grant your own request too.' He smiled, stood and lightly touched Hook's shoulder. 'And pray to our saints, Crispin and Crispinian. I think they are less busy than the blessed Virgin. God watch over you, Englishman.'

The priest walked away and Hook decided to take his advice and pray again to the two local saints and so he went to an altar beneath a painting of the two martyrs and there he prayed for the soul of Sarah, whose life he had failed to save in London. He stared up at the painting as he prayed. The two saints stood in a green field scattered with golden stars on a hill high above a white-walled city. They looked gravely and a little sadly towards Hook. They did not look like shoemakers. They were dressed in white robes and Crispin carried a shepherd's crook while Crispinian held a wicker tray of apples and pears. Their names were painted beneath each man and Hook, though he could not read, could tell which saint was which because one name was longer than the other. Crispinian looked much the friendlier man. He had a rounder face and blue eyes and a half-smile of great kindliness, while Saint Crispin appeared much sterner and was half turned

61

away, as though he had no time for an onlooker and was about to walk down the hill and into the city, and so Hook fell into the habit of praying to Crispinian each morning, though he always acknowledged Crispin too. He dropped two pennies in the jar each time he prayed.

'To look at you,' John Wilkinson said one evening, 'I wouldn't take you for a man of prayer.'

'I wasn't,' Hook said, 'till now.'

'Frightened for your soul?' the old archer asked.

Hook hesitated. He was binding arrow fledging with the silk stolen from the cathedral's altar frontal. 'I heard a voice,' he blurted out suddenly.

'A voice?' Wilkinson asked. Hook said nothing. 'God's voice?' the older man asked.

'It was in London,' Hook said.

He felt foolish for his admission, but Wilkinson took it seriously. He stared at Hook for a long time, then nodded abruptly. 'You're a lucky man, Nicholas Hook.'

'I am?'

'If God spoke to you then He must have a purpose for you. That means you might survive this siege.'

'If it was God who spoke to me,' Hook said, embarrassed.

'Why shouldn't He? He needs to speak to people, on account that the church don't listen to Him.'

'It doesn't?'

Wilkinson spat. 'The church is about money, lad, money. Priests are supposed to be shepherds, aren't they? They're meant to be looking after the flock, but they're all in the manor hall stuffing their faces with pastries, so the sheep have to look after themselves.' He pointed an arrow at Hook. 'And if the French break into the town, Hook, don't go to Saint Anthony the Lesser! Go to the castle.'

'Sir Roger . . .' Hook began.

'Wants us dead!' Wilkinson said angrily.

'Why would he want that?'

'Because he's got no money and a heap of debt, boy, so the man with the biggest purse can buy him. And because he's not a real Englishman. His family came to England with the Normans and he hates you and me because we're Saxons. And because he's crammed to the throat with Norman shit, that's why. You go to the castle, lad! That's what you do.'

The next few nights were dark, and the waning moon was a sliver like a cutthroat's blade. The Sire de Bournonville feared a night attack and ordered dogs to be tethered out in the wasteland where the houses had been burned. If the dogs barked, he said, the warning bell on the western gate was to be rung, and the dogs did bark and the bell was rung, but no Frenchmen assaulted the breach. Instead, as the dawn mist shimmered above the river, the besiegers catapulted the dogs' corpses into the town. The animals had been gelded and had their throats cut as a warning of the fate that awaited the defiant garrison.

The feast of Saint Abdus passed, and no relief force arrived, and then Saint Possidius's feast came and went, and next day was the feast of the seven holy virgins, and Hook prayed to each one, and in the next dawn he sent a plea to Saint Dunstan, the Englishman, on his feast day, and the day after that to Saint Ethelbert, who had been a king of England, and all the time he also prayed to Crispinian and to Crispin, begging their protection, and on the very next day, on the feast of Saint Hospitius, he received his answer.

When the French, who had been praying to Saint Denis, attacked Soissons.

The first Hook knew of the assault was the sound of the city's church bells clanging in frantic haste and jangling disorder. It was dark and he was momentarily confused. He slept on straw at the back of John Wilkinson's workshop and he woke to the glare of flames leaping high as the old man threw wood on the brazier to provide light. 'Don't lie there like a pregnant sow, boy,' Wilkinson said, 'they're here.'

'Mary, mother of God,' Hook felt the surge of panic like icy water seething through his body.

'I've an inkling she don't care one way or the other,' Wilkinson said. He was pulling on a mail coat, struggling to get the heavy links over his head. 'There's an arrow bag by the door,' he went on, his voice now muffled by the coat, 'full of straight ones. Left it for you. Go, boy, kill some bastards.'

'What about you?' Hook asked. He was tugging on his boots, new boots made by a skilled cobbler of Soissons.

'I'll catch up with you! String your bow, son, and go!'

Hook buckled his sword belt, strung his bow, snatched his arrow bag, then took the second bag from beside the door and ran into the tavern yard. He could hear shouting and screams, but where they came from he could not tell. Archers were pouring into the yard and he instinctively followed them towards the new defences behind the breach. The church bells were hammering the night sky with jangling noise. Dogs barked and howled.

Hook had no armour except for an ancient helmet that Wilkinson had given him and which sat on his head like a bowl. He had a padded jacket that might stop a feeble sword swing, but that was his only protection. Other archers had short mail coats and close-fitting helmets, but they all wore Burgundy's brief surcoat blazoned with the jagged red cross and Hook saw those liveries lining the new wall that was made of wicker baskets filled with earth. None of the archers was drawing a cord yet, instead they just looked towards the breach that flared with sudden light as Burgundian men-at-arms threw pitch-soaked torches into the gap of the gun-ravaged wall.

There were close to fifty men-at-arms at the new wall, but no enemy in the breach. Yet the bells still rang frantically to announce a French attack, and Hook swung around to see a glow in the sky above the city's southern rooftops, a glow that flickered lurid on the cathedral's tower as evidence that buildings burned somewhere near the Paris gate. Was that where the French attacked? The Paris gate was commanded by Sir Roger Pallaire and defended by the English men-at-arms and Hook wondered, not for the first time, why Sir Roger had not demanded that the English archers join that gate's garrison.

Instead the archers waited by the western breach where still no enemy appeared. Smithson, the centenar, was nervous. He kept fingering the silver chain that denoted his rank and glancing towards the glow of the southern fires, then back to the breach. 'Devil's turd,' he said of no one in particular.

'What's happening?' an archer demanded.

'How in God's name would I know?' Smithson snarled.

'I think they're already inside the city,' John Wilkinson

said mildly. He had brought a dozen sheaves of spare arrows that he now dropped behind the archers. The sound of screams came from somewhere in the city and a troop of Burgundian crossbowmen ran past Hook, abandoning the breach and heading towards the Paris gate. Some of the men-at-arms followed them.

'If they're inside the town,' Smithson said uncertainly, 'then we should go to the church.'

'Not to the castle?' a man demanded.

'We go to the church, I think,' Smithson said, 'as Sir Roger says. He's gentry, isn't he? He must know what he's doing.'

'Aye, and the Pope lays eggs,' Wilkinson commented.

'Now?' a man asked, 'we go now?' but Smithson said nothing. He just tugged at the silver chain and looked left and right.

Hook was staring at the breach. His heart was beating hard, his breathing was shallow and his right leg trembled. 'Help me, God,' he prayed, 'sweet Jesu protect me,' but he got no comfort from the prayer. All he could think of was that the enemy was in Soissons, or attacking Soissons and he did not know what was happening and he felt vulnerable and helpless. The bells banged inside his head, confusing him. The wide breach was dark except for the feeble flicker of dying flames from the torches, but slowly Hook became aware of other lights moving there, of shifting silver-grey lights, lights like smoke in moonlight or like the ghosts who came to earth on Allhallows Eve. The lights, Hook thought, were beautiful; they were filmy and vaporous in the darkness. He stared, wondering what the glowing shapes were, and then the silver-grey wraiths turned to red and he realised, with a start of fear, that the shifting shapes were men. He was seeing the light of the torches reflected from plate armour. 'Sergeant!' he shouted.

'What is it?' Smithson snapped back.

'The bastards are here!' Hook called, and so they were. The bastards were coming through the breach. Their plate armour was scoured bright enough to reflect the firelight and they were advancing beneath a banner of blue on which golden lilies blossomed. Their visors were closed and their long swords flashed back the flame-light. They were no longer vaporous, now they resembled men of burning metal, phantoms from the dreams of hell, death coming through the dark to Soissons. Hook could not count them, they were so many.

'Oh my God's shit,' Smithson said in panic, 'stop them!'

Hook did what he was told. He stepped back to the barricade, plucked an arrow from the linen bag and laid it on the bow's stave. The fear was suddenly gone, or else had been pushed aside by the certain knowledge of what needed to be done. Hook needed to haul back the bow's cord.

Most grown men in the prime of their strength could not pull a war bow's cord back to the ear. Most men-at-arms, despite being toughened by war and hardened by constant sword exercises, could only draw the hemp cord halfway, but Hook made it look easy. His arm flowed back, his eyes sought a mark for the arrow's bright head and he did not even think as he released. He was already reaching for the second arrow as the first, a shaft-weighted bodkin, slapped through a breastplate of shining steel and threw the man back onto the French standard-bearer.

And Hook loosed again, not thinking, only knowing that he had been told to stop this attack. He loosed shaft after shaft. He drew the cord to his right ear and was not aware of the tiny shifts his left hand made to send the white-feathered arrows on their short journey from cord to victim. He was not aware of the deaths he caused or the injuries he gave or of the arrows that glanced off armour to spin uselessly away. Most were not useless. The long bodkin heads could easily punch through armour at this close range and Hook was stronger than most archers, who were stronger than most men, and his bow was heavy. John Wilkinson, when he had first met Hook, had drawn the younger man's bow and failed to get the cord past his chin, and he had given Hook a glance of respect, and now that long, thick-bellied bow cut from the trunk of a yew in far-off Savoy, was sending death through the bell-ringing dark, except that Hook was only seeing the enemy who came across the breach where the guttering torches burned, and he did not notice the dark floods of men who surged at either edge of the wall's gap and who were already tugging at the wicker baskets. Then part of the barricade collapsed and the noise made Hook turn to see that he was the only archer left at the defences. The breach, despite the dead who lay there and the injured who crawled there, was filled with howling men. The night was lit by fire, flame red, riddled with smoke and loud with war-shouts. Hook realised then that John Wilkinson had shouted at him to run, but in the moment's excitement, the warning had not lodged in Hook's mind.

But now it did. He plucked up the arrow bag and ran.

Men howled behind him as the barricade fell and the French swarmed across its remnants and into the city.

Hook understood then how the deer felt when the hounds were in every thicket and men were beating the under-growth and arrows were whickering through the leaves. He had often wondered if an animal could know what death was. They knew fear, and they knew defiance, but beyond fear and defiance came the gut-emptying panic, the last moments of life as the hunters close in and the heart races and the mind slithers frantically. Hook felt that panic and ran. At first he just ran. The bells were still crashing, dogs were howling, men were roaring war-shouts and horns were calling. He ran into a small square, a space where leather merchants usually displayed their hides, and it was oddly deserted, but then he heard the sounds of bolts being shot and he understood that folk were hiding in their houses and barring their doors. Crashes announced where soldiers were kicking or beating those locked doors down. Go to the castle, he thought, and he ran that way, but turned a corner to see the wide space in front of the cathedral filled with men in unfamiliar liveries, their surcoats lit by the torches they carried, and he doubled back like a deer recoiling from hounds. He decided to go to Saint Antoine-le-Petit's church and sprinted down an alley, twisted into another, ran across the open space in front of the city's biggest nunnery, then turned down the street where the Goose tavern stood and saw still more men in their strange liveries, and those men blocked his way to the church. They spotted him and a growl sounded, and the growl turned into a triumphant howl as they ran towards him, and Hook, desperate as any doomed animal, bolted into an alley, leaped at the wall that blocked the end, sprawled over into a small yard that stank of sewage, scrambled across a second wall and then, surrounded by shouts and quivering with fear he sank into a dark corner and waited for the end.

A hunted deer would do that. When it saw no escape it would freeze, shiver and wait for the death it must sense. Now Hook shivered. Better to kill yourself, John Wilkinson had said, than be caught by the French and so Hook felt for his knife, but he could not draw it. He could not kill himself, and so he waited to be killed.

Then he realised his pursuers had evidently abandoned the chase. There was so much plunder for them in Soissons and so many victims, that one fugitive did not interest them and Hook, slowly recovering his senses, realised he had found a temporary refuge. He was in one of the Goose's back yards, a place where the brewery barrels were washed and repaired. A door of the tavern suddenly opened and a flaming torch illuminated the trestles and staves and tuns. A man peered into the yard, said something dismissive and went back into the tavern where a woman screamed.

Hook stayed where he was. He dared not move. The city was full of women screaming now, full of hoarse male laughter and full of crying children. A cat stalked past him. The church bells had long ceased their clangour. He knew he could not stay where he was. Dawn would reveal him. Oh God, oh God, oh God, he prayed, unaware that he prayed. Be with me now and at the hour of my death. He shivered. Hooves sounded in the street beyond the brewery yard wall, a man laughed. A woman whimpered. Clouds scurried across the moon's face and for some reason Hook thought of the badgers on Beggar's Hill, and that homely thought calmed the panic.

He stood. Perhaps there was a chance he could reach the church? It was much closer than the castle, and Sir Roger had promised to make an attempt to save the archers' lives, and, though it seemed a slender hope, it was all Hook could think of doing and so he pulled himself up the yard's wall to peer over the top. The Goose's stables were next door. No noise came from them and so he climbed onto the wall and from there he could step onto the stable roof that trembled under his weight, but by staying on the rooftop, where the ridge beam ran, he could shuffle until he reached the farther gable where he dropped into a dark alley. He was shaking again, knowing he was more vulnerable here. He moved silently, slowly, until he could peer about the alley's corner to where the church lay.

And he saw there was no escape.

The church of Saint Antoine-le-Petit was guarded by enemies. There were over thirty men-at-arms and a dozen crossbowmen in the open space in front of the church steps, all in liveries that Hook had not seen before. If Smithson

and the archers were inside the church then they were safe
enough, for they could defend the door, but it seemed plain
to Hook that the enemy must be there to prevent any archer
escaping and, he assumed, they would stop any stray archer
trying to approach the church. He thought of running for
the doorway, but guessed it would be locked and that, while
he was beating on the heavy timber, the crossbowmen would
use him for a target.

The enemy was not just guarding the church. They had
fetched barrels from some tavern and were drinking, and
they had stripped two girls naked and tied them across the
two barrels with their legs spread wide, and now the men
took it in turns to hitch up their mail coats and rape the girls
who lay silent as if they had been emptied of moans and
tears. The city was loud with women screaming, and the
sound scored across Hook's conscience like an arrowhead
scraping on slate, and perhaps that was why he did not move,
but instead stood at the corner like an animal that had no
place to run or hide. Hook wondered if the girls were dead,
they were so still, but then the nearest turned her head and
Hook remembered Sarah and flinched with guilt. The girl,
who looked no older than twelve or thirteen, stared dully
into the dark as a man jerked and grunted at her.

Then a door opened onto the alley and a flood of light
washed across Hook who turned to see a man-at-arms stagger
into the mud. The man wore a surcoat showing a silver
wheatsheaf on a green field. The man fell to his knees and
vomited as a second man, in the same livery, came to the
door and laughed. It was that second man who saw Hook
and recognised the great war bow, and so put his hand on
his sword's hilt.

Hook reacted in panic. He thrust the bow at the man with
the sword. In his head he was screaming, unable to think,
but the lunge had all his archer's strength in it and the horn

nock of the bow's tip pierced the man-at-arms's throat before his sword was even half drawn. Blood misted black and still Hook thrust so that the bow ripped clean through windpipe and muscle, skin and sinew to strike the doorjamb. The kneeling man was roaring, spraying vomit as he clawed at Hook who, still in panic, made a mewing noise of utter despair as he let go of the bow and thrust his hands at his new assailant. He felt his fingers crush eyeballs and the man began to scream, and Hook was dimly aware that the rapists outside the church were coming for him and he scrambled through the door, half tripping on the first man who lay trying to pull the bow from his ruptured throat as Hook ran across a room, burst through another door, down a passage, a third door, and he was in a yard, still not thinking, over a wall, a second wall, and there were shouts behind him and screams around him and he was in absolute terror now. He had lost his great yew bow, and had dropped the arrow bags, though he still had the sword every archer was expected to wear. He had never used it. He still wore the ragged red cross of Burgundy too, and he began to tear at the surcoat, trying to rid himself of the symbol as he looked desperately for an escape, any escape, then he scrambled over a stone wall into an alley shadowed by the overhanging houses, but in the dark he saw an open door and ran to it.

The door led into a large empty room where a guttering lantern showed a dead man sprawled across a cushioned wooden bench. The man's blood had sheeted across the flagstones. A tapestry hung on one wall and there were cupboards and a long table holding an abacus and sheets of parchment that were speared on a tall spike. Hook reckoned the dead man must have been a merchant. In one corner a ladder climbed to a higher floor and Hook went up quickly to find a plastered chamber that held a wooden bed with a pallet and blankets. A second ladder led into the attic and he clambered up and pulled the ladder into the space beneath the rafters and cursed himself for not having done the same with the first ladder. Too late now. He dared not drop back into the house and so he crouched in the bat droppings beneath the thatch. He was still shaking. Men were shouting in the houses beneath him, and for a time it seemed he must be discovered, and that discovery seemed imminent when someone climbed into the room where the bed stood, but the man only glanced briefly about before leaving, and the rest of the searchers grew bored or else found other quarry, for after a while their excited shouting died. The screaming went on, indeed the screaming became louder and it seemed to Hook, listening in puzzlement, that a whole group of women were just outside the house, all shrieking, and he flinched at the sound. He thought of Sarah in London, of Sir Martin the priest, and of the men he had just seen who had looked so bored as they raped their two silent victims.

The screaming turned into sobbing, broken only by men's laughter. Hook was shivering, not with cold, but with fear and guilt, and then he shrank into the small space under the sloping rafters because the room beneath was suddenly lit by a lantern. The light leaked through the attic's crude floorboards that were loosely laid over untrimmed beams. A man had climbed into the room and was shouting down the ladder to other men, and then a woman cried and there was the sound of a slap.

'You're a pretty one,' the man said, and Hook was so frightened that he did not even notice that the man spoke English.

'*Non*,' the woman whimpered.

'Too pretty to share. You're all mine, girl.'

Hook peered through a crack in the boards. He could see a wide-brimmed helmet that half obscured the man's shoulders, and then he saw that the woman was a white-robed nun who crouched in a corner of the room. She was whim-pering. *'Jésus,'* she cried, *'Marie, mère de Dieu!'* And the last word turned into a scream as the man drew a knife. *'Non!'* she shouted. *'Non! Non! Non!'* and the helmeted man slapped her hard enough to silence her as he pulled her upright. He put the knife at her neck, then slashed so that her habit was sliced down the front. He ripped the blade further and, despite her struggles, tore the white robe away from her and then cut at her undergarments. He threw her ruined clothes down to the lower floor and, when she was naked, pushed her onto the pallet where she curled into a ball and sobbed.

'Oh, I'm sure God was delighted with that day's work!' the voice said, though no one spoke aloud because the voice was in Hook's head. The words were those John Wilkinson had used to Hook in the cathedral, but the voice did not belong to the old archer. It was a richer, deeper voice, full of warmth, and Hook had a sudden vision of a white-robed man, smiling and carrying a tray heaped with pears and apples. It was Crispinian, the saint to whom he had addressed most of his prayers in Soissons, and now those prayers were being answered in Hook's head, and in Hook's head Crispinian looked sadly at him, and Hook understood that heaven had given him a chance to make amends. The nun in the room below had cried to Christ's mother, and the Virgin must have spoken to the saints of Soissons who now spoke to Hook, but Hook was frightened. He was hearing voices again. He did not know it, but he was kneeling. And no wonder. God was speaking to him through Saint Crispinian.

And Nicholas Hook, outlaw and archer, did not know what to do when God spoke to him. He was filled with terror.

The man in the room below threw down his helmet. He unbuckled his sword belt and tossed it aside, then he growled something at the girl before starting to haul his mail coat and its covering surcoat over his head. Hook, peering between the crude floorboards, recognised the badge on the surcoat as Sir Roger Pallaire's three hawks on a green field. What was that badge doing here? It was the victorious besiegers, not the defeated garrison, who were raping and ransacking the city, yet the three hawks were unmistakably Sir Roger's arms.

'Now,' Saint Crispinian said.

Hook did not move.

'Now!' Saint Crispin snarled in Hook's head. Saint Crispin was not as friendly as Crispinian and Hook flinched when the saint snapped the word.

The man, Hook was not sure whether it was Sir Roger himself or one of his men-at-arms, was struggling with the heavy leather-lined mail coat that was half over his head and constricting his arms.

'For God's sake!' Crispinian appealed to Hook.

'Do it, boy,' Saint Crispin said harshly.

'Save your soul, Nicholas,' Crispinian said gently.

And Hook saved his soul.

He dropped through the hole in the attic floor. He forgot his sword, instead drawing the thick-bladed knife that he had once used to eviscerate deer carcasses. He fell just behind the man who could not see because his mail coat was over his head, but he heard Hook's arrival and he turned just as Hook's blade ripped across his belly. Nicholas Hook gutted the man. The strength of an archer's right arm was in the cut and the blade went deep and the guts slithered out like wet eels sliding from a slit sack as the man gave a strangulated cry that was muffled by the heavy coat shrouding his head, and he cried again as the knife gave a second cut, upwards this time as Hook pushed his knife hand deep into the man's ruined belly to drive the blade up under the ribcage to find and puncture the would-be rapist's heart.

The man dropped back onto the bed and was dead before he hit the pallet.

And Hook, blood-wet to his elbow, stared down at his victim.

He realised later that the down-filled pallet had saved his life for it soaked up the blood that otherwise would have dripped through the floorboards to alarm the men beneath. There were two of them, both wearing Sir Roger's livery, but Hook, standing in fear over his victim, noticed that the dead man's surcoat was made of finely woven linen, much finer than the usual cheap surcoat. He moved away from the hatch in the floor. The two men were ransacking a store cupboard and seemed oblivious of the killing that had just occurred above their heads.

The dead man's mail coat was tight-linked and polished, studded with the buckles that had anchored his plate armour. Hook crouched and tugged the coat clear of the man's head and saw that he had killed Sir Roger Pallaire. Sir Roger, ostensibly a Burgundian ally, had been left alive to rape and steal, which surely meant that Sir Roger had been secretly on the side of the French. Hook tried to comprehend that betrayal, while the naked girl stared at him with eyes and mouth wide open. She looked scared and Hook feared she was about to scream and so he put a finger to his lips, but she shook her head and suddenly began to make small desperate noises, half moans, half gasps, and Hook frowned at first, then understood that silence was more suspicious than the noise of her distress. That was clever of her, he thought. He nodded at her, then cut away a blood-drenched purse attached to Sir Roger's belt. He also pulled Sir Roger's surcoat clear of the mail coat and tossed it with the purse into the attic, then reached up and gripped one of the beams. He pulled himself into the roof space, then stretched his right arm for the girl.

She turned away and Hook hissed at her to come with him, but the girl knew what she wanted. She spat at Sir Roger's corpse, then spat a second time before giving Hook her hand. He pulled her up as easily as he hauled back a bowstring. He gestured at the surcoat and purse and she scooped them up, then followed him along the attic. He pushed through the flimsy wattle screen that divided the roof space and so led her into the neighbouring attic. He trod carefully as the light diminished. He went to the very end, three houses down from where he had killed Sir Roger, and he gestured at the girl again, motioning her to crouch by the gable wall, and then, working slowly so as to make as little noise as possible, he pulled down the roof thatch.

It took maybe an hour. He not only dragged down the thatch, but forced some pegged rafters off the ridge timber, and when he had finished he reckoned it looked as though the roof had collapsed and he and the girl crept under the straw and timbers and huddled there. He had made a hiding place.

And all he could do was wait. The girl sometimes spoke, but Hook had learned little French during his stay in Soissons and he did not understand what she said. He hushed her, and after a while she leaned against him and fell asleep, though sometimes she would whimper and Hook awkwardly tried to soothe her. She was wearing Sir Roger's surcoat, still damp with his blood. Hook untied the purse's strings and saw coins, gold and silver; the price, he suspected, of betrayal.

Dawn was smoky grey. Sir Roger's gutted corpse was found before the sun came up and there was a great hue and cry and Hook heard the men ransacking the row of houses beneath him, but his hiding place was cunningly made and no one thought to look in the tangle of straw and timber. The girl woke then and Hook laid a finger on her lips and she shivered as she clung to him. Hook's fear was still there, but it had settled into a resignation, and somehow the company of the girl gave him a hope that had not been in his soul the night before. Or perhaps, he thought, the twin saints of Soissons were protecting him and he made the sign of the cross and sent a prayer of gratitude to Crispin and Crispinian. They were silent now, but he had done what they had told him to do, and then he wondered if it had been Crispinian who had spoken to him in London. That seemed unlikely, but who had it been? God? Yet that question was unimportant against his realisation that he had done what he had failed to do in London and so hope flickered inside him. Hope of redemption and survival. It was a feeble hope, small as a candle's flame in a high wind, but it was there.

The city had become quieter as the dawn approached, but as the sun rose over the cathedral the noise began again. There were screams and moans and cries. There was a gap in the ragged collapsed thatch and Hook could see down into the small square in front of the church of Saint Antoine-le-Petit. The two girls who had been tied to the barrels were gone, though the crossbowmen and men-at-arms were still there. A brindled dog sniffed at the corpse of a nun who lay with her head in a pool of black blood and with her habit pulled up above her waist. A man-at-arms rode through the square, a naked girl draped belly down across the saddle in front of him. He slapped her rump two-handed, as though he played a drum, and the watching men laughed.

Hook waited. He needed to piss badly, but dared not move, so he wet his breeches and the girl smelt it and grimaced, but had to pee herself a moment later. She began to cry softly and Hook held her close until her tears stopped. She murmured to him, and he murmured back, and neither understood the other, but both were comforted.

Then the sound of more hooves made Hook twist around to peer through a gap in the straw. He could see down into the square where a score or more of horsemen had arrived in front of the church. One man carried a banner of golden

79

lilies on a blue field, the whole surrounded by a red border blazoned with white dots. The horsemen were in armour, though none wore a helmet, and they were followed by armoured men-at-arms who came on foot.

One of the newly arrived riders wore a surcoat that showed three hawks on a green field and Hook realised the horseman must be an Englishman who had been in Sir Roger's service, and it was that man who spurred his horse to the church and, leaning from the saddle, pounded a shortened lance against the door. He shouted something, though Hook was too far away to hear, but it must have been words of reassurance because, a moment later, the church door opened and Sergeant Smithson peered out.

The two men talked, then Smithson went back into the church, and there was a long pause. Hook watched, wondering what was happening, then the church door swung open again and the English archers filed warily into the sunlight. It seemed that Sir Roger had kept his word and Hook, watching from the ravaged gable, wondered if there was any chance of joining the bowmen who now gathered in front of the Englishman's horse. Sir Roger must have agreed that the archers would be spared, for the French appeared to be welcoming them. Smithson's men piled their bows, arrow bags and swords by the church door and then, one by one, knelt to a horseman whose stallion was gaudy with the golden lilies on their blue cloth. The rider wore a gold coronet and bright polished armour and he raised a hand in what appeared to be a kindly benediction. Only John Wilkinson hung back close to the church.

If I can reach the street, Hook thought, then I can run to join my countrymen. 'No,' Saint Crispinian whispered in Hook's head, startling him. The girl was clutching him.

'No?' Hook whispered aloud.

'No,' Saint Crispinian said again, very firmly.

The girl asked Hook something and he hushed her. 'Wasn't talking to you, lass,' he whispered.

The blue and gold horseman held his mailed fist high for a few heartbeats, then abruptly dropped his hand.

And the massacre began.

The dismounted men-at-arms drew swords and attacked the kneeling archers. The first of the bowmen died swiftly because they were unprepared, but others had time to draw their short knives and fight back, but the Frenchmen were in plate armour and they carried the longer blades and they came at the archers from every side. Sir Roger's man-at-arms watched. John Wilkinson snatched up a sword from the pile by the church door, but a man-at-arms ran him through with a shortened lance, and a second Frenchman cut down through his neck so that Wilkinson's blood sprayed high on the door's stone archway, which was carved with angels and fishes. Some archers were taken alive, bludgeoned back to the ground and guarded there by the grinning men-at-arms.

The man in the golden coronet turned and rode away, followed by his standard-bearer, his squire, his page and his mounted followers. The Englishman wearing the badge of the three hawks rode with them, turning his back on the surviving archers who called out for mercy. But there was no mercy.

The French had long memories of defeat and they hated the men who drew the long war bow. At Crécy the French had outnumbered the English and had trapped them, and the French had charged across the low valley to rid the world of the impudent invaders, and it had been the archers who had defeated them by filling the sky with goose-fledged death and so cut down noble knights with their long-nosed arrows. Then, at Poitiers, the archers had ripped apart the chivalry of France and at that day's end the King of France was a prisoner, and all those insults still rankled, and so there was no mercy.

Hook and the girl listened. There were thirty or forty archers still alive and the French first chopped two fingers from each man's right hand so they could never again draw a bow. A big-bellied, wide-grinned Frenchman took the fingers with a mallet and chisel, and some of the archers took the agony in silence, while others had to be dragged protesting to the barrel on which their hands were spread. Hook thought the revenge would end there, but it had only begun. The French wanted more than fingers, they wanted pain and death.

A tall man, mounted on a high horse, watched the archers' deaths. The man had long black hair that fell below his armoured shoulders and Hook, who had the eyesight of a hawk, could clearly see the man's handsome, sun-darkened face. He had a sword-blade of a nose, a wide mouth and a long jaw shadowed by stubble. Over his armour he wore a bright surcoat that showed a golden sun from which rays snaked and shot, and on the bright sun was an eagle's head. The girl did not see the man. She had her face buried in Hook's arms. She could hear the screams, but she would not watch. She whimpered whenever a man screamed under the exquisite pain that the French exacted as revenge.

Hook watched. He reckoned the tall man who wore the eagle and the sun could have stopped the torture and murder, but the man did nothing. He sat in his saddle and watched impassively as the French stripped the surviving archers naked, then took their eyes with the points of long knives. The men-at-arms taunted the newly-blinded archers and scoured out their sockets with sharp blades. One Frenchman pretended to eat an eyeball, and the others laughed. The long-haired man did not laugh, he just observed, and his face showed nothing as the blinded men were laid flat on the cobbles to be castrated. Their screams filled the city that was already filled with screaming. It was only when the last

82

blind Englishman had been gelded that the handsome man on the handsome warhorse left the square and the archers were left to bleed to death, sightless under a summer sky. Death took a long time, and Hook shivered even though the air was warm. Saint Crispinian was silent. A naked woman, her breasts cut off and her body red with blood, collapsed amidst the dying archers and wept there until a Frenchman, tired of her tears, casually stove in her skull with a battle-axe. Dogs sniffed the dying.

The sack of the city continued all day. The cathedral and the parish churches and the nunnery and the priories were all plundered. Women and children were raped and raped again, and their menfolk were murdered and God turned His face away from Soissons. The Sire de Bournonville was executed, and he was fortunate because he died without being tortured first. The castle, supposedly a refuge, had fallen without a fight as the French, permitted into the town by the treachery of Sir Roger, found its gate open and its portcullis raised. The Burgundians died, and only Sir Roger's men, complicit in their dead leader's betrayal, had been allowed to live as the city was put to the sword. The citizens had resented their Burgundian garrison and had never abandoned their loyalty to the King of France, but now, in a welter of blood, rape and theft, the French rewarded that loyalty with massacre.

'*Je suis Melisande,*' the girl said over and over, and Hook did not understand at first, but at last realised she was saying her name.

'Melisande?' he asked.

'*Oui,*' she said.

'Nicholas.'

'Nicholas,' she repeated.

'Just Nick,' he said.

'Jusnick?'

83

'Nick.'

'Nick.' They spoke in whispers, they waited, they listened to the sound of a city screaming, and they smelt the ale and the blood.

'I don't know how we get out of this place,' Hook said to Melisande, who did not understand. She nodded anyway, then fell asleep under the straw with her head on his shoulder and Hook closed his eyes and prayed to Crispinian. Help us out of the city, he begged the saint, and help me get home. Except, he thought with sudden despair, an outlaw has no home.

'You will reach home,' Saint Crispinian said to him.

Hook paused, wondering how a saint could speak to him. Had he imagined the voice? Yet it seemed real, as real as the screams that had marked the death of archers. Then he wondered how he could escape the city because the French would surely have sentries on all the gates.

'Then use the breach,' Saint Crispinian suggested gently.

'We'll go out through the breach,' Hook said to Melisande, but she was still asleep.

As night fell Hook watched pigs, evidently released from their sties behind the city's houses, feasting on the dead archers. Soissons was quieter now, the victors' appetites slaked on bodies, ale and wine. The moon rose, but God sent high clouds that first misted the silver, then hid it, and in the darkness Hook and Melisande made their way downstairs, and out into the reeking street. It was the middle of the night and men snored in broken houses. No one guarded the breach. Melisande, swathed in Sir Roger's bloody surcoat, held Hook's hand as they clambered over the wall's rubble, and then as they crossed the low ground where the tanning pits stank and walked uphill past the abandoned besiegers' camp and so into the higher woods where no blood reeked and no corpses rotted.

84

Soissons was dead.

But Hook and Melisande lived.

'The saints talk to me,' he told her in the dawn. 'Crispinian does, anyway. The other fellow is grimmer. He sometimes speaks, but he doesn't say much.'

'Crispinian,' Melisande repeated, and seemed pleased that she understood one thing he said.

'He seems nice,' Hook said, 'and he's looking after me. Looking after you too, now, I reckon!' He smiled at her, suddenly confident. 'We must get you some proper clothes, lass. You look right strange in that coat.'

Though, if Melisande looked strange, she was also lovely. Hook did not notice that until the first dawn in the high woods when the sun shot a million lances of green-shimmering gold through leaves and branches to light a slender, high-boned face wreathed in hair as black as night. She had grey eyes, pale as moonlight, a long nose and a stubborn cast to her chin, which, as Hook was to learn, reflected her character. She was pitifully thin, but had a sinewy strength and a scorn of weakness. Her mouth was wide, expressive and talkative. Hook was eventually to discover that she had been a novice in a house of nuns who were forbidden to speak, and in those first days it seemed Melisande needed to compensate for months of enforced silence. He understood nothing, yet he listened entranced as the girl chattered on.

They stayed the first day in the woods. From time to time horsemen appeared in the valley below the beeches. They were the victors of the siege of Soissons, but they were not dressed for war. Some were hawking, others seemed to be riding for the pleasure of it, and none interfered with the few fugitives who had apparently escaped Soissons and were now walking southwards, yet still Hook did not want to risk an encounter with a Frenchman and so he stayed hidden until nightfall. He had decided to head westwards, towards England, though being an outlaw meant that England was as dangerous as France, but he did not know where else he could go. He and Melisande travelled by night, their way lit by the moon. Their food was stolen, usually a lamb Hook took in the darkness. He feared the dogs that guarded the flocks, but perhaps it was Saint Crispin with his shepherd's crook who protected him, for the dogs never stirred as Hook cut an animal's throat. He would carry the small carcass back to the deep woods where he would make a fire and cook the flesh. 'You can go away on your own,' he told Melisande one morning.

'Go?' she asked, frowning, not understanding him.

'If you want, lass. You can go!' He waved vaguely south-wards and was rewarded with a scowl and a burst of incomprehensible French, which he took to mean that Melisande would stay with him. She did stay, and her presence was both a comfort and a worry. Hook was not sure if he could escape the French countryside, and if he did he could see no future. He prayed to Saint Crispinian, and hoped the martyr could help him once he reached England, if he reached England, but Saint Crispinian was silent.

Yet if Saint Crispinian said nothing, he did send Hook and Melisande a priest who was the *curé* of a parish close to the River Oise and the priest found the two fugitives sleeping under a fallen willow among a thick stand of alders, and he took them to his home where his woman fed them. Father Michel was embittered and morose, yet he took pity on them. He spoke some English that he had learned when he had been chaplain to a French lord who had held an English prisoner in his manor. That experience of being a chaplain had left Father Michel hating everyone in authority, whether it was king, bishop or lord, and that hatred was sufficient to let him help an English archer. 'You will go to Calais,' he told Hook.

'I'm an outlaw, father.'

'Outlaw?' Eventually the priest understood, but dismissed the fear. '*Proscrit*, eh? But England is home. A large place, yes? You go home and you stay far from where you sinned. What was your sin?'

'I hit a priest.'

Father Michel laughed and clapped Hook on the back. 'That was well done! I hope it was a bishop?'

'Just a priest.'

'Next time hit a bishop, eh?'

Hook paid for his stay. He chopped firewood, cleared ditches and helped Father Michel rethatch a cow byre, while Melisande assisted the housekeeper to cook, wash and mend. 'The villagers will not betray you,' the priest assured Hook.

'Why not, father?'

'Because they fear me. I can send them to hell,' the priest said grimly. He liked to talk with Hook as a way of improving his English and one day, as Hook trimmed the pear trees behind the house, he listened as Hook haltingly admitted to hearing voices. Father Michel crossed himself. 'It could be the devil's voice?' he suggested.

'That worries me,' Hook admitted.

'But I think not,' Father Michel said gently. 'You take a lot from that tree!'

'This tree's a mess, father. You should have cut her back last winter, but this won't hurt her. You want some pears? You can't let her grow wild. Trust me. Cut and cut! And when you think you've cut too much, cut the same amount again!'

'Cut and cut, eh? If I have no pears next year I will know you are the devil's man.'

'It's Saint Crispinian who talks to me,' Hook said, lopping another branch.

'But only if God lets him,' the priest said and made the

sign of the cross, 'which means God talks to you. I am glad no saints talk to me.'

'You're glad?'

'I think those who hear voices? Either they are saints themselves or they are for burning.'

'I'm no saint,' Hook said.

'But God has chosen you. He makes very strange choices,' Father Michel said, then laughed.

Père Michel also talked with Melisande and so Hook learned something about the girl. Her father was a lord, the priest said, a lord called *le Seigneur d'Enfer*, and her mother had been a servant girl. 'So your Melisande is another nobleman's bastard,' Father Michel said, 'born to trouble.' Her noble father had arranged for Melisande to enter the nunnery in Soissons as a novice and to be a kitchen maid to the nuns. 'That is how lords hide their sins,' Father Michel explained bitterly, 'by putting their bastards in prison.'

'Prison?'

'She did not want to be a nun. You know what her name is?'

'Melisande.'

'Melisande was a Queen of Jerusalem,' Père Michel said, smiling. 'And this Melisande loves you.' Hook said nothing to that. 'Take care of her,' Père Michel said sternly on the day they left.

They went in disguise. It was difficult to hide Hook's stature, but Father Michel gave him a white penitent's robe and a leper's clapper, which was a piece of wood to which two others were attached by leather strips, and Melisande, also in a penitent's robe and with her black hair chopped raggedly short, led him north and west. They were pilgrims, it appeared, seeking a cure for Hook's disease. They lived off alms tossed by folk who did not want to go near Hook, who announced his contagious presence by rattling the clapper loudly. They still moved circumspectly, skirting the larger villages and making a wide detour to avoid the smear of smoke that marked the city of Amiens. They slept in the woods, or in cattle byres, or in haystacks, and the rain soaked them and the sun warmed them and one day, beside the River Canche, they became lovers. Melisande was silent afterwards, but she clung to Hook and he said a prayer of thanks to Saint Crispinian, who ignored him.

The next day they walked north, following a road that led across a wide field between two woods, and off to the west was a small castle half hidden by a stand of trees. They rested in the eastern woods close to a tumbledown forester's cottage with a moss-thick thatch. Barley grew in the wide field, the ears rippling prettily under the breeze. Larks tumbled above them, their song another ripple, and both Hook and Melisande dozed in the late summer's warmth.

'What are you doing here?' a harsh voice demanded. A horseman, dressed richly and with a hooded hawk on his wrist, was watching them from the wood's edge.

Melisande knelt in submission and lowered her head. 'I take my brother to Saint-Omer, lord,' she said.

The horseman, who may or may not have been a lord, took note of Hook's clapper and edged his horse away. 'What do you seek there?' he demanded.

'The blessing of Saint Audomar, lord,' Melisande said. Father Michel had told them Saint-Omer was near Calais, and that many folk sought cures from Saint Audomar's shrine in the town. Father Michel had also said it was much safer to say they were travelling to Saint-Omer than to admit they were headed for the English enclave around Calais.

'God give you a safe journey,' the horseman said grudgingly and tossed a coin into the leaf mould.

'Lord?' Melisande asked.

The rider turned his horse back. 'Yes?'

'Where are we, lord? And how far to Saint-Omer?'

'A very long day's walk,' the man said, gathering his reins, 'and why would you care what this place is called? You won't have heard of it.'

'No, lord,' Melisande said.

The man gazed at her for a heartbeat, then shrugged. 'That castle?' he said, nodding to the battlements showing above the western trees, 'is called Azincourt. I hope your brother is cured.' He gathered his reins and spurred his horse into the barley.

It was four more days before they reached the marshes about Calais. They moved cautiously, avoiding the French patrols that circled the English-held town. It was night when they reached the Nieulay bridge that led onto the causeway that approached the town. Sentries challenged them. 'I'm English!' Hook shouted and then, holding Melisande's hand, stepped cautiously into the flare of torchlight illuminating the bridge's gate.

'Where are you from, lad?' a grey-bearded man in a close-fitting helmet asked.

'We've come from Soissons,' Hook said.

'You've come from . . .' the man took a step forward to peer at Hook and his companion. 'Sweet Jesus Christ. Come on through.'

So Hook stepped through the small gate built into the larger one, and thus he and Melisande crossed into England where he was an outlaw.

But Saint Crispinian had kept his word and Hook had come home.

Even in summer the hall of Calais Castle was chilly. The thick stone walls kept the warmth at bay and so a great fire crackled in the hearth, and in front of the stone fireplace was a wide rug on which two couches stood and six hounds slept. The rest of the room was stone-flagged. Swords were racked along one wall, and iron-tipped lances rested on trestles. Sparrows flitted among the beams. The shutters at the western end of the hall were open and Hook could hear the endless stirring of the sea.

The garrison commander and his elegant lady sat on one couch. Hook had been told their names, but the words had slithered through his head and so he did not know who they were. Six men-at-arms stood behind the couch, all watching Hook and Melisande with sceptical and hostile eyes, while a priest stood at the rug's edge, looking down at the two fugitives who knelt on the stone flags. 'I do not understand,' the priest said in a nasally unpleasant voice, 'why you left Lord Slayton's service.'

'Because I refused to kill a girl, father,' Hook explained.

'And Lord Slayton wished her dead?'

'His priest did, sir.'

'Sir Giles Fallowby's son,' the man on the couch put in, and his voice suggested he did not like Sir Martin.

'So a man of God wished her dead,' the priest ignored the garrison commander's tone, 'yet you knew better?' His voice was dangerous with menace.

'She was only a girl,' Hook said.

'It was through woman,' the priest pounced fiercely on Hook's answer, 'that sin entered the world.'

The elegant lady put a long pale hand over her mouth as if to hide a yawn. There was a tiny dog on her lap, a little bundle of white fur studded with pugnacious eyes, and she stroked its head. 'I am bored,' she said, speaking to no one in particular.

There was a long silence. One of the hounds whimpered in its sleep and the garrison commander leaned forward to pat its head. He was a heavy-set, black-bearded man who now gestured impatiently towards Hook. 'Ask him about Soissons, father,' he ordered.

'I was coming to that, Sir William,' the priest said.

'Then come to it quickly,' the woman said coldly.

'Are you outlawed?' the priest asked instead and, when the archer did not answer, he repeated the question more loudly and still Hook did not answer.

'Answer him,' Sir William growled.

'I would have thought his silence was eloquence itself,' the lady said. 'Ask him about Soissons.'

The priest grimaced at her commanding tone, but obeyed. 'Tell us what happened in Soissons,' he demanded, and Hook told the tale again, how the French had entered the town by the southern gate and how they had raped and killed, and how Sir Roger Pallaire had betrayed the English archers.

'And you alone escaped?' the priest asked sourly.

'Saint Crispinian helped me,' Hook said.

'Oh! Saint Crispinian did?' the priest asked, raising an

92

eyebrow. 'How very obliging of him.' There was a snort of half-suppressed laughter from one of the men-at-arms, while the others just stared with distaste at the kneeling archer. Disbelief hung in the castle's great hall like the woodsmoke that leaked around the wide hearth's opening. Another of the men-at-arms was staring fixedly at Melisande and now leaned close to his neighbour and whispered something that made the other man laugh. 'Or did the French let you go?' the priest demanded sharply.

'No, sir!' Hook said.

'Perhaps they let you go for a reason!'

'No!'

'Even a humble archer can count men,' the priest said, 'and if our lord the king collects an army, then the French will wish to know numbers.'

'No, sir!' Hook said again.

'So they let you go, and bribed you with a whore?' the priest suggested.

'She's no whore!' Hook protested and the men-at-arms sniggered.

Melisande had not yet spoken. She had seemed overawed by the big men in their mail coats and by the supercilious priest and by the languorous woman who sprawled on the cushioned couch, but now Melisande found her tongue. She might not have understood the priest's insult, but she recognised his tone, and she suddenly straightened her back and spoke fast and defiantly. She spoke French, and spoke it so quickly that Hook did not understand one word in a hundred, but everyone else in the room spoke the language and they all listened. She spoke passionately, indignantly, and neither the garrison commander nor the priest interrupted her. Hook knew she was telling the tale of Soissons's fall, and after a while tears came to her eyes and rolled down her cheeks and her voice rose as she hammered the priest with her story. She ran out of words, gestured at Hook and her head dropped as she began to sob.

There was silence for a few heartbeats. A sergeant in a mail coat noisily opened the hall door, saw that the room was occupied, and left just as loudly. Sir William looked judiciously at Hook. 'You murdered Sir Roger Pallaire?' he asked harshly.

'I killed him, sir.'

'A good deed from an outlaw,' Sir William's wife said firmly, 'if what the girl says is true.'

'If,' the priest said.

'I believe her,' the woman said, then rose from the couch, tucked the little dog into one arm and walked to the rug's edge where she stooped and raised Melisande by the elbow. She spoke to her in soft French, then led her towards the hall's far end and so through a curtained opening.

Sir William waited till his wife was gone, then stood. 'I believe he's telling the truth, father,' he said firmly.

'He might be,' the priest conceded.

'I believe he is,' Sir William insisted.

'We could put him to the test?' the priest suggested with scarcely concealed eagerness.

'You would torture him?' Sir William asked, shocked.

'The truth is sacred, my lord,' the priest said, bowing slightly. '*Et cognoscetis veritatem,*' he declaimed, '*et veritas liberabit vos!*' He made the sign of the cross. 'You will know the truth, my lord,' he translated, 'and the truth will set you free.'

'I am free,' the black-bearded man snarled, 'and it is not our duty to rack the truth out of some poor archer. We shall leave that to others.'

'Of course, my lord,' the priest said, barely hiding his disappointment.

'Then you know where he must go.'

'Indeed, my lord.'

'So arrange it,' Sir William said before crossing to Hook and indicating that the archer should stand. 'Did you kill any of them?' he demanded.

'A lot, my lord,' Hook said, remembering the arrows flying into the half-lit breach.

'Good,' Sir William said implacably, 'but you also killed Sir Roger Pallaire. That makes you either a hero or a murderer.'

'I'm an archer,' Hook said stubbornly.

'And an archer whose tale must be heard across the water,' Sir William said, then handed Hook a silver coin. 'We've heard tales of Soissons,' he went on grimly, 'but you are the first to bring confirmation.'

'If he was there,' the priest remarked snidely.

'You heard the girl,' Sir William snarled at the priest who bridled at the admonition. Sir William turned back to Hook. 'Tell your tale in England.'

'I'm outlawed,' Hook said uncertainly.

'You'll do what you're told to do,' Sir William snapped, 'and you're going to England.'

And so Hook and Melisande were taken aboard a ship that sailed to England. They then travelled with a courier who carried messages to London and also had money that paid for ale and food on the journey. Melisande was dressed in decent clothes now, provided by Lady Bardolf, Sir William's wife, and she rode a small mare that the courier had demanded from the stables in Dover Castle. She was saddle-sore by the time they reached London where, having crossed the bridge, they surrendered their horses to the grooms in the Tower. 'You will wait here,' the courier commanded them, and would not tell Hook more, and so he and Melisande found a place to sleep in the cow byre, and no one in the great fortress seemed to know why they had been summoned there.

'You're not prisoners,' a sergeant of archers told them.

'But we're not allowed out,' Hook said.

'No, you're not allowed out,' the ventenar conceded, 'but you're not prisoners.' He grinned. 'If you were prisoners, lad, you wouldn't be cuddling that little lass every night. Where's your bow?'

'Lost it in France.'

'Then let's find you a new one,' the ventenar said. He was called Venables and he had fought for the old king at Shrewsbury where he had taken an arrow in the leg that had left him with a limp. He led Hook to an undercroft of the great keep where there were wide wooden racks holding hundreds of newly made bows. 'Pick one,' Venables said.

It was dim in the undercroft where the bowstaves, each longer than a tall man, lay close together. None was strung, though all were tipped with horn nocks ready to take their cords. Hook pulled them out one by one and ran a hand across their thick bellies. The bows, he decided, had been well made. Some were knobbly where the bowyer had let a knot stand proud rather than weaken the wood, and most had a faintly greasy feel because they had been painted with a mix of wax and tallow. A few bows were unpainted, the wood still seasoning, but those bows were not yet ready for the cord and Hook ignored them. 'They're mostly made in Kent,' Venables said, 'but a few come from London. They don't make good archers in this part of the world, boy, but they do make good bows.'

'They do,' Hook agreed. He had pulled one of the longest staves from the rack. The timber swelled to a thick belly that he gripped in his left hand as he flexed the upper limb a small amount. He took the bow to a place where sunlight shone through a rusted grating.

The stave was a thing of beauty, he thought. The yew had been cut in a southern country where the sun shone brighter, and this bow had been carved from the tree's trunk. It was close-grained and had no knots. Hook ran his hand down the wood, feeling its swell and fingering the small ridges left by the bowyer's float, the drawknife that shaped the weapon. The stave was new because the sapwood, which formed the back of the bow, was almost white. In time, he knew, it would turn to the colour of honey, but for now the bow's back, which would be farthest from him when he hauled the cord, was the shade of Melisande's breasts. The belly of the bow, made from the trunk's heartwood, was dark brown, the colour of Melisande's face, so that the bow seemed to be made of two strips of wood, one white and one brown, which were perfectly married, though in truth the stave was one single shaft of beautifully smoothed timber cut from where the heartwood and sapwood met in the yew's trunk.

God made the bow, a priest had once said in Hook's village church, as God made man and woman. The visiting priest had meant that God had married heartwood and sapwood, and it was this marriage that made the great war bow so lethal. The dark heartwood of the bow's belly was stiff and unyielding. It resisted bending, while the light-coloured sapwood of the bow's spine did not mind being pulled into a curve, yet, like the heartwood, it wanted to straighten and it possessed a springiness that, released from pressure, whipped the stave back to its normal shape. So the flexible spine pulled and the stiff belly pushed, and so the long arrow flew.

'Have to be strong to pull that one,' Venables said dubiously. 'God knows what that bowyer was thinking! Maybe he thought Goliath needed a stave, eh?'

'He didn't want to cut the stave,' Hook suggested, 'because it's perfect.'

'If you think you can draw it, lad, it's yours. Help yourself to a bracer,' Venables said, gesturing to a pile of horn bracers, 'and to a cord.' He waved towards a barrel of strings.

The cords had a faintly sticky feel because the hemp had been coated with hoof glue to protect the strings from damp. Hook found a couple of long cords and tied a loop-knot in the end of one that he hooked over the notched horn-tip of the bow's lower limb. Then, using all his strength, he flexed the bow to judge the length of cord needed, made a loop in the other end of the string and, again exerting every scrap of muscle power, bent the bow and slipped the new loop over the top horn nock. The centre of the cord, where it would lie on the horn-sliver in an arrow's nock, had been whipped with more hemp to strengthen the string where it notched into the arrows.

'Shoot it in,' Venables suggested. He was a middle-aged man in the service of the Tower's constable and he was a friendly soul, liking to spend his day chattering to anyone who would listen to his stories of battles long ago. He carried an arrow bag up to the stretch of mud and grass outside the keep and dropped it with a clatter. Hook put the bracer on his left forearm, tying its strings so the slip of horn lay on the inside of his wrist to protect his skin from the bowstring's lash. A scream sounded and was cut off. 'That's Brother Bailey,' Venables said in explanation.

'Brother Bailey?'

'Brother Bailey is a Benedictine,' Venables said, 'and the king's chief torturer. He's getting the truth out of some poor bastard.'

'They wanted to torture me in Calais,' Hook said.

'They did?'

'A priest did.'

'They're always eager to twist the rack, aren't they? I never did understand that! They tell you God loves you, then they kick the shit out of you. Well, if they do question you, lad, tell them the truth.'

'I did.'

98

'Mind you, that doesn't always help,' Venables said. The scream sounded again and he jerked his head towards the muffled noise. 'That poor bastard probably did tell the truth, but Brother Bailey does like to be certain, he does. Let's see how that stave shoots, shall we?'

Hook planted a score of arrows point down in the soil. A faded and much punctured target was propped in front of a stack of rotting hay at the top of the stretch of grass. The range was short, no more than a hundred paces, and the target was twice as wide as a man and Hook would have expected to hit that easy mark every time, but he suspected his first arrows would fly wild.

The bow was under tension, but now he had to teach it to bend. He drew it only a short way the first time and the arrow scarcely reached the target. He drew it a little further, then again, each time bringing the cord closer to his face, yet never drawing the bow to its full curve. He shot arrow after arrow, and all the time he was learning the bow's idiosyncrasies and the bow was learning to yield to his pressure, and it was an hour before he pulled the cord back to his ear and loosed the first arrow with the stave's full power.

He did not know it, but he was smiling. There was a beauty there, a beauty of yew and hemp, of silk and feathers, of steel and ash, of man and weapon, of pure power, of the bow's vicious tension that, released through fingers rubbed raw by the coarse hemp, shot the arrow to hiss in its flight and thump as it struck home. The last arrow went clean through the riddled target's centre and buried itself to its feathers in the hay. 'You've done this before,' Venables said with a grin.

'I have,' Hook agreed, 'but I've been away too long. Fingers are sore!'

'They'll harden fast, lad,' Venables said, 'and if they don't torture and kill you, then you might think of joining us! Not a bad life at the Tower. Good food, plenty of it, and not much in the way of duties.'

'I'd like that,' Hook said absent-mindedly. He was concentrating on the bow. He had thought that the weeks of travel might have diminished his strength and eroded his skill, but he was pulling easily, loosing smoothly and aiming true. There was a slight ache in his shoulder and back, and his two fingertips were scraped raw, but that was all. And he was happy, he suddenly realised. That thought checked him, made him stare in wonder at the target. Saint Crispinian had guided him into a sunlit place and had given him Melisande, and then the happiness soured as he remembered he was still an outlaw. If Sir Martin or Lord Slayton discovered that Nicholas Hook was alive and in England they would demand him and would probably hang him.

'Let's see how quick you are,' Venables suggested.

Hook pushed another handful of arrows into the turf and remembered the night of smoke and screams when the glimmering metal-clad men had come through the breach of Soissons and he had shot again and again, not thinking, not aiming, just letting the bow do its work. This new bow was stronger, more lethal, but just as quick. He did not think, he just loosed, picked a new arrow and laid it over the bow, raised the stave, hauled the cord and loosed again. A dozen arrows whickered over the turf and struck the target one after the other. If a man's spread hand had been over the central mark then each arrow would have struck it.

'Twelve,' a cheerful voice said behind him, 'one arrow for each disciple.' Hook turned to see a priest watching him. The man, who had a round, merry face framed by wispy white hair, was carrying a great leather bag in one hand and had Melisande's elbow firmly clutched in the other. 'You must be Master Hook!' the priest said, 'of course you are! I'm Father Ralph, may I try?' He put down the bag, released

Melisande's arm and reached for Hook's bow. 'Do allow me,' he pleaded, 'I used to draw the bow in my youth!'

Hook surrendered the bow and watched as Father Ralph tried to pull the cord. The priest was a well-built man, though grown rather portly from good living, but even so he only managed to pull the cord back about a hand's breadth before the stave began quivering with the effort. Father Ralph shook his head. 'I'm not the man I was!' he said, then gave the bow back and watched as Hook, apparently effortlessly, bent the long stave to unhook the string. 'It is time we all talked,' Father Ralph said very cheerfully. 'A most excellent day to you, Sergeant Venables, how are you?'

'I'm well, father, very well!' Venables grinned, bobbed his head and knuckled his forehead. 'Leg doesn't hurt much, father, not if the wind ain't in the east.'

'Then I shall pray God to send you nothing but west winds!' Father Ralph said happily, 'nothing but westerlies! Come, Master Hook! Shed light upon my darkness! Illuminate me!'

The priest, again clutching his bag, led Hook and Melisande to rooms built against the Tower's curtain wall. The chamber he chose, which was small and panelled with carved timber, had two chairs and a table and Father Ralph insisted on finding a third chair. 'Sit yourselves,' he said, 'sit, sit!'

He wished to know the full story of Soissons and so, in English and French, Hook and Melisande told their tale again. They described the assault, the rapes and the murders, and Father Ralph's pen never stopped scratching. His bag contained sheets of parchment, an ink flask and quills, and he wrote unceasingly, occasionally throwing in a question. Melisande spoke the most, her voice sounding indignant as she recounted the night's horrors. 'Tell me about the nuns,' Father Ralph said, then made a fluttery gesture as if he had been a fool and repeated the question in French. Melisande sounded ever more indignant, staring wide-eyed at Father Ralph when he motioned her to silence so his pen could catch up with her flood of words.

Hoofbeats sounded outside and, a few moments later, there was the clangour of swords striking each other. Hook, as Melisande told her story, looked through the open window to see men-at-arms practising on the ground where his arrows had flown. They were all dressed in full plate armour that made a dull sound if a blade struck. One man, distinctive because his armour was black, was being attacked by two others and he was defending himself skilfully, though Hook had the impression that the two men were not trying as hard as they might. A score of other men applauded the contest. '*Et gladius diaboli*,' Father Ralph read aloud slowly as he finished writing a sentence, '*repletus est sanguine*. Good! Oh, that is most excellent!'

'Is that Latin, father?' Hook asked.

'It is, yes! Yes, indeed! Latin! The language of God! Or perhaps He speaks Hebrew? I suppose that's more likely and it will make things rather awkward in heaven, won't it? Will we all have to learn Hebrew? Or maybe we shall find ourselves gloriously voluble in that language when we reach the heavenly pastures. I was saying how the devil's sword was slaked with blood!' Father Ralph chuckled at that sentiment, then motioned for Melisande to continue. He wrote again, his pen flying over the parchment. The sound of confident male laughter sounded from the turf outside where two other men-at-arms now fought, their swords quick in the sunlight. 'You wonder,' Father Ralph asked when he had finished yet another page, 'why I transcribe your tale into Latin?'

'Yes, father.'

'So all Christendom will know what sanguinary devils the French are! We shall copy this tale a hundred times and send it to every bishop, every abbot, every king and every prince in Christendom. Let them know the truth of Soissons! Let them know how the French treat their own people! Let them know that Satan's dwelling place is in France, eh?' He smiled.

'Satan does live there,' a harsh voice spoke behind Hook, 'and he must be driven out!' Hook twisted in his chair to see that the black-armoured man-at-arms was standing in the doorway. He had taken off his helmet and his brown hair was plastered down by sweat in which an impression of his helmet liner remained. He was a young man who looked familiar, though Hook could not place him, but then Hook saw the deep scar beside the long nose and he almost knocked the chair over as he scrambled to kneel before his king. His heart was beating fast and the terror was as great as when he had waited by the breach at Soissons. The king. That was all he could think of, this was the king.

Henry made an irritable gesture that Hook should rise, an order Hook was too nervous to obey. The king edged between the table and the wall to look at what Father Ralph had written. 'My Latin is not what it should be,' he said, 'but the gist is clear enough.'

'It confirms all the rumours we heard, sire,' Father Ralph said.

'Sir Roger Pallaire?'

'Killed by this young man, sire,' Father Ralph said, gesturing at Hook.

'He was a traitor,' the king said coldly, 'our agents in France have confirmed that.'

'He screams in hell now, sire,' Father Ralph said, 'and his screams shall not end with time itself.'

'Good,' Henry said curtly and sifted the pages. 'Nuns? Surely not?'

'Indeed, sire,' Father Ralph said. 'The brides of Christ were violated and murdered. They were dragged from their prayers to become playthings, sire. We had heard of it and we had scarce dared to believe it, but this young lady confirms it.'

The king rested his gaze on Melisande, who, like Hook, had dropped to her knees where, like Hook, she quivered with nervousness. 'Get up,' the king said to her, then looked at a crucifix hanging on the wall. He frowned and bit his lower lip. 'Why did God allow it, father?' he asked after a while, and there was both pain and puzzlement in his voice. 'Nuns? God should have protected them, surely? He should have sent angels to guard them!'

'Perhaps God wanted their fate to be a sign,' Father Ralph suggested.

'A sign?'

'Of the wickedness of the French, sire, and thus the right-eousness of your claim to that unhappy realm's crown.'

'My task, then, is to avenge the nuns,' Henry said.

'You have many tasks, sire,' Father Ralph said humbly, 'but that is certainly one.'

Henry looked at Hook and Melisande, his armoured fingers tapping on the table. Hook dared to look up once and saw the anxiety on the king's narrow face. That surprised him. He would have guessed that a king was above worry and aloof to questions of right or wrong, but it was clear that this king was pained by his need to discover God's will. 'So these two,' Henry said, still watching Hook and Melisande, 'are telling the truth?'

'I would swear to it, sire,' Father Ralph said warmly.

The king gazed at Melisande, his face betraying no emotion, then the cold eyes slid to Hook. 'Why did you alone survive?' he asked in a suddenly hard voice.

'I prayed, sire,' Hook said humbly.

'The others didn't pray?' the king asked sharply.

'Some did, sire.'

'But God chose to answer your prayers?'

'I prayed to Saint Crispinian, sire,' Hook said, paused, then plunged on with his answer, 'and he spoke to me.'

Silence again. A raven cawed outside and the clash of swords echoed from the Tower's keep. Then the King of England reached out his gauntleted hand and tipped Hook's face up so he could look into the archer's eyes. 'He spoke to you?' the king asked.

Hook hesitated. He felt as though his heart was beating at the base of his throat. Then he decided to tell the whole truth, however unlikely it sounded. 'Saint Crispinian spoke to me, sire,' he said, 'in my head.'

The king just stared at Hook. Father Ralph opened his mouth as though he were about to speak, but a mailed royal hand cautioned the priest to silence and Henry, King of England, went on staring so that Hook felt fear creep up his spine like a cold snake. 'It's warm in here,' the king said suddenly, 'you will talk with me outside.'

For a heartbeat Hook thought he must have been speaking to Father Ralph, but it was Hook the king wanted, and so Nicholas Hook went into the afternoon sunshine and walked beside his king. Henry's armour squeaked slightly as it rubbed against the greased leather beneath. His men-at-arms had instinctively approached as he appeared, but he waved them away. 'Tell me,' Henry said, 'how Crispinian spoke to you.'

Hook told how both saints had appeared to him, and how both had spoken to him, but that it was Crispinian who had been the friendly voice. He felt embarrassed to describe the conversations, but Henry took it seriously. He stopped and faced Hook. He was half a head shorter than the archer, so he had to look up to judge Hook's face, but it appeared he was more than satisfied by what he saw. 'You are blessed,' he said. 'I would wish the saints would speak to me,' he said wistfully. 'You have been spared for a purpose,' he added firmly.

'I'm just a forester, sire,' Hook said awkwardly. For a heart-beat he was tempted to tell the further truth, that he was an outlaw too, but caution checked his tongue.

'No, you are an archer,' the king insisted, 'and it was in our realm of France that the saints assisted you. You are God's instrument.'

Hook did not know what to say and so said nothing.

'God granted me the thrones of England and of France,' the king said harshly, 'and if it is His will, we shall take the throne of France back.' His mailed right fist clenched suddenly. 'If we do so decide,' he went on, 'I shall want men favoured by the saints of France. Are you a good archer?'

'I think so, sire,' Hook said diffidently.

'Venables!' the king called and the ventenar limped hurriedly across the turf and fell to his knees. 'Can he shoot?' Henry asked.

Venables grinned. 'As good as any man I ever did see, sire. As good as the man who put that arrow into your face.'

The king evidently liked Venables for he smiled at the slight insolence, then touched an iron-sheathed finger to the deep scar beside his nose. 'If he'd shot harder, Venables, you would have another king now.'

'Then God did a good deed that day, sire, in preserving you, and God be thanked for that great mercy.'

'Amen,' Henry said. He offered Hook a swift smile. 'The arrow glanced off a helmet,' he explained, 'and that took the force from it, but it still went deep.'

'You should have had your visor closed, sire,' Venables said reprovingly.

'Men should see a prince's face in battle,' Henry said firmly, then looked back to Hook. 'We shall find you a lord.'

'I'm outlawed, lord,' Hook blurted out, unable to conceal the truth any longer. 'I'm sorry, sire.'

'Outlawed?' the king asked harshly, 'for what crime?'

Hook had dropped to his knees again. 'For hitting a priest, sire.'

The king was silent and Hook dared not look up. He expected punishment, but instead, to his astonishment, the king chuckled. 'It seems that Saint Crispinian has forgiven you that grievous error, so who am I to condemn you? And in this realm,' Henry went on, his voice harder now, 'a man is what I say he is, and I say you are an archer and we shall find you a lord.' Henry, without another word, walked back to his companions and Hook let out a long breath.

Sergeant Venables climbed to his feet, flinching from the pain in his wounded leg. 'Chatted to you, did he?'

'Yes, sergeant.'

'He likes doing that. His father didn't. His father was all gloomy, but our Hal is never too grand to say a word or two to a common bastard like you or me.' Venables spoke warmly. 'So, he's finding you a new lord?'

'So he said.'

'Well, let's hope it's not Sir John.'

'Sir John?'

'Mad bastard he is,' Venables said, 'mad and bad. Sir John will have you killed in no time at all!' Venables chuckled, then nodded to the houses built against the curtain wall. 'Father Ralph is looking for you.'

Father Ralph was beckoning from the doorway. So Hook went to finish his tale.

'Jesus weeping Christ, you spavined fart! Cross it! Cross it! Don't flap it like a wet cock! Cross it! Then close me!' Sir John Cornewaille snarled at Hook.

The sword came again, slashing at Hook's waist, and this time Hook managed to cross his own blade to parry the blow and, as he did so, pushed forward, only to be thumped back by a thrust of Sir John's mailed fist. 'Keep coming,' Sir John urged him, 'crowd me, get me down on the ground, then finish me!' Instead Hook stepped back and brought up his sword to deflect the next swing of Sir John's blade. 'What in Christ's name is the matter with you?' Sir John shouted in rage. 'Have you been weakened by that French whore of yours? By that titless streak of scabby French gristle? Christ's bones, man, find a real woman! Goddington!' Sir John glanced at his centenar, 'Why don't you spread that scabby whore's skinny legs and see if she can even be humped?'

Hook felt the sudden anger then, a red mist of rage that drove him onto Sir John's blade, but the older man stepped lithely aside and flicked his sword so that the blade's flat rapped the back of Hook's skull. Hook turned, his own sword scything at Sir John, who parried easily. Sir John was in full armour, yet moved as lightly as a dancer. He lunged at Hook, and this time Hook remembered the advice and he swept the lunge aside and threw himself on his opponent, using all his weight and height to unbalance the older man, and he knew he was going to hammer Sir John onto the ground where he would beat him to a pulp, but instead he felt a thumping smack on the back of his skull, his vision went dark, the world reeled, and a second crashing blow with the heavy pommel of Sir John's sword threw him face down into the early winter stubble.

He did not hear much of what Sir John said in the next few minutes. Hook's head was painful and spinning, but as he gradually recovered his senses he heard some of the snarled peroration. 'You can feel anger before a fight! But in the fight? Keep your goddam wits about you! Anger will get you killed.' Sir John wheeled on Hook. 'Get up. Your mail's filthy. Clean it. And there's rust on the sword blade. I'll have you whipped if it's still there at sundown.'

'He won't whip you,' Goddington, the centenar, told Hook

that evening. 'He'll thump you and cut you and maybe break your bones, but it'll be in a fair fight.'

'I'll break his bones,' Hook said vengefully.

Goddington laughed. 'One man, Hook, just one man has held Sir John to a drawn fight in the last ten years. He's won every tournament in Europe. You won't beat him, you won't even come close. He's a fighter.'

'He's a bastard!' Hook said. The back of his head was matted with blood. Melisande was cleaning his mail and Hook was scrubbing at the rust on his sword blade with a stone. Both sword and mail had been supplied by Sir John Cornewaille.

'He was goading you, boy, he meant nothing,' Goddington said to Hook. 'He insults everyone, but if you're his man, and you will be, he'll fight for you too. And he'll fight for your woman.'

Next day Hook watched as Sir John put archer after archer onto the ground. When his own turn came to face Sir John he managed to trade a dozen blows before being turned, tripped and thrown down. Sir John backed away from him, scorn on his scarred face, and that scorn drove Hook to his feet and to a wild, savage charge and a searing cut with the sword that Sir John contemptuously flicked away before tripping Hook again. 'Anger, Hook,' Sir John growled, 'if you don't control it, it'll kill you, and a dead archer's no good to me. Fight cold, man. Fight cold and hard. Fight clever!' To Hook's surprise he reached out a hand and pulled Hook to his feet. 'But you're quick, Hook,' Sir John said, 'you're quick! And that's good.'

Sir John looked to be close on forty years old, but he was still the most feared tournament fighter in Europe. He was a squat, thick-chested man, bow-legged from years spent on horseback. He had the brightest blue eyes Hook had ever seen, while his flat, broken-nosed face showed the scars of battles, whether fought against rebels, Frenchmen, tavern brawlers or tournament opponents. Now, in anticipation of war with France, he was raising a company of archers and another of men-at-arms, though in Sir John's eyes, there was no great difference between the two. 'We are a company!' he shouted at the archers, 'archers and men-at-arms together! We fight for each other! No one hurts one of us and goes unhurt!' He turned and poked a metal finger into Hook's chest. 'You'll do, Hook. Give him his coat, Goddington.'

Peter Goddington brought Hook a surcoat of white linen that showed Sir John's badge; a red rampant lion with a golden star on its shoulder and a golden crown on its snarling head.

'Welcome to the company,' Sir John said, 'and to your new duties. What are your new duties, Hook?'

'To serve you, Sir John.'

'No! I've got servants who do that! Your job, Hook, is to rid the world of anyone I don't like! What is it?'

'To rid the world of anyone you don't like, Sir John.'

And that was liable to be a large part of the world. Sir John Cornewaille loved his king, he worshipped his older wife who was the king's aunt, he adored the women on whom he fathered bastards and he was devoted to his men, but the rest of the world were nearly all goddam scum who deserved to die. He tolerated his fellow Englishmen, but the Welsh were cabbage-farting dwarves, the Scots were scabby arse-suckers and the French were shrivelled turds. 'You know what you do with shrivelled turds, Hook?'

'You kill them, Sir John.'

'You get up close and kill them,' Sir John said. 'You let them smell your breath as they die. You let them see you grinning as you disembowel them. You hurt them, Hook, and then you kill them. Isn't that right, father?'

'You speak with the tongue of angels, Sir John,' Father

Christopher said blandly. He was Sir John's confessor and, like the company of archers gathered in the field, wore a mail coat, tall boots and a close-fitting helmet. There was nothing about him to suggest he was a priest, but if there had been any such evidence then he would not have been in Sir John's employment. Sir John wanted soldiers.

'You're not archers,' Sir John growled at the bowmen in the winter field. 'You shoot arrows till the putrid bastards are on top of you, and then you kill them like men-at-arms! You're no good to me if you can only shoot! I want you so close you can smell their dying farts! Ever killed a man so close you could have kissed him, Hook?'

'Yes, Sir John.'

Sir John grinned. 'Tell me about the last one? How did you do it?'

'With a knife, Sir John.'

'How! Not what with! How?'

'Ripped his belly, Sir John,' Hook said, 'straight up.'

'Did you get your hand wet, Hook?'

'Drenched, Sir John.'

'Wet with a Frenchman's blood, eh?'

'He was an English knight, Sir John.'

'God damn your bollocks, Hook, but I love you!' Sir John exclaimed. 'That's how you do it!' he shouted at the archers, 'you rip their bellies open, shove blades in their eyes, slice their throats, cut off their bollocks, drive swords up their arses, tear out their gullets, gouge their livers, skewer their kidneys, I don't care how you do it, so long as you kill them! Isn't that right, Father Christopher?'

'Our Lord and Saviour could not have expressed the sentiment more eloquently, Sir John.'

'And next year,' Sir John said, glowering at his archers, 'we might be going to war! Our king, God bless him, is the rightful King of France, but the French deny him his throne, and if God is doing what He's supposed to do then He'll let us invade France! And if that happens, we will be ready!'

No one was certain if war was coming or not. The French sent ambassadors to King Henry who sent emissaries back to France, and rumours swept England like the winter rains that seethed on the west wind. Sir John, though, was confident there would be war and he made a contract with the king as scores of other men were doing. The contract obliged Sir John to bring thirty men-at-arms and ninety archers to serve the king for twelve months, and in turn the king promised to pay wages to Sir John and his soldiers. The contract had been written in London and Hook was among the ten men who rode to Westminster when Sir John added his signature and pressed his lion seal into a blob of wax. The clerk waited for the wax to harden, then carefully cut the parchment into two unequal parts, not neatly, but zigzagging his blade randomly down the document's length. He put one ragged part into a white linen bag, and gave the other to Sir John. Now, if anyone doubted the document's provenance, the two uneven parts could be matched and neither party to the contract could forge the document and expect the forgery to go undiscovered. 'The exchequer will advance you monies, Sir John,' the clerk said.

The king was raising money by taxes, by loans and by pawning his jewels. Sir John received a bag of coins and a second bag that contained loose jewels, a golden brooch and a heavy silver box. It was not enough to allow Sir John to raise the extra men and to buy the weapons and horses he needed, and so he borrowed more money from an Italian banker in London.

Men, horses, armour and weapons had to be purchased. Sir John, his pages, squires and servants needed over fifty horses between them. Each man-at-arms was expected to own at least three horses, including a properly trained destrier for fighting, while Sir John undertook to supply every archer with a riding horse. Hay was needed to feed all the horses and had to be purchased until the spring rains greened the pastures. The men-at-arms provided their own armour and weapons, though Sir John did order a hundred short lances for use by men fighting on foot. He had also equipped his ninety archers with mail coats, helmets, good boots and a weapon to use in the close-quarter fighting when their bows were no longer useful. 'Swords won't help you much in battle,' he told his archers. 'Your enemies will be in plate armour and you can't cut plate armour with a sword. Use a poleaxe! Beat the bastards down! Then kneel on the arse-sucking scabs, lift their visors and put a knife into one of their filthy eyes.'

'Unless they are wealthy,' Father Christopher put in mildly. The priest was the oldest man in Sir John's company, over forty years old, with a round, cheerful face, a twisted smile, grey hair and eyes that were both curious and mischievous.

'Unless the arse-licking scab is wealthy,' Sir John agreed, 'in which case you take him prisoner and so make me rich!'

Sir John ordered a hundred poleaxes made for his archers. Hook, who knew how to shape wood, helped carve the long ash handles, while blacksmiths forged the heads. One side of each head was a heavy hammer, weighted with lead, which could be used to crush plate armour or, at the very least, knock an armoured man off balance. The opposing side was an axe that, in the hands of an archer, could split a helmet as though it were made of parchment, while the head of the axe was a spike thin enough to pierce the slits of a knight's visor. The upper shaft of each axe was sheathed in iron so an opponent could not cut through the handle. 'Beautiful,' Sir John said when the first weapons were delivered. He stroked the iron-clad handle as though it were a woman's flank, 'Just beautiful.'

By late spring the news came that God had done His duty by persuading the king to make an invasion of France and so Sir John's company marched south on roads lined with the white blossom of hawthorn hedges. Sir John was cheerful, animated by the prospect of war. He rode ahead, followed by his pages, his squire and a standard-bearer who carried the flag of the crowned red lion with its golden star. Three carts bore provisions, short lances, armour, spare bowstaves and sheaves of arrows. The road south led through woods that were thickly hazed with bluebells and past fields where the year's first hay had already been cut and was laid to dry in long rows. Newly shorn sheep looked naked and thin in the meadows. More bands of men joined the road, all horsemen, all in strange livery, and all going towards the south coast where the king had summoned the men who had signed his jaggedly-cut contracts. Most of the horsemen, Hook noted, were archers, outnumbering the men-at-arms by three to one. The long bows were stored in leather cases that were slung over their owners' shoulders.

Hook was happy. Sir John's men were his companions now. Peter Goddington, the centenar, was a fair man, tough with laggards, but warm in his approval of the men who shared his dream of creating the best company of archers in England. Thomas Evelgold was next in command and he, like Goddington, was an older man, almost thirty. He was a morose man, slower thinking than the centenar, but he was grudgingly helpful to the younger archers among whom Hook found his particular friends. There were the twins, Thomas and Matthew Scarlet, both a year younger than Hook, and Will of the Dale who could reduce the company to helpless laughter with his imitations of Sir John. The four drank together, ate together, laughed together and competed against each other, though it was recognised among all the archers that none could outshoot Nicholas Hook. They had practised with weapons all winter and now France was ahead and God was on their side. Father Christopher had assured them of that in a sermon preached the day before they rode. 'Our lord the king's quarrel with the French is just,' Father Christopher had said with unusual seriousness, 'and our God will not abandon him. We go to right a wrong, and the forces of heaven will march with us!' Hook did not understand the quarrel except that somewhere in the king's ancestry was a marriage that led Henry to the French throne, and perhaps he was the rightful king and perhaps he was not, but Hook did not care. He was just happy to wear the Cornewaille lion and star.

And he was happy that Melisande was one of the women chosen to ride with the company. She had a small, fine-boned mare that belonged to Sir John's wife, the sister of the late king, and she rode it well. 'We must take women with us,' Sir John had explained.

'God is merciful,' Father Christopher had murmured.

'We can't wash our own clothes!' Sir John had said. 'We can't sew! We can't cook! We must have women! Useful things, women. We don't want to be like the French! Humping each other when a sheep isn't available, so we'll take women!' He liked Melisande to ride alongside him and chatted away to her in French, making her laugh.

'He does not really hate the French,' Melisande told Hook on the evening that they arrived near a town with a large abbey. The abbey bell was summoning the faithful to prayer, but Hook did not move. He and Melisande were sitting beside a small river that flowed placidly through lush water meadows. Across the river, two fields away, another company of men-at-arms and archers was making camp. The fires of Sir John's men were already burning, hazing the trees and the distant abbey tower with smoke. 'He just likes to be rude about the French,' Melisande said.

'About everyone.'

'He is kind inside,' Melisande said, then leaned back to rest her head on his chest. When standing she barely reached his shoulder. Hook loved the fragility of her looks, though he knew that apparent frailty was deceptive for he had learned that Melisande had the supple strength of a bowstave and, like a bow that had followed the string and so been bent into a permanent curve even when unstrung, she possessed fiercely held opinions. He loved that in her. He also feared for her.

'Maybe you shouldn't come,' Hook said.

'Why? Because it is dangerous?'

'Yes.'

Melisande shrugged. 'It is safer to be French in France than to be English, I think. If they capture Alice or Matilda then they will be raped.' Alice and Matilda were her particular friends.

'And you won't be?' Hook asked.

Melisande said nothing for a while, perhaps thinking of Soissons. 'I want to come,' she finally said.

'Why?'

'To be with you,' she said, as though the answer were obvious. 'What's a centenar?'

'Like Peter Goddington? Just a man who leads archers.'

'And a ventenar?'

'Well, a centenar leads a whole lot of archers, maybe a hundred? And a ventenar is in charge of perhaps twenty of them. They're all sergeants.'

Melisande thought about that for a few seconds. 'You should be a ventenar, Nick.'

Hook smiled, but said nothing. The river was crystal clear as it flowed over a sandy bed where water crowsfoot and cress waved languidly. Mayflies were dancing and, every now and then, a splash betrayed a feeding trout. Two swans and

116

four cygnets swam beside the far bank and, as Hook watched them, he saw a shadow stir in the water beneath. 'Don't move,' he warned Melisande and, moving very slowly, took the cased bow from his shoulder.

'Sir John knows my father,' Melisande said suddenly.

'He does?' Hook asked, surprised. He unlaced the leather case and gently slid the bow free.

'Ghillebert,' Melisande said the name slowly, as if it was unfamiliar, 'the Seigneur de Lanferelle.'

Father Michel, in France, had said Melisande's father was the Seigneur d'Enfer, but Hook supposed he had misheard. 'He's a lord, eh?' he remarked.

'Lords have many children,' Melisande said, *et je suis une bâtarde.*

Hook said nothing. He braced the bowstave against the bole of an ash tree and bent the yew to loop the string over the upper nock.

'I am a bastard,' Melisande said bitterly. 'That is why he put me in the nunnery.'

'To hide you.'

'And protect me, I think,' Melisande said. 'He paid money to the abbess. He paid for my food and bed. He said I would be safe there.'

'Safe to be a servant girl?'

'My mother was a servant girl. Why not me? And I would have become a nun one day.'

'You're not a servant girl,' Hook said, 'you're a lord's daughter.' He took an arrow from his bag, choosing a bodkin with its long, sharp and heavy head. He was holding the bow horizontally on his lap and now laid the arrow on the stave and notched the feathered end on the string. The shadow stirred. 'How well do you know your father?' Hook asked.

'I have only met him twice,' Melisande said. 'Once when I was small, and I do not remember that well, and then before I went to the nunnery. I liked him.' She paused, searching for the right English words. 'In the beginning, I liked him.'

'Did he like you?' Hook asked carelessly, concentrating on the shadow rather than on Melisande. He was drawing the bow now, still holding it horizontally and unwilling to raise it vertically in case the movement sent the shadow fast upstream.

'He was so,' she paused, looking for the word, '*beau*. He was tall. And he has a beautiful badge. He wears a great yellow sun with golden rays. And on the sun there is the head of . . .'

'An eagle,' Hook interrupted.

'*Un faucon*,' Melisande said.

'A falcon then,' Hook said, and remembered the long-haired man who had watched the archers being murdered in front of the church of Saint Antoine-le-Petit. 'He was in Soissons,' he said harshly. He had paused with the bow partially drawn. The shadow drifted in the water and Hook thought it would vanish downstream, then it flicked its tail and was back under the far bank.

Melisande was staring up at Hook. 'He was there?'

'Long black hair,' Hook said.

'I did not see him!'

'You had your head buried in my shoulder most of the time,' Hook said. 'You didn't want to look. They were torturing men. Taking their eyes. Cutting them.'

Melisande was silent a long time. Hook raised the bow slightly, then she spoke again, but in a smaller voice. 'My father is called something else,' she said, 'le Seigneur d'Enfer.'

'That's the name I heard,' Hook said.

'Le Seigneur d'Enfer,' Melisande said again. 'The lord of hell. It is because Lanferelle sounds like *l'enfer*, and *l'enfer* is hell, but maybe because he is so fierce in a fight. He has sent many men to hell, I think. And some to heaven too.'

Swallows flickered fast over the river and, from the corner of his eye, Hook saw the brilliant blue flash of a kingfisher's flight. The shadow was unmoving again. He drew the cord further back, unable to pull it to the full extent because Melisande's slender body obstructed him, but even at half draw the great war bow was a dreadful weapon.

'He is not a bad man,' Melisande said as though she tried to persuade herself of that fact.

'You don't sound very certain,' Hook said.

'He is my father.'

'Who put you in a nunnery.'

'I did not want to go!' she said fiercely. 'I told him! No! No!'

Hook smiled. 'You didn't want to be a nun, eh?'

'I knew the sisters. My mother would take me to visit them. We gave them,' she paused, looking for the English words and failing to find them, '*les prunes de damas, abricots et coings.*' She shrugged. 'I do not know what those things are. Fruit? We gave the sisters fruit, but they were never kind to us. They were horrid.'

'But your father sent you there anyway,' Hook said.

'He said I should pray for him. That was my duty. But you know what I prayed for instead? I prayed he would come for me one day,' she said wistfully, 'that he would ride on his great horse through the convent gate and take me away.'

'Is that why you want to go to France?'

She shook her head. 'I want to be with you.'

'Your father won't like me.'

She dismissed that with a shrug. 'Why should he ever see us again?'

Hook aimed just beneath the shadow, though he was not thinking about his aim. Instead he was thinking about a tall man with long black hair who did nothing to stop torture

119

and agony. He was thinking about the lord of hell. 'Supper,' he said harshly, and released the cord.

The arrow leaped off the string, its white feathers bright in the sinking sun. It slashed into the water and there was a sudden thrashing, a churning turmoil that sent trout exploding upstream, and the thrashing went on as Hook jumped into the river.

The pike had been spitted by the arrow that had pinned it to the river's far bank, and Hook had to pull hard to yank the shaft free. He carried the fish back. It twisted on the arrow and tried to bite him, but once on the western bank he rapped its skull with the hilt of his knife and the huge fish died instantly. It was almost as long as his bow, a great dark hunter with savage teeth.

'*Un brochet!*' Melisande said with delight.

'A pike,' Hook said, 'and there's good eating on a pike.' He gutted the fish on the bank, spilling the offal back into the river.

Next day Sir John led a contingent of men-at-arms and archers westwards to buy grain, dried peas and smoked meat, and Sir John gave Hook the easy duty, which was to stay in a village under a fold of the hills and to guard the sacks and barrels that were being piled on a wagon, which stood outside a tavern called the Mouse and Cheese. The wagon's two draught horses were picketed on the village green. Hook's bow, unstrung, lay on an outside table beside the pot of ale that the tavern keeper had given him, but Hook was up on the wagon bed, pounding flour into a barrel. Father Christopher, dressed in shirt, breeches and boots, wandered aimlessly, peering into the cottages, petting cats and teasing the women who washed clothes in the stream that edged the village's one street. He finally came back to the Mouse and Cheese and dropped a small bag of silver coins onto the table. It was the priest's job to pay for any food that a farmer or villager might wish to sell. 'Why are you hitting the flour, young Hook?' the priest asked.

'I'm packing it down tight, father. Salt, hazel and flour!'

Father Christopher gave an exaggerated grimace of distaste. 'You're salting the flour?'

'There's a layer of salt at the bottom of the barrel,' Hook explained, 'to stop the flour getting damp, and I add the hazel to keep it fresh.' He showed Father Christopher some hazel wands he had plucked from a hedge and stripped of their leaves.

'And that works?' the priest asked.

'Of course it does! Did you never fetch flour from a mill?'

'Hook!' the priest protested, 'I'm a man of God. We don't actually work!' He laughed.

Hook thrust another pair of wands into the barrel, then stood back and dusted his hands. 'Aye, well that's a good piece of work,' he said, nodding at the flour.

Father Christopher smiled benignly, then leaned back and gazed at the sunlit woods climbing the hills above the thatched roofs. 'God, I love England,' he said, 'and God knows why young Hal wants France.'

'Because he's the King of France,' Hook said.

Father Christopher shrugged. 'He's got a claim, Hook, but so do others. If I were King of England I'd stay here. Is this your ale?'

'It is, father.'

'Be a Christian and give me some.' Father Christopher said, then raised the pot in Hook's direction and drank from it. 'But to France we go, and doubtless we'll win!'

'We will?'

'Only God knows the answer to that, Hook,' Father Christopher said, suddenly thoughtful. 'There's a powerful lot of Frenchmen! And if they stop quarrelling among

121

themselves and turn on us? Still, we have these things,' he slapped Hook's bow, 'and they don't.'

'Can I ask you something, father?' Hook said, climbing down from the wagon and sitting beside the priest.

'Oh, for Christ's blessed sake don't ask me which side God is on.'

'You told us He was on our side!'

'True, Hook, I did, and there are thousands of French priests saying the same thing to the French!' Father Christopher grinned. 'Let me give you some priestly advice, Hook. Put your trust in the yew bow, my boy, and not in any priest's words.'

Hook touched the bow, feeling the slick tallow he had rubbed into the wood. 'What do you know about Saint Crispinian, father?'

'Oh, a theological enquiry,' Father Christopher said. He drank the rest of Hook's ale, then rapped the pot on the table as a signal that he needed more. 'Not sure I remember much! I didn't really study as I should at Oxford. There were too many girls I liked.' He smiled for a moment. 'There was a brothel there, Hook, where all the girls dressed as nuns. You could hardly get inside the house because of priests! I met the Bishop of Oxford there at least half a dozen times. Happy days.' He sighed and gave Hook a sideways grin. 'So, what do I know? Well, Crispinian had a brother called Crispin, though not everyone says they were brothers. Some say they were noblemen, and some say they weren't. They might have been shoemakers, which doesn't sound like a nobleman's occupation, does it? They were certainly Romans. They lived about a thousand years ago, Hook, and of course they were martyred.'

'So Crispinian's in heaven,' Hook said.

'He and his brother live on the right hand of God,' Father Christopher confirmed, 'where I hope they get quicker service than I do!' He rapped the table again, and a girl came running from the tavern door to be greeted with a wide priestly smile. 'More ale, my lovely darling,' Father Christopher said, and rolled one of Sir John's coins down the table. 'Two pots, my sweet,' he smiled again, then sighed when the girl had gone. 'Oh, I wish I were young again.'

'You are young, father.'

'Dear God, I'm forty-three! I'll be dead soon! I'll be as dead as Crispinian, but he was a hard man to kill.'

'He was?'

Father Christopher frowned. 'I'm trying to remember. He and Crispin were tortured because they were Christians. They were racked, and they had nails driven under their fingernails, and strips of flesh cut out of them, but none of that killed them! They were singing God's praises to the torturers all the time! Not sure I could be that brave.' He made the sign of the cross, then smiled as the girl put down the ale. He waved off the coins she offered as change.

'So there they were,' he went on, enjoying his tale, 'and the man who was torturing them decided to finish them off quickly, maybe because he was tired of hearing them sing, so he tied millstones around their necks and threw them into a river. But that didn't work either because the millstones floated! So the torturer had them pulled out of the river and threw them onto a fire! And even that didn't kill them. They went on singing and the fire wouldn't touch them, and God filled the torturer with despair and the wretched man threw himself on the fire instead. He burned, but the two saints lived.'

A small group of horsemen appeared at the end of the village street. Hook glanced at them, but none was wearing Sir John Cornewaille's livery, so he turned back to the priest.

'God had saved the brothers from the torture and from the drowning and from the fire,' Father Christopher said, 'but for some reason He let them die anyway. They had their heads chopped off by the emperor, and that stopped them singing. It would, wouldn't it?'

'But it was still a miracle,' Hook said in wonderment.

'It was a miracle they survived so long,' Father Christopher agreed. 'But why are you so interested in Crispinian? He's really a French saint, not ours. He and his brother went to France, see? To do their work.'

Hook hesitated, not sure whether he wanted to confess that a headless saint talked to him, but before he could decide either way a voice sneered. 'God's belly!' the voice said, 'look who we have here! Master Nicholas Hook!'

Hook looked up to see Sir Martin leering triumphantly from his horse. There were eight horsemen and all but Sir Martin were wearing Lord Slayton's moon and stars. Thomas Perrill and his brother Robert were among the riders, as was Lord Slayton's centenar, William Snoball. Hook knew them all.

'Friends of yours?' Father Christopher asked.

'I thought you were dead, Hook,' Sir Martin said. He was in a priest's robe that was tucked up so his skinny legs could straddle the horse and, though priests were forbidden to carry edged weapons, he wore an old-fashioned sword with a wide crosspiece on the hilt. 'I hoped you were dead,' he added, 'doomed, damned and dead.' His long face grimaced in what might have been a smile.

'I live,' Hook said curtly.

'And you wear another man's livery,' Sir Martin said, 'which is not right, Hook, not right at all. It defies law and the scriptures, and Lord Slayton will not like it. Is this yours?' He pointed to the wagon.

'It is ours,' Father Christopher answered pleasantly.

Sir Martin appeared to notice Father Christopher for the first time. He peered intensely at the grey-haired man for a few heartbeats, then shook his head. 'I don't know you,' he said, 'and I don't need to know you. I need food. That's why we came, and there,' he pointed a bony finger at the wagon, 'is food. Manna from heaven. As God sent ravens to feed Elijah the Tishbite, so He has sent us Hook.' He found that amusing and laughed to himself, and in the laughter was the cackle of madness.

'But that food is ours,' Father Christopher said as though he spoke to a small child.

'But he,' Sir Martin sneered, pointing at Hook, 'he, he, he,' and with each repetition he stabbed his finger towards Hook, 'that piece of shit beside you, is Lord Slayton's man. And he is an outlaw.'

Father Christopher turned a surprised face on Hook. 'Are you?' he asked.

Hook nodded, said nothing.

'Well, well,' Father Christopher said mildly.

'An outlaw can possess nothing,' Sir Martin rasped, 'which is the commandment of the scriptures, so that food is ours.'

'I think not,' Father Christopher replied calmly, smiling.

'You may think what you like,' Sir Martin said with a sudden vehemence, 'because we'll take it anyway, and we'll take him.' He pointed to Hook.

'You know the livery?' Father Christopher asked gently, gesturing at Hook's surcoat.

'An outlaw can wear no livery,' Sir Martin said. He looked happy as he anticipated the pleasure of Hook's death. 'Tom?' he twisted in the saddle to look at the older Perrill brother, 'rip that surcoat off him, tie his hands tight and bring him.'

William Snoball had an arrow on his string. The rest of Sir Martin's archers followed his example so that half a dozen arrows were pointed at Hook as Tom Perrill slid from the saddle. 'Been waiting to do this,' Perrill said. His face, long-nosed and lantern-jawed like Sir Martin's, was lit by a grin, 'Do we hang him here, Sir Martin?'

125

'It would save Lord Slayton the trouble of a trial, wouldn't it?' the priest said. 'And remove from his lordship the temptation of mercy.' He cackled again.

Father Christopher held up a slim hand in warning, but Tom Perrill ignored the gesture. He came around the table and was just reaching for Hook when he was stopped by the sound of a sword scraping through a scabbard's throat.

Sir Martin turned.

A single horseman watched the scene from the edge of the village. There were more horsemen behind him, but they had evidently been ordered to wait.

'I really would advise you,' Father Christopher said very mildly, 'to take those arrows off their strings.'

None of the archers followed his advice. They glanced nervously at Sir Martin, but Sir Martin seemed not to know what to do, and just then the lone horseman touched his spurs to his stallion's flanks.

'Sir Martin!' William Snoball appealed for orders.

But Sir Martin said nothing. He merely watched as the man-at-arms spurred towards him, the stallion's hooves spewing puffs of dust as it cantered, and the rider drew back his sword arm and then, as he galloped past, swept once.

The flat of the blade smacked across Robert Perrill's skull. The archer, whose selection had been random, toppled slowly from the saddle to drop heavily onto the street. The arrow, released by his nerveless hand, thumped into the tavern's wall, half drilling through it. It had missed Hook by inches. Tom Perrill turned to help his brother, who stirred groggily in the dust, then went still as Sir John Cornewaille wheeled his horse. Sir John spurred again, and now Sir Martin's archers hurriedly took the arrows off their strings. Sir John slowed the stallion, then curbed it.

'Greetings, Sir John,' Father Christopher said happily.

'What's happening?' Sir John asked harshly.

126

Robert Perrill staggered to his feet, the right side of his head sheeted with blood. Tom Perrill was unmoving now, his eyes fixed on the sword that had struck his brother.

Father Christopher drank some ale, then wiped his lips. 'These men, Sir John,' he waved at Sir Martin and his archers, 'expressed a desire to take our food. I did advise them against such a course, but they insisted the food was theirs because it was under the protection of young Hook here and, according to this holy priest, Hook is an outlaw.'

'He is,' Sir Martin found his voice, 'deemed so by law and doomed thereby!'

'I know he's an outlaw,' Sir John said flatly, 'and so did the king when he gave Hook to me. Are you saying the king made a mistake?'

Sir Martin glanced at Hook with surprise, but held his ground. 'He is an outlaw,' he insisted, 'and Lord Slayton's man.'

'He is my man,' Sir John said.

'He is . . .' Sir Martin began, then faltered under Sir John's gaze.

'He is my man,' Sir John said again, his voice dangerous now, 'he fights for me, and that means I fight for him. You know who I am?' Sir John waited for an acknowledgement from the priest, but Sir Martin's gaze had dissolved into vagueness and he was now staring into the sky as though he were communing with angels. 'Tell his lordship,' Sir John went on, 'to discuss the matter with me.'

'We will, sir, we will,' William Snoball answered after glancing at Sir Martin.

'Elijah the Tishbite,' Sir Martin spoke suddenly, 'ate bread and flesh by the brook Cherith. Did you know that?' This question was asked earnestly of Sir John who merely looked bemused. 'The brook Cherith,' Sir Martin said as though he imparted a great secret, 'is where a man may hide himself.'

127

'Jesus wept,' Sir John said.

'And no wonder,' Father Christopher sighed. Then he gently lifted Hook's bow and slammed it hard down onto the table and the abrupt noise made the horses twitch and snapped Sir Martin's eyes into comprehension. 'I forgot to mention,' Father Christopher said, smiling seraphically at Sir Martin, 'that I am also a priest. So let me offer you a blessing.' He pulled out a golden crucifix that had been hidden beneath his shirt and held it towards Lord Slayton's men. 'May the peace and love of our Lord Jesus Christ,' he said, 'comfort and sustain you while you take your farting mouths and your turd-reeking presence out of our sight.' He waved a sketchy cross towards the horsemen. 'And thus farewell.'

Tom Perrill stared at Hook. For a moment it seemed his hatred might conquer his caution, but then he twisted away and helped his brother remount. Sir Martin, his face dreamy again, allowed William Snoball to lead him away. The other horsemen followed.

Sir John dropped from his saddle, took Hook's ale, and drained it. 'Remind me why you were outlawed, Hook?'

'Because I hit a priest, Sir John,' Hook admitted.

'That priest?' Sir John asked, jerking a thumb towards the retreating horsemen.

'Yes, Sir John.'

Sir John shook his head. 'You did wrong, Hook, you did very wrong. You shouldn't have hit him.'

'No, Sir John,' Hook said humbly.

'You should have slit the goddam bastard's putrid bowels open and ripped his heart out through his stinking arse,' Sir John said, looking at Father Christopher as if hoping his words might offend the priest, but Father Christopher merely smiled. 'Is the bastard mad?' Sir John demanded.

'Famously,' Father Christopher said, 'but so were half the

128

saints and most of the prophets. I can't think you'd want to go hawking with Jeremiah, Sir John?'

'Damn Jeremiah,' Sir John said, 'and damn London. I'm summoned there again, father. The king demands it.'

'May God bless your going forth, Sir John, and your returning hence.'

'And if King Harry doesn't make peace,' Sir John said, 'I'll be back soon. Very soon.'

'There'll be no peace,' Father Christopher said confidently. 'The bow is drawn and the arrow yearns to fly.'

'Let's hope it does. I need the money a good war will bring.'

'I shall pray for war, then,' Father Christopher said lightly.

'For months now,' Sir John said, 'I've prayed for nothing else.'

And now, Hook thought, Sir John's prayers were being answered. Because soon, very soon, they would be sailing to war. They would sail to play the devil's game. They would sail to France. They were going to fight.

PART TWO

Normandy

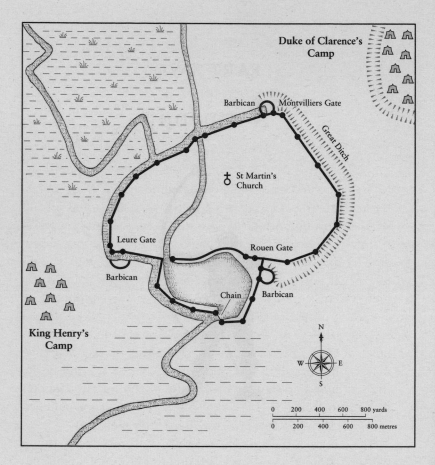

Harfleur

Nick Hook could scarce believe the world held so many ships. He first saw the fleet when Sir John's men mustered on the shore of Southampton Water so that the king's officers could count the company. Sir John had contracted to supply ninety archers and thirty men-at-arms and the king had agreed to pay Sir John the balance of the money owed for those men when the army embarked, but first the numbers and condition of Sir John's company had to be approved. Hook, standing in line with his companions, gazed in awe at the fleet. There were anchored ships as far as he could see; so many ships that their hulls hid the water. Peter Goddington, the centenar, had claimed there were fifteen hundred vessels waiting to transport the army, and Hook had not believed so many ships could exist, yet there they were.

The king's inspector, an elderly and round-faced monk with ink-stained hands, walked down the line of soldiers to make sure that Sir John had hired no cripples, boys or old men. He was accompanied by a grim-faced knight wearing the royal coat of arms, whose task was to inspect the company's weapons. He found nothing amiss, but nor did he expect to discover any shortcomings in Sir John Cornewaille's preparations. 'Sir John's indenture specifies ninety archers,' the monk said reprovingly when he reached the line's end.

'It does indeed,' Father Christopher agreed cheerfully. Sir John was in London with the king, and Father Christopher was in charge of the company's administration during Sir John's absence.

'Yet there are ninety-two archers!' the monk spoke with mock severity.

'Sir John will throw the two weakest overboard,' Father Christopher said.

'That will serve! That will serve!' the monk said. He glanced at his grim-faced companion, who nodded approval of what he had seen. 'The money will be brought to you this afternoon,' the monk assured Father Christopher. 'God bless you one and all,' he added as he mounted his horse so he could ride to where other companies were waiting for inspection. His clerks, clutching linen bags filled with parchments, scurried after him.

Hook's ship, the *Heron*, was a squat, round-bottomed merchant ship with a bluff bow, a square stern and a thick mast from which Sir John Cornewaille's lion banner flew. Close by, and looming above the *Heron*, was the king's own ship, the *Trinity Royal*, which was the size of an abbey and made even bigger by the towering wooden castles added to her bows and stern. The castles, which were painted red, blue and gold and hung with royal banners, made the *Trinity Royal* look top heavy, like a farm wagon piled too high with harvest sheaves. Her rails had been decorated with white shields on which red crosses were painted, while aloft she flew three vast flags. At her bows, on a short mast that sprang from her jaunty bowsprit, was a red banner decorated with four white circles joined by black-lettered strips. 'That flag on the bow, Hook,' Father Christopher explained, making the sign of the cross, 'is the flag of the Holy Trinity.'

Hook stared, said nothing.

'You might have thought,' Father Christopher went on slyly, 'that the Holy Trinity would require three flags, but modesty reigns in heaven and one suffices. You know the significance of the flag, Hook?'

'No, father.'

'Then I shall repair your ignorance. The outer circles are the Father, the Son and the Holy Ghost and they're joined by strips on which are written *non est*. You know what *non est* is, Hook?'

'Is not,' Melisande said quickly.

'Oh my God, she's as clever as she's beautiful,' Father Christopher said happily. He gave Melisande a slow and appreciative look that started at her face and finished at her feet. She was wearing a dress of thin linen decorated with Sir John's crest of the red lion, though the priest was hardly examining the heraldry. 'So,' he said slowly, looking back up her body, 'the Father is not the Son, who is not the Holy Ghost, who is not the Father, yet all those outer circles connect to the inner, which is God, and on the strips connecting to God's circle is the word *est*. So the Father is God, and the Son is God and the Holy Spirit is God, but they're not each other. It's really very simple.'

Hook frowned. 'I don't think it's simple.'

Father Christopher grinned. 'Of course it's not simple! I don't think anyone understands the Holy Trinity, except maybe the pope, but which pope, eh? We've got two of them now, and we're only supposed to have one! Gregory *non est* Benedict and Benedict *non est* Gregory, so let's just hope God knows which one *est* which. God, you're a pretty thing, Melisande. Wasted on Hook, you are.'

Melisande made a face at the priest who laughed, kissed his fingertips and blew the kiss to her. 'Look after her, Hook,' he said.

'I do, father.'

Father Christopher managed to tear his gaze from Melisande and stare across the water at the *Trinity Royal*, which was being nuzzled by a dozen small launches nosing into her flank like piglets suckling on a sow. Great bundles were being slung from those smaller boats into the larger. At the *Trinity Royal*'s stern, on another short mast, flew the flag of England, the red cross of Saint George on its white field. Every man in Henry's army had been given two red linen crosses, which had to be sewn on the front and back of their jupons, defacing the badge of their lord. In battle, Sir John had explained, there were too many badges, too many beasts and birds and colours, but if all the English wore one badge, Saint George's badge, then in the chaos of killing they might recognise their own compatriots.

The *Trinity Royal*'s tall mast carried the largest flag, the king's flag, the great quartered banner that twice displayed the golden leopards of England and twice the golden lilies of France. Henry claimed to be king of both countries, which was why his banner showed both, and the great fleet that filled Southampton Water would carry an army to make the banner's boast come true. It was an army, Sir John Cornewaille had told his men the night before he left for London, like no other army that had ever sailed from England. 'Our king has done it right!' he had said proudly. 'We're good!' He had grinned wolfishly. 'Our lord the king has spent money! He's pawned his royal jewels! He's bought the best army we've ever had, and we're part of it. And we're not just any part, we're the best part of it! We will not let our king down! God is on our side, isn't that right, Father?'

'Oh, God detests the French,' Father Christopher had put in confidently, as though he were intimate with God's mind.

'That's because God is no fool,' Sir John went on, 'but the

Almighty knows He made a mistake when He created the French! So He's sending us to correct it! We're God's army, and we're going to gut those devil-spawned bastards!'

Fifteen hundred ships would carry twelve thousand men and at least twice that many horses across the Channel. The men were mostly English, with some Welshmen and a few score who had come from Henry's possessions in Aquitaine. Hook could hardly imagine twelve thousand men, the number was so vast, but Father Christopher, leaning on the *Heron*'s rail, had repeated the cautionary note he had sounded outside the tavern before the confrontation with Sir Martin. 'The French can muster triple our numbers,' he said musingly, 'and maybe even more. If it comes to a fight, Hook, we'll need your arrows.'

'They won't fight us, though,' one of Sir John's men-at-arms said. He had overheard the priest's comment.

'They don't like fighting us,' Father Christopher agreed. The priest was wearing a haubergeon and had a sword hanging at his waist. 'It's not like the good old days.'

The man-at-arms, young and round-faced, grinned. 'Crécy and Poitiers?'

'That would have been grand!' Father Christopher said wistfully. 'Can you imagine being at Poitiers? Capturing the French king! It won't happen this time.'

'It won't, father?' Hook asked.

'They've learned about our archers, Hook. They stay away from us. They lock themselves up in their towns and castles and wait till we get bored. We can march around France a dozen times and they won't come out to fight, but if we can't get into their castles, what use is marching around France?'

'Then why don't they have archers?' Hook asked, but he already knew the answer because he was the answer himself. It had taken ten years to turn Nicholas Hook into an archer.

He had started at seven years old with a small bow which his father had insisted he practise every day, and every year until his father died the bows got bigger and were strung more tightly, and the young Hook had learned to draw the bow with his full body, not just his arms. 'Lay into the bow, you little bastard,' his father would say again and again, and each time strike him across the back with his big bowstave, and so Hook learned to lay into the bow and thus grew stronger and stronger. On his father's death he had taken the big bow and practised with that, shooting arrow after arrow at the butts in the church field. The arrowheads were sharpened on a post of the lych gate and the constant scraping had worn deep grooves in the stone. Nick Hook had poured his anger into those arrows, sometimes shooting till it was almost too dark to see. 'Don't snatch at the string,' Pearce the blacksmith had told him again and again, and Hook had learned the whispering release that let the string slip through his fingers, which hardened to thick leather pads. And as he drew and released, drew and released, year after year, the muscles of his back, his chest and his arms grew massive. That was one requirement, the huge muscles needed to draw the bow, while the other, which was harder to acquire, was to forget the eye.

When he first started as a boy Hook would draw the cord to his cheek and look down the arrow's length to aim, but that cheated the bow of its full power. If a bodkin was to shear through plate armour it needed all the power of the yew, and that meant drawing the cord to the ear, and then the arrow slanted across the eye, and it had taken Hook years to learn how to think his arrow to the target. He could not explain it, but no archer could. He only knew that when he drew the cord he looked at the target and the arrow flew there because he wanted it to, not because he had lined eye, arrow and target. That was why the French had no archers other than a few huntsmen, because they had no men who had spent years learning to make a length of yew and a cord of hemp into a part of themselves.

North of the *Heron*, somewhere among the tangle of moored ships, a vessel burned, sending a thick plume of smoke across the summer sky. Rumour said there had been a rebellion against the king and that the rebels had planned to burn the fleet. Father Christopher had curtly acknowledged that there had indeed been some rebels, lords all of them, but they were now dead. 'Beheaded,' he said. The burning ship, he thought, was probably an accident. 'No one will burn the *Heron*,' he had reassured the archers, and no one did. Also north of the *Heron* was the *Lady of Falmouth* and she was being loaded with horses that were swum out to the ship's side and then hoisted aboard in great leather slings. The horses rose dripping, legs dangling limp and eyes rolling white with fear, then were slowly lowered into padded stalls in the *Lady of Falmouth*'s hold. Hook saw his black gelding, Raker, lifted dripping from the sea, then Melisande's small piebald mare, Dell. Men swam among the horses, deftly fixing the slings. Sir John's great destrier, a black stallion called Lucifer, glared about him as he was lifted from the sea.

Next day Sir John Cornewaille arrived from London with the king. The French, it seemed, had sent a last embassy, but their terms had been rejected and so the fleet would sail. Sir John was rowed to the *Heron* in a small boat and he bellowed orders and greetings as he clambered over the side. A moment later trumpets sounded from the *Trinity Royal* as a barge, painted blue and gold, and with white-shafted oars, carried the king to the great ship's side. Henry was in full plate armour, burnished and polished and scoured until it reflected the sun in white flashes of dazzling light, yet he climbed the ladder as nimbly as a ship's cabin boy as the trumpeters in the stern castle raised their instruments and blew another fanfare. Cheers sounded from the *Trinity Royal*, then other ships took up the acclaim, which spread through the fleet of fifteen hundred vessels.

That afternoon, as the wind blew steady from the west, a pair of swans flew through the fleet, their wingbeats loud in the warm air. The swans flew south and Sir John, seeing them, thumped the ship's rail and gave a cheer.

'The swan,' Father Christopher announced to the bemused archers, 'is our king's private badge! The swans are leading us to victory!'

And the king must have seen the omen for himself, because, just after the swans had beaten their way past his ship, the sail of the *Trinity Royal* was hauled up the mast. The sail was painted with the royal arms; red, gold and blue. It reached halfway and the wind billowed it from its long yard, and the sound of its thrashing reached the *Heron* before, suddenly, it dropped again. It was the signal to leave and, one by one the ships hauled their anchors and set their sails. The wind was fair for France.

A wind to carry England to war.

No one knew where in France they were going to war. Some men suggested the fleet would go south to Aquitaine, others thought it would be Calais, and most had no idea at all. A few did not care, but just leaned over the side and retched.

The fleet sailed for two days and two nights beneath skies of small white clouds that scurried eastwards and beneath stars as bright as jewels. Father Christopher told stories on board the *Heron* and Hook was enthralled by the tale of Jonah and the whale, and he searched the sun-glinting sea for a sight of another such monster, but he saw none. He saw only the endless ships scattered across the heaving waters like a flock released to summer pastures.

On the second dawn Hook was standing as far forward as the ship's cramped bows permitted and he was watching the sea, hoping to find a man-swallowing fish, when Sir John silently joined him. Hook hastily knuckled his forehead and Sir John nodded companionably. Melisande was sleeping on deck, sheltered by stacks of barrels and wrapped in Hook's cloak, and Sir John smiled towards her. 'A good girl, Hook,' he said.

'Yes, Sir John.'

'And doubtless we'll bring a score of other good French girls home! New wives. See those clouds?' Sir John was staring straight ahead to where a cloud bank lay across the horizon. 'That's Normandy, Hook.'

Hook gazed, but could see nothing beneath the clouds except the foremost ships of the fleet. 'Sir John?' he asked tentatively and received an encouraging look. 'What do you know about,' he paused, 'the Seigneur d'Enfer,' he struggled with the French words.

'Lanferelle? Melisande's father?' Sir John asked.

'She told you about him?' Hook asked, surprised.

'Oh, she did,' Sir John said, smiling, 'indeed she did. Why do you want to know?'

'I'm curious,' Hook said.

'Worried because she's a lord's daughter?' Sir John asked shrewdly.

'Yes,' Hook admitted.

Sir John smiled, then pointed over the *Heron*'s bows. 'See those small sails?' Far ahead of the English fleet was another spread of ships, far fewer and all much smaller, nothing but a scatter of tiny brown sails. 'French fishermen,' Sir John said grimly, 'taking news of us to their home ports. Let's pray the bastards won't guess where we're coming ashore, because that's their chance to kill us, Hook! As we go ashore. They know we're coming! And all they need do is have two hundred men-at-arms waiting on the beach and we'll never manage a landing.'

Hook watched the tiny sails that did not appear to be moving against the sea's immensity. The western sky was still dark, the east was glowing. He wondered how the sailors of the English fleet knew where they were going. He wondered whether Saint Crispinian would ever speak to him again.

'There,' Sir John said softly. It seemed he had decided to ignore Hook's question about the Sire of Lanferelle and was instead pointing straight ahead.

And there it was. The coast of Normandy. It was nothing but a shadowed speck for now, a scrap of dark solidity where the clouds and the sea met.

'I talked to Lord Slayton,' Sir John said. Hook stayed silent. 'He can't travel to France, of course, not crippled as he is, but he was in London to wish the king well. He says you're a good man in a fight.'

Hook said nothing. The only fights that Lord Slayton would have known about were tavern brawls. They could be murderous, but it was not the same as battle.

'Lord Slayton was a good fighter too,' Sir John said, 'before he got wounded in the back. He was a bit slow on the down-stroke parry, I remember. It's always dangerous to raise a sword above your shoulder, Hook.'

'Yes, Sir John,' Hook said dutifully.

'And he did declare you outlawed,' Sir John went on, 'but that doesn't matter now. You're going to France, Hook, and you're no outlaw there. Whatever crimes you're accused of in England don't count in France, and even that doesn't matter because you're my man now.'

'Yes, Sir John,' Hook said again.

'You're my man,' Sir John said firmly, 'and Lord Slayton agreed that you are. But you've still got a quarrel. That priest wants you dead, and Lord Slayton said there were others who'd happily fillet you.'

Hook thought of the Perrill brothers. 'There are,' he admitted.

'And Lord Slayton told me other things about you,' Sir John went on. 'He said you're a murderer, a thief and a liar.'

Hook felt the old flare of anger, but it died instantly like the spume of the waves. 'I was those things,' he said defensively.

'And that you're competent,' Sir John said, 'and what you are, Hook, is what *le Seigneur d'Enfer* is. Ghillebert, Lord of Lanferelle, is competent. He's a rogue, and he's also charming, clever and sly. He speaks English!' He said the last three words as though that were a very strange accomplishment. 'He was taken prisoner in Aquitaine,' he explained, 'and held in Suffolk till his ransom was paid. That took three years. He was released ten years ago and I dare say there are plenty of small children with his long nose growing up in Suffolk. He's the only man I never beat in a tournament.'

'They say you never lost!' Hook said fiercely.

'He didn't beat me either,' Sir John said, smiling. 'We fought till we had no strength to fight more. I told you, he's good. I did put him down, though.'

'You did?' Hook asked, intrigued.

'I think he slipped. So I stepped back and gave him time to get up.'

'Why?' Hook asked.

Sir John laughed. 'In a tournament, Hook, you must display chivalry. Good manners are as important as fighting in a tournament, but not in battle. So if you see Lanferelle in battle, leave him to me.'

'Or to an arrow,' Hook said.

'He can afford the best armour, Hook. He'll have Milanese plate and your arrow will like as not get blunted. Then he'll kill you without even knowing he fought you. Leave him to me.'

Hook heard something close to admiration in Sir John's tone. 'You like him?'

Sir John nodded. 'I like him, but that won't stop me killing him. And as for him being Melisande's father, so what? He must have littered half France with his bastards. My bastards aren't lords, Hook, and nor are his.'

Hook nodded, frowning. 'At Soissons,' he began, and paused.

'Go on.'

'He just watched as archers were tortured!' Hook said indignantly.

Sir John leaned on the rail. 'We talk about chivalry, Hook, we're even chivalrous! We salute our enemies, we take their surrenders gallantly, we dress our hostility in silks and fine linen, we are the chivalry of Christendom.' He spoke wryly, then turned his extraordinarily bright blue eyes on Hook. 'But in battle, Hook, it's blood and anger and savagery and killing. God hides His face in battle.'

'This was after the battle,' Hook said.

'Battle anger is like being drunk. It doesn't go away quickly. Your girl's father is an enemy, an enemy of charm, but he's as dangerous as I am.' Sir John grinned and lightly punched Hook's shoulder. 'Leave him to me, Hook. I'll kill him. I'll hang his skull in my hall.'

The sun rose in splendour and the shadows fled and the coast of Normandy grew to reveal a line of white cliffs topped with green. All day the fleet beat southwards, helped by a shift of wind that flicked the tops of the waves white and filled the sails. Sir John was impatient. He spent the day staring at the distant coast and insisting that the shipmaster get closer.

'Rocks, my lord,' the shipmaster said laconically.

'No rocks here! Get closer! Get closer!' He was looking for some evidence that the enemy was tracking the fleet from the clifftops, but there was no sign of horsemen riding south to keep pace with the fleet's slow progress. Fishing boats still scattered ahead of the English ships that, one by one, rounded a vast headland of white chalk and entered a bay where they turned into the wind and anchored.

The bay was wide and not well sheltered. The big waves heaved from the west to roll the *Heron* and make her snub at her anchor. The shore was close here, scarce two bowshots distant, but there was little to be seen other than a beach where the waves broke white, a stretch of marsh and a steep thick-wooded hill behind. Someone said they were in the mouth of the Seine, a river that ran deep into France, but Hook could see no sign of any river. Far off to the south was another shore, too distant to be seen clearly. More ships, the laggards, rounded the great headland and gradually the bay became thick with the anchored vessels.

'*Normandie*,' Melisande said, staring at the land.

'France,' Hook said.

'*Normandie*,' Melisande insisted, as though the distinction were important.

Hook was watching the trees, wondering when a French force would appear there. It seemed clear that the English army was going to land in this bay, which was little more than a shingled cove, so why were the French not trying to stop the invasion on the beach? Yet no men or horses showed at the treeline. A hawk spiralled up the face of the hill and gulls wheeled over the breaking waves. Hook saw Sir John being rowed in a small boat to the *Trinity Royal* where sailors were busy decorating the rails with the white shields painted with the cross of Saint George. Other boats were converging on the king's ship, carrying the great lords to a council of war.

'What will happen to us?' Melisande asked.

'I don't know,' Hook admitted, but nor did he care much. He was going to war in a company he had come to love, and he had Melisande, whom he loved, though he wondered if she would leave him now she was back in her own country. 'You're going home,' he said, wanting her to deny it.

For a long time she said nothing, just gazed at the trees and beach and marsh. '*Maman* was home,' she said finally. 'I do not know where home is now.'

'With me,' Hook said awkwardly.

'Home is where you feel safe,' Melisande said. Her eyes were grey as the heron that glided above the shingle to land in the low ground beyond. Pages were kneeling on the *Heron*'s deck where they scoured the men-at-arms' plate armour. Each piece was scrubbed with sand and vinegar to burnish the steel to a rustless shine, then wiped with lanolin. Peter Goddington ordered a pot of beeswax opened and the archers smeared woollen cloths with the wax and rubbed it into their bowstaves.

'Was your mother cruel to you?' Hook asked Melisande as he waxed the huge bow.

'Cruel?' she seemed puzzled. 'Why would she be cruel?'

'Some mothers are,' Hook said, thinking of his grandmother.

'She was lovely,' Melisande said.

'My father was cruel,' he said.

'Then you must not be,' Melisande said. She frowned, evidently thinking.

'What?'

She shrugged. 'When I went to the nunnery? Before?' She stopped.

'Go on,' Hook said.

'My father? He called me to him. I was thirteen? Perhaps fourteen?' She had lowered her voice. 'He made me take off all my clothes,' she stared at Hook as she spoke, 'and I stood there for him, *nue*. He walked around me and he said no man could have me.' She paused. 'I thought he was going to . . .'

'But he didn't?'

'No,' she said quickly. 'He stroked my *épaule*,' she hesitated, finding the English word, 'shoulder. He was, how do you say? *Frissonnant?*' she held out her hands and shook them.

'Shivering?' Hook suggested

She nodded abruptly. 'Then he sent me away to the nuns. I begged him not to. I said I hated the sisters, but he said I must pray for him. That was my duty, to work hard and to pray for him.'

'And did you?'

'Every day,' she said, 'and I prayed he would come for me, but he never did.'

The sun was sinking when Sir John returned to the *Heron*. There was still no sign of any French soldiers on the shore, but the trees beyond the beach could have hidden an army. Smoke rose from the hill to the east of the cove, evidence that someone was on that height, but who or how many was impossible to say. Sir John clambered aboard and walked around the deck, sometimes thrusting a finger at a man-at-arms or archer. He pointed at Hook. 'You,' he said, then walked on. 'Everyone I pointed to,' he turned and shouted, 'will be going ashore with me. We go tonight! After dark. The rest of you? Be ready at dawn. If we're still alive you'll join us. And those of you going ashore? Armour! Weapons! We're not going to dance with the bastards! We're going to kill them!'

That night there was a three-quarters moon silvering the sea. The shadows on land were black and stark as Hook dressed for war. He had his long boots, leather breeches, a leather jerkin, a mail coat and a helmet. He wore his archer's horn bracer on his left forearm, not so much to protect his arm against the string's lash because the mail would do that, but rather to stop the string fraying on the armour's links. He had a short sword hanging from his belt, a poleaxe slung on his back, and a linen arrow bag at his right side with the feathers of twenty-four arrows poking from the opening. Five men-at-arms and twelve archers were going ashore with Sir John and they all climbed down into an open boat that sailors rowed towards the surf. Other boats from other ships were also heading for the shore. No one spoke, though now and then a voice called soft from an anchored ship, wishing them luck. If the French were in the trees, Hook thought, then they would see the boats coming. Maybe even now the French were drawing swords and winding the thick strings of their steel-shafted crossbows.

The boat began to heave in short sharp lurches as the waves steepened near the shore. The sound of the surf became louder and more ominous. The sailors were digging their blades deep in the water, trying to outrace the curling, breaking waves, but suddenly the boat seemed to surge ahead and the sea was moonlit white, shattered and violent all about them, and then the boat dropped like a stone and there was a scraping sound as its keel dragged on the shingle. The boat slewed around and the water seethed about the hull before being sucked back to sea. 'Out!' Sir John hissed, 'out!'

Other boats slammed into the beach and men leaped out and trudged up the shingle bank with drawn swords. They gathered above the thick line of weed and driftwood that marked the high tide line. Huge boulders littered the beach, their moon-shadowed sides black. Hook had expected Sir John to be in charge of this first landing, but instead it was a much younger man who waited till all the boats had discharged their passengers. The sailors shoved their launches off the beach and held them just beyond the breaking waves. If the French were waiting and awake then the boats could come to pick up the landing party, but Hook doubted many would escape. There would be blood in the sucking shingle instead. 'We stay together,' the young man said in a low voice, 'archers to the right!'

'You heard Sir John!' Sir John Cornewaille hissed. The young man was Sir John Holland, nephew to the king and Sir John Cornewaille's stepson. 'Goddington?'

'Sir John?'

'Take your archers far enough out to give us flanking cover!'

It seemed the older Sir John was really in charge, merely yielding the appearance of command to his stepson. 'Forward!' the younger Sir John called, and the line of men, forty men-at-arms on the left and forty archers on the right, advanced further up the beach.

To find defences.

At first Hook thought he was approaching a great ridge of earth at the top of the shingle, but as he drew closer he saw that the ridge was man-made and had a ditch in front of it. It was a bank thrown up to serve as a rampart, and not only was it ditched, but there were bastions jutting out onto the shingle from which crossbowmen could shoot into the flanks of any attacker advancing up the beach. The ramparts, which had hardly been eroded by wind or rain, stretched the width of the cove and Hook imagined how hard it would be to fight up their front with men-at-arms hacking down from the summit and crossbow bolts slashing from the sides, but all he could do was imagine, because the rampart, that must have taken days to make, was entirely deserted.

'Been busy little farts, haven't they?' Sir John Cornewaille remarked caustically. He kicked the rampart's summit.

'What's the point of making defences and then abandoning them?'

'They knew we'd land here?' Sir John Holland suggested cautiously.

'Then why aren't they here to greet us?' Sir John asked. 'They probably built ramparts like these on every beach in Normandy! Bastards are pissing in their breeches and digging walls. Archers! You can all whistle, can't you?'

The archers said nothing. Most were too surprised by the question to make any response.

'You can all whistle?' Sir John asked again. 'Good! And you all know the tune of "Robin Hood's Lament"?'

Every archer knew that tune. It would have been astonishing had they not, for Robin Hood was the archers' hero, the bowman who had stood up against the lords and princes and sheriffs of England. 'Right!' Sir John announced. 'We're going up the hill! Men-at-arms on the track and archers into the woods! Explore to the top of the hill! If you hear or see someone then come and find me! But whistle "Robin Hood's Lament" so I know it's an Englishman coming and not some prick-sucking Frenchman! Let's go!'

Before they could climb the hill they needed to cross a sullen stretch of moon-glossed marsh that lay behind the beach's thick bank of earth and shingle. There was a path of sorts that doglegged its way over the swampy ground, but Sir John Cornewaille insisted the archers spread either side of the track so that, if an ambush was sprung, they could shoot their arrows in from the flanks. Peter Goddington cursed as he waded between the tussocks. 'He'll have us killed,' he grumbled as newly woken birds screeched up from the marsh, their sudden wingbeats loud in the night. The surf fell and sucked on the beach.

The marsh was a bowshot wide, a little more than two hundred paces. Hook could shoot further, but so could every crossbowman in France and, as he splashed towards the dark woods that grew almost to the marsh's edge, he watched the black shadows in fear of a sudden noise that would betray the release of a bolt. The French had known the English were coming. They would have had spies counting the shipping in Southampton Water and the fishermen would have brought news that the great fleet was off the coast. And the French had taken the trouble to defend even this small cove with an elaborate earthwork, so why were they not manning it? Because, Hook thought, they were waiting in the woods. Because they wanted to kill this advance party as it crossed the marsh.

'Hook! Tom and Matt! Dale! Go right!' Goddington waved the four men towards the eastern side of the marsh. 'Head on up the hill!'

Hook splashed off to his right, followed by the twins and by William of the Dale. Behind them the men-at-arms were grouped on the track. Every man, whether lord or archer, was wearing the badge of Saint George on their surcoat. The legs of the men-at-arms were cased in plate armour that reflected the moon white and bright, while their drawn swords looked like streaks of purest silver. No crossbow bolts flew from the woods. If the French were waiting then they must be higher up the slope.

Hook climbed a short bank of crumbling earth at the marsh's northern edge. He turned to see the fleet on the moon-glittered sea, its few lanterns dull red and its masts a forest. The stars were brilliant. He turned back to the wood's edge that was black as the pit. 'Bows are no good in the trees,' he told his companions. He unstrung the stave and slipped it into the horsehide case that had been folded and tucked in his belt. Leave a bow strung too long and it followed the cord to become permanently curved and so lost its power. It was better to store the stave straight and so he slung the

151

case's leather loop over his shoulder and drew his short sword. His three companions did the same and then followed Hook into the trees.

No Frenchman waited. No sudden sword blow greeted Hook, no crossbow bolt whipped from the dark. There was nothing but the sound of the sea and the blackness under the leaves and the small sounds of a wood at night.

Hook was at home in the trees, even among these foreign trees. Thomas and Matthew Scarlet were fuller's sons, reared to a mill where great water-driven beams thumped clay into cloth to release the wool's grease. William of the Dale was a carpenter, but Hook was a forester and a huntsman and he instinctively took the lead. He could hear men off to his left and, not wanting them to mistake him for a Frenchman, headed further to his right. He could smell a boar, and remembered a winter dawn when he had put five man-killing arrows into a great tusked male that had still charged him, arrows clattering in its side, anger fierce in its small eyes, and Hook had only escaped by scrambling up an oak. The boar had died eventually, its hooves stirring the blood-soaked leaf mould as its life drained away.

'Where are we going?' Thomas Scarlet asked.

'Top of the hill,' Hook answered curtly.

'What do we do there?'

'We wait,' Hook said. He did not know the answer. He could smell woodsmoke now, the pungent scent betraying that folk were nearby. He wondered if there was a charcoal-making camp in the woods because that would explain the smell, or perhaps the unseen fire warmed crossbowmen who waited for their targets to appear on the hilltop.

'We're going to kill the turd-sucking bastards,' William of the Dale said in his uncanny imitation of Sir John. Matt Scarlet laughed.

'Quiet,' Hook said sharply, 'and go faster!' If crossbowmen

152

were waiting then it was better to move quickly rather than present an easy target, but his instincts were telling him that there was no enemy in these trees. The wood felt deserted. When he had hunted deer-poachers on Lord Slayton's land he had always felt their presence, a knowledge that came from beyond sight, smell or hearing; an instinct. Hook reckoned these woods were empty, yet there was still that smell of woodsmoke. Instinct could be wrong.

The slope flattened and the trees became sparser. Hook was still leading his companions to the east, anxious to stay well away from a nervous English archer. Then, suddenly, he had reached the summit and the trees ended to reveal a sunken road running along the ridge. 'Bows,' he told his companions, though he did not unsheathe his own stave. He had heard something off to his left, some noise that could not have been made by any of Sir John's men. It was the thump of a hoof.

The four archers crouched in the trees above the road. The hoofbeats sounded louder, but nothing could be seen. It was one horse, Hook thought, judging from the sound, and then, suddenly, the horse and its rider were visible, riding eastwards. The rider was swathed in darkness as if he wore a cloak, but Hook could see no weapons. 'Don't shoot,' he told his companions, 'he's mine.'

Hook waited till the horseman was nearly opposite his hiding place, then leaped down the bank and snatched at the bridle. The horse slewed and reared. Hook reached up with his free hand, grasped a handful of the rider's cloak and hauled downwards. The horse whinnied, but obeyed Hook's touch, while the rider gasped as he thumped hard onto the road. The man tried to scramble away, but Hook kicked him hard in the belly, and then Thomas, Matthew and William were at his side, hauling the prisoner to his feet.

'He's a monk!' William of the Dale said.

'He was riding to fetch help,' Hook said. That was a guess, but hardly a difficult surmise.

The monk began to protest, speaking too quickly for Hook to understand any of his words. He spoke loudly too. 'Shut your face,' Hook said, and the monk, as if in response, began to shout his protests, so Hook hit him once and the monk's head snapped back and blood sprang from his nose, and he went instantly quiet. He was a young man who now looked very scared.

'I told you to shut your face,' Hook said. 'You three, whistle! Whistle loud!'

William, Matthew and Thomas whistled 'Robin Hood's Lament' as Hook led the prisoner and horse back along the road that lay sunken between two tree-shrouded banks. The track curved to the left to reveal a great stone building with a tower. It looked like a church. *'Une église?'* he asked the monk.

'Un monastère,' the monk said sullenly.

'Keep whistling,' Hook said.

'What did he say?' Tom Scarlet asked.

'He said it's a monastery. Now whistle!'

Smoke came from a chimney of the monastery, explaining the smell that had haunted Hook as they climbed the hill. No one else from the landing party was in sight yet, but as Hook led his small party towards the building a gate opened and a wash of lantern light revealed a group of monks standing in the gateway. 'Arrows on strings,' Hook said, 'and keep goddam whistling, for God's sake.'

A tall, thin, grey-haired man, robed in black, advanced down the track. *'Je suis le prieur,'* he announced himself.

'What did he say?' Tom Scarlet asked.

'He says he's the prior,' Hook said, 'just keep whistling.' The prior reached out a hand as if to take the bloodied monk, but Hook turned on him and the tall man stepped hastily back. The other monks began to protest, but then more archers came from the woods and Sir John Holland and his stepfather appeared around the priory's edge with the men-at-arms.

'Well done, Hook!' Sir John Cornewaille shouted, 'got yourself a horse!'

'And a monk, Sir John,' Hook said. 'He was riding for help, leastways I think he was.'

Sir John strode to Hook's side. The prior made the sign of the cross as the men-at-arms filled the road in front of the monastery, then stepped towards Sir John and made a voluble complaint that involved frequent gestures at Hook and at the bleeding monk. Sir John tipped up the wounded man's face to inspect the broken nose by moonlight. 'They must have sent a warning of our arrival yesterday,' he said, 'so this man was plainly sent to tell someone we were landing. Did you hit him, Hook?'

'Hit him, Sir John?' Hook asked, playing dumb while he thought what answer would serve him best.

'The prior says you hit him,' Sir John said accusingly.

Hook's instinct was to lie, just as he had always lied when faced with such accusations, but he did not want to sour his service to Sir John with untruths so he nodded. 'I did, Sir John,' he said.

Sir John's face showed a hint of a smile. 'That's a pity, Hook. Our king has said he'll hang any man who hurts a priest, a nun or a monk. He's very pious is our Henry, so I want you to think very carefully about your answer. Did you hit him, Hook?'

'Oh no, Sir John,' Hook said. 'I wouldn't dream of doing that.'

'Of course you wouldn't,' Sir John said, 'he just tumbled out of his saddle, didn't he? And he fell right onto his nose.' He blandly offered that explanation to the prior before

155

pushing the bloody-nosed monk towards his brethren. 'Archers,' Sir John said, turning to his men, 'I want you all on the skyline, there,' he pointed eastwards, 'and stay on the road. I'll take the horse, Hook.'

The archers waited on the road, which fell away in front of them before rising to another tree-covered crest. The stars were fading as the dawn smeared the east. Peter Goddington gave permission for some men to sleep as others kept watch and Hook made a bed on a mossy bank and must have slept an hour before more hoofbeats woke him. It was full light now and the sun was streaming through green leaves. A dozen horsemen were on the road, one of them Sir John Cornewaille. The horses were shivering and skittish and Hook guessed they had just been swum ashore and were still uncertain of their footing. 'On to the next ridge!' Sir John shouted at the archers and Hook hastily picked up his arrow bag and cased bow. He followed the archers eastwards, and the men-at-arms, in no apparent hurry, walked their horses behind.

The view from the further ridge was astonishing. To Hook's right the sea narrowed towards the Seine's mouth. The river's southern bank was all low wooded hills. To the north were more hills, but in front of Hook, glinting under the morning sun, the road fell away through woods and fields to a town and its harbour. The harbour was small, crammed with ships, and protected by the town walls that were built clear around the port, leaving only a narrow entrance leading to a slender channel that twisted to the sea. Behind the port was the town itself, all roofs and churches ringed by a great stone wall that was obscured in places by houses that had been built outside its perimeter. The houses, which spread out on all sides of the town, could not hide the great towers that studded the wall. Hook counted the towers. Twenty-four. Banners hung from the towers and from the walls in between. The archers were much too far away to see the flags, but

156

the message of the banners was obvious; the town knew the English had landed and was proclaiming its defiance.

'Harfleur,' Sir John Cornewaille announced to the archers. 'A nest of goddamned pirates! They're villains who live there, boys! They raid our shipping, raid our coast, and we're going to scour them out of that town like rats out of a granary!'

Hook could see more now. He could see a river looping through fields to Harfleur's north. The river evidently ran clear through the town, entering under a great arch and flowing through the houses to empty itself in the walled harbour. But the citizens of Harfleur, warned the previous day of the coming of the English, must have dammed the archway so that the river was now flooding to spread a great lake about the town's northern and western sides. Harfleur, under that morning sun, looked like a walled island.

A crossbow bolt seared overhead. Hook had seen the flicker of its first appearance, down and to his left, meaning that whoever had shot the bolt was in the woods north of the road. The bolt landed somewhere in the trees behind.

'Someone doesn't like us,' one of the mounted men-at-arms said lightly.

'Anyone see where it came from?' another rider demanded sharply.

Hook and a half-dozen other archers all pointed to the same patch of dense trees and undergrowth. The road dropped in front of them, then ran level for a hundred paces to the lip of a shelf before falling again towards the flood-besieged town, and the crossbowman was somewhere on that wide wooded ledge.

'I don't suppose he'll go away,' Sir John Cornewaille remarked mildly.

'There may be more than one?' someone else suggested.

'Just one, I think,' Sir John said. 'Hook? You want to fetch the wretched man for me?'

Hook ran to his left, plunged into the trees, then turned down the short slope. He reached the wide ledge and there went more slowly, picking his way carefully to keep from making a noise. He had strung his bow. In thick trees the bow was a dubious weapon, but he did not want to encounter a crossbowman without having an arrow on the string.

The wood was oak, ash and a few maples. The undergrowth was hawthorn and holly, and there was mistletoe growing high in the oaks, something Hook noted for he rarely saw it sprouting from oak in England. His grandmother had valued oak mistletoe, using it in a score of medicines she had made for the villagers, and even for Lord Slayton when the ague struck him. Her chief use for the mistletoe had been the treatment of barren women for which she had pounded the small berries with mangrove root, the whole moistened with the urine of a mother. There had been a fecund woman in the village, Mary Carter, who had given birth to fifteen healthy children, and Hook had often been sent with a pot to request her urine, and once he had been beaten by his grandmother for coming back with the pot empty because she had refused to believe that Mary Carter was away from home. The next time Hook had pissed in the pot himself and his grandmother had never noticed the difference.

He was thinking about that, and wondering whether Melisande would become pregnant, when he heard the fierce, quick sound of a crossbow being shot. The noise was close. He crouched, crept forward and suddenly saw the shooter. It was a boy, maybe twelve or thirteen years old, who was grunting slightly as he worked the crank to span his weapon. The head of the bow had a stirrup in which the boy had placed his foot, and at its butt was the socket where he had fitted the two handles that turned to wind back the cord. It was hard work and the boy was grimacing with the effort of inching the thick cord up the weapon's stock. He was concentrating so hard that he did not notice Hook until the archer picked him up by the scruff of his coat. The boy beat at Hook, then yelped as he was slapped around the head.

'You're a rich one, aren't you?' Hook said. The boy's coat, which Hook was holding by the collar, was of finely woven woollen cloth. His breeches and shoes were expensive, and his crossbow, which Hook scooped up with his right hand, looked as though it had been made specially for the boy because it was much smaller than a man's bow. The stock was walnut and beautifully inlaid with silver and ivory chasings that depicted a deer hunt in a forest. 'They'll probably hang you, boy,' Hook said cheerfully, and walked out to the road with the boy tucked under his left arm and his own bow and the valuable crossbow held in his right. He climbed back up the hill to where grinning archers lined the ridge and mounted men-at-arms blocked the road. 'Here's the enemy, Sir John!' Hook said cheerfully, dropping the boy beside Sir John's horse.

'A brave enemy,' a horseman said admiringly and Hook looked up to see the king. Henry was in plate armour and wore a surcoat showing his royal arms. He wore a helmet ringed with a golden crown, though his visor was lifted to reveal his long-nosed face with its deep dark pit of a scar. Hook dropped to his knees and dragged the boy down with him.

'*Votre nom?*' the king demanded of the boy, who did not answer, but just glared up at Henry. Hook cuffed him around the head again.

'Philippe,' the boy said sullenly.

'Philippe?' Henry asked, 'just Philippe?'

'Philippe de Rouelles,' the boy answered, defiant now.

'It seems that Master Philippe is the only man in France

159

who dares face us!' the king said loudly enough for everyone on the hilltop to hear. 'He shoots two crossbow bolts at us! You try to kill your own king, boy,' Henry went on, speaking French again, 'and I am king here. I am King of Normandy, King of Aquitaine, King of Picardy, and King of France. I am your king.' He swung his leg over the saddle and dropped to the grass. A squire spurred forward to take the reins of the king's horse as Henry took two steps to stand above Philippe de Rouelles. 'You tried to kill your king,' he said, and drew his sword. The blade made a hissing noise as it scraped through the scabbard's throat. 'What do you do with a boy who tries to kill a king?' Henry demanded loudly.

'You kill him, sire,' a horseman growled.

The king's blade rose. Philippe was shaking and his eyes were tear-bright, but his face was still stubbornly defiant. Then he flinched as the blade flashed down.

It stopped an inch above his shoulder. Henry smiled. He tapped the blade once, then tapped it again on the boy's other shoulder. 'You're a brave subject,' he said lightly. 'Rise, Sir Philippe.' The horsemen laughed as Hook hauled the wide-eyed boy to his feet.

Henry was wearing a golden chain about his neck from which hung a thick ivory pendant decorated with an antelope made of jet. The antelope was another of his personal badges, though Hook, seeing the badge, neither knew what the beast was nor that it was the king's private insignia. Henry now lifted the chain from his neck and draped it over Philippe's head. 'A keepsake of a day on which you should have died, boy,' Henry said. Philippe said nothing, but just looked from the rich gift to the man who had given it to him. 'Your father is the Sire of Rouelles?' the king asked.

'Yes, lord,' Philippe said in a voice scarce more than a whisper.

'Then tell your father his rightful king has come and that

his king is merciful. Now go, Sir Philippe.' Henry dropped his sword back into its black scabbard. The boy glanced at the crossbow in Hook's hand. 'No, no,' the king said, 'we keep your bow. Your punishment will be whatever your father deems appropriate for its loss. Let him go,' the king ordered Hook. He appeared not to recognise the archer with whom he had spoken in the Tower.

Henry watched the boy run down the slope, then climbed back into his saddle. 'The French send a lad to do their work,' he said sourly.

'And when he grows, sire,' Sir John said equally sourly, 'we'll have to kill him.'

'He is our subject,' the king said loudly, 'and this is our land! These people are ours!' He stared at Harfleur for a long time. The town might be his by right, but the folk inside had a different opinion. Their gates were shut, their walls were hung with defiant banners and their valley was flooded. Harfleur, it seemed, was determined to fight.

'Let's get the army ashore,' Henry said.

And the fight for France had begun.

The army began to come ashore on Thursday, August fifteenth, the feast of Saint Alipius, and it took till Saturday, the feast of Saint Agapetus, until the last man, horse, gun and cargo had been brought to the boulder-strewn beach. The horses staggered when they were swum ashore. They whinnied and cavorted, eyes white, until grooms calmed them. Archers cut a wider road up from the beach to the monastery where the king had his quarters. Henry spent hours on the beach, encouraging and chivvying the work, or else he rode to the crest where Philippe de Rouelles had tried to kill him and from there he stared eastwards at Harfleur. Sir John Cornewaille's men guarded the ridge, but no French came to drive the English back into the sea. A

161

few horsemen rode from the town, but they stayed well out of bowshot, content to gaze at the enemy on the skyline.

The flood waters spread about Harfleur. Some of the houses built outside the walls were flooded so that only their rooftops showed above the water, but two wide stretches of dry ground remained in the base of the bowl where the town sat. The nearer stretch led to one of Harfleur's three gates and, from his eyrie high on the hill, Hook could see the enemy making the finishing touches to a huge bastion that protected that gate. The bastion was like a small castle blocking the road, so that any attack on the gate would first have to take that new and massive fortification.

On the Friday afternoon, the feast of Saint Hyacinth, Hook and a dozen men were sent to retrieve Sir John's last horses, which were swum ashore from the *Lady of Falmouth*. The animals floundered on the shingle and the archers ran ropes through their bridles to keep them together. Melisande had come with Hook and she stroked the nose of Dell, her small piebald mare that had been a gift from Sir John's wife. She murmured soothing words to the mare. 'That horse don't speak French, Melisande!' Matthew Scarlet said, 'she's an English mare!'

'She's learning French,' Melisande said.

'Language of the devil,' William of the Dale said in his imitation of Sir John, and the other archers laughed. Matthew Scarlet, one of the twins, was leading Lucifer, Sir John's big battle-charger, who now lunged away from him. One of Sir John's grooms ran to help. Hook had a leading rein with eight horses attached and he pulled them towards Melisande, intending to add Dell to his string. He called her name, but Melisande was staring up the beach, frowning, and Hook looked to see where she was gazing.

A group of men-at-arms was kneeling on the stones as a priest prayed and for a moment he thought that was what

162

had caught her eye, then he saw a second priest just beyond one of the great boulders. It was Sir Martin, and with him were the Perrill brothers, and the three men were looking at Melisande, and Hook had the impression, no more, that they had made obscene gestures. 'Melisande,' he said, and she turned to him.

Sir Martin grinned. He was gazing at Hook now and he slowly lifted his right hand and folded back his fingers so that only the longest finger protruded, and then, still slowly, he slipped his left fist over that one finger and, holding his hands together, made the sign of the cross towards Hook and Melisande. 'Bastard,' Hook said softly.

'Who is it?' Melisande asked.

'They're enemies,' Hook said. The Perrill brothers were laughing.

Tom and Matthew Scarlet came to stand with Hook. 'You know them?' Tom Scarlet asked.

'I know them.'

Sir Martin again made the sign of the cross before turning away in response to a shout. 'He's a priest?' Tom Scarlet asked in a tone of disbelief.

'A priest,' Hook said, 'a rapist and gentry born. But he was bitten by the devil's dog and he's dangerous.'

'And you know him?'

'I know him,' Hook said, then turned on the twins. 'You all look after Melisande,' he said fiercely.

'We do,' Matthew Scarlet said, 'you know that.'

'What did he want?' Melisande asked.

'You,' Hook said, and that night he gave her the small crossbow and its bag of bolts. 'Practise with it,' he said.

Next day, on the feast of Saint Agapetus, the eight great guns were hauled up from the beach. One gun, which was named the King's Daughter, needed two wagons for its massive hooped barrel which was longer than three bowstaves and had a gaping mouth large enough to take a barrel of ale. The other cannon were smaller, but all needed teams of over twenty horses to drag them to the hilltop.

Patrols rode north, bringing back supplies and commandeering farm wagons that would carry the provisions and tents and arrows and newly-felled oaks, which would be trimmed and shaped to make the catapults that would add their missiles to the shaped gun-stones that all had to be carried up the hill by yet more wagons. But, at last, the whole army and all its horses and all its supplies was ashore, and under a bright afternoon sun the cumbersome wagons were lined on the road beside the monastery and the army of England, banners flying, assembled around them. There were nine thousand archers and three thousand men-at-arms, all of them mounted, and there were pages and squires and women and servants and priests and yet more spare horses, and the flags snapped bright in the midday wind as the king, mounted on a snow-white gelding, rode along his red-crossed army. The sun glinted from the crown that surmounted his helmet. He reached the skyline above the town and he stared for a few minutes, then nodded to Sir John Holland who would have the honour of leading the vanguard. 'With God's blessing, Sir John!' the king called, 'on to Harfleur!'

Trumpets sounded, drums beat, and the horsemen of England spilled over the edge of the hill. They wore the cross of Saint George and above their helmeted heads their lords' banners were gold and red and blue and yellow and green and to anyone watching from Harfleur's walls it must have seemed as though the hills were pouring an armoured mass towards their town.

'How many people live in the town?' Melisande asked Hook. She rode beside him, and hanging by her saddle was the ivory and silver inlaid crossbow Hook had given her.

'Sir John reckons they've only got about a hundred soldiers in the town,' Hook said.

'Is that all?'

'But they have the townsfolk as well,' Hook said, 'and there must be two thousand of them? Maybe three thousand!'

'But all these men!' Melisande said and twisted in her saddle to look at the long lines of horsemen who filled the space on either side of the road. Mounted drummers beat on their instruments, making a noise to warn the citizens of Harfleur that their rightful king was coming in wrath.

Yet Henry of England was not the only person approaching the town. Even as the English spilled down the slope towards the dry ground to Harfleur's west, another cavalcade was riding from the east. They were a long way off, but clearly visible; a column of men-at-arms and wagons, a long line of reinforcements riding towards the ramparts. 'That,' Sir John Cornewaille said, watching the distant men, 'is a pity.'

'They're bringing guns,' Peter Goddington remarked.

'As I said,' Sir John said with surprising mildness, 'it is a pity.' He spurred Lucifer to the head of the column and other lords, all wanting the honour of being the first to face the defiant town, raced after him. Hook watched the riders gallop down the hill and onto the flat ground, then saw the great blossom of black smoke billow and grow from Harfleur's wall. A few seconds later the sound of the gun punched the summer air, a flat crack that seemed to linger in the bowl of the hills in which the port was built. The gun-stone struck the meadows where the horsemen rode, ricocheted upwards in a flurry of turf then plunged harmlessly into the trees beyond.

And Harfleur was under siege.

It seemed to Hook that he never stopped digging in the first few days of the siege. It was midden trenches first. 'Our ma fell into a shit-pit once,' Tom Scarlet said, 'she was drunk. She dropped some beads in it and then tried to fish them out with a rake.'

'They were nice beads,' Matthew Scarlet put in, 'bits of old silver, weren't they?'

'Coins,' his twin said, 'which our dad found in a buried jar. He bored them through and hung them on a scrap of bowstring.'

'Which broke,' Matt said.

'So ma tried to fish them out with a rake,' Tom picked up the tale, 'and fell right in, head first!'

'She got the beads back,' Matt said.

'She sobered up quick enough,' Tom Scarlet went on, 'but she couldn't stop laughing. Our dad took her down the duck pond and pushed her in. He made her take all her clothes off and then the ducks all flew away. They would, wouldn't they? A naked woman splashing about and laughing. Whole village was laughing!'

The first thing the king had ordered was the burning of

the houses outside the town's walls so that nothing would stand between the ramparts and his guns. The job was done at night, so that the flames burst into the darkness to light the defiant banners on Harfleur's pale walls, and all next day the smoke of the smouldering buildings lingered in the flooded bowl of hills that cradled the port and reminded Hook of the smoke that had veiled the land around Soissons.

'Of course the priest wasn't happy,' Matthew Scarlet continued his brother's story, 'but our parish priest always was a rank piece of piss. He had our mother up in front of the manor court! Breaking the peace, he said, but his lord-ship gave her three shillings to buy cloth for new clothes and a kiss for being happy. He said she could go swimming in his shit any time she wanted.'

'Did she ever?' Peter Scoyle asked. Scoyle was a rarity, a bowman born and bred in London. He had been a comb-maker's apprentice and had been convicted of causing a murderous affray, but had been pardoned on condition that he served in the king's army.

'She never did,' Tom Scarlet said, 'she always said that one bath in shit was enough for a lifetime.'

'One bath is enough for any lifetime!' Father Christopher had evidently heard the twins telling their tale. 'Beware of cleanliness, boys! The blessed Saint Jerome warns us that a clean body means an unclean soul, and the holy Saint Agnes was proud of never having washed in her life.'

'Melisande won't approve,' Hook said, 'she likes being clean.'

'Warn her!' Father Christopher said seriously, 'the physi-cians all agree, Hook, that washing weakens the skin. It lets in disease!'

Then, when the pits were dug, Hook and a hundred other archers rode north up the valley of the River Lézarde and dug again, this time making a great dam across the valley.

They demolished a dozen half-timbered houses in a village and used the beams to strengthen the huge earthen bank that stopped up the river. The Lézarde was small and the summer had been dry, but it still took four days of hard digging to make a barrier high enough to divert most of the river water westwards. By the time Hook and his companions went back to Harfleur the flood waters had partly subsided, though the ground about the town was still waterlogged and the river itself still spilled over its banks to make a wide lake north of the town.

Next they dug pits for guns. Two cannon, one called Londoner because the citizens of London had paid for it, were already in place and their gun-stones were biting at the huge bastion the defenders had built outside the Leure Gate. The Duke of Clarence, who was the king's brother, had marched clear around the town and his forces, which were a third of the English army, were attacking Harfleur's eastern side. They had their own guns that had been fortuitously captured from a supply convoy making for Harfleur. The Dutch gunners, hired to defend Harfleur from its English enemies, happily took English coin and turned their cannon against the town's defenders. Harfleur was surrounded now. No more reinforcements could reach the town unless they fought their way past the English army or sailed past the fleet of royal warships that guarded the harbour entrance.

On the day that the gun-pits were finished Hook and forty other archers climbed the hill to the west of the encampment, following the road by which the army had approached Harfleur. Huge oaks lined the nearest crest, and they were ordered to fell those trees and lop off the straightest limbs, which were to be sawn to the length of a bowstave and loaded onto wagons. The day was hot. A half-dozen archers stayed by the road with the huge two-handled saws while the rest spread along the crest. Peter Goddington marked the trees he wanted felled, and assigned a pair of archers to each. Hook and Will of the Dale were almost the farthest south, with only the Scarlet twins closer to the sea. Melisande was with Hook. Her hands were raw from washing clothes and there were still more clothes to be boiled and scrubbed back in the encampment, but Sir John's steward had let her accompany Hook. She carried the small crossbow on her back and never left Sir John's company without the weapon. 'I will shoot that priest if he touches me,' she had told Hook, 'and I'll shoot his friends.' Hook had nodded, but said nothing. She might, he thought, shoot one of them, but the weapon took so long to reload that she had no chance of defending herself against more than one man.

The trees muffled the occasional sound of a cannon firing and dulled the crash of the gun-stones striking home on Harfleur's walls. The axes were loud. 'Why did we come so far from the camp?' Melisande asked.

'Because we've chopped down all the big trees that are closer,' Hook said. He was stripped to the waist, his huge muscles driving the axe deep into an oak's trunk so that the chips flew.

'And we're not that far away from the camp,' Will of the Dale added. He was standing back, letting Hook do the work and Hook did not mind. He was used to wielding a forester's axe.

Melisande spanned the crossbow. She found it hard work, but she would not let Hook or Will help her crank the twin handles. She was sweating by the time the pawl clicked to hold the cord under its full tension. She laid a bolt in the groove, then aimed at a tree no more than ten paces away. She frowned, bit her lower lip, then pulled the trigger and watched as the bolt flew a yard wide to skitter through the undergrowth beyond. 'Don't laugh,' she said before either man had any chance to laugh.

'I'm not laughing,' Hook said, grinning at Will.

'I wouldn't dare,' Will said.

'I will learn,' Melisande said.

'You'll learn better if you keep your eyes open,' Hook said.

'It's hard,' she said.

'Look down the arrow,' Will advised her, 'hold the bow firm and pull the trigger nice and slowly. And may God bless you when you shoot,' he added the last words in Father Christopher's sly voice.

She nodded, then cranked the bow again. It took a long time before it clicked, then instead of shooting it she laid the weapon on the leaf mould and just watched Hook and she thought how he made felling a great oak look easy, just as he made shooting a bow seem simple.

'I'll see if the twins need help,' Will of the Dale said, 'because you don't, Nick.'

'I don't,' Hook agreed, 'so go and help them. They're fuller's sons which means they've never done a proper day's work in their lives.'

Will picked up his axe, his arrow bag and his cased bow and disappeared among the southern trees. Melisande watched him go, then looked down at the cocked crossbow as though she had never seen such a thing before. 'Father Christopher was talking to me,' she said quietly.

'Was he?' Hook asked. He looked up at the tree, then back to the cut he had made. 'This great thing will fall in a minute,' he warned her. He went to the back side of the trunk and buried the axe in the wood. He wrenched the blade free. 'So what did Father Christopher want?'

'He wanted to know if we would marry.'

'Us? Marry?' The axe chopped again and a wedge of wood came away when Hook pulled the blade back. Any moment now, he thought. He could sense the tension in the oak, the silent tearing of the timber that preceded the tree's death. He stepped away to stand beside Melisande who was well clear of the trunk. He noticed the crossbow was still cocked and almost told her that she would weaken the weapon by leaving the shank stressed, but then decided that might not be a bad thing. A weakened shank would make it easier for her to span. 'Marry?' he asked again.

'That's what he said.'

'What did you say?'

'I didn't know,' she said, staring at the ground, 'maybe?'

'Maybe,' Hook echoed her, and just then the timber cracked and ripped and the huge oak fell, slowly at first, then faster as it crashed through leaves and branches to shudder down. Birds shrieked. For a moment the woods were full of alarm, then all that was left was the ringing sound of the other axes along the ridge. 'I think, maybe,' Hook said slowly, 'that it's a good idea.'

'You do?'

He nodded. 'I do.'

She looked at him, said nothing for a while, then picked up the crossbow. 'I look down the arrow,' she said, 'and hold the bow tight?'

'And you squeeze gently,' he said. 'Hold your breath while you squeeze, and don't look at the bolt, just look at the place where you want the bolt to go.'

She nodded, laid a bolt in the groove and aimed at the same tree she had missed before. It was a couple of paces closer now. Hook watched her, saw the concentration on her face and saw her flinch in anticipation of the weapon's kick. She held her breath, closed her eyes and pulled the trigger and the bolt flashed past the tree's edge and vanished down the gentle farther slope. Melisande stared forlorn at where it had gone.

'You haven't got that many bolts,' Hook said, 'and those are special.'

'Special?'

'They're smaller than most,' he said, 'they're made specially to fit that bow.'

'I should find the ones I shot?'

He grinned. 'I'll chop off a couple of these boughs, and you should find those two bolts.'

'I have nine left.'

'Eleven would be better.'

She laid the crossbow on the ground and picked her way down the slope to vanish in the sunlit green of the undergrowth. Hook cocked the crossbow, winding the cord back easily, hoping that the continual stress would weaken the stave and so help Melisande, then he went back to lopping branches. He wondered why the king had demanded so many pieces of straight timber the height of a bowstave. Not his business, he decided. He made short work of a second branch, then a third. The great trunk would be sawn eventually, but for the moment he would leave it where it had fallen. He lopped off more of the smaller branches, and heard the long collapse of another tree somewhere along the ridge. Pigeons clattered through the leaves. He thought he might have to go and help Melisande find the bolts because she had been gone far too long, but just as he had that thought she came running back, her face alarmed and her eyes wide. She pointed down the westwards slope. 'There are men!' she said.

'Course there are men,' Hook said, and sliced off a limb the size of a man's arm with a one-handed stroke of the axe. 'We're all over the place.'

'Men-at-arms,' Melisande hissed, *'chevaliers*!'

'Probably our fellows,' Hook said. Mounted men-at-arms patrolled the surrounding countryside every day, looking for supplies and watching for the French army that everyone expected would come to Harfleur's relief.

'They are French!' Melisande hissed.

Hook doubted it, but he swung the axe to bury its blade in the fallen trunk, then jumped down and took her arm. 'Let's have a look.'

There were indeed men. There were horsemen in a fern-thick gully that twisted through the high wood. Hook could see a dozen of them in single file, following a track through the trees, but he sensed there were more riders behind them. And he saw, too, that Melisande was right. The horsemen were not wearing the cross of Saint George. They had surcoats, but none of the badges was familiar, and the riders were armoured in plate and all wore helmets. They had their visors raised and Hook could see the leading horseman's eyes glitter in the steel's shadow. The man held up his hand to check the column, then stared intently up the slope, trying to discover exactly where the sound of axe blows came from, and as he stared, so more horsemen appeared from the far trees.

'French,' Melisande whispered.

'They are,' Hook said softly. Most of the horsemen carried drawn swords.

'What do you do?' Melisande asked, still whispering, 'hide?'

'No,' Hook said, because he knew what he must do. The knowledge was instinctive and he did not doubt it, nor did he hesitate. He led her back to the felled tree, snatched up the cocked crossbow, then ran along the ridge. 'The French!' he shouted. 'They're coming! Get back to the wagons! Fast!' He shouted it over and over. 'Back to the wagons!' He first ran to his right, away from the wagons, to find Tom Scarlet and Will of the Dale standing and staring. 'Will,' Hook said, 'use Sir John's voice. Tell them the French are here, and get everyone back to the wagons.'

Will of the Dale just gaped at him.

'Use Sir John's voice!' Hook said harshly, shaking the

carpenter by the shoulders. 'The goddam French are coming! Now go! Where's Matt?' he asked the last question of Tom Scarlet, who mutely pointed southwards.

Will of the Dale was obeying Hook. He was hurrying back along the crest and using his imitation of Sir John's harsh voice to pull the archers back to where the big wagons waited on the road. Peter Goddington, confused by the mimicry, searched for Sir John and found Hook, Melisande and Tom Scarlet instead. 'What in God's name is happening?' Goddington demanded angrily.

'French, sergeant,' Hook said, pointing down the western slope.

'Don't be daft, Hook,' Goddington said, 'there are no goddam French here.'

'I saw them,' Hook said. 'Men-at-arms. They're in armour and carrying swords.'

'They were our men, you fool,' Goddington insisted. 'Probably a forage party.'

The centenar was so sure of himself that Hook was beginning to doubt what he had seen, and his uncertainty was increased because the horsemen, though they must have heard the shouting on the crest, had not reacted. He had expected the men-at-arms to spur up the slope and burst through the trees, but none had appeared. Yet he stuck to his story. 'There were about twenty of them,' he told Goddington, 'armoured, and with strange livery. Melisande saw them too.'

The sergeant glanced at Melisande and decided her opinion was worthless. 'I'll have a look,' he said grudgingly. 'Where did you say they were?'

'In the trees down that slope,' Hook said, pointing. 'They're not on the road. They're in the trees, like they didn't want to be seen.'

'You'd better not be dreaming,' the centenar grumbled and went down the slope.

175

'Where's Matt?' Hook asked Tom Scarlet again.

'He went to look at the sea,' Tom Scarlet answered.

'Matt!' Hook bellowed, cupping his hands.

There was no answer. The warm wind sighed in the branches and chaffinches made a busy noise somewhere down the eastern slope. A gun sounded from the siege lines, the echo rumbling in the bowl of the hills and melding with the crash of the stone's impact. Hook could not hear the clink of bridles or the thump of hooves and he wondered if he had imagined the horsemen. The shouting on the crest had ended, suggesting that the bemused archers must have assembled back at the wagons.

'We'd never seen the sea before,' Tom Scarlet said nervously, 'not before we sailed here. Matt wanted to look again.'

'Matt!' Hook shouted again, but again there was no answer.

Peter Goddington had vanished over the crest's lip. Hook gave the crossbow to Melisande and then uncased his bow, strung it, and put an arrow across the stave. He walked to the gully's lip and gazed down into the ferns. Peter Goddington was alone in the gully. There was not a horseman in sight and the centenar looked up and gave Hook a glance of pure disgust. 'Nothing here, you fool,' he shouted, and just then Hook saw the two horsemen come from the trees on the right.

'Behind you!' he shouted, and Goddington began to run up the slope as Hook raised the bow, hauled the cord back and loosed just as the man-at-arms nearest the centenar swerved left. The arrow, a bodkin, glanced off the espalier that armoured the man's shoulder. The sword chopped down and Hook, as he pulled another arrow from the bag, saw blood bright and sudden in the glowing green woodland, he saw Peter Goddington's head turn red, saw him stumble as the second Frenchman, his sword held rigid as a lance, took the centenar in the back. Goddington fell.

Hook loosed again. The white feathers streaked through shadow and sunlight and the bodkin head, shafted with oak, slammed through the second man's breastplate and hurled him back in his tall saddle. More horsemen were coming now, spurring from the thick trees to put their horses at the slope, and Tom Scarlet was tugging at Hook's arm. 'Nick! Nick!'

And suddenly it was panic because there were more riders to their left, between them and the sea, and Hook seized Melisande's sleeve and dragged her back. He had not seen that southernmost column, and Hook realised the French had come in at least two parties and he had seen only one, and he ran desperately, hearing the hooves loud and getting louder, and he dragged Melisande fast to one side, dodging like a hare pursued by hounds, but then a horseman galloped in front of him and slewed about in a slithering flurry of leaf mould. Hook twisted to his left to find refuge by the bole of a great hollow oak. It was really no refuge at all, because he was cornered now, and still more horsemen came and a rider laughed from his saddle as the men-at-arms surrounded Melisande and the two archers.

'Matt!' Tom said, and Hook saw that Matthew Scarlet was already a prisoner. A Frenchman in blue and green livery had him by his jacket's collar, dragging him alongside his horse.

'Archers,' a horseman said. The word was the same in French and English, and there was no mistaking the pleasure with which the man spoke.

'*Père!*' Melisande gasped, '*Père?*'

And that was when Hook saw the falcon stooping against the sun. The livery was newly embroidered and bright, almost as bright as the sword blade that reached towards him. The blade came within a hand's breadth of his throat, then suddenly stopped. The rider, sitting straight-legged in his destrier's saddle, stared down at Hook. The haunch of a roe deer, newly killed, hung from his saddle's pommel and its blood had dripped onto the scale-armoured foot of the horseman, who was Ghillebert, Seigneur de Lanferelle, the lord of hell.

He was a lord in splendour, mounted on a magnificent stallion and wearing plate armour that shone like the sun. He alone among the horsemen was bareheaded so that his long black hair hung sleek almost to his waist. His face was like polished metal, hard edged, bronze dark, with a hawk's nose and hooded eyes that showed amusement as he stared first at Hook who was trapped by the sword blade, then at Melisande who had raised the cocked crossbow. If Lanferelle was astonished at discovering his daughter in a high Norman wood he did not show it. He offered her a flicker of a wry smile, then said something in French and the girl fumbled in the pouch and took out a bolt that she laid in the weapon's groove. Ghillebert, Lord of Lanferelle, could easily have stopped her, but he merely smiled again as the now loaded weapon was raised once more to point at his face. He spoke, much too fast for Hook to understand, and Melisande answered just as fast, but passionately.

There was a shout from behind Hook, far behind, from where the road dropped to the English camp. The Lord of Lanferelle gestured to his men, gave an order, and they rode towards the shout. Half of the men, who numbered eighteen, wore the livery of the hawk and sun, the rest had the same blue and green livery as the man holding Matt Scarlet prisoner, and that man, together with a squire wearing Lanferelle's badge were the only ones who stayed with le Seigneur d'Enfer.

'Three English archers,' Lanferelle spoke in English suddenly, and Hook remembered how this Frenchman had learned English when he was a prisoner waiting for his ransom to be collected, 'three goddam archers, and I give gold to my men for bringing me the fingers of goddam archers.' Lanferelle grinned suddenly, his teeth very white against his sun-darkened skin. 'There are fingerless peasants all across Normandy and Picardy because my men cheat.' He seemed proud of that, because he gave a sudden braying laugh. 'You know she is my daughter?'

'I know,' Hook said.

'She's the prettiest of them! I have nine that I know of, but only one from my wife. But this one,' he looked at Melisande who still held the crossbow on him, 'this one I thought to protect from the world.'

'I know,' Hook said again.

'She was supposed to pray for my soul,' Lanferelle said, 'but it seems I must breed other daughters if my soul is to be saved.'

Melisande spat some fast words that only made Lanferelle smile more. 'I put you in the convent,' he said, still speaking English, 'because you were too pretty to be humped by some sweaty peasant and too ill-born to be married to a gentleman. But now it seems you found the peasant anyway,' he gave Hook a derisive glance, 'and the fruit is picked, eh? But picked or not,' he said, 'you are still my possession.'

'She's mine,' Hook said, and was ignored.

'So what shall I do? Take you back to the nunnery?' Lanferelle asked, then grinned delightedly when Melisande raised the crossbow an inch higher. 'You won't shoot,' he said.

'I will,' Hook said, but it was a barren threat for he had no arrow on his string and knew he would be given no time to pull one from the bag.

'Who do you serve?' Lanferelle asked.

'Sir John Corncwaillc,' Hook said proudly.

Lanferelle was pleased. 'Sir John! Ah, there's a man. His mother must have slept with a Frenchman! Sir John! I like

Sir John,' he smiled. 'But what of Melisande, eh? What of my little novice?'

'I hated the convent,' she spat at him, using English.

Lanferelle frowned as though her sudden outburst puzzled him. 'You were safe there,' he said, 'and your soul was safe.'

'Safe!' Melisande protested, 'in Soissons? Every nun was raped or killed!'

'You were raped?' Lanferelle asked, his voice dangerous.

'Nicholas stopped him,' she said, gesturing at Hook, 'he killed him first.'

The dark eyes brooded on Hook for an instant, then returned to Melisande. 'So what do you want?' he asked, almost angrily. 'You want a husband? Someone to look after you? How about him?' Lanferelle jerked his head towards his squire. 'Maybe you should marry him? He's gently born, but not too gently. His mother was a saddler's daughter.' The squire, who plainly did not understand a word that was being said, stared dumbly at Melisande. He wore no helmet, but had an aventail instead, a hood of chain mail that framed a sweaty face scarred by childhood pox. His nose had been flattened in some fight and he had thick, wet-looking lips. Melisande grimaced and spoke urgently in French, so urgently that Hook only understood part of what she said. She was scornful and tearful at the same time, and her words appeared to amuse her father. 'She says she will stay with you,' Lanferelle translated for Hook, 'but that depends upon my wishes. It depends on whether I let you live.'

Hook was thinking that he could lunge upwards with the bowstave and drive the horn-nocked tip into Lanferelle's throat, or else into the soft tissue under his chin and keep driving the shaft so that it pierced the Frenchman's brain.

'No,' the voice spoke in his head. It was almost a whisper, but unmistakably the voice of Saint Crispinian who had been silent for so long. 'No,' the saint said again.

Hook almost fell to his knees in gratitude. His saint had returned. Lanferelle was smiling. 'Were you thinking to attack me, Englishman?'

'Yes,' Hook admitted.

'And I would have killed you,' Lanferelle said, 'and maybe I will anyway?' He stared towards the place where the wagons waited beside the road. Those wagons were hidden by the thick summer foliage, but shouts were loud and Hook could hear the sharp sound of bowstrings being loosed. 'How many of you are there?' Lanferelle asked.

Hook thought about lying, but decided Lanferelle would discover the truth soon enough. 'Forty archers,' he admitted.

'No men-at-arms?'

'None,' Hook said.

Lanferelle shrugged as if the information were not that important. 'So, you capture Harfleur, and what then? Do you march on Paris? On Rouen? You don't know. But I know. You will march somewhere. Your Henry has not spent all that money to capture one little harbour! He wants more. And when you march, Englishman, we shall be around you and in front of you and behind you, and you will die in ones and twos until there are only a few of you left, and then we shall close on you like wolves on a flock. And will my daughter die because you will be too weak to protect her?'

'I protected her in Soissons,' Hook said, 'you didn't.'

A tremor of anger showed on Lanferelle's face. The sword tip quivered, but there was also an uncertainty in the Frenchman's eyes. 'I looked for her,' he said. He sounded defensive.

'Not well enough,' Hook responded fiercely, 'and I found her.'

'God led him to me,' Melisande spoke in English for the first time.

'Oh! God?' Lanferelle had recovered his poise and sounded amused. 'You think God is on your side, Englishman?'

'I know He is,' Hook said stoutly.

'And you know what they call me?'

'The Lord of Hell,' Hook said.

Lanferelle nodded. 'It is a name, Englishman, just a name to frighten the ignorant. But despite that name I want my soul in heaven when I die, and for that I need people to pray for me. I need masses said, I need prayers chanted and I need nuns and priests on their knees.' He nodded at Melisande. 'Why should she not pray for me?'

'I do,' Melisande said.

'But will God listen to her prayers?' Lanferelle asked. 'She deserted God for you, and that is her choice, but let us see what God wants, Englishman. Hold up your hand.' He paused and Hook did not move. 'You want to live?' Lanferelle snarled. 'Hold up your hand! Not that one!' He wanted Hook's right hand, the hand with the fingertips hardened to calluses by the friction of the bow's cord.

Hook held up his right hand.

'Spread your fingers,' Lanferelle ordered and moved his sword slowly so that the blade's tip just touched Hook's palm. 'I could kill you,' Lanferelle said, 'but my daughter likes you and I have an affection for her. But you took her blood without my permission, and blood demands blood.' He moved his wrist, only his wrist, but so deftly and so strongly that the blade's tip moved an arrow's length in the air, and moved so fast that Hook had no chance to evade before the blade sliced off his smallest finger. The blood welled and ran. Melisande screamed, but did not pull the crossbow's trigger. Hook felt no pain for a heartbeat, then the agony streaked through his arm.

'There,' Lanferelle said, amused, 'I leave you the fingers for the string, yes? For her sake. But when the wolves close on you, Englishman, you and I shall play our game. If you win, you keep her, but if you lose, she goes to his marriage bed,' he jerked his head at his slack-mouthed squire. 'It's a stinking bed and he ruts like a boar. He grunts. Do you agree to our game?'

'God will give us victory,' Hook said. His hand was all pain, but he had kept the hurt from showing on his face.

'Let me tell you something,' Lanferelle said, leaning from his saddle. 'God does not give a cow's wet turd about your king or mine. Do you agree to our game? We fight for Melisande, yes?'

'Yes,' Hook said.

'Then put your arrows down,' Lanferelle said, 'and throw your bows away.'

Hook understood that the Frenchman did not want an arrow in his back as he rode away, and so he and Tom Scarlet threw their bowstaves into the tangled leaves of the felled oak, then dropped their arrow bags.

Lanferelle smiled. 'We have an agreement, Englishman! The prize is Melisande, but we must seal it with blood, yes?'

'It is sealed,' Hook said, holding up his blood-soaked hand.

'We are playing for a life,' Lanferelle said, 'not for blood,' and with that he touched a knee to his stallion, which turned obediently and the Lord of Hell swept his sword with the swivelling horse and the blade's tip ripped through Matt Scarlet's throat to fill the greenwood with a spray of red and a jet of blood, and Tom Scarlet cried aloud and Lanferelle laughed as he spurred eastwards followed by his two men.

'Matt!' Tom Scarlet dropped to his knees beside his twin brother, but Matthew Scarlet was dying as fast as the blood that pumped from his torn and bubbling throat.

The hoofbeats faded. There was no more shouting from where the wagons were parked. Melisande was crying.

Hook fetched the bows. The French had gone. He used an axe to make a grave under an oak tree, a wide grave, wide enough for Matt Scarlet and Peter Goddington to lie together on the ridge above the sea.

Above Harfleur, where the guns tore the walls into rubble.

It was hard and ceaseless work. Hook and the archers cut timber and split timber and sawed timber to shore up the gun-pits and trenches. New gun-pits were made, closer to the town, but the precious weapons had to be protected from Harfleur's defenders and so the archers constructed thick screens of wooden baulks that stood in front of the cannons' mouths. Each screen was made from oak trunks thick as a girl's waist, and they were sloped backwards so that they would deflect the enemy's missiles skywards. The cleverest thing about the screens, Hook thought, was how they were mounted on frames so that they could swivel. An order was given when a gun was at last ready to fire and men would turn a great windlass that hauled down the top of the screen and so raised the lower edge to expose the cannon's black-ened muzzle. The gun would fire and the world would vanish in a sickening, stinking, thick cloud of smoke that smelt exactly like rotted eggs, and the sound of the gun-stone striking the wall would be lost in the echo of the great cannon's bellow, and then the windlass would be released and the screen would thump down to protect the gun and its Dutch gunners again.

The enemy had learned to watch for the opening screens and would wait for that moment before shooting their own guns and springolts, so the English guns were also protected by enormous wicker baskets filled with earth and by more timber baulks, and sometimes a screen would be raised even though a gun was not ready to be fired, just to trick the enemy into loosing their missiles, which would thump harmlessly into the baskets and oak trunks. Then, when the gun was ready, the wicker basket immediately in front of the barrel was rolled clear, the screen was raised, and the noise could be heard far up the Lézarde's flooded valley.

The enemy also possessed cannon, but their guns were much smaller, firing a stone no bigger than an apple and lacking the weight to smash through the heavy screens. Their springolts, giant crossbows that shot thick bolts, had even less power. Hook, delivering a wagon of timber to reinforce the trenches, had a springolt bolt hit one of his horses plumb on the chest. The missile buried itself in the horse's body, ripping through lungs, heart and belly so that the beast simply collapsed, feet spreading in a sudden pool of blood. The heat shimmered off the blood and off the flooded land and off the marshes beside the wide glittering sea.

Trenches defended the besiegers from the enemy's guns and springolts, though there was small defence against the ballista that hurled stones high in the air so that they fell almost vertically. The English had their own catapults, made from the timber cut on the slopes above the port, and those machines rained both stones and festering animal corpses into Harfleur. From the hill Hook could see shattered roofs and two broken church towers. He could see the wall broken open so that the rubble spilled into the ditch, and he could see the giant bastion defending the gate being ripped and frayed and broken and battered. That bastion had been constructed from earth and timber, and the English gun-stones chopped and gnawed at its two towers, which flanked a short, thick curtain wall.

'We'll be making a sow next,' Sir John told his archers, 'our lord the king is in a hurry!'

'There's a great hole in their town wall, Sir John,' Thomas Evelgold remarked. He had replaced Peter Goddington as the centenar.

'And behind that gap is a new wall,' Sir John said, 'and to attack it we'd have to get past their barbican.' The barbican was the twin-towered bastion protecting the Leure Gate. 'You want their bastard crossbowmen shooting at you from the side? That barbican has to go, so we'll be making a sow. We'll have to fell more trees! Hook, I want you.'

The other archers watched as Sir John took Hook aside. 'There'll be no more French men-at-arms in the hills,' Sir John said, 'we've got our own men out there now, and we've got more men watching for a relief force, but they're seeing nothing.' That was a puzzle. August was ending and still the French had sent no army to relieve the besieged town. English horsemen rode every day to scout the roads from the north and the east, but the country stayed empty. Sometimes a small force of French men-at-arms challenged the patrols, but there was no cloud of dust to betray a marching army. 'So tell me what you did on the ridge,' Sir John said, 'the day poor Peter Goddington died.'

'I just warned our fellows,' Hook said.

'No, you didn't. You told them to get back to the wagons, is that right?'

'Yes, Sir John.'

'Why?' Sir John asked belligerently.

Hook frowned as he remembered. At the time it had seemed an obvious precaution, but he had not thought why it was so obvious. 'Our bows were no good in the trees,' he now said slowly, 'but if they were back at the wagons they could shoot. They needed space to shoot.'

'Which is just what happened,' Sir John said. The archers, gathering at the wagons, had driven the raiders away with two volleys. 'So you did the right thing, Hook. The bastards only came to make mischief. They wanted to kill a few men and have a look at what progress we were making, and you saw them off!'

'I wasn't there, Sir John,' Hook said, 'it was the other archers what drove them off.'

'You were with the Sire of Lanferelle, I know. And he let you live.' Sir John gave Hook an appraising look. 'Why?'

'He wants to kill me later,' Hook said, not sure that was the right answer, 'or maybe it's because of Melisande?'

'He's a cat,' Sir John said, 'and you're his mouse. A wounded mouse,' he glanced at Hook's right hand, which was still bandaged. 'You can still shoot?'

'Good as ever, Sir John.'

'So I'm making you a ventenar. Which means I'm doubling your pay.'

'Me!' Hook stared at Sir John.

Sir John did not answer straightaway. He had turned a critical eye on his men-at-arms, who were practising sword strokes against tree trunks. Practise, practise, practise was one of Sir John's constant refrains. He claimed to strike a thousand blows a day in never-ending practice and he demanded the same of his men. 'Put some muscle into it, Ralph,' he shouted at one man, then turned back to Hook. 'Did you think about what to do when you saw the French?'

'No.'

'That's why I'm making you a sergeant. I don't want men who have to think about what to do, but just do it. Tom Evelgold's now your centenar, so you can take his company. I tell him what to do, he tells you what to do, and you tell your archers what to do. If they don't do it, you thump the bastards, and if they still don't do it, I thump you.'

'Yes, Sir John.'

Sir John's battered face grinned. 'You're good, young Hook, and you're something else.' He pointed at Hook's bandaged hand. 'You're lucky. Here,' he took a thin silver chain from a pouch and dropped it into Hook's hand. 'Your badge of office. And tomorrow you build a sow.'

'What's a sow, Sir John?'

'It's a pig to build, I'll tell you that much,' Sir John said, 'a goddam pig!'

It began to rain that night. The rain came from the sea, carried on a cold west wind. It began softly, pattering on the besiegers' tents, and then the wind rose to tear at the banners on their makeshift poles and the rain hardened and came at an angle and drenched the ground into a morass of mud. The flood waters, which had largely subsided, began to rise again and the midden overflowed. The gunners cursed and raised awnings over their weapons, while every archer carefully hid his bowstrings from the soaking rain.

There was no need for Hook to carry a bow. His job was to raise the sow and it was, as Sir John had promised, a pig of a job. It was not intricate work, not even skilled, but it needed strength and it had to be done in full view of the defenders and within range of their cannons, springolts, catapults and crossbows.

The sow was a giant shield, shaped like the toe of a shoe, behind and beneath which men could work safe from enemy missiles, and it would have to be built strong enough to withstand the repeated strike of gun-stones.

A white-haired Welshman, Dafydd ap Traharn, supervised the work. 'I come from Pontygwaith,' he told the archers, 'and in Pontygwaith we know more about building things than all you miserable English bastards put together!' He had planned to run two wagons loaded with earth and stones to the place where the sow would be built and use the wagons to protect the archers from enemy missiles, but the rain had softened the ground and the wagons had become bogged down. 'We'll have to dig,' he said with the relish of a man who knew he would not have to wield a spade himself. 'We know about digging in Pontygwaith, know more than all you English fart-makers put together!'

'That's because you were digging graves for all the Welshmen we killed,' Will of the Dale retorted.

'Burying you *sais*, we were,' Dafydd ap Traharn replied happily. Later, as he chatted with Hook, he cheerfully admitted he had been a rebel against the English king just fifteen years before. 'Now that Owain Glyn Dwr,' he said warmly, 'what a man!'

'What happened to him?'

'He's still alive, boy!' Dafydd ap Traharn said, 'still alive!' Glyn Dwr's rebellion had burned for over a decade, giving young Henry, Prince of Wales and now King of England, a long education in warfare. The revolt had been defeated and some of the Welsh leaders had been dragged on hurdles through London to their executions, but Owain Glyn Dwr himself had never been captured. 'We have magicians in Wales,' Dafydd ap Traharn lowered his voice and leaned close to Hook as he spoke, 'and they can turn a man invisible!'

'I'd like to see that,' Hook said wistfully.

'Well, you can't, can you? That's the whole thing about being invisible, you can't see them! Why, Owain Glyn Dwr could be here right now and you couldn't see him! And that's what has happened to him, see? He's living in luxury, boy, with women and apples, but if an Englishman gets within a mile of him, he turns invisible!'

'So what's a rebel Welshman doing with this army?' Hook asked.

'A man has to live,' Dafydd ap Traharn said, 'and eating an enemy's loaf of bread is better than staring into an empty oven. There's dozens of Glyn Dwr's men in this army, boy, and we'll fight as hard for Henry as we ever did for Owain.' He grinned. 'Mind you, there are a few of Owain Glyn Dwr's men in France as well, and they'll fight against us.'

'Archers?'

'God be praised, no. Archers can't afford to run away to

France, can they now? No, it's the gentry who lost their land who went to France, not the archers. Have you ever faced an archer in battle?'

'God be praised, no,' Hook said.

'It is not what I would call a happy experience,' Dafydd ap Traharn said grimly. 'My God, boy, but we Welsh don't take fright easily, but when Henry's archers shot at Shrewsbury it was death from the sky. Like hail, it was, only hail with steel points, and hail that never stopped, and men were dying all around me and their screams were like tortured gulls on a black shore. An archer is a terrible thing.'

'I'm an archer.'

'You're a digger now, boy,' Dafydd ap Traharn said, grinning, 'so dig.'

They dug a trench away from a gun-pit, digging it towards the walls of Harfleur, and the defenders saw the trench being made and rained crossbow bolts and gun-stones on the work. The defenders' catapults tried to lob stones onto the new trench, but the missiles went wide, landing in showers of splattering mud. After thirty paces of new trench had been made Dafydd ap Traharn declared himself satisfied and ordered a new pit to be excavated. It had to be big, square and deep, and so the archers hacked and shovelled till they reached a layer of chalk. The new pit's side seeped water so that they slopped about in muck as they raised a parapet of tree trunks on three sides of the pit, only leaving the rear that led to the English camp unprotected. They laid the trunks flat, four abreast, and piled more on top, so that a man could stand upright in the pit and be invisible to the enemy on Harfleur's walls. 'Tonight,' Dafydd ap Traharn said, 'we'll make a roof and our lovely sow will be finished.'

They made the roof at night because the pit was close enough to the walls to be within easy range of a crossbow, but the enemy must have guessed what was happening and

190

they shot blind through the rain-soaked darkness and three men were wounded by the short, sharp bolts that spat from the night. It took all that night to lay long trunks over the pit and then to cover those timbers with a thick layer of earth and chalk rubble before adding a final covering of more tree trunks. 'And now the real work begins,' Dafydd ap Traharn said, 'which means we have to use Welshmen.'

'The real work?' Hook asked.

'We're going to make a mine, lad. We're going to dig deep.'

The rain ended at dawn. A chill wind came from the west and the rain slid away across France and the sun fought against cloud as the enemy gunners hammered the newly-made sow with gun-stones that wasted their power on the thick log parapet. Hook and his archers slept, sheltering under the crude cabins they had made from tree boughs, earth and ferns. When Hook woke he found Melisande scrubbing his mail coat with sand and vinegar. '*Rouille*,' she said in explanation.

'Rust?'

'That's what I said.'

'You can polish my coat, darling,' Will of the Dale said as he crawled from his shelter.

'Do your own, William,' Melisande said. 'I cleaned Tom's, though.'

'Well done,' Hook said. All the archers were worried about Thomas Scarlet whose customary cheerfulness had been buried with his twin brother. Scarlet scowled these days, or else sat by himself, brooding. 'All he wants,' Hook said quietly, 'is to meet your father again.'

'Then Thomas will die,' Melisande said bleakly.

'He loves you,' Hook said.

'My father?'

'He let you live. He let you stay with me.'

191

'He let you live too,' she said, almost resentfully.

'I know.'

She paused. Her grey eyes watched Harfleur, which was ringed with gunsmoke like a sea fog shrouding a cliff. Hook put his wet boots to dry beside the campfire. The burning wood spat and shot sparks. It was willow, and willow always protested against burning. 'He loved my mother, I think,' Melisande said wistfully.

'Did he?'

'She was beautiful,' Melisande said, 'and she loved him. She said he was so beautiful too. A beautiful man.'

'Handsome,' Hook allowed.

'Beautiful,' Melisande insisted.

'When you met him in the trees,' Hook asked, 'did you want him to take you away?'

She gave an abrupt shake of her head. 'No,' she said, 'I think he is a bad angel. And I think he is in my head like the saint is in yours,' she turned to look at him, 'and I wish he would go away.'

'You think about him? Is that it?'

'I always wanted him to love me,' she said harshly, and started scouring the mail again.

'As he loved your mother?'

'No! *Non!*' She was angry, and for a while she said nothing, then relented. 'Life is hard, Nicholas, you know that. It is work and work and work and worry where the food will come from and it is more work, and a lord, any lord, can stop all that. They can wave their hand and there is no more work, no more worry, just *facile.*'

'Easy?'

'And I wanted that.'

'Tell him you want that.'

'He is beautiful,' Melisande said, 'but he is not kind. I know that. And I love you. *Je t'aime.*' She said the last words decidedly, without apparent affection, but Hook was struck dumb by them. He watched archers bringing firewood to the camp. Melisande grimaced with the effort of scrubbing the sand on the mail coat. 'You know of Sir Robert Knolles?' she asked suddenly.

'Of course I do,' Hook said. Every archer knew of Sir Robert, who had died rich not many years before.

'He was an archer once,' Melisande said.

'That's how he started,' Hook agreed, wondering how Melisande knew of the legendary Sir Robert.

'And he became a knight,' Melisande said, 'he led armies! And now Sir John has made you a ventenar.'

'A ventenar isn't a knight,' Hook said, smiling.

'But Sir Robert was a ventenar once!' Melisande said fiercely, 'and then he became a centenar, and then a man-at-arms, and after that a knight! Alice told me. And if he could do it, why not you?'

That vision was so astonishing that Hook could only stare at her for a moment. 'Me? A man-at-arms?' he finally said.

'Why not?'

'I'm not born to that!'

'Nor was Sir Robert.'

'Well, it does happen,' Hook said dubiously. He knew of other archers who had led companies and become rich. Sir Robert was the most famous, but archers also remembered Thomas of Hookton who had died as lord of a thousand acres. 'But it doesn't happen often,' Hook went on, 'and it takes money.'

'And what is war to you men but money? They talk without end of prisoners? Of ransoms?' Melisande pointed her brush at him and grinned mischievously. 'Capture my father. We'll ransom him. We'll take his money.'

'You'd like that, would you?' Hook asked.

'Yes,' she said vengefully, 'I would like that.'

Hook tried to imagine being rich. Of receiving a ransom that would be more than most men could earn in a lifetime, and then he forgot that dream as John Fletcher, who was one of the older archers and a man who had shown some resentment at Hook's promotion, suddenly flinched and ran towards the midden trench. Fletcher's face looked pale. 'Fletch is ill,' Hook said.

'And poor Alice was horribly sick this morning,' Melisande said, wrinkling her nose in distaste *'la diarrhée*!'

Hook decided he did not want to know more about Alice Godewyne's sickness, and he was saved from further details by Sir John Cornewaille's arrival. 'Are we awake?' the knight bellowed, 'are we awake and breathing?'

'We are now, Sir John,' Hook answered for the archers.

'Then down to the trenches! Down to the trenches! Let's get this goddam siege done!'

Hook donned his damp boots and half-scrubbed mail, pulled on his helmet and surcoat, then went to the trenches. The siege went on.

The sow shuddered each time a gun-stone struck its sloping face. The logs that formed the face were battered, split, and bristling with springolt bolts, but the enemy's missiles had failed to break the heavy shield or even weaken it, and beneath the layers of timber and earth the Welsh miners went to work.

Other shafts were being driven on Harfleur's eastern side where the Duke of Clarence's forces were camped, and from both east and west the guns roared and the stones clawed at the walls, the mangonels and trebuchets dropped boulders into the town, smoke and dust erupted and plumed from the narrow streets while the mines crept towards the ramparts. The eastern shafts were being driven under the walls where great caverns, shored with timber, would be clawed out of the chalk and, when the time came, the timber supports would be burned away so that the caverns would collapse and bring down the ramparts above. The western mine, its entrance guarded by the sow Hook had helped make, was intended to tunnel under the vast battered bastion that protected the Leure Gate. Bring that barbican down and the English army could attack the breach beside the gate without any danger of being assaulted on their flank by the barbican's garrison. So the Welshmen dug and the archers guarded their sow and the town suffered.

The barbican had been made from great oak trunks that had been sunk into the earth and then hooped with iron. The trunks had formed the outline of two squat round towers joined by a brief curtain wall, and their interior had been rammed with earth and rubble, the whole protected by a flooded ditch facing the besiegers. The English guns had splintered the nearest timbers so that the earth had spilled out to make a steep unstable ramp that filled one part of the ditch, yet still the bastion resisted. Its ruin was manned by crossbowmen and men-at-arms, and its banners hung defiantly from what remained of its wooden ramparts. Each night, when the English guns ceased fire, the defenders made repairs and the dawn would reveal a new timber palisade and the guns would have to begin their slow work of demolition again. Other guns fired at the town itself.

When Hook had first seen Harfleur it had looked almost magical to him: a town of tight roofs and church steeples all girdled by a white, tower-studded wall that had glowed in the August sun. It had looked like the painted town in the picture of Saint Crispin and Saint Crispinian in Soissons Cathedral, the picture he had stared at for so long as he said his prayers.

Now the painted town was a battered heap of stones, mud, smoke and shattered houses. Long stretches of the walls still stood and still flaunted their derisive banners that displayed the badges of the garrison's leaders, images of the saints and invocations to God, but eight of the towers had been collapsed into the town ditch, and one long length of rampart had been beaten into wreckage close to the Leure Gate. The great missiles lobbed into the town by the catapults smashed houses and started fires so that a pall of smoke hung constantly above the besieged town. A church steeple had fallen, taking its bells in a mighty cacophony, and still the boulders and gun-stones hammered at the already hammered town.

And still the defenders fought back. Each dawn Hook led men into the pits that defended the English guns and in every dawn he saw where the garrison had been working. They were making a new wall behind the broken rampart and they shored up the collapsing barbican with new timbers. English heralds, holding their white wands and gaudy in their coloured coats, rode to the enemy walls to offer terms, but the enemy commanders rebuffed the heralds each time. 'What they're hoping,' Father Christopher told Hook one early September morning, 'is that their king will lead an army to their rescue.'

'I thought the French king was mad?'

'Oh, so he is! He believes he is made of glass!' Father Christopher said mockingly. The priest visited the trenches every morning, offering blessings and jests to the archers. 'It's true! He thinks he's made of glass and will shatter if he falls. He also chews rugs and tells his troubles to the moon.'

'So he won't be leading any army here, father,' Hook said, smiling.

'But the mad king has sons, Hook, and they're all blood-thirsty little scum. Any one of them would love to grind our bones to powder.'

'Will they try?'

'God knows, Hook, God alone knows and He isn't telling me. But I do know there's an army gathering at Rouen.'

'Is that far?'

'See that road?' The priest pointed to the faint remains of a road that had once led from the Leure Gate, but which was now only a scar in a muddy, missile-battered landscape. 'Follow that,' Father Christopher said, 'and turn right when

197

it reaches the hill and keep going, and after fifty miles you'll find a great bridge and a huge city. That's Rouen, Hook. Fifty miles? An army can march that in three days!'

'So they come,' Hook said, 'and we'll kill them.'

'King Harold said much the same just before Hastings,' Father Christopher said gently.

'Did Harold have archers?' Hook asked.

'Just men-at-arms, I think.'

'Well, then,' Hook said and grinned.

The priest raised his head to peer at Harfleur. 'We should have captured the place by now,' he said wistfully. 'It's taking much too long.' He turned because a passing man-at-arms had greeted him cheerfully. Father Christopher returned the greeting and made a sketchy sign of blessing towards the hurrying man. 'You know who that was, Hook?'

Hook looked at the retreating figure who wore a bright surcoat of red and white. 'No, father, no idea.'

'Geoffrey Chaucer's son,' the priest said proudly.

'Who?'

'You've not heard of Geoffrey Chaucer?' Father Christopher asked. 'The poet?'

'Oh, I thought he might be someone useful,' Hook said, then slammed a hand onto the priest's shoulder and so forced him to crouch. A heartbeat later a crossbow bolt slapped into the muddy back of the trench where Father Christopher had been standing. 'That's Catface,' Hook explained, 'he's useful.'

'Catface?'

'A bastard on the barbican, father. He's got a face like a polecat. I can see him raise his bow.'

'You can't shoot him?'

'Twenty paces too far off, father,' Hook said, and peered between two battered wicker baskets filled with disintegrating earth that formed the parapet. He waved, and a figure on the bastion waved back. 'I always let him know I'm still living.'

'Polecat,' Father Christopher said musingly. 'You know Rob Pole is ill?'

'So's Fletch. And Dick Godewyne's wife.'

'Alice? Is she sick too?'

'Horrible, I hear.'

'Rob Pole can't stop shitting,' the priest said, 'and nothing but blood and mucky water comes out.'

'God help us,' Hook said, 'Fletch is the same.'

'I'd better start praying,' Father Christopher said earnestly, 'we can't lose men to sickness. Are you feeling well?'

'I am.'

'God be praised for that. And your hand? How's your hand?'

'It throbs, father,' Hook said, holding up his right hand, which was still bandaged. Melisande had covered the wound with honey, then wrapped it.

'Throbbing is a good sign,' the priest said. He leaned forward and sniffed at the bandage, 'and it smells good! Well, it stinks of mud, sweat and shit, but so do we all. It doesn't smell rotten, and that's the important thing. How's your piss? Is it cloudy? Strong-coloured? Feeble?'

'Just normal, father.'

'That's grand, Hook. We can't lose you!'

And strange to tell, Hook thought, but he reckoned the priest was telling the truth because he knew he was doing his ventenar's job well. He had expected to be embarrassed by the small authority, and had feared that some of the older men would deliberately ignore his orders, but if there was any resentment it was muted and his commands were obeyed readily enough. He wore the silver chain with pride.

The weather had turned hot again, baking the mud into a crust that crumbled into fine dust with every footstep.

Harfleur crumbled too, yet still the garrison defied the besiegers. The king would come to the archers' pits four or five times a day and stare at the ramparts. At the beginning of the siege he had chatted with the archers, but now his face was drawn and his lips thin and the archers gave him and his small entourage space. They watched him stare and they could read from his scarred face that he did not think an assault could break through the new inner walls. Any such attack would have to stumble over the ruins of the burned houses, suffer the bolts spitting from the barbican, then cross the great town ditch before climbing the wreckage of the gun-shattered wall and all the time the crossbow bolts would slash in from the flanks, and once across the wall's ruins the attackers would be faced with the new inner wall that was made from thick baskets of earth, and from baulks of timber and stones fetched from the fallen buildings inside the town. 'We need another length of wall down,' Hook overheard the king say, 'and then we attack instantly into the new breach.'

'Can't be done, sire,' Sir John Cornewaille said grimly. 'This is the only dry approach we've got.' The flood waters had receded, but they still ringed much of the town, restricting the English attacks to the two places where the mine shafts were being hacked towards the town.

'Then bring down the barbican,' the king insisted, 'and beat the gate beyond into splinters.' He stared, long-nosed and grim-faced, at the stubborn barbican, then suddenly became aware of the anxious archers and men-at-arms watching him. 'God didn't bring us this far to fail!' he shouted confidently. 'The town will be ours, fellows, and soon! There will be ale and good food! It will all be ours soon!'

All day the chalk and soil was dragged from the mine shaft while the timbers, cut to a bowstave's length, were carried inside to support the tunnel. The guns kept up their

200

fire, shrouding the besiegers' lines with smoke, punching their eardrums with noise and pounding the already pounded defences.

'How are your ears?' Sir John greeted Hook on an early September morning.

'My ears, Sir John?'

'Those ugly things on the sides of your head.'

'Nothing wrong with them, Sir John.'

'Then come with me.'

Sir John, his fine armour and surcoat covered in dust, led Hook back through a trench and so to the mine's entrance beneath the sow. The shaft sloped sharply down for fifteen paces, then the tunnel levelled. It was two paces wide and as high as a bowstave. Rushlights burned from small brackets nailed to the timber supports, but as Hook followed Sir John he noted how the small flames grew feebler the deeper they went. Every few paces Sir John stopped and flattened himself against the tunnel's side and Hook did the same to let some miner pass with a load of excavated chalk. Dust hung in the air, while the floor was a slurry of water and chalk dust. 'All right, boys,' Sir John said when he reached the tunnel's end, 'time to rest. Everyone stay still and silent!'

The far end of the tunnel was lit by horn-shielded lanterns hanging from the last beam to be propped into place. Two miners had been using pick-axes on the tunnel's face and they gratefully put down their tools and sank to the floor as Dafydd ap Traharn, supervising the work, nodded a greeting to Hook. Sir John crouched near the grey-haired Welshman and motioned for Hook to squat. 'Listen,' Sir John hissed.

Hook listened. A miner coughed. 'Shh,' Sir John said.

Sometimes, in the long woods that fell from Lord Slayton's pastures to the river, Hook would stand quite motionless, just listening. He knew every sound of those trees, whether it was a deer's hoof-fall, a boar snuffling, a woodpecker drumming, the clack of a raven's bill as it preened its feathers or just the wind in the leaves, and from those sounds his ear would find the discordant note, the signal that told him a trespasser was prowling the undergrowth. Now he listened in just the same way, ignoring the breathing of the half-dozen men, letting his mind wander, just allowing the silence to fill his head and so alert him to the smallest disturbance. He listened a long time.

'My ears ring all the time,' Sir John whispered, 'I think because I've got beaten on the helmet with blades too much and . . .' Hook held up an impatient hand, unaware that he was ordering a Knight of the Garter to silence. Sir John obeyed anyway. Hook listened, heard something and then heard it again. 'Someone's digging,' he said.

'Oh, the bastards,' Sir John said quietly. 'Are you sure?'

Now that he had identified the sound Hook was surprised no one else could hear the rhythmic thunk of picks striking chalk. The garrison was making a counter-mine, driving their own tunnel towards the besiegers in hope of intercepting the English tunnel before it could be finished. 'Maybe two tunnels,' Hook said. The sound was slightly irregular, as if two mismatched rhythms were mixing.

'That's what I thought,' Dafydd ap Traharn said, 'but I wasn't sure. The ears play tricks underground, they do.'

'Busy little bastards, aren't they?' Sir John said vengefully. He looked at Dafydd ap Traharn. 'How far to go?'

'Twenty paces, Sir John, say two days. Another two to make the chamber. One to fill it with incendiaries.'

'They're still a long way off,' Sir John said. 'Maybe they won't find this tunnel?'

'They'll be listening too, Sir John. And the closer they get the clearer they hear us.'

'Putrid stinking prickless rancid bastards,' Sir John said to no one in particular. He nodded at Hook. 'I still can't hear them.'

'They're there,' Hook said confidently. They spoke in whispers, shrouded by a darkness scarce relieved by the rushlight lanterns flickering in the foul air.

One of the miners spoke in Welsh. Dafydd ap Traharn silenced him with a cautionary hand. 'He's worried what happens if the enemy breaks into the tunnel, Sir John.'

'Make a chamber here,' Sir John said, 'big enough for six or seven men. We'll have archers and men-at-arms standing guard here. Have your own weapons at hand, but for the moment, keep digging. Let's bring that bastard barbican down.' The mine shaft was aiming for the northernmost tower of the obstinate bastion in hope of tumbling it to fill the flooded ditch. A cavern would be made beneath the tower, a cavern supported by timber baulks that would be burned away so that the roof would collapse and, with it, the tower. Sir John slapped the miners on their shoulders. 'Well done, boys,' he said, 'God is with you.' He beckoned to Hook and the two of them went back towards the sow. 'I hope to God He is with us,' Sir John grumbled, then stopped and frowned as he contemplated the tunnel's entrance. 'We'll have to put some defences here,' he said.

'In the sow?'

'If the bastards break into our tunnel, Hook, they'll come swarming out of that hole like rats smelling a free breakfast. We'll put a wall here and garrison it with archers.'

Hook watched two men carry pit supports into the tunnel. 'A wall here will slow the work, Sir John,' he said.

'God damn you, Hook, I know that!' Sir John snapped, then gazed at the tunnel's mouth. 'We need to end this siege! It's gone on too long. Men are getting sick. We need to be away from this stinking place.'

'Barrels?' Hook suggested.

'Barrels?' Sir John echoed with another snarl.

'Fill three or four barrels with stones and soil,' Hook said patiently, 'and if the French come, just roll the barrels into the entrance and stand them upright. Half a dozen archers can take care of any bastard that tries to get past them.'

Sir John stared at the entrance for a few heartbeats, then nodded. 'Your mother wasn't wasting her time when she spread her thighs, Hook. Good man. I want the barrels in place by sundown.'

The barrels were in place by dusk. Hook, waiting to be relieved, went to the trench beside the sow and watched the broken walls that were lit red by the sun sinking beyond the tree-stripped hills. Behind him, in the English camp, a man played a flute plaintively, repeating the same phrase over and over as though trying to get it right. Hook was tired. He wanted to eat and sleep, nothing more, and he paid small attention as a man-at-arms came to stand beside him at the parapet. The man was wearing a close-fitting helmet that half shadowed his face, but otherwise had no armour, just a leather jerkin, but his muddied boots were well made and a golden chain at his neck denoted his high status. 'Is that a dead dog?' the man asked, nodding towards a furry corpse lying halfway between the English forward trench and the French barbican. Three ravens were pecking at the dead beast.

'The French shoot them,' Hook said. 'The dogs run out of our lines and the crossbowmen shoot them. Then they vanish in the night.'

'The dogs?'

'They're food for the French,' Hook explained curtly. 'Fresh meat.'

'Ah, of course,' the man said. He watched the ravens for a while. 'I've never eaten dog.'

'Tastes a bit like hare,' Hook said, 'but stringier.' Then he

204

glanced at the man and saw the deep-pitted scar beside the long nose. 'Sire,' he added hastily, and dropped to one knee.

'Stand up, stand up,' the king said. He stared at the barbican, which now resembled little more than a heap of earth with a wall of battered tree trunks rammed into its crumbling forward slope. 'We must take that barbican,' he said absently, speaking to himself. Hook was watching the bastion, looking for the telltale flicker of movement that would warn him of a crossbowman taking aim, but he reckoned the king was safe enough because the French usually went quiet as the sun sank beneath the western horizon, and this evening was no different. The guns and catapults of both sides were silent. 'I remember the first day of the siege,' the king said, sounding almost puzzled, 'and the church bells were always ringing in the town. I thought they were being defiant, then I realised they were burying their dead. But they don't ring any more.'

'Too many dead, sire,' Hook said awkwardly, 'or maybe there's no bells left.' There was something about talking to a king that made his thoughts stumble.

'It must be ended quickly,' the king said earnestly, then stepped back from the parapet. 'Does the saint still speak to you?' he asked, and Hook was so astonished that the king remembered him that he said nothing, just nodded hastily. 'That's good,' Henry said, 'because if God is on our side then nothing can prevail against us. Remember that!' He gave Hook a half smile. 'And we will prevail,' Henry added softly, almost as though he spoke to himself. Then he walked down the trench leading back to the sow where a dozen men waited for him.

Hook went to bed.

Next morning, when a gun fired, the earth trembled.

Hook was in the mine, down at the lowest level where

Sir John had led him to listen again, and suddenly the earth shuddered and the rushlights flickered dark.

Everyone crouched in the half dark, listening. A miner began coughing wetly and Hook waited until the echo of the cough had died away. Listening. Listening for death, listening.

A second gun fired and the earth seemed to quiver as the tiny flames spluttered again and dust jarred from the roof and gobbets of earth spattered down to splash in the tunnel's slurry. The rumble of the gun's noise seemed to last for ever, then there was a moaning sound, a creaking, as though the oaken supports were bending under the weight of the earth they carried.

'Hook?' Sir John asked.

There was a scratching noise, so faint that Hook wondered if he imagined it, but then there was a muffled crack followed by silence. After a while the scratching started again, and this time Hook was sure he heard it. The men in the tunnel watched him anxiously. He crossed to the further wall and pressed an ear against the chalk.

Scratching. Hook looked at Dafydd ap Traharn. 'How are you digging now, sir?' he asked.

'The way we always do,' the Welshman said, puzzled.

'Show me, sir?'

The Welshman took a pick and went to the tunnel's face where, instead of swinging the pick to bury its blade in the soft rock, he dragged it down a natural cleft. He dragged it again, deepening the cleft, and then pushed the blade into the hole and tried to lever out a chunk of stone, but the hole was not deep enough and so he scratched the steel point down the groove again. He scratched it. He was working quietly, trying not to alert the French as the tunnel went closer to the ravaged walls, and Hook realised that was the sound he was hearing. Both teams of tunnellers were trying to work silently.

'They're very close,' Hook said.

'*Cymorth ni, O Arglwydd*,' a miner muttered and crossed himself.

'How close?' Sir John demanded, ignoring the plea for God's help.

'Can't tell, Sir John.'

'God damn the goddam bastards,' Sir John spat.

'They may be above us,' Dafydd ap Traharn suggested, 'or below.'

'You'll know when they're really close,' Hook said, 'you'll hear the scratching loud.'

'Scratching?' the Welshman asked.

'It's what I hear, sir.'

'They'll hack their way through the last few feet,' Dafydd ap Traharn said grimly, 'and come on us like demons.'

'We have our own demons waiting for them,' Sir John said. 'We're not abandoning this tunnel! We need it! We'll fight the bastards underground. It will save us digging them graves, won't it?'

The war bows were too long to use in the tunnel and so at midday Sir John brought a half-dozen crossbows. 'If they break in,' he told Hook, 'greet them with these. Then use your poleaxes.'

The scratching was louder, so loud that Dafydd ap Traharn decided there was no longer any purpose in trying to be silent and so his men began to swing their pickaxes, filling the tunnel's end with noise and a fine choking dust. Every now and then a blade struck flint and a spark would fly fierce and bright across the gloomy shaft. The sparks looked like shooting stars and Hook remembered his grandmother crossing herself whenever she saw such a star, then she would say a prayer and she claimed such prayers, carried by the hurrying stars, were more effective. He closed his eyes when the sparks flew and prayed for Melisande and for

Father Christopher and for his brother, Michael. Michael, at least, was in England, far from the Perrill brothers and their mad priest father. 'Another day's work,' Dafydd ap Traharn said, interrupting Hook's thoughts of home, 'and we can start making the cavern. Then we'll bring down their tower like the walls of Jericho!'

The men-at-arms and the archers sat at the tunnel's edge, drawing in their feet to let the labourers carry out the excavated spoil and bring in the new timbers to support the roof. They listened to the sounds of the French miners. Those noises were louder, inescapable and ominous. They came from the north where the enemy had to be driving a counter-mine to intercept the English work and, in the dust-shrouded light of the small flames, Hook constantly watched the far wall, expecting to see a great hole appear through which an armoured enemy would erupt. Sir John spent much of the afternoon in the tunnel, his sword drawn and face shadowed. 'We have to fight them back into their hole,' he said, 'and then collapse their work. Jesus, it smells like a midden down here!'

'It is a midden,' Dafydd ap Traharn said. Some of the labourers had fallen ill and constantly fouled the wet slurry underfoot.

Sir John left late in the day and, an hour later, sent other men to relieve the mine's guards. Those new men came stooping down the tunnel, their shadows flickering monstrously in the half darkness. 'Christ on his cross,' a voice grumbled, 'can't breathe this air.'

'You have crossbows for us?' another voice demanded.

'We've got them,' Hook acknowledged, 'and they're cocked.'

'Leave them for us,' the man said, then peered at the archers he was relieving. 'Hook? Is that you?'

'Sir Edward!' Hook said. He laid the crossbow on the floor and stood, smiling.

'It is you!' Sir Edward Derwent, Lord Slayton's man who, in London, had saved Hook from the manor court and its inevitable punishment, was smiling back in the dirty light. 'I heard you were here,' he said, 'how are you?'

'Still alive, Sir Edward,' Hook said, grinning.

'God be praised for that, though God knows how anyone survives down here.' Sir Edward, his scar-ravaged face half hidden by his helmet, listened to the ominous noises. 'They sound close!'

'We think they are,' Hook said.

'It's deceptive,' Dafydd ap Traharn put in. 'They could be ten paces away still. It's hard to tell with sounds underground.'

'So they could be a hand's breadth away?' Sir Edward enquired sourly.

'Oh, they could be!' the Welshman said dourly.

Sir Edward looked at the drawn crossbows. 'And the idea is to welcome them with bolts?' he asked, 'then kill the bastards?'

'The idea is to keep me alive,' Dafydd ap Traharn said, 'and you're blocking the tunnel, you are! There are too many of you! There's work to be done.'

Sir John's men-at-arms had already gone, and now Hook sent his archers after them. He lingered a moment. 'I wish you a quiet night,' he said to Sir Edward.

'Dear God, I echo that prayer,' Sir Edward said. He grinned. 'It's good to see you, Hook.'

'A pleasure to see you, sir,' Hook said, 'and thank you.'

'Go and rest, man,' Sir Edward said.

Hook nodded. He hefted his poleaxe and, with a farewell nod to Dafydd ap Traharn, edged past Sir Edward's men, one of whom tried to trip him and Hook saw the lantern jaw and sunken eyes and, for a moment, in the half darkness, he thought it was Sir Martin, then realised it was the priest's elder son, Tom Perrill. Both brothers were there, stooping under the beams, but Hook ignored them, knowing that neither would attack him while Sir Edward was present.

He trudged up the tunnel towards the fading daylight far ahead. He was thinking of Melisande, of the stew she would have ready, and of songs around the campfire when the world shattered.

Noise thudded about his ears. It started as a thunderous growl that billowed just behind him, then there was a rending noise as though the earth itself was splitting apart, and he turned to see dust boiling towards him, a dark cloud of dust rolling in the shaft's dark light, and men like monstrous shadows were lumbering in that darkness. There was shouting, the sound of steel on armour, and a scream. The first scream.

The French had broken through.

Hook instinctively started back towards the fighting, then remembered the barrels and wondered if he should block the tunnel's entrance. He hesitated. A man was screeching from the dark, a horrible noise, like the sound of a clumsily gelded beast. There was another rumbling and Hook had a glimpse of more men dropping from the tunnel's roof, then more dust surged towards him, obliterating his sight, but in the dust a figure lurched towards him. It was a man-at-arms, sword drawn. His visor was closed, he held his sword two-handed, and somehow the dust and half-light made him look like some enormous earth-giant come from nightmare's bowels. His plate armour was coated in chalk and earth, and Hook stared, petrified by the unnatural vision, but then the man bellowed and that sound startled Hook to reality just as the man-at-arms lunged the sword at his belly. Hook twisted to one side and rammed the poleaxe straight at the steel-shrouded face. The spear point slid off the pig-snouted visor, but the top edge of the heavy hammer cracked into the helmet, crushing the metal. Hook had used all his archer's strength in that blow and the earth-giant reeled backwards, blood welling from his visor's holes, and Hook remembered all those lessons in Sir John's meadows and closed on the man fast, getting inside the sword's reach so the enemy could not swing the blade, and he rammed the poleaxe like a quarterstaff, driving the man down onto the floor. Hook had no room to swing the poleaxe, but strength made up for that and he slammed the axe blade onto the man's sword elbow, breaking it, then slid the spear point into the gap between the enemy's helmet and breastplate. The Frenchman wore an aventail, a mail hood, to protect that gap, but the steel spike ripped easily through the links and gouged into the man's throat, and then more men were coming towards Hook as the earth-giant, shrunken to normal size now, writhed on the mine floor where his blood spilt into the chalk, black draining into white.

The men coming up the tunnel were fighting each other. Hook dragged the blade free of the dying earth-giant and rammed the spear point at a man in a strange surcoat. The blade glanced off plate armour, ripping the coat and the man turned, beast-faced visor pointing at Hook, and brought his sword around, but it caught on one of the mine's timber supports and Hook lunged again with the poleaxe, this time hooking the axe blade around the man's ankle and then pulling hard so that the Frenchman lost his balance. A Welsh miner staggered towards Hook, guts spilling from an opened belly. Hook shouldered him aside and pushed the spear point under the fallen man's breastplate, the gap just visible through the torn linen. He pushed and twisted the long haft, trying to drive the blade up into the man's stomach and chest, but something blocked the blade, and then another rush of men pushed him backwards. They were Lord Slayton's men, retreating from the French, though a handful of the enemy was among them. Men wrestled in the dark, tripped over the dead and the dying, and slipped in sewage. Two men-at-arms forced Hook back against the side of the tunnel and he again thrust the poleaxe like a quarterstaff, two-handed, but a rush of men pushed his enemies aside as archers and miners fled to the sow.

'Hold them!' Sir Edward's voice bellowed from further down the mine.

The barrels. Hook, momentarily free of enemies, turned and ran towards the mine entrance. He made it to where the shaft sloped gently up towards the surface, but there a foot tripped him and he sprawled heavily onto the chalk. He twisted aside and tried to climb to his feet, but a boot kicked him in the belly. Hook twisted again to see Tom and Robert Perrill standing over him.

'Quick,' Tom Perrill shouted at his brother.

Robert lifted a sword, point downwards, aimed at Hook's throat.

'I'll have your woman,' Tom Perrill said, though Hook could scarcely hear him over the shouts and screams echoing up the tunnel. More shouts sounded from the sow where attackers fought a bitter sudden battle against startled defenders. Then Robert Perrill's sword came down and Hook rolled again, throwing himself against his enemies' feet and he heaved up so that Robert Perrill tumbled against the far wall and the poleaxe was still in Hook's hand as he scrambled to his feet and turned on Thomas Perrill, who simply ran away.

'Coward!' Hook shouted, and looked down to Robert who was flailing the sword uselessly and screaming, screaming, and Hook suddenly understood why. The earth was quivering as another scream, thin as a blade, sounded in Hook's ears.

'Down!' Saint Crispinian said.

And the earth was shaking now, and the thin scream was lost in thunder, only the thunder was not from the sky, but from the earth, and Hook obeyed the saint, crouching down beside Robert Perrill as the tunnel roof collapsed.

It seemed to last for ever. Timbers cracked, the noise groaned and boomed, and the earth fell.

Hook closed his eyes. The thin scream was back, but it was inside his head. It was fear, his own scream, his terror of death. He was breathing dust. At the last day, he knew, the dead would rise from the earth. They would come from their graves, the earth making way for their flesh and bones, and they would face east towards the shining holy city of Jerusalem, and the sky in the east would be brighter than the sun and a great terror would swamp the newly resurrected dead as they stood in their winding sheets. There would be screaming and crying, folk flinching from the sudden dazzle of new light, but all the dead priests of the parish would have been buried with their feet towards the west so that when they rose from their tombs they would face their frightened congregations and could call out reassurance. And for some reason, as the earth collapsed to make Hook's grave, he thought of Sir Martin, and wondered whether that twisted, sour, long-jawed face would be the first he would see on the last day when trumpets filled the heavens and God came in glory to take His people.

A roof timber slammed down, and the earth fell and Hook was crouched and the thunder was all around him and the scream in his head died to a whimper.

And then there was silence.

Sudden, utter, black silence.

Hook breathed.

'Oh, God,' Robert Perrill moaned.

Something pressed on Hook's back. It was heavy, and seemed immovable, but it was not crushing him. The darkness was absolute.

'Oh, God, please,' Perrill said.

The earth shuddered again and there was a muffled bang. A gun, Hook thought, and now he could even hear voices, but they were very far off. His mouth was full of grit. He spat.

The poleaxe was still in Hook's right hand, but he could not move it. The weapon was trapped by something. He let go of it and felt around him, conscious that he was in a small, tight space. His fingers groped across Perrill's head. 'Help me,' Perrill said.

Hook said nothing.

He felt behind him and realised a roof timber had half fallen and somehow left this small space where he crouched and breathed. The timber slanted down and it was that rough oak that was pressing into his spine. 'What do I do?' he asked aloud.

'You're not far from the surface,' Saint Crispinian said.

'You must help me,' Perrill said.

If I move I die, Hook thought.

'Nick! Help me,' Perrill said, 'please!'

'Just push up,' Saint Crispinian said.

'Show some courage,' Saint Crispin said in his harsher voice.

'For God's sake, help me,' Perrill moaned.

'Move to your right,' Saint Crispinian said, 'and don't be frightened.'

Hook moved slowly. Earth fell.

'Now dig your way out,' Saint Crispinian said, 'like a mole.'

'Moles die,' Hook said, and he wanted to explain how they trapped moles by blocking their tunnels and then digging out the frightened animals, but the saint did not want to listen.

'You're not going to die,' the saint said impatiently, 'not if you dig.'

So Hook pushed upwards, scrabbling at the earth with both hands, and the soil caved in, filling his mouth and he wanted to scream, but he could not scream, and he pushed with his legs, using all the strength in his body, and the earth collapsed around him and he was certain he would die here, except that suddenly, quite suddenly, he was breathing clean air. His grave had been very shallow, nothing but a shroud of fallen soil and he was half standing in open air and was astonished to discover that full night had not yet fallen. It seemed to be raining, except the sky was clear, and then he realised the French were shooting crossbow bolts from the barbican and from the half-wrecked walls. They were not shooting at him, but at men peering from the English trenches and around the edges of the sow.

Hook was up to his waist in earth. He reached down beside his right leg and took hold of Robert Perrill's leather jerkin. He pulled, and the earth was loose enough to let him drag the choking archer up into the last of the daylight. A crossbow bolt thumped into the soil a few inches from Hook and he went very still.

He was in what looked like a crude trench and the high sides of the trench gave him some protection from the French bolts. The town's defenders were cheering. They had seen the tunnel's collapse and they saw the English trying to rescue anyone who might have survived the catastrophe and so they were filling the twilight with crossbow bolts to drive those rescuers back.

'Oh, God,' Robert Perrill sighed.

'You're alive,' Hook said.

'Nick?'

'We have to wait,' Hook said.

Robert Perrill choked and spat out earth. 'Wait?'

'Can't move till dark,' Hook said, 'they're shooting at us.'

'My brother!'

'He ran away,' Hook said. He wondered what had happened to Sir Edward. Had that deeper part of the mine collapsed? Or had the French killed all the men in the tunnel? The enemy had driven their own shaft above the English excavation and then dropped into the tunnel and Hook imagined the sudden fight, the death in the darkness and the pain of dying in the ready-made grave. 'You were going to kill me,' he said to Robert Perrill.

Perrill said nothing. He was half lying on the trench floor, but his legs were still buried. He had lost his sword.

'You were going to kill me,' Hook said again.

'My brother was.'

'You held the sword,' Hook said.

Perrill wiped dirt from his face. 'I'm sorry, Nick,' he said.

Hook snorted, said nothing.

'Sir Martin said he'd pay us,' Perrill admitted.

'Your father?' Hook sneered.

Perrill hesitated, then nodded. 'Yes.'

'Because he hates me?'

'Your mother rejected him,' Perrill said.

Hook laughed. 'And your mother whored herself,' he said flatly.

'He told her she'd go to heaven,' Perrill said, 'that if you do it with a priest you go to heaven. That's what he said.'

'He's mad,' Hook said flatly, 'moon-touched mad.'

Perrill ignored that. 'He gave her money, he still does, and he'll give us money.'

'To kill me?' Hook asked, though the French were trying hard enough to save Sir Martin the trouble. The crossbow bolts were thudding and spitting, some tumbling end over end down the crude trench made by the collapsed tunnel.

'He wants your woman,' Robert Perrill said.

'How much is he paying you?'

'A mark each,' Perrill said, eager to help Hook now.

A mark. One hundred and sixty pennies, or three hundred and twenty pence if both brothers were paid. Fifty-three days' pay for an archer. The price of Hook's life and Melisande's misery. 'So you have to kill me?' Hook asked, 'then take my girl?'

'He wants that.'

'He's an evil mad bastard,' Hook said.

'He can be kind,' Perrill said pathetically. 'Do you remember John Luttock's daughter?'

'Of course I remember her.'

'He took her away, but he paid John in the end, gave him the girl's dowry.'

'A hundred and sixty pennies for raping her?'

'No!' Perrill was puzzled by the question. 'I think it was two pounds, might have been more. John was happy.'

The light was fading fast now. The French had saved their loaded guns for the moment when their counter-mine pierced the English tunnel and now they fired shot after shot from Harfleur's walls. The smoke billowed like thunderclouds to darken the already dark sky as the gun-stones bounced and thudded off the sow's stout flanks.

'Robert!' a voice shouted from the sow.

'That's Tom!' Robert Perrill said, recognising his brother's voice. He took a breath to call back, but Hook stopped his mouth with a hand.

'Keep quiet,' Hook snarled. A crossbow bolt tumbled down the trench and smacked into Hook's mail. It had lost its force and bounced away as another bolt struck sparks from a lump of flint nearby. 'What happens now?' Hook asked, taking his hand away from Robert Perrill's mouth.

'What do you mean?'

'I take you back and you try and kill me again.'

'No!' Perrill said. 'Get me out of here, Nick! I can't move!'

'So what happens now?' Hook asked again. Crossbow bolts

were cracking into the sow so frequently that it sounded like hail on a timber roof.

'I won't kill you,' Perrill said.

'What should I do?' Hook asked.

'Pull me out, Nick, please,' Perrill said.

'I wasn't talking to you. What should I do?'

'What do you think?' Saint Crispin, the harsher brother, said in a mocking voice.

'It's murder,' Hook said.

'I won't kill you!' Perrill insisted.

'You think we saved the girl so she could be raped?' Saint Crispinian asked.

'Get me out of this muck,' Perrill said, 'please!'

Instead Hook reached out and found one of the spent crossbow bolts. It was as long as his forearm, as thick as two thumbs and fledged with stiff leather vanes. The point was rusted, but still sharp.

He killed Perrill the easiest way. He smacked him hard around the head, and while the archer was still recovering from the blow, drove the bolt down through one eye. It went in easily, glancing off the socket, and Hook kept driving the thick shaft into Perrill's brain until the rusted point scraped against the back of Perrill's skull. The archer twisted and jerked, choked and quivered, but he died quickly enough.

'Robert!' Tom Perrill shouted from the sow.

A springolt bolt struck a masonry chimney breast left standing in the scorched remains of a burned house. The bolt spun into the falling darkness, end over end, soaring over the English trenches to fall far beyond. Hook wiped his wounded right hand on Robert Perrill's tunic, cleaning off the muck that had spurted from the dead man's eye, then heaved himself free of the soil. It was very nearly night and the smoke of the gunshots still shrouded what little light remained. He stepped over Perrill and staggered towards the sow, his legs slow to find their strength again. Crossbow bolts flicked past him, but their aim was wild now and Hook reached the sow safely. He held on to its flank as he walked, then dropped into the safety of the trench. Lanterns lit his dirt-crusted face and men stared at him.

'How many others survived?' a man-at-arms asked.

'Don't know,' Hook said.

'Here,' a priest brought him a pot and Hook drank. He had not realised how thirsty he was until he tasted the ale.

'My brother?' Thomas Perrill was among the men staring at Hook.

'Killed by a crossbow bolt,' Hook said curtly and stared up into Perrill's long face. 'Straight through the eye,' he added brutally. Perrill stared at him, and then Sir John Cornewaille pushed through the small crowd in the sow's pit.

'Hook!'

'I'm alive, Sir John.'

'You don't look it. Come.' Sir John grasped Hook's arm and led him towards the camp. 'What happened?'

'They came from above,' Hook said. 'I was on my way out when the roof fell in.'

'It fell on you?'

'Yes, Sir John.'

'Someone loves you, Hook.'

'Saint Crispinian does,' Hook said, then he saw Melisande in the light of a campfire and went to her embrace.

And afterwards, in the darkness, had nightmares.

Sir John's men started dying next morning. A man-at-arms and two archers, all three of them struck by the sickness that turned bowels into sewers of filthy water. Alice Godewyne died. A dozen other men-at-arms were sick, as were at least twenty archers. The army was being ravaged

219

by the plague and the stench of shit hung over the camp, and the French built their walls higher every night and in the dawn men struggled to the gun-pits and trenches where they vomited and voided their bowels.

Father Christopher caught the sickness. Melisande found him shivering in his tent, face pale, lying in his own filth and too weak to move. 'I ate some nuts,' he told her.

'Nuts?'

'*Les noix*,' he explained in a voice that was like a breathless groan. 'I didn't know.'

'Didn't know?'

'The doctors tell me now that you shouldn't eat nuts or cabbage. Not with the sickness about. I ate nuts.'

Melisande washed him. 'You'll make me sicker,' he complained, but was too weak to prevent her from cleaning him. She found him a blanket, though Father Christopher threw it off when the day's warmth became insufferable. Much of the low land in which Harfleur stood was still flooded and the heat seemed to shimmer off the shallow water and made the air thick as steam. The guns still fired, but less frequently because the Dutch gunners had also been struck by the murrain. No one was spared. Men in the king's household fell ill, great lords were struck down and the angels of death hovered on dark wings above the English camp.

Melisande found blackberries and begged some barley from Sir John's cooks. She boiled the berries and barley to reduce the liquid that she then sweetened with honey and spooned into Father Christopher's mouth. 'I'm going to die,' he told her weakly.

'No,' she said decisively, 'you are not.'

The king's own physician, Master Colnet, came to Father Christopher's tent. He was a young, serious man with a pale face and a small nose with which he smelt Father Christopher's faeces. He offered no judgement on what he had determined from the odours, instead he briskly opened a vein in the priest's arm and bled him copiously. 'The girl's ministrations will do no harm,' he said.

'God bless her,' Father Christopher said weakly.

'The king sent you wine,' Master Colnet said.

'Thank his majesty for me.'

'It's excellent wine,' Colnet said, binding the cut arm with practised skill, 'though it didn't help the bishop.'

'Bangor's dead?'

'Not Bangor, Norwich. He died yesterday.'

'Dear God,' Father Christopher said.

'I bled him too,' Master Colnet said, 'and thought he would live, but God decreed otherwise. I shall come back tomorrow.'

The Bishop of Norwich's body was cut into quarters, then boiled in a giant cauldron to flense the flesh from the bones. The filthy steaming liquid was poured away and the bones were wrapped in linen and nailed in a coffin that was carried to the shore so the bishop could be taken home to be buried in the diocese he had taken such care to avoid in life. Most of the dead were simply dropped into pits dug wherever there was a patch of ground high enough to hold an unflooded grave, but as more men died the grave-pits were abandoned and the corpses were carried to the tidal flats and thrown into the shallow creeks where they were at the mercy of wild dogs, gulls and eternity. The stench of the dead and the stink of shit and the reek of smouldering fires filled the encampment.

Two mornings after Hook had stumbled away from the fallen mine there was a sudden flurry of gunshots from the walls of Harfleur. The garrison had loaded their cannon and now fired them all at the same time so that the battered town was edged with smoke. Defenders cheered from the walls and waved derisive flags.

'A ship got through to them,' Sir John explained.

'A ship?' Hook asked.

'For Christ's sake, you know what a ship is!'

'But how?'

'Our goddam fleet was asleep, that's how! Now the goddam bastards have got food. God damn the bastards.' It seemed God had changed sides, for the defences of Harfleur, though battered and broken, were constantly replenished and rebuilt. New walls backed the broken old, and every night the garrison deepened the defensive ditch and raised new obstacles in the shattered breaches. The intensity of the crossbow bolts did not let up, proof that the town had been well stocked, or else that the ship that had evaded the blockade had brought a new supply. The English, meanwhile, grew more ill. Sir John ducked into Father Christopher's tent and stared at the priest. 'How is he?' he asked Melisande.

She shrugged. As far as Hook could tell the priest was already dead, for he lay unmoving on his back, his mouth slackly open and his skin greyish pale.

'Is he breathing?' Sir John demanded.

Melisande nodded.

'God help us,' Sir John said and backed out of the tent, 'God help us,' he said again, and stared at the town. It should have fallen two weeks ago, yet there it lay, defiant still, the wreckage of its wall and towers protecting the new barricades that had been built behind.

There was some good news. Sir Edward Derwent was a prisoner in Harfleur, as was Dafydd ap Traharn. The heralds, returning from another vain attempt to persuade the garrison to surrender, told how the men trapped in the mine's far end had surrendered. The collapsed mine had been abandoned, though on Harfleur's eastern side, where the king's brother led the siege, other shafts were still being driven towards the walls. The best news was that the French were making no effort to relieve the town. English patrols were riding far

222

into the countryside to find grain, and there was no sign of an enemy army coming to strike at the disease-weakened English. Harfleur, it seemed, had been left to rot, though it appeared now that the besiegers would be destroyed first.

'All that money,' Sir John said bleakly, 'and all we've done is march a couple of miles to become lords of graves and shit-pits.'

'So why don't we just leave it?' Hook asked. 'Just march away?'

'A goddam stupid question,' Sir John said. 'The place might surrender tomorrow! And all Christendom is watching. If we abandon the siege we look weak. And besides, even if we did march inland we won't necessarily find the French. They've learned to fear English armies and they know the quickest way to get rid of us is to hide themselves in fortresses. So we might just abandon this siege to start another. No, we have to take this goddam town.'

'Then why don't we attack?' Hook asked.

'Because we'll lose too many men,' Sir John said. 'Imagine it, Hook. Crossbows, springolts, guns, all tearing into us as we advance, killing us while we fill the ditch, and then we get over the wall's rubble to find a new ditch, a new wall, and more crossbows, more guns, more catapults. We can't afford to lose a hundred dead and four hundred crippled. We came here to conquer France, not die in this rancid shit-hole.' He kicked at the hard ground, then stared at the sea where six English ships lay at anchor off the harbour entrance. 'If I commanded Harfleur's garrison,' he said ruefully, 'I know just what I'd do now.'

'What's that?'

'Attack,' Sir John said. 'Kick us while we're half crippled. We speak of chivalry, Hook, and we are chivalrous. We fight so politely! Yet you know how to win a battle?'

'Fight dirty, Sir John.'

'Fight filthy, Hook. Fight like the devil and send chivalry to hell. He's no fool.'

'The devil?'

Sir John shook his head. 'No, Raoul de Gaucourt. He commands the garrison,' Sir John nodded towards Harfleur. 'He's a gentleman, Hook, but he's also a fighter. And he's no fool. And if I were Raoul de Gaucourt I'd kick the shit out of us right now.'

And next day Raoul de Gaucourt did.

'Wake up, Nick!' It was Thomas Evelgold bellowing at him. The centenar slapped Hook's shelter, shaking it so hard that scraps of dead leaves and pieces of turf fell onto Hook and Melisande. 'God damn you, wake up!' Evelgold shouted again.

Hook opened his eyes to darkness. 'Tom?' he called, but Evelgold had already moved on to wake other archers.

A second voice was shouting for the men to assemble. 'Armour! Weapons! Hurry! Goddam now! I want you all here, now! Now!'

'What is it?' Melisande asked.

'Don't know,' Hook said. He fumbled to find his mail coat. The stink of the leather lining was overpowering as he pulled it over his head. He forced the unwieldy garment down his chest. 'Sword belt?'

'Here,' Melisande was kneeling. The campfires were being revived and their flames reflected red from her wide open eyes.

Hook put on the short surcoat with its cross of Saint George, the badge that every man was required to wear in the siege-works. He pulled on his boots, the once good boots that he had bought in Soissons but which were now coming apart at the seams. He strapped on his belt, slid the bow from its cover and snatched up an arrow bag. He had tied a long leather strap to the poleaxe and he slung that over his shoulder, then ducked into the night. 'I'll be back,' he called to Melisande.

'*Casque!*' she shouted after him, '*casque!*' He reached back and took the helmet from her. He felt a sudden urge to tell her he loved her, but Melisande had disappeared back into the shelter and Hook said nothing. He sensed the night was ending. The stars were pale, which meant dawn would soon stain the sky above the obstinate city, but ahead of him there was tumult. The flames in the siege-works leaped higher, casting grotesque shadows across the broken ground.

'Come to me! Come to me!' Sir John was shouting beside the largest campfire. The archers were gathering quickly, but the men-at-arms, who needed more time to buckle on their plate armour, were slower to arrive. Sir John had chosen to forgo his expensive plate armour and was dressed like the archers in mail coat and jupon. 'Evelgold! Hook! Magot! Candeler! Brutte!' Sir John called. Walter Magot, Piers Candeler and Thomas Brutte were the other three ventenars.

'Here, Sir John!' Evelgold responded.

'Bastards have made a sally,' Sir John said urgently. That explained the shouting and the sound of steel clashing with steel that came from the forward trenches. Harfleur's garrison had sallied out to attack the sow and gun-pits. 'We have to kill the bastards,' Sir John said. 'We're going to attack straight down to the sow. Some of us are, but not you, Hook! You know the Savage?'

'Yes, Sir John,' Hook said, adjusting the buckle of his sword belt. The Savage was a catapult, a great wooden beast that hurled stones into Harfleur and, of all the siege engines, it lay closest to the sea at the right-hand end of the English lines.

'Take your men there,' Sir John said, 'and work your way in towards the sow, got that?'

226

'Yes, Sir John,' Hook said again. He strung the bow by bracing one end on the ground and looping the cord over the upper nock.

'Then go! Go now!' Sir John snarled, 'and kill the bastards!' He turned. 'Where's my banner! I want my banner! Bring me my goddamned banner!'

Hook led sixteen men now. It should have been twenty-three, but seven were either dead or ill. He wondered how seventeen men were supposed to fight their way along trenches and gun-pits swarming with an enemy who had sallied from the Leure Gate. It was evident the French had captured large stretches of the siege-works because, as Hook led his men down the southwards track, he could see more fires springing up in the English gun-pits and the shapes of men scurrying in front of those flames. Groups of men-at-arms and archers crossed Hook's path, all going towards the fighting. Hook could hear the clash of blades now.

'What do we do, Nick?' Will of the Dale asked.

'You heard Sir John. Start at the Savage, work our way in,' Hook said, and was surprised that he sounded confident. Sir John's orders had been vague and given hurriedly, and Hook had simply obeyed by leading his men towards the Savage, but only now was he trying to work out what he was supposed to do. Sir John was assembling his men-at-arms and had kept most of the archers, presumably for an attack on the sow that seemed to have fallen into the enemy's possession, but why detach Hook? Because, Hook decided, Sir John needed flank protection. Sir John and his men were the beaters and they would drive the game across Hook's front where the archers could cut them down. Hook, recognising the plan's simplicity, felt a surge of pride. Sir John could have sent his centenar Tom Evelgold or any of the other ventenars, all of whom were older and more senior, but Sir John had chosen Hook.

Fires burned at the Savage, but they had not been set by the French. They were the campfires of the men who guarded the pit in which the catapult sat, and their flames lit the monstrously gaunt beams of the giant engine. A dozen archers, the sentries who guarded the machine through the night, waited with strung bows and, as they saw men coming down the slope, turned those bows towards Hook. 'Saint George!' Hook bellowed, 'Saint George!'

The bows dropped. The sentries were nervous. 'What's happening?' one of them demanded of Hook.

'French are out.'

'I know, but what's happening?'

'I don't know!' Hook snapped, then turned to count his men. He did it in the old way of the country, like a shepherd counting his flock, just as his father had taught him. Yain, tain, eddero, he counted and got to bumfit, which was fifteen, and looked for the extra man and saw two. Tain-o-bumfit? Then he saw that the seventeenth man was short and slight and carried a crossbow. 'For God's sake, girl, go back,' he called, and then he forgot Melisande because Tom Scarlet shouted a warning and Hook whipped around to see a band of men running towards the Savage down the wide trench that snaked to the catapult from the nearest gun-pit. Some of the approaching men carried torches that streamed sparks and the bright flames reflected from helmets, swords and axes.

'No crosses!' Tom Scarlet warned, meaning that none of the men in the trench was wearing the cross of Saint George. They were French and, seeing the archers outlined by the fires burning in the Savage's pit, they began shouting their challenge. 'Saint Denis! Harfleur!'

'Bows!' Hook shouted, and his men instinctively spread out. 'Kill them!' he shouted.

The range was short, less than fifty paces, and the attackers made themselves into an easy target because they were constricted by the trench's walls. The first arrows drilled into them and the thuds of the heads striking home instantly silenced the enemy's shouting. The sound of the bows was sharp, each release of the string followed by the briefest fluttering rush as the feathers caught the air. In the darkness those feathers made small white flickers that stopped abruptly as the arrows slapped home. To Hook it seemed as if time had slowed. He was plucking arrows from his bag, laying them over the stave, bringing up the bow, hauling the cord, releasing, and he felt no excitement, no fear and no exhilaration. He knew exactly where each arrow would go before he even pulled it from the bag. He aimed at the approaching men's bellies and, in the flame-light, he saw those men doubling over as his arrows struck.

The enemy's charge ended as surely as though they had run into a stone wall. The trench was wide enough for six men to walk abreast and all the leading Frenchmen were on the ground, spitted by arrows, and the men behind tripped on them and, in their turn, were hit by arrows. Some glanced off plate armour, but others sliced straight through the metal, and even an arrow that failed to pierce the plate had sufficient force to knock a man backwards. If the enemy could have spread out they might have reached the Savage, but the trench walls constricted them and the feathered bodkins ripped in from the dark and so the attacking party turned and ran back, leaving a dark mass behind, not all of it motionless. 'Denton! Furnays! Cobbold!' Hook called, 'make sure those bastards are dead 'uns. The rest of you, after me!'

The three men jumped into the trench, drew their swords and approached the wounded enemy. Hook meanwhile stayed above the trench, advancing beside it with an arrow on his cord. He could see men fighting around the distant sow and in the wide pit where the biggest gun, the great bombard called the King's Daughter, was dug in. Fire burned bright there, but it was none of Hook's business. His job was to be on Sir John's flank.

The ground was rough, churned up by digging and by the strike of French missiles. The boulders slung by the big catapults in Harfleur littered the path, as did the remnants of the houses that had been burned when the siege began, but the dawn was now seeping a faint light in the east, just enough to cast shadows from the obstacles. A crossbow bolt whipped past Hook's head and he sensed it had come from the nearest gun-pit where a cannon called the Redeemer was emplaced. 'Will! Keep those bastards busy.'

'What bastards?'

'The ones who've captured the Redeemer!' Hook said, and grabbed Will of the Dale's arm and turned him towards the gun-pit, which was a black shadow twenty paces beyond the trench. It had been protected from the springolts and guns of Harfleur by one of the ingenious wooden screens that loomed high in the darkness, but the tilting screen had not kept the enemy from capturing the cannon. 'Put as many arrows into the pit as you can,' Hook told Will, 'but stop shooting when we reach the gun.' Hook pushed six men towards Will. 'You obey Will,' he told them, 'and you look after Melisande,' he added to Will, for she was still with the group. 'The rest of you, after me.'

Another crossbow bolt hissed close by, but Hook's men were moving fast now. Will of the Dale and his half-dozen men were moving eastwards to shoot their arrows through the opening at the back of the pit, while Hook was running to the Redeemer's flank. He jumped down into the wide trench and waited for his six men to join him. 'No bows from now on,' he told them.

'No bows? We're archers!' Will Sclate grumbled. Will Sclate always grumbled. He was not a popular man, too morose to be easy company and too slow-witted to join in the incessant chatter among the archers, but he was big and hugely strong. He had grown up on one of Sir John's estates, a labourer's son who might have expected to work the fields his whole life, but Sir John had seen the boy's strength and insisted he learn the longbow. Now, as an archer, he earned far more than any labourer, but he was as slow and stubborn as the clay fields he had once worked with hoe and beetle.

'You're a soldier,' Hook snapped at him, 'and you're going to use hand weapons.'

'What are we doing?' Geoffrey Horrocks asked. He was the youngest of Sir John's archers, just seventeen, the son of a falconer.

'We're going to kill some bastards,' Hook said. He slung the bow across his body and hefted the poleaxe instead. 'And we go fast! After me! Now!'

He scrambled up the face of the trench and over the wreckage of the soil-filled wicker baskets that formed the trench's parapet. He could see flame-light in the Redeemer's pit and he could hear the sharp thin noise of bowstrings being released from his left where Will of the Dale's men were lined beside the stone stump of a wrecked chimney. A shout came from the pit, then another, then a screech as an arrowhead scraped against the cannon's flank. Seven archers were shooting into the pit. In one minute they could easily loose sixty or seventy arrows, and those arrows were flickering through the half-light, filling the gun-pit with hissing death and forcing the French to crouch for protection.

Then Hook and his men came at them from the flank. The Frenchmen did not see him because the arrows were whistling and thumping around them, and they were crouching to find what little protection the pit offered. The massive wooden screen gave splendid protection on the face that looked towards Harfleur, but the pit had never been designed to protect men being attacked from the rear and Will's arrows were streaking down the trench and through the wide gap. Then Hook leaped across the parapet at the pit's side and he prayed the arrows would stop.

They must have stopped because none of his men was struck by an arrow. The archers were shouting a challenge as they followed Hook over the wicker baskets, and still shouting as they started the killing. Hook was swinging the poleaxe as he landed and its lead-weighted hammer head crashed into a crouching Frenchman's helmet and Hook sensed rather than saw the metal crumpling under the massive blow that collapsed metal, skull and brain. A man reared up to his right, but Sclate hurled him back with contemptuous ease as Hook sprawled on the far side of the cannon. He had leaped clean across the Redeemer's barrel.

He hit the far side of the pit hard, lost his footing and fell heavily. A surge of fear flared cold in his veins. The biggest fear was that he was on the ground and vulnerable, another that he might have damaged the bow slung on his back, but later, when he remembered the fight, he realised he had also felt elation. In memory it was all a blur of screaming men, bright blades and ringing metal, but in that welter of impressions there was a cold hard centre in which Nick Hook regained his feet and saw a man-at-arms at the front of the pit. The man was wearing plate armour half covered by a surcoat that displayed a red heart pierced by a burning lance. He was holding a sword. His visor was raised and his eyes reflected the small flames of the fallen torches and Hook saw fear in those eyes, and Hook felt no pity because of that fear. Kill or be killed, Sir John always said, and Hook ran at the man, poleaxe levelled, the haft held in both his hands, and he ignored the feeble defensive sword-swing the man offered and lunged the spear point at the Frenchman's midriff. The blade scraped off the bottom rim of the breastplate and jarred on the faulds, the plate strips worn on a leather skirt designed to stop a sword thrust into the lower belly. But no fauld could resist a poleaxe thrust and Hook saw the man's terrified eyes open wide, and saw his mouth make a great hole as the spear point ripped through steel, leather, mail undershirt, skin, muscle and guts to ram against the Frenchman's spine. The man made a mewing noise and Hook was bellowing a challenge as the thrust pushed his victim back against the gunpit's face. Hook hauled the poleaxe back, and the flailing man came with it, his flesh trapping the point, and Hook put his boot into the mess of blood and armour, braced his leg and tugged till the blade came free. He lunged it forward again, but checked the blow as the man fell to his knees. Hook whipped around, ready to defend himself, but the fight was already over. There had only been eight men in the pit. They must have been left there by the larger French party advancing towards the Savage and, when that party had been thrown back by arrows, these eight had been forgotten. Their job had been to wreck the cannon, a job they had been trying to do with a huge axe that lay abandoned beside the windlass that tilted the heavy protective screen on its massive axle. They had managed to chop the windlass into splinters, but now all but one of them was dead.

'Can't hurt a cannon with an axe!' Tom Scarlet said derisively. The one living Frenchman moaned.

'Anyone hurt?' Hook demanded.

'I twisted my ankle,' Horrocks said. He was panting and his eyes were wide with astonishment or fear.

'You'll mend,' Hook said abruptly. 'Are we all here?' His men were all present, and Will of the Dale was running up the trench with Melisande and his six archers. The wounded Frenchman whimpered and drew his legs up. He had been wearing no armour except a padded haubergeon and Will Sclate had driven an axe deep into his chest so that the linen padding had spilt out and was now soaked with blood. Hook could see a mess of lungs and splintered ribs. Blood bubbled black from the man's mouth as he moaned again. 'Put him out of his misery,' Hook demanded, but his archers just stared at him. 'Oh, for Christ's sake,' Hook said. He stepped over a corpse, put the poleaxe's spike at the man's neck, lunged once and so did the job himself.

Will of the Dale stared at the carnage in the pit. 'Last time the silly bastards do that!' he said. He tried to speak lightly, imitating Sir John, but there was a squawk in his voice and horror in his eyes.

Melisande was close behind Will. She stared dumbly at the dead Frenchmen, next at the blood dripping thick from Hook's poleaxe, then up into his eyes. 'You shouldn't be here,' he told her harshly.

'I can't stay in the camp,' she said, 'that priest might come.'

'We'll look after her, Nick,' Will of the Dale said, his voice still strained. He took a step forward and lifted one of the fallen torches, though there was enough light in the east now to make the flames unnecessary. 'Look what they did,' he said.

The Frenchmen had used their big axe to chop through the iron bands that hooped the Redeemer's barrel. Hook had not noticed the damage before, but now he saw that two of the metal rings had been hacked clean through, which meant the gun was probably useless because, if it was fired, the barrel would expand, split and kill every man in the pit. That was none of Hook's business. 'Search the bastards,' he ordered his men. The three archers who had plundered the bodies of the first French casualties had found silver chains, coins, brooches and a dagger with a jewelled hilt. Those valuables were all in an arrow bag to which new riches were now added. 'We'll share it out later,' Hook decreed. 'Now come on, get out of here! Bows!'

His bow had been undamaged by his fall. He took it in his left hand, slung the poleaxe on his shoulder, and laid an arrow on the cord. He climbed the pit's side into a grey dawn streaked by dark smoke.

In front of him a battle raged around the sow and around the pit that held the King's Daughter. The French had captured both, but the English had streamed from their camp and now outnumbered the raiding party, which was being forced inexorably back. Trumpets blew, the signal for the French to break off their fight and retreat to Harfleur. Flames licked at the sow's heavy timbers and at the swinging screen sheltering the bombard. Men-at-arms were hacking at each other, blades flashing reflected light as they slashed and thrust. Hook looked for Sir John's rampant lion banner and saw it to his left. He saw too that Sir John's men were fighting across the main trench, driving back the large group of French who now formed the attackers' left wing. 'Bows!' Hook called.

He hauled the cord back, drawing it to his right ear. The French had been summoned back to the town, but they dared not turn and run for fear of the close English pursuit, and so they were fighting hard, trying to drive Sir John's men back into the trench. They were half facing away from Hook and had no idea that he was on their flank. 'Aim true,' Hook shouted, wanting none of his arrows to fall on Englishmen, then he released, took another bodkin and that new arrow was only half drawn as the first drove into an enemy's back. Hook drew full again, saw a Frenchman turn towards the new threat, released, and the arrow slapped into the man's face, and suddenly the enemy was running, defeated by the unexpected attack from their flank.

A crossbow bolt flashed in front of Hook. A springolt bolt, much larger, churned up a spout of earth as a gun fired from Harfleur's wall. The stone banged into the ground just behind the archers as yet more bolts flickered through the smoke. The crossbow bolts made a fluttering noise and Hook reckoned their leather fledgings were twisted out of shape, perhaps because they had been badly stored. The bolts were not flying true, but they were still coming too close. Hook glanced at the barbican and saw the enemy crossbowmen taking aim from its summit. He turned and sped an arrow towards them, then called to his men. 'Stop shooting! Get to the trench!'

The French were retreating fast now, but they had done what they had set out to do, which was to damage the siege-works. Three of the cannon, including the King's Daughter, would never fire again, and all along the trenches parapets had been thrown down and men killed. And now, from the broken ramparts, the defenders jeered at the English as the returning raiding party negotiated the deep ditch in front of the broken barbican. Arrows still followed the French and some men were struck and slid into the ditch's bottom, but the sally had been a success. The English works burned and the garrison's insults stung.

'Bastards,' Sir John was saying repeatedly. 'They caught us sleeping, the bastards!'

'The Savage isn't touched,' Hook reported stoically, 'but they broke the Redeemer.'

'We'll break them, the goddam bastards!' Sir John said.

'And none of us was hurt,' Hook added.

'We'll hurt them, by Christ,' Sir John vowed. His face was twisted by anger. The siege was already bogged down, but now the enemy had delivered another hard blow to the English hopes. Sir John shuddered as an enemy man-at-arms, taken prisoner, was ushered down the trench. For a heart-beat it looked as though Sir John would unleash his fury on the hapless man, but then he saw Melisande and released his frustration on her instead. 'What in the name of suffering Christ is she doing here?' he demanded of Hook. 'Jesus Christ on the cross, are you turd-witted? Can't be without your woman for a goddamned minute?'

'It was not Nick!' Melisande called defiantly. She was

236

holding the crossbow, though she had not shot with it. 'It was not Nick,' she said again, 'and he did tell me to go away.'

Sir John's courtesy towards women overcame his anger. He grunted what might have been an apology, and then Melisande was explaining herself, talking in fast French, gesturing towards the camp, and as she spoke Sir John's face showed a renewed anger. He turned on Hook. 'Why didn't you tell me?'

'Tell you what, Sir John?'

'That a bastard priest has threatened her?'

'I fight my own battles,' Hook said sullenly.

'No!' Sir John thrust a gauntleted hand to strike Hook's shoulder. 'You fight my battles, Hook,' he punched Hook's shoulder again, 'that's what I pay you for. But if you fight mine, then I fight yours, you understand? We are a company!' Sir John shouted the last four words so loudly that men fifty yards down the trench turned to watch him. 'We are a company! No one threatens any one of us without threatening all of us! Your girl should be able to walk naked through the whole army and not a man will dare touch her because she belongs to us! She belongs to our company! By Christ I'll kill the holy bastard for this! I'll rip the spine out of his goddam throat and feed his shrivelled prick to the dogs! No one threatens us, no one!'

Sir John, with his real enemies safely back behind their smoke-rimmed ramparts, was looking for a fight. And Hook had just given him one.

Hook watched as Melisande spooned honey into Father Christopher's mouth. The priest was sitting, his back supported by a barrel that had come from England filled with smoked herrings. He was skeletally thin, his face was pale and tired and he was plainly as weak as a fledgling, but he was alive.

'Cobbett's dead,' Hook said, 'and Robert Fletcher.'

'Poor Robert,' Father Christopher said, 'how's his brother?'

'Still alive,' Hook said, 'but he's sick.'

'Who else?'

'Pearson's dead, Hull is, Borrow and John Taylor.'

'God have mercy on them all,' the priest said and made the sign of the cross. 'The men-at-arms?'

'John Gaffney, Peter Dance, Sir Thomas Peters,' Hook said, 'all dead.'

'God has turned His face from us,' Father Christopher said bleakly. 'Does your saint still speak to you?'

'Not now,' Hook admitted.

Father Christopher sighed. He closed his eyes momentarily. 'We have sinned,' he said grimly.

'We were told God was on our side,' Hook said stubbornly.

'We believed that,' the priest said, 'we surely believed that, and we came here with that assurance in our hearts, but the French will believe the same thing. And now God is revealing Himself. We should not have come here.'

'You should not,' Melisande said firmly.

'Harfleur will fall,' Hook insisted.

'It probably will,' Father Christopher allowed, then paused as Melisande wiped a trickle of honey from his chin. 'If the French don't march to its relief? Yes, it will fall eventually, but what then? How much of the army is left?'

'Enough,' Hook said.

Father Christopher offered a tired smile. 'Enough to do what? To march on Rouen and make another siege? To capture Paris? We'll scarce be able to defend ourselves if the French do come here! So what will we do? We'll go into Harfleur and remake its walls, and then sail home. We've failed, Hook. We've failed.'

Hook sat in silence. One of the remaining English cannons

fired, the sound flat and lingering in the warm air. Somewhere in the camp a man sang. 'We can't just go home,' he said after a while.

'We can,' Father Christopher said, 'and we most certainly will. All this money for nothing! For Harfleur, maybe. And what will it cost to rebuild those walls?' He shrugged.

'Maybe we should abandon the siege,' Hook suggested morosely.

The priest shook his head. 'Henry will never do that. He has to win! That way he proves God's favour, and besides, abandoning the siege makes him look weak.' He was silent for a while, then frowned. 'His father took the throne by force, and Henry fears others might do the same if he shows weakness.'

'Eat, don't talk,' Melisande said briskly.

'I've eaten enough, my dear,' Father Christopher said.

'You should eat more.'

'I will. This evening. *Merci*.'

'God's sparing you, father,' Hook said.

'Perhaps He doesn't want me in heaven?' Father Christopher suggested with a wan smile, 'or perhaps He is giving me time to become a better priest.'

'You are a good priest,' Hook said warmly.

'I shall tell Saint Peter that when he asks if I deserve to be in heaven. Ask Nick Hook, I shall say. And Saint Peter will ask me, who is Nick Hook? Oh, I shall say, he's a thief, a rogue, and probably a murderer, but ask him anyway.'

Hook grinned. 'I'm honest now, father.'

'Thou art not far from the kingdom of heaven, young Hook, but let us hope it's many a long day before we meet there. And at least we'll be spared Sir Martin's company.'

Melisande sneered. 'He is a coward. *Un poltron!*'

'Most men are cowards when they meet Sir John,' Father Christopher said mildly.

'He had nothing to say!' Melisande said.

Sir John had gone to the shelters where Lord Slayton's men were camped. He had taken Hook and Melisande with him, and he had bellowed that any man who wished to kill Hook could do so right there and then. 'Come and take his woman,' Sir John had shouted. 'Who wants her?'

Lord Slayton's archers, his men-at-arms and his camp followers had been cleaning armour, preparing food or just resting, but all had turned to watch the show. They watched in silence.

'Come and take her!' Sir John shouted. 'She's yours! You can take turns like dogs rutting a bitch! Come on! She's a pretty thing! You want to hump her? She's yours!' He waited, but not one of Lord Slayton's men moved. Then Sir John had pointed at Hook. 'You can all have her! But first you have to kill my ventenar!'

Still no one moved. No one even met Sir John's eyes.

'Which man is being paid to kill you?' Sir John had asked Hook.

'That one,' Hook said, pointing at Tom Perrill.

'Then come here,' Sir John had invited Perrill, 'come and kill him. I'll give you his woman if you do.' Perrill had not moved. He was half hiding behind William Snoball who, as Lord Slayton's steward, had some small authority, but Snoball dared not confront Sir John Cornewaille. 'There is just one thing,' Sir John had added, 'which is that you have to kill both Hook and me before you get the woman. So come on! Fight me first!' He had drawn his sword and waited.

No one had moved, no one had spoken. Sir Martin had been watching from behind some men-at-arms. 'Is that the priest?' Sir John had demanded of Hook.

'That's him.'

'My name is John Cornewaille,' Sir John had shouted,

'and some of you know who I am. And Hook is my man. He is my man! He is under my protection, as is this girl!' He had put his free arm around Melisande's shoulders, then pointed his sword blade at Sir Martin. 'You, priest, come here.'

Sir Martin had not moved.

'You can come here,' Sir John said, 'or I can come and fetch you.'

Sir Martin, long face twitching, had sidled away from the protective men-at-arms. He looked around as if seeking a place to run, but Sir John had snarled at him to come closer and he had obeyed. 'He's a priest!' Sir John had called, 'so he's a witness to this oath. I swear by this sword and by the bones of Saint Credan, that if a hair of Hook's head is touched, if he is attacked, if he is wounded, if he is killed, then I shall find you and I shall kill you.'

Sir Martin had been peering at Sir John as though he were a curious specimen in a fairground display; a five-legged cow, perhaps, or a woman with a beard. Now, still with a puzzled expression, the priest raised both hands to heaven. 'Forgive him, Lord, forgive him!' he called.

'Priest,' Sir John began.

'Knight!' Sir Martin had retorted with surprising force. 'The devil rides one horse and Christ the other. You know what that means?'

'I know what this means,' Sir John had held his sword blade towards the priest's throat, 'it means that if one of you cabbage-shitting rat-humping turds touches Hook or his woman then he will have to reckon with me. And I will tear your farting bowels out of your putrid arses with my bare hands, I will make you die screaming, I will send your shit-ridden souls to hell, I will kill you!'

Silence. Sir John had sheathed his sword, the hilt thumping loud onto the scabbard's throat. He stared at Sir Martin, daring the priest to challenge him, but Sir Martin had drifted away into one of his reveries. 'Let's go,' Sir John had said and, when they were out of earshot of the shelters, he had laughed. 'That's settled that.'

'Thank you,' Melisande had said, her relief obvious.

'Thank me? I enjoyed that, lass.'

'He probably did enjoy it,' Father Christopher said when the tale was told to him, 'but he'd have enjoyed it more if one of them had offered a fight. He does love a fight.'

'Who's Saint Credan?' Hook asked.

'He was a Saxon,' Father Christopher said, 'and when the Normans came they reckoned he shouldn't be a saint at all because he was a Saxon peasant like you, Hook, so they burned his bones, but the bones turned to gold. Sir John likes him, I have no idea why.' He frowned. 'He's not as simple as he likes to pretend.'

'He's a good man,' Hook said.

'He probably is,' Father Christopher agreed, 'but don't let him hear you say that.'

'And you're recovering, father.'

'Thanks to God and to your woman, Hook, yes, I am.' The priest reached out and took Melisande's hand. 'And it's time you made an honest woman of her, Hook.'

'I am honest,' Melisande said.

'Then it's time you tamed Master Hook,' Father Christopher said. Melisande looked at Hook and for a moment her face betrayed nothing, then she nodded. 'Maybe that's why God spared me,' Father Christopher said, 'to marry the two of you. We shall do the deed, young Hook, before we leave France.'

And it seemed that must be soon because Harfleur stood undefeated, the army of England was dying of disease and the year was inexorably passing. It was already September. In a few weeks the autumn rains would come, and the cold would come, and the harvest would be safely gathered behind fortress walls, and so the campaign season would end. Time was running out.

England had gone to war. And she was losing.

That evening Thomas Evelgold tossed a big sack to Hook. Hook jerked aside, thinking the sack would flatten him, but it was surprisingly light and merely rolled off his shoulder. 'Tow,' Evelgold said in explanation.

'Tow?'

'Tow,' Evelgold said, 'for fire arrows. One sheaf of arrows for each archer. Sir John wants it done by midnight, and we're to be down in the trench before dawn. Belly's boiling pitch for us.' Belly was Andrew Belcher, Sir John's steward who supervised the kitchen servants and sumpters. 'Have you ever made a fire arrow?' Evelgold asked.

'Never,' Hook confessed.

'Use the broadheads, tie a fistful of tow up by the head, dip it in pitch and aim high. We need two dozen apiece.' Evelgold carried more sacks to the other groups while Hook pulled out handfuls of the greasy tow, which was simply clumps of unwashed fleece straight off the sheep's back. A flea jumped from the wool and vanished up his sleeve.

He divided the tow into seventeen equal sections and each of his archers divided their share into twenty-four, one lump of fleece for each arrow. Hook cut up some spare bowstrings and his men used the lengths of cord to bind the bouquets of dirty wool to the arrowheads, then they lined up by Belly's cauldron to dip the tow into the boiling pitch. They propped the arrows upright against tree stumps or barrels to let the sticky pitch solidify. 'What's happening in the dawn?' Hook asked Evelgold.

'The French kicked our arses this morning,' Evelgold said grimly, 'so we have to kick theirs tomorrow morning.' He shrugged as if he did not expect to achieve much. 'You lose any more men today?'

'Cobbett and Fletch. Matson can't last long.'

Evelgold swore. 'Good men,' he said grimly, 'and dying, for what?' He spat towards a campfire. 'When the pitch is dry,' he went on, 'tease it out a bit. It lets it catch the fire easier.'

The camp was restless all night. Men were carrying faggots to the forward trench nearest to the enemy's barbican. The faggots were great bundles of wood, bound with rope, and the sight of them made it clear enough what was intended at dawn. A flooded ditch protected the barbican and it would need to be filled if men were to cross and assault the battered fortress.

Sir John's men-at-arms were ordered to put on full armour. Thirty men-at-arms had sailed from Southampton Water on the day the swans had flown low through the fleet to signify good fortune, but only nineteen were now fit to serve. Six had died, the other five were vomiting and shitting and shivering. The fit men-at-arms were being helped by squires and pages who buckled plates of armour over padded leather jerkins that had been wiped with grease so the shrouding metal would move easily. Sword belts were strapped over jupons, though most men-at-arms chose to carry poleaxes or shortened lances. A priest from Sir William Porter's household heard confessions and gave blessings. Sir William was Sir John's closest friend and also his brother-in-arms, which meant they fought side by side and had sworn to protect each other, to ransom each other if, by misfortune, either were taken prisoner, and to protect the other man's widow if either were to die. Sir William was a studious looking man, thin-faced and pale-eyed. His hair, before he hid it with a snout-visored helm, was thinning. He seemed out of place in armour, as though his natural home was a library or perhaps a courtroom, but he was Sir John's chosen battle companion and that spoke volumes about his courage. He adjusted his helmet and pushed up the visor before nodding a nervous greeting to Sir John's archers.

Those archers were armoured and armed. Most men, like Hook, wore a padded haubergeon sewn with metal plates over a mail coat. They had helmets and a few had aventails, the hood of mail that was worn beneath the helmet and fell across the shoulders. Their bow arms were protected by bracers, they wore swords and carried three arrow bags, two of which contained the tow-headed fire arrows. Some chose to carry an axe as well as a bow, but most, like Hook, preferred the poleaxe. All the men, whether lords, knights, men-at-arms or archers, wore the red cross of Saint George on their jupons.

'God be with you,' Sir William saluted the archers, who murmured a dutiful response.

'And the devil take the French!' Sir John called as he strode from his tent. He was in a high mood, the prospect of action giving his eyes a gleam. 'It's a simple enough job this morning!' he said dismissively. 'We just have to take the barbican away from the bastards! Let's do it before break-fast!'

Melisande had given Hook a lump cut from a flitch of bacon and a piece of bread, which he ate as Sir John's company filed downhill towards the siege-works. It was still dark. The wind was brisk and cool from the east, bringing the scent of the salt marshes to cut the cloying smell of the dead. The arrows clattered in their bags as the archers followed the winding paths. Fires glowed in the siege lines, and on the defences of Harfleur where, Hook knew, the garrison would be repairing the damage done during the previous day. 'God bless you,' a priest called as the bowmen filed past, 'God be with you! God preserve you!'

The French must have sensed something evil was brewing

for they used a pair of catapults to lob two light carcasses across the ramparts. The carcasses were great balls of cloth and tinder soaked in pitch and sulphur and they wheeled and sparked as they arced through the night sky, then fell in a great gout of flame that burst bright when the wicker-strapped balls landed. The firelight reflected off helmets in the English trenches and those gleams provoked the cross-bowmen on the walls to start shooting. The bolts whispered overhead or thumped into the parapets. Insults were shouted from the walls, but the shouts were half-hearted, as though the garrison was tired and uncertain.

The English trench was crowded. The archers with the fire arrows were ordered to the front, and behind them more archers waited with bundles of faggots. Sir John Holland, the king's nephew, was in charge of the attack, though again, as when he had led the scouting party ashore before the invasion, he was accompanied by his stepfather, Sir John Cornewaille. 'When I give the command,' the younger Sir John said, 'the archers will loose fire arrows at the barbican. We want to set it alight!'

Iron braziers had been placed every few yards along the trench. They were heaped with burning sea-coal that gave off pungent fumes.

'Drown them with fire!' Sir John Holland urged the archers, 'smoke them out like rats! And when they're blinded by smoke we fill in the ditch and take the barbican by assault!' He made it sound easy.

The remaining English guns had been loaded with stones coated with pitch. The Dutch gunners waited, their linstocks glowing. Dawn seemed to take for ever. The defenders got tired of shooting crossbow bolts and their insults, with their bolts, faded away. Both sides waited. A cockerel crowed in the camp and soon a score of birds was calling. Pageboys carrying spare sheaves of arrows waited in the saps behind the trench where priests were saying mass and hearing confessions. Men took it in turns to kneel and receive the wafers along with God's blessing. 'Your sins are forgiven,' a priest murmured to Hook, who hoped it was true. He had not confessed to Robert Perrill's murder and, as he took the host, he wondered if that deception would condemn him. He almost blurted out his guilt, but the priest was already gesturing the next man forward so Hook stood and moved away. The wafer stuck to his palate and he said a sudden, silent prayer to Saint Crispinian. Did Harfleur have a guardian saint, he wondered, and was that saint beseeching God to kill the English?

A stir in the trench made Hook turn to see the king edging through the crowded ranks. He wore full battle armour, though he had yet to pull on his helmet. His breast and back plates were covered with a surcoat on which the royal arms were blazoned bright, crossed by the red of Saint George. The king carried a broad-bladed war-axe as well as his sheathed sword. He had no shield, but nor did any other knight or man-at-arms. Their plate armour was protection enough and iron-bound shields were a relic of olden days. The king nodded companionably to the archers. 'Take the barbican,' he said as he walked along the trench, 'and the city must surely fall. God be with you.' He repeated the phrases as he worked his way along the trench, followed by a squire and two men-at-arms. 'I shall go with you,' he said as he neared Hook. 'If God wants me to rule France then He will protect us! God be with you! And keep me company, fellows, as we take back what is rightfully ours!'

'String your bows,' Sir John Holland said when the king had gone past, 'won't be long now!' Hook braced one end of his big bow against his right foot and bent it so that he could loop the string about the upper nock.

'Shoot high with the fire arrows!' Thomas Evelgold

growled. 'You can't do a full draw or you'll scorch your hand! So shoot high! And make sure the pitch is well alight before you loose!'

The grey light seeped brighter. Hook, gazing between two gabions of the battered parapet, could see that the barbican was a wreck. Its great iron-bound timbers that had once formed such a formidable wall had been broken and driven in by gunfire, yet the enemy had patched the gaps with more timbers so that the whole outlying fort now resembled an ugly hill studded with wooden baulks. The summit, which had once stood close to forty feet high, was half that now, yet it was still a formidable obstacle. The face was steep, the ditch deep, and there was room at the top for forty or fifty crossbowmen and men-at-arms. Banners hung down the ruined face, displaying saints and coats of arms. Once in a while a helmeted face would peer past a timber as the men on the ragged top watched for the expected assault.

'You start shooting your fire arrows when the guns fire!' Sir John Cornewaille reminded his men. 'That's the signal! Shoot steadily! If you see a man trying to extinguish the fires, kill the bastard!'

The coals in the nearest brazier shifted, provoking a spurt of light and a galaxy of sparks. A page crouched beside the iron basket with a handful of kindling that he would pile on the coals to make the flames to light the pitch-soaked arrows. Gulls wheeled and flocked above the salt marsh where the bodies of the dead were thrown into the tidal creeks. The gulls of Normandy were getting fat on English dead. The wafer was still stuck in Hook's dry mouth.

'Any moment now,' Sir William Porter said as though that would be a comfort to the waiting men.

There was a creaking sound and Hook looked to his left to see men turning the windlass that lifted the tilting screen in front of the nearest gun. The French saw it too and a springolt bolt whipped from the ramparts to thump into the lifting screen. A gunner pulled a gabion away from the cannon's black mouth.

And the gun fired.

The pitch that coated the stone had caught fire from the powder's explosion so that the gun-stone looked like a sear of dull light as it whipped from the smoke to flash across the broken ground and crash into the barbican.

'Now!' Sir John Holland called and the page piled the kindling onto the coals so that bright flames burst from the brazier. 'Don't let the arrows touch each other,' Evelgold advised as the archers held the first missiles in the newly roused fire. More guns fired. A timber on the barbican shattered and a spill of earth scumbled down the steep face. Hook waited till his pitch bouquet was well alight, then placed the arrow on the string. He feared the ash shaft would burn through, so he hauled fast, winced as the flames burned his left hand, aimed high and released quickly. Other fire arrows were already arcing towards the barbican, their flight slow and awkward. His own arrow leaped off the string and trailed sparks as it fluttered. It fell short. Other arrows were thumping into the splintered timbers of the barbican. The cannon smoke drifted like a screen between the archers and their target.

'Keep shooting,' Sir John Holland called.

Hook took the rag he used to wax his bow from a pouch and wrapped it about his left hand to protect himself from the flames. His second arrow flew true, striking one of the broken baulks of wood. The burning missiles curved through the early light in showers of fire, and the barbican was already dotted with small flames as more and more arrows fell. Hook saw defenders moving on the makeshift rampart and guessed they were pouring water or earth down the barbican's face and so he took a broadhead and shot it fast and true. Then he loosed his last fire arrow and saw that the flames were spreading and smoke was writhing from the broken barbican in a hundred places. One of the banners was alight, its linen flaring sudden and bright. He loosed three more broadheads at the ramparts, and just then a trumpet called from a few yards down the trench and the men carrying the bundled faggots pushed past him, climbed the parapet and ran forward.

'After them!' Sir John Holland shouted, 'give them arrows!'

The archers and men-at-arms scrambled from the trench. Now Hook could shoot over the heads of the men in front, aiming at the crossbowmen who suddenly crowded the barbican's smoke-wreathed parapet. 'Arrows,' he bellowed, and a page brought him a fresh bag. He was shooting instinctively now, sending bodkin after bodkin at the defenders who were little more than shadows in the thickening smoke. There were shouts from the ditch's edge. Men were dying there, but their faggots were filling the deep hole.

'For Harry and Saint George!' Sir John Cornewaille bellowed. 'Standard-bearer!'

'I'm here!' A squire, given the task of carrying Sir John's banner, called back.

'Forward!'

The men-at-arms went with Sir John, shouting as they advanced over the uneven, broken and scorched ground. The archers came behind. The trumpet still sounded. Other men were advancing to the left and right. The bowmen who had filled the ditch had run to either side and were now shooting arrows up at the rampart. Crossbow bolts smacked into men. One of Sir John's men opened his mouth suddenly, clutched his belly and, without a sound, doubled over and fell. Another man-at-arms, the son of an earl, had blood dripping from his helmet and a bolt sticking from his open visor. He staggered, then fell to his knees. He shook off Hook's helping hand and, with the bolt still in his shattered face, managed to stand and run forward again.

'Shout louder, you bastards!' Sir John called, and the attackers gave a ragged cry of Saint George. 'Louder!'

A gun punched rancid smoke from the town's walls and its stone slashed diagonally across the rough ground where the attackers advanced. A man-at-arms was struck on the thigh and he spun around, blood splashing high on his jupon, and the gun-stone kept going, disembowelling a page and still it flew, blood drops trailing, to vanish somewhere over the marshes. An archer's bow snapped at the full draw and he cursed. 'Don't give the bastards time! Kill them!' Sir John Cornewaille bellowed as he jumped down onto the faggots that filled the ditch.

And now the shouting was constant as the first attackers staggered on the uneven faggots that did not entirely fill the moat. Crossbow bolts hissed down, and the defenders added stones and lengths of timber that they hurled from the barbican's high rampart. Two more guns fired from the town walls, belching smoke, their stones slashing harmlessly behind the attackers. Trumpets were calling in Harfleur and the crossbows were shooting from the walls. So long as the attackers were close to the barbican they were safe from the missiles loosed from the town, but some men were trying to clamber up the bastion's eroded flanks and there they were in full sight of Harfleur's defenders.

Hook emptied his arrow bag at the men on the barbican's summit, then looked around for a page with more arrows, but could see none. 'Horrocks,' he shouted at his youngest archer, 'go and find arrows!' He saw a wounded archer, not one of his men, sitting a few paces away and he took a handful of arrows from the man's bag and trapped one between his thumb and the bowstave. The English banners were at the foot of the barbican and most of the men-at-arms were on its lower slopes, trying to climb between the flames that burned fiercely to blind the defenders with smoke. It was like trying to scramble up the face of a crumbling bluff, but a bluff in which fires burned and smoke writhed. The French were bellowing defiance. Their best weapons now were the stones they hurled down the face and Hook saw a man-at-arms tumble back, his helmet half crushed by a boulder. The king was there, or at least his standard was bright against the smoke and Hook wondered if the king had been the man he saw falling with a crushed helmet. What would happen if the king died? But at least he was there, in the fight, and Hook felt a surge of pride that England had a fighting king and not some half-mad monarch who circled his body with straps because he believed he was made of glass.

Sir John's banner was on the right now, joined there by the three bells on Sir William Porter's flag. Hook shouted at his men to follow as he ran to the ditch's edge. He jumped in, landing on the corpse of a man in plate armour. A crossbow bolt had pierced the man's aventail, spreading blood from his ravaged throat. Someone had already stripped the body of sword and helmet. Hook negotiated the uncertain faggots and hauled himself up the far side where the smoke was thick. He loosed three arrows, then put his last one across the bowstave. The flames were growing stronger as they fed on the barbican's broken timbers and those fires, designed to blind the defenders, were now a barrier to the attackers. Arrows hissed overhead, evidence that the pages had found more and brought them to the archers, but Hook was too committed to the attack now to go back and replenish his arrow bag. He ran to his right, dodging bodies, unaware of the crossbow bolts that struck around him. He saw Sir John precariously perched on top of some iron-bound timbers from where he stared upwards at the men who taunted the attackers. One of those defenders appeared briefly and hoisted a boulder over his head, ready to hurl it down at Sir John, and Hook paused, drew, released, and his arrow caught the man in his armpit so that he turned slowly and fell back out of sight.

A gust of the east wind swirled the smoke away from the barbican's right-hand flank and Hook saw an opening there, a cave in the half-collapsed tower that had defended the seaward side. He slung the bow and took the poleaxe off his shoulder. He shouted incoherently as he ran, then as he jumped up the barbican's face and scrabbled for a foothold in the steep rubble slope. He was at the right-hand edge of the broken fort and he could see down the southern face of Harfleur where the harbour lay. Defenders on the walls could also see him, and their crossbow bolts thumped into the barbican, but Hook had rolled into the cave that was a ledge of rubble sheltered by collapsed timbers. There was scarce room to move in the space that was little more than a wild dog's den. Now what? Hook wondered. The crossbow bolts were hissing just beyond his shallow refuge. He could hear men shouting and it seemed to Hook that the French shouted louder, evidence they believed they were winning. He leaned slightly outwards trying to get a glimpse of Sir John, but just then an eddy of wind blew a great gout of smoke to shroud Hook's eyrie.

Yet just to his right, towards the face of the barbican, he saw the metal hoops that strapped three great tree trunks together, and the hoops, he thought, made a ladder upwards and the smoke was hiding him and so he leaped across and clung to the timbers with his left hand while his boots found a small foothold on another of the iron rings. He reached up with the poleaxe and hooked it over the top ring and hauled himself up, up, and he was nearly at the top and the French had not seen him because of the smoke and because they were watching the howling mass of Englishmen who were trying to clamber up the barbican's centre where the slope was the least precipitous. Bolts, stones and broken timbers rained down on them, while the English arrows flitted through the smoke in answer.

'Hook!' a voice roared beneath him. 'Hook, you bastard! Pull me up!'

It was Sir John Cornewaille. Hook lowered the poleaxe, let Sir John grip the hammer head and then hauled him across to the timbers.

'You don't get ahead of me, Hook,' Sir John growled, 'and what in Christ's name are you doing here? You're meant to be shooting arrows.'

'I wanted to see what was on the other side of this ruin,' Hook said. Flames crept up the timbers, getting closer to Sir John's feet.

'You wanted to see . . .' Sir John began, then gave a bark of laughter. 'I'm getting goddam roasted. Pull me up more.' Hook again used the poleaxe to lift Sir John, this time to the top of the timbers. The two of them were like flies on a broken, burning pillar, perched just below the makeshift parapet, but still unseen by the defenders. 'Sweet Jesus Christ and all his piss-drinking saints, but this seems a good enough place to die,' Sir John said, and slipped the sling of his battle-axe off his shoulder. 'Are you going to die with me, Hook?'

'Looks like it, Sir John.'

'Good man. Push me up first, then join me, and let's die well, Hook, let's die very well.'

Hook took hold of the back of Sir John's sword belt and, when he got the nod, heaved. Sir John vanished upwards, tumbled over the wall and gave his war-shout. 'Harry and Saint George!' And for Harry, Saint George and Saint Crispinian, Hook followed.

And screamed.

'You won't die here,' Saint Crispinian said.

Hook hardly heard the voice because he was screaming a battle cry that was part terror and part exhilaration.

Hook and Sir John had reached the top of the barbican where the remnants of the fighting platform lay. The English bombardment had shattered the barbican's face so that the earth and rubble filling had spilled out and what had once been the fighting platform was now a crude lumpy space. The rearward wall, looking towards the city's Leure Gate, was much less damaged and served as a screen to hide what happened on the broken, rough summit from the defenders of Harfleur's walls. That summit was now a treacherous heap of earth, stones and burning timbers, which was crammed with crossbowmen and men-at-arms. Hook and Sir John had come from their left flank, and now Sir John attacked the enemy like the avenging angel.

He was fast. That was why he was the most feared tournament fighter in Christendom. In the time it took a man to strike a blow, Sir John gave two. Hook saw it because, once again, it seemed to him that time itself had slowed. He was moving to Sir John's right, aware suddenly that Saint

Crispinian had broken his silence and feeling a great surge of relief that the saint was still his patron. Hook lunged with his poleaxe as Sir John used his double-bladed battle-axe in short brutal strokes. The first smashed the roundel protecting a man-at-arms's knee, the second, a rising slash, gutted a crossbowman, and the third felled the man-at-arms whose knee had been broken. Another man-at-arms turned to drive a sword at Sir John, but Hook's poleaxe sliced into his side, piercing the edge of his breastplate and throwing him back on the men behind. Hook just kept ramming, driving the man back, crushing him into his comrades, and Sir John was making a whooping noise, a sound of pure joy. Hook was screaming, though he was not aware of it, and using his huge archer's strength to push the enemy back while Sir John was taking advantage of their confusion to chop, wound and kill.

Hook wrenched the poleaxe back, but the spear point was trapped in the man's armour. 'Take this!' Sir John said sharply, thrusting the axe at Hook, and later, much later when the fight was over, Hook marvelled at Sir John's utter calm in the middle of a fight. Sir John had seen Hook's predicament and solved it, even though he was under attack himself. He gave Hook the axe and, in the time it took Hook to take it, Sir John drew his sword. It was Sir John's favourite sword, the one he called Darling, and it was a heavier blade than most, strong enough to survive hard lunges into steel plate. Sir John used it to keep the enemy off balance, letting Hook do the killing now. Hook's first blow drove the axe into a helmet, wrenching the whole visor loose so it hung askew. 'Cheap steel!' Sir John said, and his sword flickered at men's faces, making them retreat, and Hook drove the blade into an armoured belly and saw the blood well out bright and fast. 'Flag!' Sir John bellowed. 'Bring me my goddam flag!'

Hook was standing with his feet apart, driving the axe at men who were hardly fighting back. They were hampered by the bodies at their feet and cowed by Sir John's sheer skill and ferocity. A determined man could have attacked into Sir John's sword and Hook's axe, but instead the defenders tried to back away from the blades while the Frenchmen behind pushed them forward. 'Trois!' Sir John was counting the men he had wounded or killed, 'quatre! Come on, you goddam bastards! I'm hungry!' Hook's axe was the more dangerous weapon because of its power. The blade crumpled armour like parchment or chopped into flesh like a slaughterman's cleaver, and Hook was grimacing as he swung and the enemy thought he was smiling, and that smile was more frightening than the blade. The sheer press of Frenchmen made it impossible for their crossbowmen to take aim, while the surviving rear wall and the obscuring smoke hid the fight from the bowmen on the towers of the Leure Gate. Sir John was shouting and Hook was keening a mad noise and their blades were red. Hook was not trying to kill now, he was just thrusting the enemy back and putting men on the ground to make a barrier. A fallen man-at-arms made an upwards cut with his sword, but Hook saw the lunge coming, took a half-step to one side, slammed the axe down hard onto the man's visor, heard the gurgling noise as the heavy blade crushed steel into flesh, swung the axe back to dent a man's breastplate and then rammed the weapon forward to push a third man backwards.

'My flag!' Sir John shouted again, 'I want these bastards to know who's killing them!'

His standard-bearer suddenly tumbled over the wall behind, and with him came more men-at-arms wearing Sir John's lion. 'Kill the bastards!' Sir John screamed, but the bastards had taken enough. They were spilling through a gap in the rearward wall of the barbican and scrambling down a ladder or hurling themselves at a steep slope of spilt rubble before running through the smoke for the town's gate. The rising sun was lighting that smoke. Screaming

Englishmen were killing the last defenders who could not reach the gap in time. One man held out his glove in token of surrender, but an archer beat him down with a long-hafted hammer and another skewered him with a poleaxe.

'Enough!' a voice shouted. 'Enough! Enough!'

'Hold your blows!' Sir John called. 'Hold it, I said!'

'God be thanked!' the man who had first called to end the killing said, and Hook saw it was the king who, sword in hand, suddenly knelt on the rubble and crossed himself. The king's surcoat, its bright badge crossed by Saint George's red, was scorched. A springolt bolt thumped into one of the timbers facing the town, making the wall quiver. 'Extinguish the flames!' the king called, getting to his feet. He pulled off his helmet and its leather liner so that his thick cropped hair stuck up in small, sweat-dark clumps. 'And someone have pity on that man!' He gestured at the Frenchman who had tried to surrender, and who now writhed and moaned as blood soaked the faulds just beneath his breastplate. The poleaxe was still embedded in his belly. A man-at-arms drew a knife, felt for the gap in the armour protecting the dying man's throat and stabbed home once before working the blade around inside the gullet. The man convulsed, blood bubbled from the holes in his dented visor, then he gave a spasm and was still. 'God be thanked,' the king said again. An archer suddenly fell to his knees and Hook thought the man was praying, but instead he vomited. Crossbow bolts were striking the barbican's rear wall, their strikes sounding like flails beating on a threshing floor. The king's banner was flying from the barbican now and the heavy cloth twitched as the bolts ripped and tore at the weave. 'Sir John,' the king said, 'I must thank you.'

'For doing my duty, sire?' Sir John asked, going to one knee, 'and this man helped,' he added, gesturing at Hook.

Hook also dropped to one knee. The king gave him a

glance, but showed no recognition. 'My thanks to you all,' Henry said curtly, then turned away. 'Send heralds!' he ordered one of his entourage, 'and tell them to yield the town! And bring water for the flames!'

Water was poured on the flames, but the fire had penetrated deep into the barbican's shattered timbers and they smouldered on, seeping a constant and choking smoke about the captured bastion. Its ragged summit was garrisoned by archers now, and that night they manhandled the Messenger, one of the smaller cannon, up to its summit, and that gun splintered the timbers of the Leure Gate with its first shot.

The heralds had ridden to that gate after the barbican's capture, and they had patiently explained that the English would now demolish the great gate and its towers and that the fall of Harfleur was thus inevitable, and that the garrison should therefore do the sensible, even the honourable, thing and surrender before more men died. If they refused to surrender, the heralds declared, then the law of God decreed that every man, woman and child in Harfleur would be given to the pleasure of the English. 'Think of your pretty daughters,' a herald called to the garrison's commanders, 'and for their sake, yield!'

But the garrison would not surrender, and so the English dug new gun-pits closer to the town, and they hammered the exposed Leure Gate, demolishing the towers on either side and bringing down its stone arch, yet still the defenders fought back.

And the first chill wind of summer's end brought rain.

And the sickness did not end and Henry's army died in blood, vomit and watery shit.

And Harfleur remained French.

It all had to be done again. Another assault, this time on the wreckage of the Leure Gate and, to make sure the defenders could not concentrate their men on that southwestern corner of the ramparts, the forces of the Duke of Clarence would assault the Montivilliers Gate on the town's far side.

This time, Sir John said, they were going into the town. 'The goddam bastards won't surrender! So you know what you can do with the bastards! If it's got a prick, you kill it, if it's got tits, you hump it! Everything in that town is yours! Every coin, every ale-pot, every woman! They're yours! Now go and get them!'

And so the twin assaults streamed across the filled-in ditches and the arrows rained from the sky and the trumpets blared a challenge to the uncaring sun and the killing began again. And again it was Sir John Holland who led, which meant that Sir John Cornewaille's men were in the front of the attack that swiftly captured the ruins of the Leure Gate and there, abruptly, were stopped.

The gate had once led into a closely-packed street of over-hanging houses, but the garrison had pulled those buildings down to clear a killing space, behind which they had made a new barricade that had been mostly protected from the English gun-stones by the remnants of the old wall and gate. The Messenger, mounted on the barbican's summit, had managed to shoot some stones at the fresh work, but it could only manage three shots a day and the French repaired the damage between each shot. The new wall was built from masonry blocks, roof timbers and rubble-filled baskets, and behind it were crossbowmen, and as soon as the English men-at-arms appeared across the ruin of the Leure Gate the bolts began to fly.

Archers shot back, but the French had been cunning. The new wall had been made with chinks and holes through which the crossbowmen could shoot, and which were small enough to defeat the aim of most arrows. Hook, crouching in the rubble of the old gate, reckoned that for every crossbowman shooting there were another three or four men spanning spare bows so that the bolts never stopped. Most crossbowmen were lucky to shoot two bolts a minute, but the bolts were coming from the loopholes far more frequently and still more missiles spat from the high windows of the half-ruined houses behind the wall. This, Hook knew, was how Soissons should have been defended.

'We'll have to bring up a gun,' Sir John snarled from another place in the ruined wall, but instead led a charge against the barricade, shouting at his archers to smother it in arrows. They did, but the crossbow bolts kept coming and even if the bolts failed to pierce armour they threw a man back by sheer force and when, at last, a half-dozen men managed to reach the wall and tried to pull down its timbers and stones, a cauldron was tipped over its coping and a stream of boiling fish oil spilled down onto the attackers. They ran and limped back, some gasping from the pain of the scalding, and Sir John, his armour slick with the oil, came back with them and dropped into the gate's rubble and let loose a stream of impotent curses. The French were cheering. They waved taunting flags above their new low wall. A smoky haze shimmered behind the new rampart, promising that more heated oil would greet any new attack. The English catapults were trying to drop stones on the new wall, but most of the missiles flew long to crash down among the already shattered houses.

The sun climbed. The late summer's heat had returned and both attackers and defenders roasted in their armour. Boys brought water and ale. Men-at-arms, resting in the shelter of the Leure Gate's ruins, took off their helmets. Their hair was matted flat and their faces running with sweat. The archers crouched in the stones, sometimes shooting if a man showed himself, but for long periods neither side would loose an arrow or a bolt, but just wait for a target.

261

'Bastards,' Sir John spat at the enemy.

Hook saw two defenders struggling to remove an earth-filled basket from a section of the new wall. He half stood and loosed an arrow, just as a dozen other archers did the same. The two men fell back, each struck by arrows, but the basket fell with them and Hook saw a cannon barrel, squat and low, and he flattened himself in the gate's ruins just as the cannon fired. The air whistled and screamed, stone chips were whipping in smoke, and a man gave a terrible long cry that turned to a whimper as the space in front of the wall was obscured by the thick smoke. 'Oh, my God,' Will of the Dale said.

'You hurt, Will?'

'No. Just tired of this place.'

The French had loaded their cannon with a mass of small stones that had flayed the attackers. A man-at-arms was dead, a small hole punched clean through the top of his helmet. An archer staggered back towards the barbican, one hand clamped over an empty, bloody eye socket.

'We're all going to die here,' Will said.

'No,' Hook said fiercely, though he did not believe his protest. The gun smoke cleared slowly and Hook saw that the earth-filled basket was back in its embrasure.

'Bastards,' Sir John spat again.

'We're not giving up!' the king was shouting. He wanted to assemble a mass of men-at-arms and attempt to over-whelm the wall with numbers and his men were carrying orders to the Englishmen scattered in the old wall's ruins. 'Archers to the flanks!' a man shouted, 'to the flanks!'

A French trumpeter began playing a short sharp melody. It was three notes, rising and falling, repeated over and over. There was something taunting in the sound.

'Kill that bastard!' Sir John shouted, but the bastard was hidden behind the wall.

'Move!' the king shouted.

Hook took a deep breath, then scrambled to his right. No crossbow bolts spat from the defences. The garrison was waiting, he thought. Perhaps they were running short of bolts and so they were keeping what they had to greet the next assault. He sheltered by a stub of broken wall and just then the French trumpeter stood on the new rampart and raised his instrument to his lips, and Hook stood too, and the cord came back to his right ear, he loosed, and the string whipped his bracer and the goose-fledged arrow flew true and the bodkin point took the trumpeter in the throat and drove clean through his neck so that it stood proud at his nape. The braying trumpet screeched horribly and then ended abruptly as the man fell backwards. More English arrows flitted above him as he disappeared behind the wall, leaving a fading spray of misted blood and the dying echo of the trumpet's truncated call.

'Well done, that archer!' Sir John shouted.

Hook waited. The day became still hotter under a sun that was a great furnace in a sky clouded only by the shreds of smoke from the beleaguered city. The French had stopped shooting altogether, which only convinced Hook that they were saving their missiles for the assault they knew was coming. Priests picked their way among the ruins of the old wall, shriving the dead and the dying, while behind the wall, in the space between the ruined Leure Gate and the shattered barbican, the men-at-arms assembled under their lords' banners. That force, at least four hundred strong, was easily visible to the defenders, but still they did not shoot.

One of Sir John's pages, a boy of ten or eleven with a shock of bright blond hair and wide blue eyes, brought two skins of water to the archers. 'We need arrows, boy,' Hook told him.

'I'll bring some,' the boy said.

Hook tipped the skin to his mouth. 'Why aren't the men-at-arms moving?' he asked no one in particular. The king had assembled his assault force and the archers were in place, but a curious lassitude had settled over the attackers.

'A messenger came,' the page said nervously. He was a high-born lad, sent to Sir John's household to learn a warrior's ways, and in time he would doubtless be a great lord in shining armour mounted on a caparisoned horse, but for now he was nervous of the hard-faced archers who would one day be under his command.

'A messenger?'

'From the Duke of Clarence,' the page said, taking back the water-skin.

The duke, camped on the far side of Harfleur, was also attacking the city, though no sounds betrayed any fighting from that far-off gate. 'So what did the messenger tell us?' Hook asked the page.

'That the attack failed,' the boy said.

'Sweet Jesus,' Hook said in disgust. So now, he reckoned, the king was waiting until his brother could mount another assault, and then the English would make one last effort, from both east and west, to overwhelm the stubborn defenders. And so Hook and his archers waited. If the king had sent new orders to his brother then they would take at least two hours to reach him, for the messenger had to ride far around the city's north side and cross the flooded river by boat.

'What's happening?' Sclate, the slow-witted labourer with a giant's strength, asked.

'I don't know,' Hook confessed. Sweat trickled down his face and stung his eyes. The air seemed to be filled with dust that coated his throat and made him thirsty again. The light, reflecting from the shattered chalk of the broken walls, was dazzling. He was tired. He unstrung the bow to take the tension from the stave.

'Are we attacking again?' Sclate asked.

'I reckon we attack when the duke assaults the far side,' Hook suggested. 'Be a couple of hours yet.'

'They'll be ready for us,' Sclate said gloomily.

The garrison would be ready. Ready with cannons and crossbows and springolts and boiling oil. That was what waited for the men wearing the red cross. The men-at-arms were sitting now, resting before they were ordered into the killing ground. The bright banners hung slack from their poles and a strange silence wrapped Harfleur. Waiting. Waiting.

'When we attack!' Sir John's voice broke the silence. He was striding along the front of the sheltering archers, careless that he was fully exposed to the enemy, but the French crossbowmen, doubtless under orders to conserve their bolts, ignored him. 'When we attack,' he called again, 'you advance! You keep shooting! But you keep going forward! When we go over the wall I want archers with us! We're going to have to hunt these bastards through their goddam streets! I want you all there! And good hunting! This is a day to kill our king's enemies, so kill them!'

And when the killing was done, Hook wondered, how many English would be left? The army that had sailed from Southampton Water had been small enough, but now? Now, he reckoned, there would just be half an army, many of them sick men, crammed into the ruins of Harfleur as the French army at last stirred itself to fight. Rumours said that enemy army was vast, a horde of men eager to wipe out the impudent English invaders, though God seemed to be doing that already by sickness.

'Let's get it over with,' Will of the Dale grumbled.

'Or let them keep the goddam town,' Tom Scarlet suggested, 'it's a shit-heap now.'

And what if the assault failed? Hook wondered. What if

Harfleur did not fall? Then the remnants of Henry's army would sail back to England, defeated. The campaign had begun so well, with all the panoply of banners and hope, and now it was blood and faeces and despair.

Another trumpeter began playing the same mocking notes from the city. Sir John, stalking back past his archers, turned and snarled towards the defenders. 'I want that prick-sucking bastard killed! I want him killed!' The last four words were screamed at the wall, loud enough for any Frenchmen to hear.

Then, unexpectedly, a man clambered onto the wall's top. He was not the trumpeter, who still blew from his place behind the wall. The man on the wall was unarmed, and he stood and waved both hands at the English.

Archers stood, began to draw.

'No!' Sir John bellowed. 'No! No! No! Bows down! Bows down! Bows down!'

The trumpet note wavered, faded and stopped.

The man on the wall held his empty hands high above his head.

And, miraculously, suddenly, astonishingly, it was all over.

The soldiers of Harfleur's garrison did not want to surrender, but the townspeople had suffered enough. They were hungry. Their houses had been crushed and burned by English missiles, disease was spreading, they saw an inevitable defeat and knew that vengeful enemies would rape their daughters. The town council insisted that the city yield and, without the support of the men of Harfleur who shot crossbows from the walls and without the food prepared by the women, the garrison could not prolong the fight.

The Sire de Gaucourt, who had led the defence, asked for a three-day truce in which he could send a messenger to the French king to discover whether or not a relief force was coming to the city's help. If not, then he would surrender on condition that the English army did not sack and rape the town. Henry agreed, and so priests and nobles gathered at the breach by the Leure Gate, and the leading men came from the town, and they all swore solemn oaths to abide by the terms of the truce. Afterwards, and after Henry had taken hostages to ensure that the garrison kept its word, a herald rode close under the walls and shouted up at the townsfolk who had watched the ceremony. He called in French. 'You have nothing to fear! The King of England has not come to destroy you! We are good Christians and Harfleur is not Soissons! You have nothing to fear!'

Smoke drifted from the city to haze the late summer sky. It seemed strange that no guns fired, that no trebuchets thumped as they launched their missiles, and that the fighting had stopped. The dying did not stop. The corpses were still carried to the creeks and thrown to the gulls, and it seemed there would be no end to the sickness.

And there was no French relief force.

The French army was gathering to the east, but the message came back that it would not march to relieve Harfleur and so, on the next Sunday, the feast of Saint Vincent, the city surrendered.

A pavilion was erected on the hillside behind the English encampment and a throne was placed under the canopy and draped with cloth of gold. English banners flanked the pavilion, which was filled with the high nobility in their finest clothes. A man held aloft the king's great helm, which was ringed with a golden crown, while archers lined a long path that led across the rubble of the siege-works to the ruined gate that had resisted so many attacks. Behind the archers were the rest of Henry's army, spectators to the day's drama.

The King of England, crowned with a simple circlet of

gold and wearing a surcoat blazoned with the French royal coat of arms, sat enthroned in silence. He was watching and waiting, and perhaps wondering what he must do next. He had come to Normandy and won this surrender, but that victory had cost him half his army.

Hook was at the Leure Gate where Sir John commanded a force of ten men-at-arms and forty archers. Sir John, clad in plate armour that had been scoured to a shine, was mounted on his great destrier, Lucifer, who had been draped in a dazzling linen trapper resplendent with Sir John's crest, and the same lion was modelled in painted wood to rear savagely from the crest of Sir John's helmet. The men-at-arms were also in armour, but the archers were in leather jerkins and stained breeches. All the bowmen carried halters of rough rope, the kind that a peasant might use to lead a cow to market. 'Treat them courteously,' Sir John told his bowmen. 'They fought well! They're men!'

'I thought they were all scum-sucking cabbage shitters,' Will of the Dale said quietly, but not quietly enough.

Sir John turned Lucifer. 'They are that!' he said, 'but they fought like Englishmen! So treat them like Englishmen!'

A section of the new wall had been demolished and, just after Sir John spoke, some three dozen men emerged from the gap. They had been ordered to approach the King of England barefoot and in plain linen shirts and hose. Now, nervous and apprehensive, they walked slowly and cautiously towards the waiting archers.

'Nooses!' Sir John ordered.

Hook and the other archers tied nooses in the ropes. Sir John beckoned a squire and handed his reins to the man, then slid out of his tall saddle. He patted Lucifer on the nose, then walked towards the approaching Frenchmen.

He singled out one man, a tall man with a hooked nose and a short black beard. The man was pale, and Hook guessed he was sick, but he was forcing himself to lead the Frenchmen out of the town and to keep what small dignity he had left. The bearded man beckoned to his companions to pause while he approached Sir John alone. The two men stopped a pace apart, the Englishman glorious in armour and heraldry, his sword hilt polished, his armour gleaming, while the Frenchman was in the common, ill-fitting clothes decreed by King Henry. Sir John, his visor raised, said something that Hook did not catch, then the two men embraced.

Sir John left his right arm about the Frenchman's shoulders as he led him towards the archers. 'This is the Sire de Gaucourt,' he announced, 'the leader of our enemies these last five weeks, and he has fought bravely! He deserves better than this, but our king commands and we must obey. Hook, give me the noose!'

Hook held out the halter. The Frenchman gave him an appraising look and Hook felt compelled to nod his head in respectful acknowledgement.

'I am sorry,' Sir John said in French.

'It is necessary,' Raoul de Gaucourt said harshly.

'Is it?' Sir John asked.

'We must be humiliated so that the rest of France knows what fate waits for them if they resist your king,' de Gaucourt said. He gave a wan smile then cast an appraising eye over the English army that waited to watch his humiliating walk to the king's throne. 'Though I doubt your king has the power to frighten France any more,' he went on. 'You call this a victory, Sir John?' he asked, beckoning at the battered walls he had defended so bravely. Sir John did not answer. Instead he lifted the noose to place it about de Gaucourt's head, but the Frenchman took it from him. 'Allow me,' he said, and put the rope about his own neck.

The other Frenchmen had ropes placed about their necks, and then Sir John, satisfied, pulled himself back into Lucifer's

269

saddle. He nodded to de Gaucourt, then spurred his horse along the path made between the watching English soldiers.

The Frenchmen walked the path in silence. Some, the merchants, were old men, while others, mostly soldiers, were young and strong. They were the knights and burgesses, the men who had defied the King of England, and the nooses about their necks proclaimed that their lives were now at Henry's mercy. They climbed the hillside, then knelt humbly before the throne canopied in cloth of gold. Henry gazed at them a long time. The wind lifted the silk banners and drifted smoke from the city's ruins. The assembled English nobles waited, expecting the king to announce the death sentence on the kneeling men. 'I am the rightful king of this realm,' Henry said, 'and your resistance was treason.'

A look of pain showed briefly on de Gaucourt's face. He ignored the accusation of treason and instead held out a thick bunch of heavy keys. 'The keys of Harfleur, sire,' he said, 'which are yours.'

The king did not take the offered keys. 'Your defiance,' he said sternly, 'was contrary to man's law and to God's law.' Some of the older merchants were shaking in fear and one had tears running down his face. 'But God,' Henry went on loftily, 'is merciful.' He lifted the keys at last, 'and we shall be merciful. Your lives are not forfeit.'

A cheer sounded from the English army when the cross of Saint George was hoisted over the town. Next day Henry of England walked barefoot to the church of Saint Martin to give thanks to God for a victory, yet many who watched his humble pilgrimage reckoned that his triumph was a virtual defeat. He had wasted so much time before Harfleur's walls and the sickness had torn his army apart, and the campaign season was almost over.

The English army moved inside the walls. They burned their encampment and dragged catapults and cannon through

270

the ruined gate. Sir John's men quartered themselves in a row of houses, taverns and warehouses beside the wall-enclosed harbour where Hook found space in the attic of a tavern called *Le Paon*. '*Le paon* is a bird,' Melisande had explained, 'with a big tail!' She had spread her arms wide.

'No bird's got a tail that big!' Hook said.

'*Le paon* does,' she insisted.

'Must be a French bird then,' Hook said, 'not an English one.'

Harfleur was now English. The cross of Saint George flew from the ruined stump of Saint Martin's tower, and the people of the city, who had suffered so much, were now given more suffering.

They were expelled. The city, the king declared, would be resettled by English people, just as Calais had been, and to make room for those new inhabitants over two thousand men, women and children were driven from the city. The sick were taken in carts, the rest walked, and two hundred mounted Englishmen guarded the sad column's progress along the north bank of the Seine. The English soldiers were there to protect the refugees from their own countrymen who would otherwise have robbed and raped. Men-at-arms led the procession and archers flanked it.

Hook was one of the archers. He had been reunited with his black gelding, Raker, who was fretful and needed constant curbing. Hook's surcoat was washed clean, though the red cross of Saint George had faded to a dull pink. Beneath the surcoat he wore a coat of good mail that he had taken from a French corpse and an aventail that Sir John had given him, and over the aventail's hood he now had a bascinet that was another gift from a corpse. The bascinet was a helmet with a wide brim designed to deflect a downwards blade, though like other archers Hook had hacked off the brim on the right side to make a space for his bow's cord when he drew it to the full. His sword hung at his side, his cased bow was slung across his shoulder, while his arrow bag hung from the saddle's cantle. To his right, beyond the refugees, the narrowing river rippled sun-bright, while to the left were meadows stripped of livestock by English forage parties and, beyond those pastures, gentle wooded hills still heavy in their full summer leaf. Melisande had stayed in Harfleur, but Father Christopher had insisted on accompanying the refugees. He was mounted on Sir John's great destrier, Lucifer. Sir John wanted the horse exercised, and Father Christopher was happy to oblige. 'You shouldn't have come, father,' Hook told him.

'You're a doctor of medicine now, Hook?'

'You're supposed to rest, father.'

'There'll be rest enough in heaven,' Father Christopher said happily. He was still pale, but he was eating again. He was wearing a priest's robe, something he had done more frequently since his recovery. 'I learned something during that illness,' the priest said in apparent seriousness.

'Aye? What was that?'

'In heaven, Hook, there will be no shitting.'

Hook laughed. 'But will there be women, father?'

'In abundance, young Hook, but what if they're all good women?'

'You mean the bad ones will all be in the devil's cellar, father?'

'That is a worry,' Father Christopher said with a smile, 'but I trust God to make suitable arrangements.' He grinned, happy to be alive and riding under a September sun beside a hedge thick with blackberries. A corncrake's grating cry echoed from the hills. Just after dawn, when the protesting refugees had been forced out of Harfleur, a stag had appeared on the Rouen road resplendent in his new antlers. Hook had taken it as a good omen, but Father Christopher, looking up at the dark branches of a dead elm tree, now found a gloomy one. 'The swallows are gathering early,' he said.

'A bad winter then,' Hook said.

'It means summer's end, Hook, and with it go our hopes. Like those swallows, we will disappear.'

'Back to England?'

'And to disappointment,' the priest said sadly. 'The king has debts to pay, and he can't pay them. If he had carried home a victory then it wouldn't matter.'

'We won, father,' Hook said, 'we captured Harfleur.'

'We used a pack of wolfhounds to kill a hare,' Father Christopher said, 'and out there,' he nodded eastwards, 'there's a much larger pack of hounds gathering.'

Some of that larger pack appeared at midday. The front of the long column of refugees had stopped in some meadows beside the river and now the tail of the column crowded in behind them. What had checked their progress was a band of enemy horsemen who barred the road where it led through the gate of a walled town. The townsfolk watched from the walls. The enemy had a single banner, a great white flag on which a red and double-headed eagle spread its long talons. The French men-at-arms were dressed for battle, their polished armour gleaming beneath bright surcoats, but few wore helmets and those who did had their visors raised, a clear sign that they expected no fighting. Hook guessed there were a hundred enemy and they were here under an arranged truce to receive the refugees, who were to be taken to Rouen in a fleet of barges that was moored on the river's northern bank. 'Dear God,' Father Christopher said, staring at the eagle banner, which lifted and fell in the wind that drove ripples across the river. 'That's the marshal,' Father Christopher explained, making the sign of the cross.

'The marshal?'

'Jean de Maingre, Lord of Boucicault, Marshal of France,'

Father Christopher said the name and titles slowly, his voice betraying admiration for the man who wore the badge of the double-headed eagle.

'Never heard of him, father,' Hook said cheerfully.

'France is ruled by a madman,' the priest said, 'and the royal dukes are young and headstrong, but our enemies do have the marshal, and the marshal is a man to fear.'

Sir William Porter, Sir John Cornewaille's brother-in-arms, led the English contingent and he now rode bareheaded to greet the marshal who, in turn, spurred his destrier towards Sir William. The Frenchman, who was a big man on a tall horse, towered over the Englishman as the two spoke, and Hook, watching from a distance, thought they laughed together. Then, invited by a gesture from the courtly Sir William, the Marshal of France kicked his horse towards the English troops. He ignored the French civilians and instead rode slowly down the ragged line of men-at-arms and archers.

The marshal wore no helmet. His hair was dark brown, cut bluntly short and greying at the temples, and it framed a face of such ferocity that Hook was taken aback. It was a square, blunt face, scarred and broken, beaten by battle and by life, but undefeated. A hard face, a man's face, a warrior's face, with keen dark eyes that searched men and horses for clues to their condition. His mouth was set in a grim line, but suddenly smiled when he saw Father Christopher, and in the smile Hook saw a man who might inspire other men to great loyalty and victory. 'A priest on a destrier!' the marshal said, amused. 'We mount our priests on knackered mares, not on war chargers!'

'We English have so many destriers, sire,' Father Christopher answered, 'that we can spare them for men of God.'

The marshal looked appraisingly at Lucifer. 'A good horse,' he said, 'whose is it?'

'Sir John Cornewaille's,' the priest answered.

'Ah!' the marshal was pleased. 'You will give the good Sir John my compliments! Tell him I am glad he has visited France and that I hope he will carry fond memories of it back to England. And that he will carry them very soon.' The marshal smiled at Father Christopher, then looked at Hook with apparent interest, taking in the archer's weapons and armour, before holding out a steel-gauntleted hand. 'Do me the honour,' he said, 'and lend me your bow.'

Father Christopher translated for Hook who had under-stood anyway, but had not responded because he was not certain quite what he should do. 'Let him have the bow, Hook,' Father Christopher said, 'and string it first.'

Hook uncased the great stave, placed its lower end in his left stirrup and looped the noose about the upper nock. He could feel the raw power in the tensed yew stave. It some-times seemed to him that the wood came alive when he strung the bow. It seemed to quiver in anticipation. The marshal was still holding out his hand and Hook stretched the bow towards him.

'It is a large bow,' Boucicault said in very careful English.

'One of the largest I've seen,' Father Christopher said, 'and it's carried by a very strong archer.'

A dozen French men-at-arms had followed the marshal and they watched from a few paces away as he held the stave in his left hand and tentatively pulled on the string with his right. His eyebrows lifted in surprise at the effort it took, and he gave Hook an appreciative glance. He looked back to the bow, hesitated, then raised it as though there were an imaginary arrow on the string. He took a breath, then pulled.

English archers watched, half smiling, knowing that only a trained archer could pull such a bow to the full draw. The cord went back halfway and stopped, then Boucicault hauled again and the string kept going back, back until it had reached

275

his mouth, and Hook could see the strain showing on the Frenchman's face, but Boucicault was not finished. He gave a small grimace, pulled again, and the cord went all the way to his right ear, and he held it there at the full draw and looked at Hook with a raised eyebrow.

Hook could not help it. He laughed, and suddenly the English archers were cheering the French marshal, whose face showed pure delight as he slowly relaxed his grip and handed the bow back to Hook. Hook, grinning, took the stave and half bowed in his saddle. 'Englishman,' Boucicault called, 'here!' he tossed Hook a coin and, still smiling delightedly, rode on down the line of applauding archers.

'I told you,' Father Christopher said, smiling, 'he's a man.'

'A generous man,' Hook said, staring at the coin. It was gold, the size of a shilling, and he guessed it was worth a year's wages. He pushed the gold into his pouch, which held spare arrowheads and three spare cords.

'A good and generous man,' Father Christopher agreed, 'but not a man to be your enemy.'

'Nor am I,' a voice intruded, and Hook twisted in his saddle to see that one of the men-at-arms who had followed the marshal was the Sire de Lanferelle who now leaned on his saddle's pommel to stare at Hook. He looked down at Hook's missing finger and a suggestion of a smile showed on his face. 'Are you my son-in-law yet?'

'No, sire,' Hook said and named Lanferelle to Father Christopher.

The Frenchman looked speculatively at the priest. 'You've been ill, father.'

'I have,' Father Christopher agreed.

'Is this a judgement of God? Did He in His mercy strike your army as a punishment for your king's wickedness?'

'Wickedness?' Father Christopher asked gently.

'In coming to France,' Lanferelle said, then straightened

in his saddle. His hair was oiled so that it hung sleek, raven black and shining to his waist, which was encircled by a silver-plated sword belt. His face, so strikingly handsome, was even darker after a summer in the sun, making his eyes seem unnaturally bright. 'Yet I hope you stay in France, father.'

'Is that an invitation?'

'It is!' Lanferelle smiled, showing very white teeth. 'How many men do you have now?'

'We are counted as the grains of sand on the seashore,' the priest answered blithely, 'and are as numerous as the multitudinous stars of the firmament, and are as many as the biting fleas in a French whore's crotch.'

'And just about as dangerous,' Lanferelle said, unbitten by the priest's defiant words. 'You number what? Fewer than ten thousand now? And I hear your king is sending the sick men home?'

'He sends men home,' Father Christopher said, 'because we have enough to do whatever must be done.'

Hook wondered how Lanferelle knew that the sick were being sent home, then supposed that French spies must be watching Harfleur from the surrounding hills and would have seen the litters being carried onto the English ships that could at last come right into the walled harbour.

'And your king brings in reinforcements,' Lanferelle said, 'but how many of his men must he leave in Harfleur to protect its broken walls? A thousand?' He smiled again. 'It is such a little army, father.'

'But at least it fights,' Father Christopher said, 'whereas your army slumbers in Rouen.'

'But our army,' Lanferelle said, his voice suddenly harsh, 'truly does number as the fleas in a Parisian whore's crotch.' He gathered his reins. 'I do hope you stay, father, and come to where the fleas can feed on English blood.' He nodded to

Hook. 'Give Melisande my compliments. And give her something else.' He turned in his saddle. 'Jean! *Venez!*' The same dull-faced squire who had gazed at Melisande in the woods above Harfleur spurred to his master and, on Lanferelle's orders, fumbled his jupon over his head. The Sire de Lanferelle took the gaudy garment with its bright sun and proud falcon and folded it into a square that he threw at Hook. 'If it comes to a battle,' he said, 'tell Melisande to wear that. It might be sufficient to protect her. I would regret her death. Good day to you both.' And with that he rode on after the marshal.

Clouds gathered the next day, piling above the sea and slowly drifting to make a pall over Harfleur. The archers were busy making temporary repairs to the breached walls, building timber palisades that must serve as a defence until masons came from England to remake the ramparts properly. Men were still falling ill and the battered streets stank of sewage that oozed into the River Lézarde that once again ran free through a stone channel bisecting the town, and thence into the tight harbour that smelt like a cesspit.

The king sent a challenge to the dauphin, offering to fight him face-to-face and the winner would inherit the crown of France from the mad King Charles. 'He won't accept,' Sir John Cornewaille said. Sir John had come to watch the archers pound stakes into the ground to support the new palisade. 'The dauphin's a fat, lazy bastard, and our Henry is a warrior. It would be like a wolf fighting a piglet.'

'And if the dauphin doesn't agree to fight, Sir John?' Thomas Evelgold asked.

'We'll go home, I suppose,' Sir John said unhappily. That was the opinion throughout the army. The days were shortening and becoming colder, and soon the autumn rains would arrive and that would mean the end of the campaign season. And even if Henry had wanted to continue the campaign his army was too small and the French army was too big, and sensible men, experienced men, declared that only a fool would dare defy those odds. 'If we had another six or seven thousand men,' Sir John said, 'I dare say we could bloody their goddam noses, but we won't. We'll leave a garrison to hold this shit-hole and the rest of us will sail home.'

Reinforcements still arrived, but they were not many, not nearly enough to make up the numbers who had died or who were sick, but the boats brought them into the stinking harbour and the uncertain newcomers came down the gangplanks to stare wide-eyed at the broken roofs and the shattered churches and the scorched rubble. 'Most of us will be going home soon,' Sir John told his men, 'and the newcomers can defend Harfleur.' He spoke sourly. The capture of Harfleur was not enough to compensate for the money spent and the lives lost. Sir John wanted more, as rumour said the king did, but every other great lord, the royal dukes, the earls, the bishops, the captains, all advised the king to go home.

'There's no choice,' Thomas Evelgold told Hook one evening. The great lords were at a council of war, meeting the king in an attempt to beat sense into his ambitious head, and the army waited on the council's decision. It was a beautiful evening, a sinking sun casting shadows long over the harbour. Hook and Evelgold were sitting at a table outside *Le Paon*, drinking ale that had been brought from England because the breweries of Harfleur had all been destroyed. 'We have to go home,' Evelgold said, evidently thinking of the heated discussion that was doubtless being waged in the guild hall beside Saint Martin's church.

'Maybe we stay as part of the garrison?' Hook suggested.

'Christ, no!' Evelgold said harshly, then crossed himself. 'That goddam great army of the French? They'll take this town back with no trouble! They'll beat down our palisades in three days, then kill every man here.'

Hook said nothing. He was watching the harbour's narrow entrance where an arriving ship was being propelled by huge sweeps because the wind had fallen to a whisper. Gulls wheeled above the ship's single mast and over her high, richly gilded castles. 'The *Holy Ghost*,' Evelgold said, nodding at the ship.

The *Holy Ghost* was a new ship, built with the king's money to support his invading army, but now she was chiefly employed in taking diseased men home to England. She crept closer and closer to the quay. Hook could see men on her deck, but they were not nearly as many as the ship had brought on her previous voyage and he guessed these might be the last reinforcements to arrive.

'Fifteen hundred ships brought us here,' Evelgold said, 'but we won't need that many to take us home.' He laughed bitterly. 'What a waste of a goddamned summer.' The sun glinted reflections from the gilding on the *Holy Ghost*'s two castles. The passengers on board stared at the shore. 'Welcome to Normandy,' Evelgold said. 'Will your woman go back to England?'

'She will.'

'Thought you were getting married?'

'I think we are.'

'Do it in England, Hook.'

'Why England?'

'Because it's God's country, not like this goddam place.'

Centenars and men-at-arms had come to the quay to discover if any of the newcomers belonged to their companies. Lord Slayton's centenar, William Snoball, was one of them, and he greeted Hook civilly. 'I'm surprised to see you here, Master Snoball,' Hook said.

'Why?'

'Who's stewarding while you're here?'

'John Willetts. He can manage well enough without me. And his lordship wanted me to come.'

'Because you've got experience,' Evelgold put in.

'Aye there's that,' Snoball agreed, 'and his lordship wanted me to keep an eye on,' he hesitated, 'well, you know.'

'Sir Martin?' Hook asked. 'And why in God's name did he send him?'

'Why do you think?' Snoball answered harshly.

Hook mimed drawing a knife across his throat. 'Is that what he hopes?'

'He hopes Sir Martin will minister to our souls,' Snoball said distantly and then, perhaps thinking he had betrayed too much, walked some distance down the wharf.

Hook watched the *Holy Ghost* creep closer. 'Are we expecting any new men?' he asked.

'None that I know of, Sir John hasn't said anything.'

'He's not happy,' Hook said.

'Because he's crazy, moon-touched. Daft as a hare.' Thomas Evelgold brooded for a moment. 'He wants to march into France! Man's daft! He wants us all dead! But it's all right for him, isn't it?'

'All right?'

'He won't be killed, will he? What happens if we march into France to find a battle? The gentry don't get killed, Hook, they get taken prisoner! But no one will ransom you and me. We get slaughtered, Hook, while their lordships go off to some comfortable castle and get fed and given whores. Sir John don't care. He just wants a fight! But he knows he'll like as not live through a battle. He should give a thought to us.' Evelgold drained his ale. 'Still, won't happen. We'll all be home by Saint Martin's feast day.'

'The king wants to march,' Hook said.

'The king can count as well as you and me,' Evelgold said dismissively, 'and he won't march.'

Lines were hurled from the *Holy Ghost* to be caught by men ashore, and slowly, laboriously, the great ship was hauled in to the quay. Gangplanks were lowered and then the newcomers, looking unnaturally clean, were chivvied ashore. There were around sixty archers, all carrying cased bows, arrow bags and bundles. The red crosses of Saint George on their jupons looked very bright. A priest came down the nearer gangplank, fell to his knees on the wharf and made the sign of the cross. Behind him were four archers wearing the Slayton moon and stars and one of them had springy gold hair sticking wildly from beneath his helmet's brim. For a heartbeat Hook did not believe what he saw, then he stood and shouted. 'Michael! Michael!'

It was his younger brother. Michael saw him and grinned. 'My brother,' Hook explained to Evelgold, then strode to meet Michael. They embraced. 'My God, it is you,' Hook said.

William Snoball called Michael's name, but Hook turned on the steward. 'He'll come when he's ready, Master Snoball. Where are you quartered?'

Snoball grudgingly told him and Hook promised to bring his brother, then took Michael to the table and poured a pot of ale. Thomas Evelgold left them alone. 'What in God's name are you doing here?' Hook demanded.

'Lord Slayton sent his last archers,' Michael said, grinning, 'he reckoned you all needed help. I didn't even know you were here!'

Then there was a catching up of news. Hook said that Robert Perrill had been killed in the siege, though he did not say how, and Michael told how their grandmother had died, a fact that did not trouble Hook in the least. 'She was a bitter old bitch,' he said.

'She looked after us, though,' Michael said.

'She looked after you, not me.'

Then Melisande came from the tavern and she was introduced, and Hook felt a sudden, wild and unfamiliar happiness. The two people he loved most were with him, and he had money in his pockets, and all seemed well with the world. The campaign in France might be over, and over before it had gained any great victory, but he was still happy. 'I'll ask Sir John if you can join us,' he told Michael.

'I don't think Lord Slayton will allow that,' Michael said.

'Aye, well, we can only ask.'

'So what's going to happen here?' Michael wanted to know.

'I reckon some poor bastards will be left here to defend this town,' Hook said, 'and the rest of us will go home.'

'Go home?' Michael frowned. 'But we just got here!'

'That's what folk are saying. The lords are trying to make the decision now, but it's too late in the year to go marching inland and, besides, the French army's too big. We'll be going home.'

'I hope not,' Michael said. He grinned. 'I didn't come this far to go home again. I want to fight.'

'No, you don't,' Hook said, and surprised himself by saying it. Melisande was also surprised, looking at him curiously.

'I don't?'

'It's blood,' Hook said, 'and men crying for their mothers, and too much screaming, and pain and bastards in metal trying to kill you.'

Michael was taken aback. 'They say we just shoot arrows at them,' he said falteringly.

'Aye, you do, but in the end, brother, you have to get close. Close enough to see their eyes. Close enough to kill them.'

'And Nicholas is good at that,' Melisande said flatly.

'Not every man is,' Hook said, suspecting that Michael, with his generous and trusting nature, lacked the ruthlessness to get close and commit slaughter.

'Maybe just one battle,' Michael said wistfully, 'not a very big one.'

Hook took Michael through the town at sundown. Lord Slayton's men had found houses close to the Montivilliers Gate and Hook led his brother there and so into the yard of a merchant's house where the archers were quartered. His old companions went silent as the Hook brothers appeared. There was no sign of Sir Martin, but Tom Perrill, dark and brooding, was sitting against a wall, and he stared expressionless at the two Hooks. William Snoball sensed trouble and stood up.

'Michael's joining you,' Hook announced loudly, 'and Sir John Cornewaille wants you to know that my brother is under his protection.' Sir John had said no such thing, but none of Lord Slayton's men would know that.

Tom Perrill gave a mocking laugh, but said nothing. William Snoball confronted Hook. 'There'll be no trouble,' he agreed.

'There will indeed be no trouble!' A voice echoed the statement and Hook turned to see Sir Edward Derwent, Lord Slayton's captain who had been captured in the mine, standing in the courtyard entrance. Sir Edward had been freed when the town surrendered, and Hook reckoned he must have been at the council of war because he was dressed in his finest clothes. Sir Edward now strode to the courtyard's centre. 'There will be no trouble!' he said again. 'None of you will fight each other, because your job is to fight the French!'

'I thought we were going home,' Snoball said, puzzled.

'Well, you're not,' Sir Edward said. 'The king wants more, and what the king wants, he gets.'

'We're staying here?' Hook asked, incredulous. 'In Harfleur?'

'No, Hook,' Sir Edward said, 'we're marching.' He sounded

grim, as though he disapproved of the decision. But Henry was king and, as Sir Edward had said, what the king wanted the king got.

And what Henry wanted was more war.

And so the army would march into France.

PART THREE

To the River of
Swords

There were to be no heavy wagons taken on the march. Instead the baggage would be carried by men, packhorses, and light carts. 'We have to travel fast,' Sir John explained.

'It's pride,' Father Christopher told Hook later, 'nothing but pride.'

'Pride?'

'The king can't just crawl back to England with nothing but Harfleur to show for his money! He has to do more than merely kick the French dog, he feels a need to pull its tail as well.'

The French dog did appear to be sleeping. Reports said the enemy army grew ever larger, but it showed no sign of stirring from around Rouen, and so the King of England had decided he would show Christendom that he could march from Harfleur to Calais with impunity. 'It isn't that far,' Sir John told his men, 'maybe a week's march.'

'And what do we gain from a week's march through France?' Hook asked Father Christopher.

'Nothing,' the priest said bluntly.

'So why do it?'

'To show that we can. To show that the French are helpless.'

'And we travel without the big wagons?'

Father Christopher grinned. 'We don't want the helpless French to catch us, do we? That would be a disaster, young Hook! So we can't take two hundred heavy wains with us, that would slow us down far too much, so it will be horses, spurs and the devil take the hindmost.'

'This is important!' Sir John had told his men. He had stormed into the *Paon*'s taproom and hammered one of the barrels with the hilt of his sword. 'Are you awake? Are you listening? You take food for eight days! And all the arrows you can carry! You take weapons, armour, arrows and food, and nothing else! If I see any man carrying anything other than weapons, armour, arrows and food I'll shove that useless baggage down his goddam gullet and pull it out of his goddam arse! We have to travel fast!'

'It all happened before,' Father Christopher told Hook next morning.

'Before?'

'You don't know your history, Hook?'

'I know my grandfather was murdered, and my father too.'

'I do so love a happy family,' the priest said, 'but think back to your great-grandfather's time, when Edward was king. The third Edward. He was here in Normandy and decided to make a quick march to Calais, only he got trapped halfway.'

'And died?'

'Oh, good God, no, he beat the French! You've surely heard of Crécy?'

'Oh, I've heard of Crécy!' Hook said. Every archer knew of Crécy, the battle where the bowmen of England had cut down the nobility of France.

'So you know it was a glorious battle, Hook, in which God favoured the English, but God's favour is a fickle thing.'

'Are you telling me He's not on our side?'

'I'm telling you that God is on the side of whoever wins, Hook.'

Hook considered that for a moment. He was sharpening arrowheads, slithering the bodkins and broadheads against a stone. He thought of all the tales he had heard as a child when old men had spoken of the arrow-storms of Crécy and Poitiers, then flourished a bodkin at Father Christopher. 'If we meet the French,' he said stoutly, 'we'll win. We'll punch these through their armour, father.'

'I have a grievous suspicion that the king agrees with you,' the priest said gently. 'He really does believe God is on his side, but his brother evidently does not.'

'Which brother?' Hook asked. The Duke of Clarence and the Duke of Gloucester were both with the army.

'Clarence,' Father Christopher said. 'He's sailing home.'

Hook frowned at that news. The duke, according to some men, was an even better soldier than his older brother. Hook inspected a bodkin. Most of the long narrow head was dark with rust, but the point was now shining metal and wickedly sharp. He tested it by pricking the ball of his hand, then wet his fingers and smoothed out the fledging. 'Why's he going?'

'I suspect he disapproves of his brother's decision,' Father Christopher said blandly. 'Officially, of course, the duke is ill, but he looked remarkably well for an ailing man. And, of course, if Henry is killed, God forbid, Clarence will become King Thomas.'

'Our Harry won't die,' Hook said fiercely.

'He very well might if the French catch us,' the priest said tartly, 'but even our Henry has listened to advice. He was told to go home, he wanted to march to Paris, but he's settled for Calais instead. And with God's help, Hook, we should reach Calais long before the French can reach us.'

'You make it sound as if we're running away.'

'Not quite,' the priest said, 'but almost. Think of your lovely Melisande.'

Hook frowned, puzzled. 'Melisande?'

'The French are gathered at her bellybutton, Hook, and we are perched on her right nipple. What we plan to do is run to her left nipple and hope to God the French don't make it to her cleavage before us.'

'And if they do?'

'Then the cleavage will become the valley of the shadow of death,' Father Christopher said, 'so pray that we march fast and that the French go on sleeping.'

'You can't be fussy!' Sir John had told his archers in the taproom. 'We can't pack arrows in barrels, we don't have the carts to carry barrels! And you can't use discs! So bundle them, bundle them tight!'

Bundled arrows suffered from crushed fledgings, and crushed fledgings made arrows inaccurate, but there was no choice but to bind the arrows in tight sheaves that could be hung from a saddle or across a packhorse's back. It took two days to tie the sheaves, for the king was demanding that every available arrow be carried on the journey and that meant carrying hundreds of thousands of arrows. As many as possible were heaped on the light farm carts that would accompany the army, but there were not enough such vehicles, so even men-at-arms were ordered to tie the bundles behind their saddles. There were just five thousand archers marching to Calais and in one minute those men were capable of shooting sixty or seventy thousand arrows, and no battle was ever won in a minute. 'If we take every arrow we've got, there still won't be enough,' Thomas Evelgold grumbled, 'and then we'll be throwing rocks at the bastards.'

A garrison was left at Harfleur. It was a strong force of over three hundred men-at-arms and almost a thousand archers, though it was short of horses because the king demanded that the garrison give up every beast except the knights' war-trained destriers. The horses were needed to carry arrows. The new defenders of Harfleur were left perilously short of arrows themselves, but new ones were expected to arrive any day from England where foresters cut ash shafts, blacksmiths forged bodkins and broadheads, and fledgers bound on the goose feathers.

'We will march swiftly!' a priest with a booming voice shouted. It was the day before the army marched and the priest was visiting every street in Harfleur with a parchment on which the king's orders had been written. The priest's job was to make certain every man understood the king's commands. 'There will be no straggling! Above all, the property of the church is sacred! Any man who plunders church property will be hanged! God is with us, and we march to show that by His grace we are the masters of France!'

'You heard him!' Sir John shouted as the priest walked on. 'Keep your thieving hands off church property! Don't rape nuns! God doesn't like it, and nor do I!'

That night, in the church of Saint Martin, Father Christopher made Hook and Melisande man and wife. Melisande cried and Hook, as he knelt and gazed at the candles guttering on the altar, wished Saint Crispinian would speak to him, but the saint said nothing. He wished he had thought to summon his brother to the church, but there had been no opportunity. Father Christopher had simply insisted that it was time Hook made Melisande his wife and so had taken them to the broken-spired church. 'God be with you,' the priest said when the brief ceremony was done.

'He has been,' Melisande said.

'Then pray that He stays with you, because we need God's help now.' The priest turned and bowed to the altar. 'By

God we need it,' he added ominously, 'the Burgundians have marched.'

'To help us?' Hook asked. It seemed so long ago that he had worn the ragged red cross of Burgundy and watched as the troops of France had massacred a city.

'No,' Father Christopher said, 'to help France.'

'But . . .' Hook began, then his voice trailed away.

'They have made up their family quarrel,' Father Christopher said, 'and so turned against us.'

'And we're still going to march?' Hook asked.

'The king insists,' Father Christopher said bleakly. 'We are a small army at the edge of a great land,' he went on, 'but at least you two are joined now for all time. Even death cannot separate you.'

'Thanks be to God,' Melisande said, and made the sign of the cross.

Next day, the eighth day of October, a Tuesday, the feast day of Saint Benedicta, under a clear sky, the army marched.

They went north, following the coastline, and Hook felt the army's spirits rise as they rode away from the smell of shit and death. Men grinned for no apparent reason, friends teased each other cheerfully, and some put spurs to horses and just galloped for the sheer joy of being in open country again.

Sir John Cornewaille commanded the army's vanguard, and his own men were in the van of the van and so rode at the very front of the column. Sir John's banner flew between the cross of Saint George and the flag of the Holy Trinity, the three standards guarded by Sir John's men-at-arms and followed by four mounted drummers who beat incessantly. The archers rode ahead, scouting the path, and watching for an enemy whose first appearance was an ambush, though none of Sir John's men was involved. The

French had waited until the well-armed and vigilant vanguard had gone by, then had sallied from Montivilliers, a walled town close to the road. Crossbowmen shot from the woods and a group of men-at-arms charged the column and there was a flurry of fighting before the attackers, who numbered fewer than fifty men, were beaten off, though not before they had managed to take a half-dozen prisoners and leave two English dead.

That skirmish occurred on the first day, but thereafter the French seemed to fall back into sleep and so the English men-at-arms rode unarmoured, their mail and plate carried by the sumpter horses. The riders' different coloured jerkins gave the mounted column a holiday appearance, enhanced by the banners flying at the head of every contingent. The women, pages and servants rode behind the men-at-arms, leading packhorses loaded with armour, food and the great bundles of arrows. Sir John's company had two light carts, one loaded with food and plate armour, the other heaped with arrows. When Hook turned in his saddle he saw a filmy cloud of dust pluming over the low hills and heavy woods. The dust marked the trail of England's army as it twisted through the small valleys leading towards the River Somme, and to Hook it appeared to be a large army, but in truth it was a defiant band of fewer than ten thousand men, and only looked larger because there were over twenty thousand horses.

On the Sunday they dropped out of the small, tight hills into a more open and flatter countryside. Sir John had suggested that this was the day they should reach the Somme, and had added that the Somme was the only major obstacle on their journey. Cross that river and they would have a mere three days' marching to Calais. 'So there won't be a battle?' Michael Hook asked his brother. Lord Slayton's men were also in the vanguard, though Sir Martin and Thomas Perrill stayed well clear of Sir John and his men.

'They say no,' Hook said, 'but who knows?'

'The French won't stop us?'

'They don't seem to be trying, do they?' Hook said, nodding at the empty country ahead. He and the rest of Sir John's archers were a half-mile in front of the column, leading the way to the river. 'Maybe the French are happy to see us go?' he suggested. 'They're just leaving us be, perhaps?'

'You've been to Calais,' Michael said, impressed that his elder brother had travelled so far and seen so much since last they were together.

'Strange little town, it is,' Hook said, 'a vast wall and a great castle and a huddle of houses. But it's the way home, Michael, the way home!'

'I just got here,' Michael said ruefully.

'Maybe we'll come back next year,' Hook said, 'and finish the job. Look!' He pointed far ahead to where, in the smudges of brown, golden and yellow leaves, a sheen of light glittered. 'That might be the river.'

'Or a lake,' Michael suggested.

'We're looking for a place called Blanchetaque,' Hook said.

'They have the funniest names,' Michael said, grinning.

'There's a ford at Blanchetaque,' Hook said. 'We cross that and we're as good as home.'

He turned as hooves sounded loud behind and saw Sir John and a half-dozen men-at-arms galloping towards him. Sir John, bareheaded and wearing mail, slowed Lucifer. He was looking off to the left where the sea showed beyond a low ridge. 'See that, Hook?' he asked cheerfully.

'Sir John?'

Sir John pointed to a tiny white lump on the sea's horizon. 'Gris-Nez! The Grey Nose, Hook.'

'What's that, Sir John?'

'A headland, Hook, just a half-day's ride from Calais! See how close we are?'

'Three days' ride?' Hook asked.

'Two days on a horse like Lucifer,' Sir John said, smoothing the destrier's mane. He turned to look at the nearer countryside. 'Is that the river?'

'I think so, Sir John.'

'Then Blanchetaque can't be far! That's where the third Edward crossed the Somme on his way to Crécy! Maybe your great-grandfather was with him, Hook.'

'He was a shepherd, Sir John, never drew a bow in his life.'

'He used a sling,' Michael said, sounding nervous because he spoke to Sir John.

'Like David and Goliath, eh?' Sir John said, still gazing at the distant headland. 'I hear you got church married, Hook!'

'Yes, Sir John.'

'Women do like that,' Sir John said, sounding gloomy, 'and we like women!' He cheered up. 'She's a good girl, Hook.' He stared at the land ahead. 'Not a goddam Frenchman in sight.'

'There's a horseman down there,' Michael said very diffidently.

'There's a what?' Sir John snapped.

'Down there,' Michael said, pointing to a stand of trees a mile ahead, 'a horseman, sir.'

Sir John stared and saw nothing, but Hook could now see the man who was motionless on his horse in the deep shade of the full-leafed wood. 'He's there, Sir John,' Hook confirmed.

'Bastard's watching us. Can you flush him out, Hook? He might know whether the goddam French are guarding the ford. Don't chase him away, I want him driven to us.'

Hook looked at the land to his right, searching for the dead ground that would let him circle behind the horseman unseen. 'I reckon so, Sir John,' he said.

'Do it, man.'

Hook took his brother, Scoyle the Londoner and Tom Scarlet, and he rode away from the half-hidden horseman, going back towards the approaching army and then down a slight incline that took him from the man's sight. After that he turned east off the road and kicked Raker's flanks to gallop across a stretch of grassland. They were still hidden from their quarry. Ahead of the four horsemen were copses and thickets. The fields here had no hedges, only ditches, and the horses jumped them easily. The land was nearly flat, but had just enough swell and dip to hide the four archers as Hook turned north again. Off to his right a man was ploughing a field. His two oxen were struggling to drag the big plough that was set low because winter wheat was always sown deeper. 'He needs some rain!' Michael shouted.

'It would help!' Hook answered.

The horses thumped up an almost imperceptible rise and the landscape that Hook had held in his head revealed itself. He did not turn to the wood where the horseman was hidden, but kept going northwards to cut the man off from the Somme. Perhaps the man had already ridden away? In all likelihood he was simply some local gentleman who wanted to watch the enemy pass, but the gentry knew more of what happened in their neighbouring regions than the peasantry and that was why Sir John wanted to question the man.

Raker was tiring, blowing and fractious, and Hook curbed the horse. 'Bows,' he said, uncasing his own and stringing it by supporting one end in his bucket stirrup.

'Thought we weren't supposed to kill him,' Tom Scarlet said.

'If the bastard's a gentleman,' Hook said, and he supposed the man was because he was mounted on horseback, 'then he'll be sword trained. If you come at him with a blade he'll like as not slash your head off. But he won't like facing an arrow, will he?' He locked an arrow on the stave with his left thumb.

He patted Raker's neck, then kicked the horse forward again. Now they were coming at the wood from the road's far side. He could see that Sir John had stayed on the slight crest, not wanting to spring the man out of his hiding place, but the lone Frenchman had scented trouble, or else he had simply watched for the approaching English long enough, because he suddenly broke cover and spurred his horse north towards the river. 'God damn him,' Hook said.

Sir John saw the man ride away and immediately spurred forward with his men-at-arms, but the English horses were tired and the Frenchman's mount was well rested. 'They've no chance of catching him,' Scoyle said.

Hook ignored that pessimism. Instead he turned Raker and banged his heels back. The Frenchman was following the road that curved to the right and Hook could gallop across the chord of that curve. He knew he could not out-gallop the man and so stood no chance of catching him, but he did have a chance of getting close enough to use the bow. The man turned in his saddle and saw Hook and his men and slashed his spurs back, and Hook kicked as well and the hooves hammered the hard ground and Hook saw that the fugitive would be hidden by trees in a moment and so he hauled on Raker's reins, pulled his feet from the stirrups and threw himself out of the saddle. He stumbled, fell to one knee, and the bow was already rising in his left hand and he caught the string, nocked the arrow and pulled back.

'Too far,' Scoyle said, reining in his horse, 'don't waste a good arrow.'

'Much too far,' Michael agreed.

But the bow was huge and Hook did not think about his aim. He just watched the distant horseman, willed where he wanted the arrow to go, then hauled and released and the cord twanged and slashed against his unprotected wrist and the arrow fluttered a heartbeat before its fledging caught the air and tautened its flight.

'Tuppence says you'll miss by twenty paces,' Tom Scarlet said.

The arrow drew its curve in the sky, its white fledging a diminishing flicker in the autumn light. The far horseman galloped, unaware of the broadhead that flew high before starting its hissing descent. It fell fast, plunging, losing its momentum, and the horseman turned again to watch for his pursuers and as he did so the barbed arrow slapped into his horse's belly and sliced into blood and flesh. The horse twisted hard and sudden with the awful pain and Hook saw the man lose his balance and fall from the saddle.

'Sweet Jesu!' Michael said in pure admiration.

'Come on!' Hook gathered Raker's reins and hauled himself into the saddle and kicked back before he had found the stirrups and for a moment he thought he would fall off himself, but he managed to thrust his right boot into the bucket and saw the Frenchman was remounting his horse. Hook had wounded the horse, not killed it, but the animal was bleeding because the broadhead was designed to rip and tear through flesh, and the harder the Frenchman rode the beast the more blood it would lose.

The horseman spurred his wounded mount to vanish among the trees and a moment later Hook was on the road and among the same trees and he saw the Frenchman was a hundred paces ahead and his horse was faltering, leaving a trail of blood. The man saw his pursuers and slid out of his saddle because his horse could go no further. He turned to run into the woods and Hook shouted. *'Non!'*

He let Raker slow to a stop. Hook's bow was drawn and there was another arrow on the string, and this arrow was aimed at the horseman who gave a resigned nod. He wore a sword, but no armour. His clothes, as Hook drew nearer, looked to be of fine quality; good broadcloth and a tight-woven linen shirt and expensive boots. He was a fine-looking man, perhaps thirty years old, with a wide face and a trimmed beard and pale green eyes that were fixed on the arrow's head. 'Just stay where you are,' Hook said. The man might not speak English, but he understood the message of the tensioned bow and its bodkin arrow, and so he obeyed, caressing the nose of his dying horse. The horse gave a pathetic whinny, then its forelegs crumpled and it fell onto the track. The man crouched and stroked, speaking softly to the dying beast.

'You almost let him get away, Hook!' Sir John shouted as he arrived.

'Nearly, Sir John.'

'So let's see what the bastard knows,' Sir John said, and slid out of his saddle. 'Someone kill that poor horse!' he demanded. 'Put the animal out of its misery!'

The job was done with a poleaxe blow to the horse's forehead, then Sir John talked with the prisoner. He treated the man with an exquisite politeness, and the Frenchman, in turn, was loquacious, but there was no denying that whatever he revealed was causing Sir John dismay. 'I want a horse for Sir Jules,' Sir John turned on the archers with that demand. 'He's going to meet the king.'

Sir Jules was taken to the king and the army stopped.

The vanguard was only five miles from the ford at Blanchetaque, and Calais was just three days' march north of that ford. In three days' time, eight days after they had left Harfleur, the army should have marched through the gates of Calais and Henry would have been able to claim, if not a victory, at least a humiliation of the French. But that humiliation depended on crossing the wide tidal ford of Blanchetaque.

And the French were already there. Charles d'Albret, the Constable of France, was on the Somme's northern bank, and the prisoner, who was in the constable's service, described how the ford had been planted with sharpened stakes, and how six thousand men were waiting on the further bank to stop the English crossing.

'It can't be done,' Sir John said bleakly that evening. 'The bastards are there.'

The bastards had blocked the river and, as night fell, the clouded sky reflected the campfires of the French force that guarded the Blanchetaque ford. 'The ford's only crossable when the tide's low,' Sir John explained, 'and even then we can only advance twenty men abreast. And twenty men can't fight off six thousand.'

No one spoke for a while, then Father Christopher asked the question that every man in Sir John's company wanted to ask even though they dreaded the answer. 'So what do we do, Sir John?'

'Find another ford, of course.'

'Where, pray?'

'Inland,' Sir John said grimly.

'We march towards the bellybutton,' Father Christopher said.

'We do what?' Sir John asked, staring as though the priest were mad.

'Nothing, Sir John, nothing!' Father Christopher said.

So now England's army, with only enough food for three more days, must march deep into France to cross a river. And if they could not cross the river they would die, and if they did cross the river they might still die because going inland would take time, and time would give the French army the opportunity to wake from its slumber and march. The dash up the coast had failed and now Henry and his little army must plunge into France.

302

And next morning, under a heavy grey sky, they headed east.

Hope had sustained the army, but now despair crept in. Disease returned. Men were forever dismounting, running to one side and dropping their breeches so that the rearguard rode through the stink of shit. Men rode silently and sullenly. Rain came in bands from the ocean, sweeping inland, leaving the column wet and dripping.

Every ford across the Somme was staked and guarded. The bridges had been destroyed, and a French army now shadowed the English. It was not the main army, not the great assembly of men-at-arms and crossbowmen that had gathered in Rouen, but a smaller force that was more than adequate to block any attempted crossing of a barricaded ford. They were in sight every day, men-at-arms and crossbowmen, all of them mounted, riding along the river's northern bank to keep pace with the English on the southern. More than once Sir John led archers and men-at-arms in a headlong gallop to try and seize a ford before the French reached it, but the French were always waiting. They had put garrisons at every crossing.

Food became scarce, though the small unwalled towns grudgingly yielded baskets of bread, cheese and smoked fish rather than be attacked and burned. And each day the army became hungrier and marched deeper into enemy country.

'Why don't we just go back to Harfleur?' Thomas Evelgold grumbled.

'Because that would be running away,' Hook said.

'That's better than dying,' Evelgold said.

There were also enemies on the English side of the river. French men-at-arms watched the passing column from low hilltops to the south. They were usually in small bands, perhaps six or seven men, and if a force of English knights rode towards them they would invariably draw away, though once in a while an enemy might raise his lance as a signal that he was offering single combat. Then, perhaps, an Englishman would respond and the two men would gallop together, there would be a clatter of iron-shod lances on armour and one man would topple slowly from his horse. Once two men skewered each other and both died, each impaled on his enemy's lance. Sometimes a band of French would charge together, as many as forty or fifty men-at-arms, attacking a weak point in the marching column to kill a few men before galloping away.

Other Frenchmen were busy ahead of the column, taking away the harvest to leave nothing for the invaders. The food, collected from barns and granaries, was taken to Amiens, a city the English skirted on the day they should have arrived in Calais. The bags that had held food were now empty. Hook, riding in a thin drizzle, had stared at the distant white vision of Amiens Cathedral towering above the city and he had thought of all the food inside the walls. He was hungry. They were all hungry.

Next day they camped near a castle that stood atop a white chalk cliff. Sir John's men-at-arms had captured a pair of enemy knights who had strayed too close to the vanguard and the prisoners had boasted how the French would defeat Henry's small army. They had even repeated the boasts to Henry himself, and Sir John brought his archers orders from the king. He stood amidst their campfires. 'Tomorrow morning,' he said, 'every man is to cut a stake as long as a bowstave. Longer if you can! Cut a stake as thick as your arm and sharpen both ends.'

Rain hissed in the fire. Hook's archers had eaten poorly on a hare that Tom Scarlet had killed with an arrow and that Melisande had roasted over the fire, which was surrounded by flat stones on which she had made flat cakes from a mix of oats and acorns. They had a few nuts and some hard green apples. There was no ale left, no wine either, so they took water from a stream. Melisande was now swathed in Hook's enormous mail coat and huddled beside him.

'Stakes?' Thomas Evelgold enquired cautiously.

'The French, may they rot in hell,' Sir John said as he walked closer to the biggest fire, 'have decided how to beat you. You! The archers! They fear you! Are you all listening to me?'

The archers watched him in silence. Sir John was wearing a leather hat and a thick leather coat. Rainwater dripped from the brim and hems. He carried a shortened lance, one cut down so that a man-at-arms could use it on foot. 'We're listening, Sir John,' Evelgold growled.

'Instructions have been sent from Rouen!' Sir John announced. 'The Marshal of France has a plan! And the plan is to kill you, the archers, first, then kill the rest of us.'

'Take the gentry prisoner, you mean,' Evelgold said, but too quietly for Sir John to hear.

'They're assembling knights on well-armoured horses,' Sir John said, 'and the riders will have the best armour they can find! Milanese armour! And you all know about Milanese armour.'

Hook knew that the armour made in Milan, wherever that was, had the reputation of being the best in Christendom. It was said that Milanese plate would resist the heaviest bodkin, but luckily such armour was rare because it was so expensive. Hook had been told that a complete suit of Milanese plate would cost close to a hundred pounds, over ten years' pay for an archer, and a heavy outlay for most men-at-arms, who thought themselves rich if they had forty pounds a year.

'So they'll armour their horses and wear Milanese plate,'

Sir John went on, 'and charge you, the archers! They want to get in among you with swords and maces.' The archers were listening intently now, imagining the big horses with steel faces and padded flanks wheeling and rearing among their panicked ranks. 'If they send a thousand horsemen you'll be lucky to stop a hundred of them! And the rest will just slaughter you, except they won't, because you'll have stakes!' He lifted the shortened lance to show what he meant, then thrust its butt end onto the leaf mould and slanted the shaft so that the iron-tipped point was about breast height. 'That's how you'll drive the stake into the ground,' he told them. 'If a horse charges home onto that it'll get impaled, and that's how you stop a man in Milanese armour! So tomorrow morning you all cut a stake. One man, one stake, and you sharpen both ends.'

'Tomorrow, Sir John?' Evelgold asked. He sounded sceptical. 'Are they that close?'

'They could be anywhere,' Sir John said. 'From tomorrow's dawn you ride in mail and leather, you wear helmets, you keep your strings dry, and you carry a stake.'

Next morning Hook cut a bough from an oak and sharpened the green wood with his poleaxe blade. 'When we left England,' Will of the Dale said ruefully, 'they said we were the best army ever gathered! Now we're down to wet strings, acorn cakes, and stakes! Goddamned stakes!'

The long oak stake was awkward to carry on horseback. The horses were tired, wet and hungry, and the rain came again, harder, blowing from behind and pattering the river's surface into a myriad dimples. The French were on the far bank. They were always on the far bank.

Then new orders came from the king and the vanguard turned away from the river to climb a long damp slope that led to a wide plateau of wet, featureless land. 'Where are we going now?' Hook asked as the river disappeared from sight.

'God knows,' Father Christopher said.

'And He's not telling you, father?'

'Does your saint tell you anything?'

'Not a word.'

'So God alone knows where we are,' Father Christopher said, 'but only God.' The plateau had clay soil and the road was soon churned into a morass of mud on which the rain fell incessantly. It was growing colder, and the plateau had few trees, which meant fuel for fires was scarce. Some archers in another company burned their sharpened stakes for warmth at night and the army paused to watch those men being whipped. Their ventenar had his ears cut off.

The French horsemen sensed the despair in Henry's army. They rode just to the south, tracking the army, and the English men-at-arms were too tired and their horses too hungry to accept the implied challenge of the raised lances, and so the French grew bolder, riding ever closer. 'Don't waste your arrows!' Sir John told his archers.

'One less Frenchman to kill in a battle,' Hook suggested.

Sir John smiled tiredly. 'It's a matter of honour, Hook.' He nodded towards a Frenchman who trotted less than a quarter-mile away. The man was quite alone and rode with an upright lance as an invitation for some Englishman to fight him. 'He's sworn to do some deed of great valour,' Sir John explained, 'like killing me or another knight, and that's a noble ambition.'

'It saves him from an arrow?' Hook responded dourly.

'Yes, Hook, it does. Let him live. He's a brave man.'

More brave men approached that afternoon, but still no Englishmen responded, and so the Frenchmen became still bolder, riding close enough to recognise men they had met in tournaments across Europe. They chatted. There were maybe a dozen such French knights visible at any one time, and one of them, mounted on a tall and sprightly black horse that took the heavy soil with a high-stepping energy, spurred his way to the vanguard's front. 'Sir John!' the rider called. He was the Sire de Lanferelle, his long hair wet and lank.

'Lanferelle!'

'If I give you oats for your horse, you'll match my lance?'

'If you give me oats,' Sir John called back, 'my archers will eat!'

Lanferelle laughed. Sir John veered away from the road to ride beside the Frenchman and the two talked amicably. 'They look like friends,' Melisande said.

'Maybe they are,' Hook suggested.

'And they will kill each other in battle?'

'Englishman!' It was Lanferelle who called to Hook and who now rode towards the archers. 'Sir John says you married my daughter!'

'I did,' Hook said.

'And without my blessing,' Lanferelle said, sounding amused. He looked at Melisande. 'You have the jupon I gave you?'

'*Oui*,' she said.

'Wear it,' her father said harshly, 'if there's a battle, wear it.'

'Because it will save me?' she asked bitterly. 'The novice's robe didn't protect me in Soissons.'

'Damn Soissons, girl,' Lanferelle said, 'and what happened there will happen to these men. They're doomed!' He swept his arm to indicate the muddy, slow column. 'The goddams are all doomed! I will take pleasure in saving you.'

'For what?'

'For whatever choice I make for you,' Lanferelle said. 'You've tasted your freedom, and look where it has led you!' He smiled, his teeth surprisingly white. 'You can come now? I shall take you away before we slaughter this army.'

'I stay with Nicholas,' she said.

'Then stay with the goddams,' Lanferelle said harshly, 'and

when your Nicholas is dead I shall take you away.' He wheeled his horse and, after a few more words with Sir John, rode south.

'The goddams?' Hook asked.

'It's what the French call you English,' she said, then looked at Sir John. 'Are we doomed?' she asked.

Sir John smiled ruefully. 'It depends on whether their army catches us, and if it catches us, whether it can beat us. We're still alive!'

'Will it catch us?' Melisande asked.

Sir John pointed north. 'There was a small French army on the river's northern bank,' he explained, 'and they were keeping pace with us. They were making sure we couldn't cross. They were driving us towards their bigger army. But here, my dear, the river curves north. A great curve! We're cutting across country, but that smaller army has to ride all the way around and it will take them three or four days, and tomorrow we'll be at the river and there'll be no small army on the other side and if we find a ford or, God willing, a bridge, we'll be across the Somme and riding for the taverns of Calais! We'll go home!'

Yet each day they covered less ground. There was no grazing for the horses, and no oats, and every day more men dismounted to lead their weakening, tiring mounts. In the first week of the march the towns had given food to the passing army, but now the few small walled towns shut their gates and refused to offer any help. They knew the English could not spare the time to assault their ramparts, however decrepit, and so they watched the disconsolate column pass by and offered prayers that God would utterly destroy the weakened invaders.

And God's displeasure was the last thing Henry dared risk, so that, on their last day on the plateau, the day before they would ride down into the valley of the Somme again, when a priest came to complain that an Englishman had stolen his church's pyx, the king ordered the whole column to halt. Centenars and ventenars were commanded to search their men. The missing pyx, which was a copper-gilt box in which consecrated wafers were held, was evidently of little value, but the king was determined to find it. 'Some poor bastard probably stole it to get the wafers,' Tom Scarlet suggested, 'he ate the wafers and threw the pyx away.'

'Well, Hook?' Sir John demanded.

'None of us has it, Sir John.'

'One goddam pyx,' Sir John snarled, 'a pox on the pyx, father!'

'If you say so, Sir John,' Father Christopher said.

'Give the French a chance to catch us because of one goddam pyx!'

'God will reward us if we discover the item,' Father Christopher suggested, 'indeed, He has already lifted the rain!' It was true. Since the search had begun the rain had ended and a weak sun was struggling to clear the clouds and shine on the waterlogged land.

And then the pyx was found.

It had been hidden in the sleeve of an archer's jerkin, a spare jerkin that he had evidently kept wrapped and tied to his horse's pommel, though the archer himself claimed that he had seen neither jerkin nor pyx before. 'They all claim innocence,' a royal chaplain told the king, 'just hang him, sire.'

'We will hang him,' the king agreed vigorously, 'and we'll let every man see him hanged! This is what happens when you sin against God! Hang him!'

'No!' Hook protested.

Because the man being dragged to the tree where the king and his entourage waited was his brother Michael.

For whom the rope waited.

*   *   *

310

The king's men dragged Michael to the base of the elm tree where Henry and his courtiers waited on horseback beside the country priest who had first complained about the theft of his pyx. The army, commanded to attend, was gathered in a vast circle, though few except those in the foremost ranks could see what happened. Two soldiers in mail coats half covered by the royal coat-of-arms had pinioned Michael Hook's arms and were half pulling and half pushing him towards the king. They hardly needed to use force for Michael was going willingly enough. He just looked bemused.

'No!' Hook shouted.

'Shut your mouth,' Thomas Evelgold growled.

If the king heard Hook's protest he showed no sign of it. His face was unmoving, hard-planed, shaven raw, implacable.

'He . . .' Hook began, intending to say his brother had not, could not, have stolen a pyx, but Evelgold turned fast and slammed his fist into Hook's stomach, driving the wind from him.

'Next time, I break your jaw,' Evelgold said.

'My brother,' Hook panted, suddenly straining to draw breath.

'Quiet!' Sir John snarled from in front of his company.

'You offend God, you risk our whole campaign!' the king spoke to Michael, his voice like gravel. 'How can we expect God to be on our side if we offend Him? You have put England itself at risk.'

'I didn't steal it!' Michael pleaded.

'Whose company is he?' the king demanded.

Sir Edward Derwent stepped forward. 'One of Lord Slayton's archers, sire,' he said, bowing his greying head, 'and I doubt, sire, that he is a thief.'

'The pyx was in his keeping?'

'It was found in his belongings, sire,' Sir Edward said carefully.

'The jerkin wasn't mine, lord!' Michael said.

'You are certain the pyx was in his baggage?' the king asked Sir Edward, ignoring the fair-haired young archer who had dropped to his knees.

'It was, sire, though how it arrived there, I cannot tell.'

'Who discovered it?'

'Sire, me, sire,' Sir Martin, his priest's robe discoloured by clay, stepped out of the crowd. 'It was me, sire,' he said, dropping to one knee. 'And he's a good boy, sire, he's a Christian boy, sire.'

Sir Edward might have protested Michael's innocence all day and not moved the king to doubt, but a priest's word carried far more weight. Henry gathered his reins and leaned forward in his saddle. 'Are you saying he did not take the pyx?'

'He . . .' Hook began, and Evelgold hit him so hard in the belly that Hook doubled over.

'The pyx was found in his baggage, sire,' Sir Martin said.

'Then?' the king started, then checked. He looked puzzled. One moment the priest had suggested Michael's innocence, now he suggested the opposite.

'It is incontrovertible, sire,' Sir Martin said, managing to sound mournful, 'that the pyx was among his belongings. It saddens me, sire, it galls my heart.'

'It angers me,' the king shouted, 'and it angers God! We risk His displeasure, His wrath, for a copper box! Hang him!'

'Sire!' Michael called, but there was no pity, no appeal and no hope. The rope was already tied about a branch, the noose was pushed over Michael's head and two men hauled on the bitter end to hoist him into the air.

Hook's brother made a choking noise as he thrashed desperately, his legs jerking and thrusting, and slowly, very slowly the thrashing turned to spasms, to quivers, and the choking noise became short harsh gasps and finally faded to nothing. It took twenty minutes, and the king watched every twitch, and only when he was satisfied that the thief was dead did he take his eyes from the body. He dismounted then and, in front of his army, went on one knee to the astonished country priest. 'We beg your forgiveness,' he said loudly and speaking in English, a language the priest did not understand, 'and the forgiveness of Almighty God.' He held out the pyx in both hands and the priest, frightened by what he had seen, took it nervously, then a look of astonishment came to his face because the little box was much heavier than it had ever been before. The King of England had filled it with coin.

'Leave the body there!' Henry commanded, getting to his feet. 'And march! Let us march!' He took his horse's reins, put a foot into the stirrup and swung himself lithely into the saddle. He rode away, followed by his entourage, and Hook moved towards the tree where his brother's body hung.

'Where the hell are you going?' Sir John asked harshly.

'I'll bury him,' Hook said.

'You're a goddamned fool, Hook,' Sir John said, then hit Hook's face with a mailed hand, 'what are you?'

'He didn't do it!' Hook protested.

Sir John struck him again, much harder, gouging scratches of blood into Hook's cheek. 'It doesn't matter that he didn't do it,' he snarled. 'God needed a sacrifice, and He got one. Maybe we'll live because your brother died.'

'He didn't steal, he's never stolen, he's honest!' Hook said.

The gloved hand hammered Hook's other cheek. 'And you do not protest at the decisions of our king,' Sir John said, 'and you do not bury him because the king doesn't want him buried! You are lucky, Hook, not to be hanging beside your brother with piss running down your goddam leg. Now get on your horse and ride.'

'The priest lied!'

'That is your business,' Sir John said, 'not mine, and it is certainly not the king's business. Get on your horse or I'll have your goddam ears cut off.'

Hook got on his horse. The other archers avoided him, sensing his ill-luck. Only Melisande rode with him.

Sir John's men were first on the road. Hook, bitter and dazed, was unaware that he was passing Lord Slayton's men until Melisande hissed, and only then did he notice the archers who had once been his comrades. Thomas Perrill was grinning triumphantly and pointing to his eye, a reminder of his suspicion that Hook had murdered his brother, while Sir Martin stared at Melisande, then glanced at Hook and could not resist a smile when he saw the archer's tears.

'You will kill them all,' Melisande promised him.

If the French did not do the job for him, Hook thought. They rode on downhill, going now towards the Somme and towards the army's only hope; an unguarded ford or bridge.

It started to rain again.

There was not one ford across the Somme, but two, and, better still, neither was guarded. The shadowing French army on the river's north bank had still not marched the full distance about the great looping curve and the English, arriving at the edge of a vast marsh that bordered the Somme, could see nothing but empty countryside beyond the river.

The first scouts to explore the fords reported that the river was flowing high because of the rain, but not so high as to make the fords impassable, yet to reach the crossings the army had to negotiate two causeways that ran arrow-straight across the wide marsh. Those causeways were over a mile long; twin roads that had been raised above the mire by embankments, and the French had broken both so that at the centre of each was a great gap where the causeways had been demolished to leave a morass of treacherous, sucking ground. The scouts had crossed those stretches of bog, but reported that their horses had sunk over their knees, and that none of the army's wagons could hope to negotiate the terrain. 'Then we remake the causeways,' the king ordered.

It took the best part of a day. Much of the army was ordered to dismantle a nearby village so that the beams, rafters and joists could be used as foundations for the repairs. Bundled thatch, faggots and earth were then thrown on top of the timbers to make new embankments while the men of the rearguard formed a battle line to protect the work against any surprise attack from the south. There was no such attack. French horsemen watched from a distance, but those enemy riders were few and made no attempt to interfere.

Hook took no part in the work because the vanguard had been ordered to cross the river before any repairs were made. They left their horses behind, walked to the causeway's gap and jumped down into the bog where they struggled across to the causeway's next stretch, which led to the river bank. They waded the Somme, the archers holding bows and arrow bags above their heads. Hook shivered as he went further into the river. He could not swim and he felt tremors of fear as the water crept over his waist and up to his chest, but then, as he pushed against the slow pressure of the current, the riverbed began to rise again. The footing was firm enough, though a few men slipped and one man-at-arms was swept downstream, his cries fading fast as his mail coat dragged him under. Then Hook was wading through reeds and climbing a short muddy bluff to reach the northern bank. The first men were across the Somme.

Sir John ordered his archers to go a half-mile north to where a straggling hedge and ditch snaked between two wide pastures. 'If the goddam French come,' Sir John said bleakly, 'just kill them.'

'You expecting their army, Sir John?' Thomas Evelgold asked.

'The one that was tracking us along the river?' Sir John asked, 'those bastards will get here soon enough. But their larger army? God only knows. Let's hope they think we're still south of the river.'

And even if it was only the smaller army that came, Hook thought, these few archers of the vanguard could not hope

316

to stop it. He sat by a stretch of flooded ditch, beneath a dead alder, staring north, his mind wandering. He had been a bad brother, he decided. He had never looked after Michael properly and, if he was truthful with himself, he would admit that his brother's trusting character and unending optimism had grated on him. He gave a nod when Thomas Scarlet, who had lost his own twin brother to Lanferelle's sword, squatted beside him. 'I'm sorry about Michael,' Scarlet said awkwardly, 'he was a good lad.'

'He was,' Hook said.

'Matt was too.'

'Aye, he was. A good archer.'

'He was,' Scarlet said, 'he was.'

They looked north in silence. Sir John had said that the first evidence of a French force would be mounted scouts, but no horsemen were visible.

'Michael always snatched at the string,' Hook said. 'I tried to teach him, but he couldn't stop it. He always snatched. Spoiled his aim, it did.'

'It does,' Scarlet said.

'He never learned,' Hook said, 'and he didn't steal that goddamned box either.'

'He didn't seem like a thief.'

'He wasn't! But I know who did steal it, and I'll cut his goddam throat.'

'Don't hang for it, Nick.'

Hook grimaced. 'If the French catch us, it won't matter, will it? I'll either be hanged or chopped down.' Hook had a sudden vision of the archers dying in their tortured agony in front of the little church in Soissons. He shivered.

'But we've crossed the river,' Scarlet said firmly, 'and that's good. How far now?'

'Father Christopher says it's a week's marching from here, maybe a day or two longer.'

'That's what they said a couple of weeks ago,' Scarlet said ruefully, 'but doesn't matter. We can go hungry for a week.'

Geoffrey Horrocks, the youngest archer, brought a helmet filled with hazelnuts. 'Found them up the hedge,' he said, 'you want to share them out, sergeant?' he asked Hook.

'You do it, lad. Tell them it's supper.'

'And tomorrow's breakfast,' Scarlet said.

'If I had a net we could catch some sparrows, ' Hook said.

'Sparrow pie,' Scarlet said wistfully.

They fell silent. The rain had stopped, though the keen wind was chilling the wet archers to the bone. A flock of black starlings, so thick that they looked like a writhing cloud, rose and fell two fields away. Behind Hook, far across the river, men laboured to remake the causeways.

'He was a grown man, you know.'

'What did you say, Tom?' Hook asked, startled from half-waking thoughts.

'Nothing,' Scarlet said, 'I was falling asleep till you woke me.'

'He was a very good man,' the voice said quietly, 'and he's resting in heaven now.'

Saint Crispinian, Hook thought, and his view of the country was misted by tears. You're still with me, he wanted to say.

'In heaven there are no tears,' the saint went on, 'and no sickness. There's no dying and no masters. There's no hunger. Michael is in joy.'

'You all right, Nick?' Tom Scarlet asked.

'I'm all right,' Hook said, and thought that Crispinian knew all about brothers. He had suffered and died with his own brother, Crispin, and they were both with Michael now, and somehow that seemed good.

It took the best part of the day to restore the two causeways and then the army began to cross in two long lines of horses and wagons and archers and servants and women. The king, resplendent in armour and crown, galloped past Hook's ditch. He was followed by a score of nobles who curbed their horses and, like Hook, gazed northwards. But the French army that had been keeping pace along the river's northern bank had fallen far behind and there was no enemy in sight. The English were across the river and now had entered territory claimed by the Duke of Burgundy, though it was still France. But between the army and England there were now no major obstacles unless the French army intervened.

'We march on,' Henry told his commanders.

They would march north again, north and west. They would march towards Calais, towards England and to safety. They marched.

They left the wide River Somme behind, but next day, because the army was footsore, sick and hungry, the king ordered a halt. The rain had cleared and the sun shone through wispy clouds. The army was now in well-wooded country so there was fuel for fires and the encampment took on a holiday air as men hung their clothes to dry on makeshift hurdles. Sentries were set, but it seemed as though England's army was all alone in the vastness of France. Not one Frenchman appeared. Men scavenged the woods for nuts, mushrooms and berries. Hook hoped to find a deer or a boar, but the animals, like the enemy, were nowhere to be seen.

'We might just have escaped,' Father Christopher greeted Hook on his return from his abortive hunt.

'The king must think so,' Hook said.

'Why?'

'Giving us a day's halt?'

'Our gracious king,' the priest said, 'is so mad that he might just be hoping the French will catch us.'

'Mad? Like the French king?'

'The French king is really mad,' Father Christopher said, 'no, our king is just convinced of God's favour.'

'Is that madness?'

Father Christopher paused as Melisande came to join them. She leaned on Hook, saying nothing. She was thinner than Hook had ever seen her, but the whole army was thin now; thin, hungry and ill. Somehow Hook and his wife had both avoided the bowel-emptying sickness, though many others had caught the disease and the camp stank of it. Hook put his arm about her, holding her close and thinking suddenly that she had become the most precious thing in all his world. 'I hope to God we have escaped,' Hook said.

'And our king half hopes that,' Father Christopher said, 'and half hopes that he can prove God's favour.'

'And that's his madness?'

'Beware of certainty. There are men in the French army, Hook, who are as convinced as Henry that God is on their side. They're good men too. They pray, they give alms, they confess their sins and they vow never to sin again. They are very good men. Can they be wrong in their conviction?'

'You tell me, father,' Hook said.

Father Christopher sighed. 'If I understood God, Hook, I would understand everything because God is everything. He is the stars and the sand, the wind and the calm, the sparrow and the sparrowhawk. He knows everything, He knows my fate and He knows your fate, and if I understood all that, what would I be?'

'You would be God,' Melisande said.

'And that I cannot be,' Father Christopher said, 'because we cannot comprehend everything. Only God does that, so beware of a man who says he knows God's will. He is like a horse that believes it controls its rider.'

'And our king believes that?'

'He believes he is God's favourite,' Father Christopher said, 'and perhaps he is. He is a king, after all, anointed and blessed.'

'God made him a king,' Melisande said.

'His father's sword made him a king,' Father Christopher said tartly, 'but, of course, God could have guided that sword.' He made the sign of the cross. 'Yet there are those,' he spoke softly now, 'who say his father had no right to the throne. And the sins of the fathers are visited on their sons.'

'You're saying . . .' Hook began, then checked his tongue because the conversation was veering dangerously close to treason.

'I'm saying,' Father Christopher said firmly, 'that I pray we get home to England before the French find us.'

'They've lost us, father,' Hook said, hoping he was right.

Father Christopher smiled gently. 'They may not know where we are, Hook, but they know where we're going. So they don't need to find us, do they? All they need do is get ahead of us and let us find them.'

'And we're resting for the day,' Hook said grimly.

'So we are,' the priest said, 'which means we must pray that our enemy is at least two days' march behind us.'

Next day they rode on. Hook was one of the scouts who ranged two miles ahead of the vanguard and looked for the enemy. He liked being a scout. It meant he could put his sharpened stake on a wagon and ride free in front of the army. The clouds were thickening again and the wind was cold. There had been a frost whitening the grass when the camp stirred, though it had vanished quickly enough. The beech leaves had turned to a dull red-gold and the oaks to the colour of bronze, while some trees had already shed their foliage. The lower pastures were half flooded from the recent rain, while the fields that had been deep-ploughed for winter wheat showed long streaks of silvery water between the ridges left by the ploughshare. Hook's men were following a drover's path that led past villages, but the hovels were all empty. There was no livestock and no grain. Someone, he thought, knew the English were on this road and had stripped the countryside bare, but whoever had organised that deprivation had vanished. There was no sign of an enemy.

It began to rain again at midday. It was just a drizzle, but it penetrated every gap in Hook's clothing. Raker, his horse, went slowly. The whole army was going slowly, incapable of speed. They passed a town and Hook, so dulled now to what he saw, scarce looked at the walls with their brightly defiant banners. He just rode on, following the road, leaving the town and its battlements behind until, quite suddenly, Hook knew they were doomed.

He and his men had breasted a small rise and in front of them was a wide grassy valley, its far side rising gently to the horizon where there was a church tower and a spread of woods. The valley was pastureland, empty of life now, but scarred across the valley floor was the evidence of their approaching doom.

Hook curbed Raker and stared.

Because right across his front, stretching from east to west, was a smear of mud, a great wide scar of churned land where every blade of grass had vanished. Water glinted from the myriad holes left by the hooves of horses. The ground was a mess, churned and rutted and broken and pitted, because an army had marched through the valley.

It must have been a great army, Hook thought. Thousands of horses had left the tracks that were newly made. He rode to the edge of the scar and saw the clarity of the hoofprints so distinctly that in places he could see the marks left by the horseshoe nails. He stared westwards, to where that vanished army had gone, but he saw nothing, only the path by which the thousands of men had travelled. The scarred earth turned north at the valley's end.

'Sweet Jesus,' Tom Scarlet said in awe, 'there must be thousands of the bastards.'

'Ride back,' Hook told Peter Scoyle, 'find Sir John, tell him about this.'

'Tell him about what?' Scoyle asked.

Hook remembered Scoyle was a Londoner. 'What do you think that is?' He pointed at the scarred earth.

'A muddy mess,' Scoyle said.

'Tell Sir John the enemy was here within the last day.'

'They were?'

'Go!' Hook said impatiently, then turned back to stare at the myriad hoofprints. There were thousands upon thousands, so many they had trampled the valley into a quagmire. He had seen the drovers' roads in England after the vast herds of cattle had been driven down to their slaughter in London, and as a boy he had been amazed by the size of the herds, but these tracks were far greater than any left by those doomed animals. Every man in France, he thought, and maybe every man in Burgundy, had ridden across this valley, and they had passed within the last day. So somewhere to the west or north, somewhere between this place and Calais, that great host waited.

'They have to be watching us,' he said.

'Sweet Jesus,' Tom Scarlet said again, and made the sign of the cross. Both archers looked at the further woods, but no glint of reflected sunlight betrayed a man in armour. Yet Hook was sure the enemy must have scouts who were shadowing England's tired army.

Sir John arrived with a dozen men-at-arms. He said nothing as he stared at the tracks and then, as Hook had done, he looked westwards and then northwards. 'So they're here,' he finally said, sounding resigned.

'That's not the small army that was following us along the river,' Hook said.

'Of course it goddam well isn't,' Sir John said, looking at the rutted fields. 'That's the might of France, Hook,' he said sarcastically.

'And they must be watching us, Sir John,' Hook said.

'You need a shave, Hook,' Sir John said harshly. 'You look like a goddamned vagabond.'

'Yes, Sir John.'

'And of course the cabbage-shitting farts are watching us. So fly the banners! And damn them! Damn them, damn them, damn them!' He shouted the mild curses, startling Lucifer who flicked back his ears. 'Damn them and keep going!' Sir John said.

Because there was no choice. And next day, though there was still no sign of the enemy army, there came proof that the French knew exactly where the English were because three heralds waited on the road. They were in their bright liveries, carrying the long white wands of their office, and Hook greeted them politely and sent for Sir John again, and Sir John took the three heralds to the king.

'What did those fancy bastards want?' Will of the Dale asked.

'They wanted to invite us all to breakfast,' Hook said. 'Bacon, bread, fried goose liver, pease pudding, good ale.'

Will grinned. 'I'd strangle my own mother for a bowl of beans now, just plain beans.'

'Beans, bread and bacon,' Hook said wistfully.

'Roast ox,' Will said, 'with juices dripping.'

'Just a lump of bread would do,' Hook said. He knew the three Frenchmen would learn much from their visit. Heralds were supposed to be above faction, mere observers and messengers, but the three men would surely tell the French commanders of the English troops scurrying off the road to lower their breeches and void their bowels, of the sagging horses, of the bedraggled, silent army that travelled north and west so slowly.

'They challenged us to battle,' Father Christopher said after the heralds had left. The chaplain, inevitably, knew what had happened when the three French emissaries met the king. 'It was all exceedingly polite,' he told Hook and his archers, 'everyone bowed very prettily, exchanged charming compliments, agreed the weather was most inclement, and then our guests issued their challenge.'

'Nice of them,' Hook said sarcastically.

'The niceties are important,' the priest said chidingly, 'you don't dance with a woman without asking her first, not in polite society, so now the Constable of France and the Duke of Bourbon and the Duke of Orleans are inviting us to dance.'

'Who are they?' Tom Scarlet asked.

'The constable is Charles d'Albret, and pray he doesn't dance face to face with you, Tom, and the dukes are great men. The Duke of Bourbon is an old friend of yours, Hook.'

'Of mine?'

'He led the army that ruined Soissons.'

'Jesus,' Hook said, and again thought of the blind archers bleeding to death on the cobblestones.

'And each of the dukes,' Father Christopher went on, 'probably leads a contingent greater than our whole army.'

'And the king accepted their invitation?' Hook asked.

'Oh willingly!' Father Christopher said. 'He loves to dance, though he declined to name a place for the dance. He said the French would doubtless have no trouble finding us.'

And now, because he knew the French would have no such trouble, and because his army might have to fight at any moment, the king ordered every man to ride in full panoply. They were to wear armour and surcoats, though most armour and jupons were now so stained or rusted and ragged that they would hardly impress an enemy, let alone overawe one. And still no enemy appeared.

No enemy showed on the feast day of Saint Cordula, the British virgin who had been slaughtered by pagans, nor the next day, the feast of Saint Felix who had been beheaded for refusing to yield the holy scriptures in his possession. The army had been marching for more than two weeks, and the next day was the feast of Saint Raphael who Father Christopher said was one of the seven archangels who stand before the throne of God. 'And you know what tomorrow is?' Father Christopher asked Hook on Saint Raphael's Day.

Hook had to think about his answer which, when it came, was uncertain. 'Is it a Wednesday?'

'No,' Father Christopher said, smiling, 'tomorrow is a Friday.'

'Then I know tomorrow's Friday,' Hook said, grinning, 'and you'll make us all eat fish, father. Maybe a nice fat trout? Or an eel?'

'Tomorrow,' Father Christopher said gently, 'is the feast day of Saint Crispin and Saint Crispinian.'

'Oh, dear God,' Hook said, and felt as though cold water had suddenly washed his heart, though he could not tell whether that was fear or the sudden certitude that such a day presaged a real and beneficial significance.

'And it might be a good day to say your prayers,' the priest suggested.

'I will, father,' Hook promised, and he began praying that very moment. Let us reach your day, he prayed to Saint Crispinian, without seeing the French, and I will know we are safe. Let us escape, he prayed, and take us safe home. Blind the French to our presence, he begged, and he added that prayer to Saint Raphael who was the patron saint of the blind. Just take us safe home, he prayed, and he vowed to Saint Crispinian that he would make a pilgrimage to

Soissons if the saint took him home and he would put money into a jar in the cathedral, enough money to pay for the altar frontal that John Wilkinson had torn apart so long ago. Just take us home, he prayed, take us all home and make us safe.

And that day, Saint Raphael's Day, Thursday the twenty-fourth of October, 1415, Hook's prayers were answered.

They were riding through a region of small, steep hills and fast-flowing streams, guided by a local man, a fuller, who knew the tangle of bewildering tracks that laced the countryside. He led Hook and the vanguard's scouts along a wagon path that twisted beneath trees. The road to Calais was some distance to the west, but it could not be followed because it led to Hesdin, a walled town on the bank of a small river, and the bridge there was guarded by a barbican, and so the guide took them towards another crossing. 'You go north after the river,' the man said, 'just go north and you find the road again. You understand?' He was frightened of the archers and even more scared of the men-at-arms in royal livery who rode just behind and made the decisions about whether the fuller could be trusted.

'I understand,' Hook said.

'Just go north,' the man insisted. The path dropped into a valley where a village lay on the southern bank of a river. '*La Rivière Ternoise*,' the man said, then pointed to the far bank where the hills climbed steeply. 'You go up there,' he said, 'and find the road to Saint-Omer.'

'Saint-Omer?'

'*Oui!*' the guide said and Hook remembered his journey with Melisande when Saint-Omer had been their goal and Calais had lain not far beyond. So close, he thought. The nervous fuller said something else and Hook only half heard and asked him to say it again. 'The local people,' the man said, 'call the Ternoise the River of Swords.'

327

That name sent a shiver through Hook. 'Why?'

The man shrugged. 'They are all mad,' he said, 'it's just a river.'

The river was shallow despite the recent rain and the knight commanding the men-at-arms ordered Hook to take his archers across the ford and up the further slope. 'Wait at the crest,' he said and Hook obediently kicked Raker down to the River of Swords. His archers followed him, splashing through water that barely reached their horses' bellies. The slope beyond the river was steep and he and his men climbed it slowly on their tired horses. The rain had stopped, though every now and then a spatter of drizzle would sweep from a sky that grew ever darker. The clouds were low, almost black, and the air above the eastern horizon was the colour of soot. 'It's going to fairly piss down,' Hook said to Will of the Dale.

'Looks like it,' Will answered apprehensively. The air was oppressive, thick, full of a strange menace.

Hook was scarcely halfway up the slope before a whole band of men-at-arms splashed through the river and spurred up the hill behind him. Hook turned in the saddle and saw the column closing up on the Ternoise's far bank as though a sudden sense of urgency had overtaken the army. Sir John, his standard-bearer close behind, thumped past Hook, riding for the crest that was outlined against the slate-dark sky and a moment later the king himself galloped up the slope on a horse the colour of night. 'What's happening?' Tom Scarlet asked.

'God knows,' Hook said. The king, his companions and every other man-at-arms had curbed their horses at the hill's crest from where they now gazed northwards.

Then Hook himself reached the skyline and he too stared.

Ahead of him the ground fell away to a village that lay in a small green valley. A road climbed from the village, leading onto a wide reach of land that was bare earth beneath the glowering sky. That bare plateau had been ploughed, and on either side of the newly cut furrows were thick woods. The battlements of a small castle just showed above the trees to the west. A banner flew from the castellated tower, but it was too far away to see what badge it showed.

Something about the lay of the land was familiar, then Hook remembered it. 'I've been here before,' he said to no one in particular. 'Me and Melisande, we were here.'

'You were?' Tom Scarlet answered, but he was not really paying attention.

'We met a horseman here,' Hook said, staring north in a daze, 'and he told us the name of the place, but I can't remember it.'

'Must have a name, I suppose,' Scarlet said absently.

More Englishmen reached the crest and stopped there to stare. No one spoke much and many made the sign of the cross.

Because in front of them, and as numerous as the sands on the shore or as the stars in the sky, was the enemy. The forces of France and Burgundy were at the ploughland's far end and they were a multitude. Their bright banners boasted of their numbers and their banners were uncountable.

The might of France blocked the road to Calais and the English were trapped.

Henry, Earl of Chester, Duke of Aquitaine, Lord of Ireland and King of England, was given a new and savage energy by the sight of the enemy. 'Form battle!' he shouted. 'Form battle!' He galloped his horse across the face of his gathering army. 'Obey your leaders! They know where you should be, form on their standards! By the grace of God we fight this day! Form battle!'

The sun was low behind the lowering clouds and the

French army was still gathering under banners as thick as trees. 'If every banner is a lord,' Thomas Evelgold said, 'and if every lord leads ten men, how many men is that?'

'Goddam thousands,' Hook said.

'And ten's a low number,' the centenar said, 'very low. More like a hundred men for every banner, maybe two hundred!'

'Sweet Jesus,' Hook said and tried counting the enemy flags, but they were too many. All he knew was that the enemy was vast and England's army was small. 'God help us,' he could not resist saying, and once again he had the shivering recollection of the blood and screams in Soissons.

'Someone has to help us,' Evelgold said briskly, then turned to his archers. 'We're on the right. Dismount! Stakes and bows! Look lively now! I want boys for the horses! Come on, don't dawdle! Move your goddam bones! We've got some dying to do!'

The horses were left in the pastures beside the village as the army climbed the shallow slope to the plateau. The enemy could not be seen from the small valley, but as Hook breasted the rise onto the ploughland the French were visible again and he felt his fears crawl back. What he saw was a proper army. Not a sickly, dishevelled band of fugitives, but a proud, massed army come to punish the men who had dared invade France.

The English vanguard was on the right now, and its archers were furthest to the right where they were joined by half the archers who had formed the army's centre. The other half joined the rearguard who now formed on the left. So the wings of the army were each a mass of archers who flanked the men-at-arms who made a line between them.

'Sweet Christ,' Tom Scarlet said, 'I've seen more men at a horse fair.'

He was pointing to the English men-at-arms. There

330

were fewer than a thousand of them and they made a pathetically small line at the centre of the array. The archers were far more numerous. Over two thousand were now assembled on each flank. 'Stakes!' A knight wearing a green surcoat galloped along the face of the archers, 'plant your stakes, lads!'

Sir John, who had formed with the men-at-arms in the line's centre, walked to where the archers readied their stakes. 'We wait to see if they attack,' he explained, 'and if not we'll fight them in the morning!'

'Why don't we just run away in the dark?' a man asked.

'I didn't hear that question!' Sir John shouted, then went on down the line, telling men to be ready for a French assault.

The archers were not in close array like the men-at-arms who waited shoulder to armoured shoulder in a line four men deep. The bowmen, instead, needed room to pull their long bowstaves and, in response to shouted orders, had moved some paces ahead of the men-at-arms where they scattered, each man finding a space. Hook was at the very front with the rest of Sir John's men. He reckoned around two hundred archers were in line with him, the rest were behind in a dozen loose ranks where they now hammered their stakes so that the points faced towards the French. Once the stakes were in place the exposed point needed re-sharpening after the hammering it had received. 'Stand in front of your stake!' the green-surcoated man shouted. 'Don't let the enemy see it!'

'Bastards aren't blind,' Will of the Dale grumbled, 'they must have seen what we were doing.'

The French were watching. They were a half-mile away, still arriving, a mass of colour on horseback beneath banners brighter than the sky, which was becoming ever darker as the clouds thickened. Most of the French were milling around the skyline where tents were being erected, but hundreds rode southwards to gaze at England's army.

'I bet the bastards are laughing at us,' Tom Scarlet said. 'They're probably pissing themselves with laughter.'

The nearest enemy horsemen were just a quarter-mile away, standing or walking their horses in the ploughland, and just gazing at the small army that faced them. To left and right the woods looked black in the fading evening light. Some archers, their stakes hammered home, were going into those woods to empty their bowels in the thick undergrowth of hawthorn, holly and hazel, but most archers just stared back at the enemy and Hook reckoned Tom Scarlet was right. The French had to be laughing. They already had at least four or five men for every Englishman, and their forces were still arriving at the northern end of the field. Hook dropped to one knee on the wet ground, made the sign of the cross, and prayed to Saint Crispinian. He was not the only archer who prayed. Dozens of men were on their knees, as were some men-at-arms. Priests were walking among the doomed army, offering blessings, while the French walked their horses across the ploughland, and Hook, opening his eyes, imagined their laughter, their scorn at this pathetic army that had defied them, had tried to escape them and now was trapped by them. 'Save us,' he prayed to Saint Crispinian, but the saint said nothing in reply and Hook thought his prayer must have been lost in the great dark emptiness beyond the ominous clouds.

It began to rain properly. It was a cold, heavy rain and, as the wind dropped, the drops fell with a malevolent intensity that made the archers hurriedly unstring their bows and coil the cords into their hats and helmets to keep them from being soaked. The English heralds had ridden ahead of the array to be met by their French colleagues, and Hook saw the men bow to each other from their saddles. After a while the English heralds rode back, their grey horses spattered with mud from hooves to belly.

'No fight tonight, boys!' Sir John brought that news to the archers. 'We stay where we are! No fires up here! You're to stay silent! The enemy will do us the honour of fighting tomorrow, so try and sleep! No fight tonight!' He rode on down the archers' line, his voice fading in the seethe of the hard rain.

Hook was still on one knee. 'I will fight on your day,' he told the saint, 'on your feast day. Look after us. Keep Melisande safe. Keep us all safe. I beg you. In the name of the Father, I beg you. Take us safe home.'

There was no answer, just the intense hiss of rain and a distant grumble of thunder.

'On your knees, Hook?' It was Tom Perrill who sneered the words.

Hook stood and turned to face his enemy, but Tom Evelgold had already placed himself between the two archers. 'You want words with Hook?' the centenar challenged Perrill.

'I hope you live through tomorrow, Hook,' Perrill said, ignoring Evelgold.

'I hope we all live through tomorrow,' Hook said. He felt a terrible hatred of Perrill, but had no energy to make a fight of it in this wet dusk.

'Because we're not finished,' Perrill said.

'Nor are we,' Hook agreed.

'And you murdered my brother,' Perrill said, staring at Hook. 'You say you didn't, but you did, and your brother's death makes nothing even. I promised my mother something and you know what that promise was.' Rain dripped from the rim of his helmet.

'You should forgive each other,' Evelgold said. 'If we're fighting tomorrow we should be friends. We have enemies enough.'

'I have a promise to keep,' Perrill said stubbornly.

'To your mother?' Hook asked. 'Does a promise to a whore count?' He could not resist the jibe.

Perrill grimaced, but kept his temper. 'She hates your family and she wants it dead. And you're the last one.'

'The French will like as not make your mother happy,' Evelgold said.

'One of us will,' Perrill said, 'me or them,' he nodded to the enemy army, though kept his eyes on Hook, 'but I'll not kill you while they fight us. That's what I came to tell you. You're frightened enough,' he sneered, 'without watching your back.'

'You've said your words,' Evelgold said, 'now go.'

'So a truce,' Perrill suggested, ignoring the centenar, 'till this is over.'

'I'll not kill you while they fight us,' Hook agreed.

'Nor tonight,' Perrill demanded.

'Nor tonight,' Hook said.

'So sleep well, Hook. It might be your last night on earth,' Perrill said, then walked away.

'Why does he hate you?' Evelgold asked.

'It goes back to my grandfather. We just hate each other. The Hooks and the Perrills, they just hate each other.'

'Well, you'll both be dead by this time tomorrow,' Evelgold said heavily, 'we all will be. So make your confession and take mass before the fight. And your men are sentries tonight. Walter's men take first watch, you take second. You're to go halfway up the field,' he nodded at the ploughland, 'and you're not to make any noise. No one is. No shouting, no singing, no music.'

'Why not?'

'How the goddam hell would I know? If a gentleman makes a noise the king will take away his horse and harness, and if an archer squeals he'll have his ears cut off. King's orders. So you stand watch, and God help you if the French come.'

'They won't, will they? Not at night?'

'Sir John doesn't think so. But he still wants sentries.' Evelgold shrugged as if to suggest that sentries would do no good, then, with nothing more to say, he walked away.

More French came to see their enemy before the night hid them. Rain swept across the plough, the sound of it drowning any laughter from the enemy. Tomorrow was Saint Crispin and Saint Crispinian's Day, and Hook reckoned it would be his last.

It rained through the night. A hard cold rain. Sir John Cornewaille ran through that rain to the cottage in Maisoncelles where the king had his quarters, but though the king's youngest brother, Humphrey, Duke of Gloucester and Thomas, Duke of York, were in the tiny smoke-filled room, neither knew where the king of England had gone.

'Probably praying, Sir John,' the Duke of York said.

'God's ears are getting a battering tonight, your grace,' Sir John said dourly.

'Add your voice to the cacophony,' the duke said. He was the grandson of the third Edward and had been cousin to the second Richard whose throne had been usurped by the king's father, but he had proved his loyalty to the usurper's son and, because his piety matched the king's, he was deep in Henry's confidence. 'I believe his majesty is testing the temper of the men,' the duke said.

'The men will do,' Sir John said. He was uncomfortable with the duke whose learning and sanctity lent him an aloof distant air. 'They're cold,' he went on, 'they're sour, they're wet, they're hungry, they're sick, but they'll fight like mad dogs tomorrow. I wouldn't want to fight them.'

'You wouldn't advise,' Humphrey, Duke of Gloucester

began, then hesitated and decided to say no more. Sir John knew what question had gone unsaid. Would he advise the king to slip away in the night? No, he would not, but he did not voice that opinion. The king would not run, not now. The king believed God was his supporter, and in the morning God would be required to prove that with a miracle.

'I'll leave your graces to arm,' Sir John said

'You have a message for his majesty?' the Duke of York asked.

'Only to wish him God's blessings,' Sir John said. In truth he had gone to test the king's temper, though he did not really doubt Henry's resolve. He said his farewells and went back to the cowshed that was his own quarters. It was a miserable stinking hovel, but Sir John knew he was fortunate to have found it on a night when most men would be exposed to thunder, lightning, rain and wintry cold.

Rain beat on the fragile roof, leaked through the thatch and puddled on the floor where a paltry fire gave off more smoke than light. Richard Cartwright, Sir John's armourer, was waiting. He looked more priestlike than any priest, with a grave, dignified face and a quaint, fluttering courtesy. 'Now, Sir John?' he asked.

'Now,' Sir John said, and dropped his wet cloak beside the fire.

He had taken off the armour he had worn during the day and Cartwright had dried it, scoured it for rust and polished it. Now he used cloths he had kept dry in a horsehide bag to wipe dry the leather breeches and jerkin that Sir John wore. The leather was supple deerhide, and the two expensive garments had been made by a tailor in London so that they fitted Sir John like a second skin. Cartwright said nothing as he wiped handfuls of lanolin onto the deerhide.

Sir John was lost in his own thoughts. He had done this so often, stood with his hands outstretched as Cartwright made the leather arms and legs slippery so that the armour above would move easily. He thought back to tournaments and battles, to the excitement that always accompanied the anticipation of those contests, but he sensed no excitement tonight. The rain hammered, the cold wind gusted drops through the cowshed door, and Sir John thought of the thousands of Frenchmen whose armourers were also readying them for battle. So many thousands, he thought. Too many.

'You spoke, Sir John?' Cartwright said.

'Did I?'

'I'm sure I misheard, Sir John. Raise your arms, please.' Cartwright dropped a mail haubergeon over Sir John's head. The chain mail was close-linked, sleeveless and dropped to Sir John's groin. The armholes were wide, so that Sir John would not be hampered by its constriction. 'Forgive me, Sir John,' Cartwright murmured as he always did when he knelt in front of his master and laced the front and back hems of the haubergeon between Sir John's legs. Sir John said nothing.

Cartwright also kept silent as he buckled the cuisses to Sir John's thighs. The front ones slightly overlapped the back ones, and Sir John flexed his legs to make sure the steel plates moved smoothly against each other. He did not ask for any adjustment because Cartwright knew precisely what he was doing. Next came the greaves to protect Sir John's calves, and the roundels for his knees, and the plate-covered boots that were buckled to the greaves.

Cartwright stood and strapped the skirt into place. The skirt was leather, covered with mail and then plated with overlapping strips of steel to protect Sir John's groin. Sir John was thinking of his archers trying to sleep in the driving rain. They would be tired, wet and cold in the morning, but he did not doubt they would fight. He heard stones scraping on blades. Arrows, swords and axes were being sharpened.

The breastplate and backplate came next, the heaviest pieces, made of Bordeaux steel like the rest of the plate, and Cartwright deftly secured the buckles, then strapped on the rerebraces that covered Sir John's upper arms, the vambraces for his forearms, more roundels for the elbows, and then, with a bow, offered Sir John the plate-covered gauntlets that had their leather palms cut out so Sir John could feel his weapons' hilts with bare hands. Espaliers covered the vulnerable place where breastplate and backplate joined, then Cartwright strapped the hinged bevor about Sir John's neck. Some men wore a chain aventail to cover the space between helmet and breastplate, but the finely shaped steel bevor was better than any mail, though Sir John frowned irritably when he tried to turn his head.

'Should I loosen the straps, Sir John?'

'No, no,' Sir John said.

'Your arms, Sir John?' Cartwright hinted gently, and then pulled the surcoat over his master's head, helped Sir John's arms into the wide sleeves, then smoothed the linen that was embroidered with the crowned lion and blazoned with the cross of Saint George. Cartwright buckled the sword belt into place and hung the big sword, Darling, which was Sir John's favourite, from its studs. 'You will entrust the scabbard with me, Sir John, in the morning?' Cartwright asked.

'Of course.' Sir John always discarded his scabbard before a fight because a scabbard could tangle a man's legs. When battle was close Darling would rest in a leather loop, her blade bare.

A leather hood was laced over Sir John's head, and it was done. The hood would help cushion the helmet which Sir John took, then handed back to Cartwright. 'Take the visor off,' he ordered.

'But . . .'

'Take it off!'

338

Once, in a tournament in Lyons, Sir John had managed to knock closed the visor of an opposing swordsman and the man's subsequent half-blindness had made him easy to defeat. Tomorrow, he thought, an Englishman would need every small advantage he could find.

'I believe the enemy have crossbows,' Cartwright said humbly.

'Take it off.'

The visor was removed and Cartwright, with a small bow, handed the helmet back to Sir John. Sir John would put it on later and Cartwright would buckle the helm to the espaliers, but for now Sir John was ready.

It rained. Out in the dark a horse whinnied and thunder sounded. Sir John picked up the strip of purple and white silk that was his wife's favour and kissed it before stuffing the silk into the narrow space between bevor and breast-plate. Some men tied their women's favours about their necks and Sir John, off balance, had once grabbed such a favour and so pulled an enemy off his horse and then killed him. If, tomorrow, an enemy seized the purple and white it would come free easily and not topple Sir John. Every small advantage. Sir John flexed his arms and found every-thing satisfactory, and so gave a grim smile. 'Thank you, Cartwright,' he said.

Cartwright bowed his head and spoke the words he had always spoken, right from the very first time he had armoured his master. 'Sir John,' he said, 'you are dressed to kill.'

As were thirty thousand Frenchmen.

'What you should do,' Hook told Melisande, 'is go away. Go tonight. Take all our coins, whatever you can carry, and go.'

'Go where?' she demanded.

'Find your father,' Hook said. They were talking in the English encampment, which lay in the lower ground south

339

of the long ploughed field. The small cottages of the village had been taken by lords, and Hook could hear the sound of hammers on steel as the armourers made the last adjustments to expensive plate. The sound was sharp, drowned by the seethe of the unending rain. To the east of the village the army's wagons were parked, their spoked wheels lit by the few fires that struggled to survive the downpour. The French army was out of sight from the low ground, but their presence was betrayed by the dull glow of their campfires reflecting from the underside of the dark clouds. Those clouds were suddenly thrown into clear view by a fork of lightning that zigzagged into the eastern woods. A moment later a clap of thunder filled the universe like the sound of some monstrous cannon.

'I chose to be with you,' Melisande said stubbornly.

'We're going to die,' Hook said.

'No,' she protested, but without much conviction.

'You talked to Father Christopher,' Hook said remorselessly, 'and he talked to the heralds. He reckons there are thirty thousand Frenchmen. We've got six thousand men.'

Melisande huddled closer to Hook, trying to find shelter under the cloak they shared. They had their backs to an oak tree, but it offered small protection against the rain. 'Melisande was married to a king of Jerusalem,' she said. Hook said nothing, letting her say whatever it was she needed to say. 'And the king died,' she went on, 'and all the men said she must go to a convent and say prayers, but she didn't! She made herself queen, and she was a great queen!'

'You're my queen,' Hook said.

Melisande ignored the clumsy compliment. 'And when I was in the convent? I had one friend. She was older, much older, Sister Beatrice, and she told me to go away. She told me I had to find my own life, and I didn't think I could, but then you came. Now I shall do what Queen Melisande did. I shall do what I want.' She shivered. 'I will stay with you.'

'I'm an archer,' Hook said bleakly, 'just an archer.'

'No, you are a ventenar! Tomorrow, who knows, maybe a centenar? And one day you will have land. We will have land.'

'Tomorrow is Saint Crispinian's Day,' Hook said, unable to imagine owning land.

'And he has not forgotten you! Tomorrow he will be with you,' Melisande said.

Hook hoped that was true. 'Do one thing for me,' he said, 'wear your father's jupon.'

She hesitated, then he felt her nod. 'I will,' she promised.

'Hook!' Thomas Evelgold's voice barked from the darkness. 'Time to take your boys forward!' Tom Evelgold paused, waiting for a response, and Melisande clutched Hook. 'Hook!' Evelgold shouted again.

'I'm coming!'

'I'll see you again,' Melisande said, 'before . . .' her voice trailed away.

'You'll see me again,' Hook said, and he kissed her fiercely before relinquishing the cloak to her. 'I'm coming!' he shouted to Tom Evelgold again.

None of his archers had been sleeping because none could sleep in the drenching rain beneath the thunder. They grumbled as they followed Hook up the gentle slope to the great stretch of black ploughland where, for a long while, they blundered around searching for the picquet they were to relieve. Hook finally discovered Walter Magot and his men a hundred paces ahead of where the sharpened stakes were still positioned. 'Tell me you left me a big fire and a pot of broth,' Magot greeted him.

'Thick broth, Walter, barley, beef and parsnips. Couple of turnips in it as well.'

'You'll hear the French,' Magot said. 'They're walking their horses. If they get too close you sing out and they go away.'

Hook peered northwards. The fires in the French camp were bright despite the rain, their flames reflected in rain-driven flickers from the water standing in the furrows and the same distant firelight outlined men leading horses in the field. 'They want the horses warm for the morning,' Hook said.

'Bastards want to charge us, don't they?' Magot said. 'Come morning, all those big men on big goddam horses.'

'So pray it stops raining,' Hook said.

'Christ, pray it does,' Magot said fervently. In rain like this the bowstrings would get wet and feeble, stealing power from the arrows. 'Stay warm, Nick,' Magot said, then led his men away to the dubious comforts of the encampment.

Hook crouched under the lash of wind and rain. Lightning staggered across the sky to stab down in the valley beyond the vast French camp and in its sudden light he had a vision of tents and banners. So many tents, so many banners, so many men come to the killing place. A horse whinnied. Scores of horses were being walked in the plough-land and Hook, when they came close, could hear their big hooves sucking in the wet soil. A couple of men came too close and both times he called out and the French servants veered away. The rain slackened from time to time, lifting its veil of noise so Hook could clearly hear the sound of laughter and singing from the enemy camp. The English camp was silent. Hook doubted many men on either side would be sleeping. It was not just the weather that would keep them awake, but the knowledge that in the morning they must fight. Armourers would be sharpening weapons and Hook felt a shiver in his heart as he thought of what the dawn must bring. 'Be with us,' he prayed to Saint Crispinian, then he remembered the advice of the priest in

Soissons Cathedral, that heaven paid closer attention to those prayers that asked for blessings on others, and so he prayed for Melisande and for Father Christopher, that they would live through the next day's turmoil.

Lightning staggered across the clouds, stark and white, and the thunder cracked overhead and the rain settled into a new and venomous intensity, falling so thick that the lights of the French camp faded. 'Who goes there?' Tom Scarlet suddenly shouted.

'Friend!' a man called back.

Another flicker of lightning revealed a man-at-arms approaching from the English encampment. He was wearing a mail coat and plate leggings and the sudden lightning lasted long enough for Hook to see the man had no surcoat and, instead of a helmet, wore a wide-brimmed leather hat. 'Who are you?' Hook demanded.

'Swan,' the man said, 'John Swan. Whose men are you?'

'Sir John Cornewaille's,' Hook answered.

'If every man in the army was like Sir John,' Swan said, 'then the French would be wise to run away!' He almost had to shout to make himself heard above the rain's malevolence. None of the archers responded. 'Are your bows strung?' Swan asked.

'In this weather, sir? No!' Hook answered.

'What if it rains like this in the morning?'

Hook shrugged. 'We'll shorten strings, sir, and shoot away, but the cords will stretch.'

'And eventually they'll break,' Will of the Dale added.

'They unravel,' Tom Scarlet said in explanation.

'So what will happen in the morning?' Swan asked. He had crouched near the archers who were clearly uncomfortable in the presence of this stranger.

'You tell us, sir,' Hook said.

'I want to know what you think,' Swan said forcibly. There

was an embarrassed silence because none of the archers wanted to share his fears. A gust of laughter and cheering sounded from the French camp. 'In the morning,' Swan said, 'many of the French will be drunk. We'll be sober.'

'Aye, only because we've got no ale,' Tom Scarlet said.

'So what do you think will happen?' Swan insisted.

There was another silence. 'Drunken goddam bastards will attack us,' Hook finally said.

'And then?'

'Then we kill the goddam drunken bastards,' Tom Scarlet said.

'And so win the battle?' Swan asked.

Again no one answered. Hook wondered why Swan had sought them out to have this forced conversation. Eventually, as none of his men spoke, Hook did. 'That's up to God, sir,' he said awkwardly.

'God is on our side,' Swan said very forcefully.

'We do hope that, sir,' Tom Scarlet said dubiously.

'Amen,' Will of the Dale put in.

'God is on our side,' Swan said even more forcefully, 'because our king's cause is just. If the gates of hell were opened in tomorrow's dawn and Satan's legions come to attack us, we shall still win. God is with us.'

And Hook remembered that far-off sunlit day in Southampton Water when the two swans had beaten past the waiting fleet and he remembered, too, that the swan was one of the badges of Henry, King of England.

'You believe that?' Swan asked, 'that our king's cause is just?'

None of the other archers answered, but Hook recognised the voice now. 'I don't know if the king's cause is just,' he said harshly.

There was a silence for a few heartbeats and Hook sensed the man who called himself Swan stiffen with indignation.

344

'Why should it not be?' Swan asked, his voice dangerously cold.

'Because on the day before we crossed the Somme,' Hook said, 'the king hanged a man for theft.'

'The man stole from the church,' Swan said dismissively, 'so of course he had to die.'

'But he never stole the box,' Hook said.

'He didn't,' Tom Scarlet added.

'He never stole that box,' Hook said harshly, 'yet the king hanged him. And hanging an innocent man is a sin. So why should God be on the side of a sinner? Tell me that, sir? Tell me why God would favour a king who murders an innocent man?'

There was another silence. The rain had eased a little and Hook could hear music coming from the French camp, then a burst of laughter. There had to be lamps inside the enemy's tents because their canvas glowed yellow. The man called Swan shifted slightly, his plate leggings creaking. 'If the man was innocent,' Swan said in a low voice, 'then the king did wrong.'

'He was innocent,' Hook said stubbornly, 'and I'd stake my life on that.' He paused, wondering if he dared go further, then decided to take the risk. 'Hell, sir, I'd wager the king's life on that!'

There was a hiss as the man called Swan took a sudden inward breath, but he said nothing.

'He was a good boy,' Will of the Dale said.

'And he never even got a trial!' Tom Scarlet said indignantly. 'At home, sir, at least we get to say our piece at the manor court before they hang us!'

'Aye! We're Englishmen,' Will of the Dale said, 'and we have rights!'

'You know the man's name?' Swan asked after a pause.

'Michael Hook,' Hook said.

'If he was innocent,' Swan said slowly, as if he were thinking about his response even as he spoke it, 'then the king will have masses sung for his soul, he will endow a chantry for him, and he will pray himself every day for the soul of Michael Hook.'

Another sharp fork of lightning stabbed the earth and Hook saw the dark scar beside the king's nose where a bodkin arrow had hit him at Shrewsbury. 'He was innocent, sir,' Hook said, 'and the priest who said otherwise lied. It was a family quarrel.'

'Then the masses will be sung, the chantry will be endowed, and Michael Hook will go to heaven with a king's prayers,' the king promised, 'and tomorrow, by God's grace, we will fight those Frenchmen and teach them that God and Englishmen are not to be mocked. We will win. Here,' he thrust something at Hook, who took it and found it was a full leather bottle. 'Wine,' the king said, 'to warm you through the rest of the night.' He walked away, his armoured feet squelching in the thick soil.

'He was a weird goddam fellow,' Geoffrey Horrocks said when the man called Swan was well out of earshot.

'I just hope he's goddam right,' Tom Scarlet put in.

'Goddam rain,' Will of the Dale grumbled. 'Sweet Jesus, I hate this goddam rain.'

'How can we win tomorrow?' Scarlet asked.

'You shoot well, Tom, and you hope God loves you,' Hook said, and he wished Saint Crispinian would break his silence, but the saint said nothing.

'If the goddamned French do get in among us tomorrow,' Tom Scarlet said, then faltered.

'What, Tom?' Hook asked.

'Nothing.'

'Say it!'

'I was going to say I'd kill you and you could kill me

before they torture us, but that would be difficult, wouldn't it? I mean you'd be dead and you'd find it really hard to kill me if you were dead.' Scarlet had sounded serious, but then began to laugh and suddenly they were all laughing helplessly, though none really knew why. Dead men laughing, but that, Hook thought, was better than weeping.

They shared the wine, which did nothing to warm them, and slowly, grey as mail, the dawn relieved the dark. Hook went into the eastern woods to empty his bowels and saw a small village just beyond the trees. French men-at-arms had quartered themselves in the hovels and now were mounting horses and riding towards the main encampment. Back on the plateau Hook watched the French forming their battles under their damp standards.

And the English did the same. Nine hundred men-at-arms and five thousand archers came to the field of Azincourt in the dawn, and across from them, across the furrows that had been deep ploughed to receive the winter wheat, thirty thousand Frenchmen waited.

To do battle on Saint Crispin's Day.

PART FOUR

Saint Crispin's Day

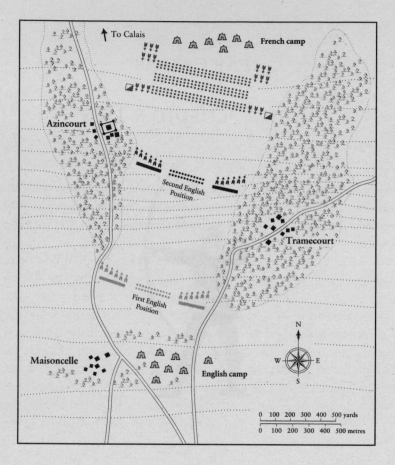

To Calais

French camp

Azincourt

Second English Position

Tramecourt

First English Position

N

W E

S

Maisoncelle

English camp

0   100 200 300 400 500 yards

0   100 200 300 400 500 metres

Azincourt

Dawn was cold and grey. A few spatters of rain blew fitfully across the ploughed field, but Hook sensed the night's downpours had ended. Small patches of mist clung to the furrows and lingered in the dripping trees.

The drummers behind the centre of the English line were beating a quick rhythm that was punctuated by the flaring sound of trumpets. The musicians were massed where the king's banner, the largest in the army, was flanked by the cross of Saint George, by the banner of Edward the Confessor and by the flag of the Holy Trinity. That quartet of banners, all flown from extra long poles, was in the middle of the centre battle, while the flanking battles, the rearguard and vanguard, were similarly dominated by their leaders' standards. There were at least fifty other flags flying in the damp air above Henry's men-at-arms, but those English standards were as nothing to the array of silk and linen that was flaunted by the French. 'Count the banners,' Thomas Evelgold had suggested as a way of estimating the French numbers, 'and reckon every flag is a lord with twenty men.' Some French lords would have fewer men-at-arms and most would have far more, but Tom Evelgold was certain his method would yield an approximation of the enemy's numbers, except that even Hook, with his good eyesight, could not distinguish the separate flags. There were simply too many. 'There are thousands of the bastards,' Evelgold said unhappily, 'and look at all those goddam crossbowmen!' The French archers were on the enemy's flanks, but some way behind the leading men-at-arms.

'You wait!' an elderly man-at-arms, grey-haired and mounted on a mud-spattered gelding, shouted at the archers. He was just one of the numerous men who had come to offer advice or orders. 'You wait,' he called again, 'till I throw my baton in the air!' The man held up a short, thick staff that was wrapped in green cloth and surmounted by golden finials. 'That's the signal to shoot arrows! No one is to shoot before that! You watch for my baton!'

'Who's that?' Hook asked Evelgold.

'Sir Thomas Erpingham.'

'Who's he?'

'The man who throws the baton,' Evelgold said.

'I shall throw it high!' Sir Thomas shouted, 'like this!' He threw the baton vigorously so that it circled high in the rain above him. He lunged to catch it as it fell, but missed. Hook wondered if that was a bad omen.

'Fetch it, Horrocks,' Evelgold said, 'and look lively, lad!' Horrocks could not run, the furrows and ridges were too thick with mud and so his feet sank up to his ankles, but he retrieved the green stick and held it to the grey-haired knight. Sir Thomas thanked him, then moved down the line of archers to shout his orders again. Hook noticed how Sir Thomas's horse struggled in the ploughed land. 'They must have set the share deep,' Evelgold said.

'Winter wheat,' Hook said.

'What's that got to do with it?'

'Always plough deeper for winter wheat,' Hook explained.

'I never had to plough,' Evelgold said. He had been a tanner before he was appointed as a ventenar to Sir John.

'Plough deep in autumn and shallow in spring,' Hook said.

'I suppose it'll save the bastards from digging us graves,' Evelgold said dourly, 'they can just roll us into those big furrows and kick the soil over us.'

'Sky's clearing,' Hook said. Off to the west, above the ramparts of the small castle of Azincourt that just showed above the woodland, the light was brightening.

'At least the bowstrings will be dry,' Evelgold remarked, 'which means we might kill a few of the goddam bastards before they slaughter us.'

The enemy flew more banners and they also had more musicians. The English trumpeters were playing brief series of defiant notes, then pausing to let the drummers beat their sharp, insistent rhythm, but the French trumpets never stopped. They clawed at English ears, a braying sound that rose and fell on the cold wind. Most of the French army was on foot, like the English, but on either wing Hook could see masses of mounted knights. The horses wore long linen trappers embroidered with coats of arms. Their riders were trying to keep the beasts warm by walking them up and down. Lances pricked the sky. 'The goddam bastards will come soon,' Tom Scarlet said.

'Maybe,' Hook said, 'maybe not.' He half wished the French would come and get the ordeal over, and he half wished he was safely back in England, abed.

'Don't string up till they move,' Evelgold called to Sir John's archers. He had offered the advice at least six times already, but none of the bowmen seemed to notice. They shivered and watched the enemy. 'Shit!' Evelgold added.

'What?' Hook asked, alarmed.

'I just stepped in some.'

'That's supposed to bring you luck,' Hook said.

'Then I'd better dance in the goddam stuff.'

Priests were saying mass among the archers and, one by one, the men went to receive the bread of life and have their sins forgiven. The king was ostentatiously kneeling bareheaded before one of his chaplains out in front of the centre battle. He had ridden the line once, mounted on a small white horse, and the gilded crown that circled his battle-helm had looked unnaturally bright in the morning's gloom. He had chivvied men into position and leaned out of his saddle to tug at an archer's stake to ensure it was well bedded in the soil. 'God is with us, fellows!' he had called to the archers. The bowmen had started to kneel in deference, but he had waved them up. 'God is on our side! Be confident!'

'Wish God has sent more Englishmen,' a voice had dared to call from among the bowmen.

'Never wish that!' the king had sounded cheerful. 'God's providence is sufficient! We are enough to do His work!'

Hook hoped to God the king was right as he went back to kneel before Father Christopher who was dressed in a black priestly robe over which he wore a mud-spattered chasuble embroidered with white doves, green crosses and the Cornewaille red lions. 'I've sinned, father,' Hook said, and he made a confession he had never made before; that he had murdered Robert Perrill and still planned to murder both Thomas Perrill and Sir Martin. It was hard to say the words, but Hook was driven to it by the thought, almost a certainty, that this was his last day on earth.

Father Christopher's hands tightened on Hook's head. 'Why did you commit murder?' he asked.

'The Perrills murdered my grandfather, my father and my brother,' Hook said.

'And now you have murdered one of them,' Father Christopher said sternly. 'Nick, it must finish.'

'I hate them, father.'

'It's a day of battle,' Father Christopher said, 'and you should go to your enemies and beg their forgiveness and make your peace.' The priest paused, but Hook said nothing. 'Other men are doing that,' Father Christopher went on. 'They're seeking out their enemies and making their peace. You should do the same.'

'I promised not to kill him in the battle,' Hook said.

'That's not enough, Nick. You want to go to God's judgement with hatred in your heart?'

'I can't make peace with them,' Hook said, 'not after they killed Michael.'

'Christ forgave His enemies, Nick, and we are to be like Christ.'

'I'm not Christ, father. I'm Nick Hook.'

'And God loves you,' Father Christopher sighed, then made the sign of the cross on Nick's head. 'You will not murder either man, Nick. That is a command from God. You understand me? You will not go into this battle with hatred in your heart. That way God will look gently on you. Promise me you will think no murder, Nick.'

It was a struggle. Hook was silent for a while, then he nodded abruptly. 'I won't kill them, father,' he said unhappily.

'Not today, not tomorrow, not ever. You swear that?'

There was another pause. Hook was thinking of the long years, of the embedded hatred, of the loathing he felt for Sir Martin and for Tom Perrill, and then he thought of what he had to face this day and he knew that if he were to go to heaven then he must give Father Christopher the solemn promise. He nodded abruptly. 'I swear it,' he said.

Father Christopher's hands tightened on Hook's bare scalp again. 'Your penance is to shoot well this day, Nicholas Hook. Shoot well for God and your king. *Te absolvo*,' he said. 'Your sins are forgiven. Now look up at me.'

Hook looked up. The rain had finally stopped. He stared

355

into Father Christopher's eyes as the priest took a sliver of charcoal and carefully wrote on Hook's forehead. 'There,' he said when he was finished.

'What's that, father?'

Father Christopher smiled, 'I've written IHC Nazar on your forehead. Some folk believe it protects a man from sudden death.'

'What does it mean, father?'

'It's the name of Christ, the Nazarene.'

'Write it on Melisande's forehead, father.'

'I will, Hook, of course I will. Now ready yourself for the body of Christ.' Hook received the sacrament and then, as other men were doing and as the king had done, he took a pinch of wet earth and swallowed it with the wafer to show he was ready for death. The gesture proclaimed he was prepared to receive the earth as the earth might have to receive him. 'God bless you, Nick,' Father Christopher said.

'I hope we meet when it's over, father,' Hook said, pulling the helmet over his aventail.

'I pray that too,' the priest said.

'The shit-eating bastards must come soon,' Will of the Dale grumbled when Hook rejoined his men, yet the French showed no sign of wanting to attack. They waited, their deep ranks almost filling the wide space between the woods. The English heralds, resplendent in their liveries and holding their long white wands, had ridden halfway to the enemy's line where they had been met by French and Burgundian heralds and now they all made a bright group that sat on their horses at the edge of the trees beside a tumbledown hovel with a mossy roof. They would observe the battle together and at its end they would decree the winner.

'Come on, you goddam bastards,' a man grumbled.

But the goddam bastards did not come. Their trumpets howled, but the long steel ranks showed no sign of being ready to advance. They waited. The trapper-bright horses milled about to hide the crossbowmen behind. A brief ray of sunlight shone on the centre of their line and Hook saw the oriflamme, the red forked pennant that announced to the French that they were to take no prisoners. Kill everyone.

'Evelgold! Hook! Magot! Candeler!' Now it was Sir John Cornewaille's turn to pace in front of the archers. 'Come here! The four of you!'

Hook joined the other three sergeants. It was extraordinarily hard to walk through the deep plough because the clay soil had turned to a viscous reddish mud that clung to his boots. It was even harder for Sir John who was wearing full plate armour, sixty pounds of steel, so that he lurched as he walked, forced to drag each steel-plated foot out of the earth's sucking grip. Sir John struggled to a place some forty or fifty paces ahead of the archers and there waited for his sergeants. 'You always want to look at your own army,' he greeted them, 'to see it as the enemy does. Have a look.'

Hook turned to stare at a mud-spattered, rusted and bedraggled army. His army. The centre of the line was made of three battles, each of around three hundred men-at-arms. The central battle was commanded by the king, the one on the far right by Lord Camoys, while the left-hand battle was led by the Duke of York. Between the three battles were two small groups of archers, while on either flank were the much larger contingents of bowmen. Those two flanking groups, with their stakes, were angled ahead of the line's centre so that their arrows could fly in from the sides. 'So what do the French do?' Sir John demanded.

'Attack,' Evelgold said dourly.

'Attack what and why?' Sir John asked harshly. None of the four archers answered, instead they gazed at their own small army and wondered what reply Sir John wanted. 'Think!' Sir John growled, his bright blue eyes darting between his sergeants. 'You're a Frenchman! You live in some shit-spattered manor with rats in the damp walls and mice dancing in the roof. What do you want?'

'Money,' Hook suggested.

'So what do you attack?'

'The flags,' Thomas Evelgold said.

'Because that's where the money is,' Sir John said. 'The goddamned bastards are flying the oriflamme,' he went on, 'but that means nothing. They want prisoners. They want rich prisoners. They want the king, the Duke of York, the Duke of Gloucester, they want me, they want ransoms! There's no profit in slaughtering archers, so the bastards will attack the men-at-arms. They'll attack the flags, but some might come for you so drive them into the centre with arrows. That's what you do! Drive their flanks into the centre. Because that's where I can kill them.'

'If we've got enough arrows,' Evelgold said doubtfully.

'Save enough!' Sir John said forcibly, 'because if you run out of arrows you're going to have to fight them hand to hand and they're trained to that, you're not.'

'You trained us, Sir John,' Hook said, remembering the winter of practice with swords and axes.

'You're half-trained, but the other archers?' Sir John asked derisively, and Hook, looking at the waiting men, knew they were no match for French men-at-arms. The archers were tailors and cordwainers, fullers and carpenters, millers and butchers. They were tradesmen who possessed a superb skill, the ability to draw the cord of a yew bow to their ear and send the arrow on its deathwards journey. They were killers, but they were not men hardened to war by tournaments and trained from childhood in the discipline of blades. Many of them had no armour other than a padded jacket, and some did not even possess that small protection. 'God keep the French from getting among them!' Sir John said.

None of the sergeants responded. They were thinking of what would happen when French men-at-arms, clad in steel, came to kill them. Hook shivered, then was distracted by the sight of five horsemen riding under the English royal banner towards the waiting French army. 'What are they doing, Sir John?' Evelgold asked.

'The king has sent them to make an appeal for peace,' Sir John said, 'they'll demand that the French yield the crown to Henry, and then we'll agree not to slaughter them.'

Evelgold just stared at Sir John as if he did not believe what he had heard. Hook suppressed a laugh and Sir John shrugged. 'So they won't accept the terms,' he said, 'and that means we fight, but it doesn't mean that they'll attack us.'

'They won't?' Magot asked.

'We have to get past them to reach Calais, so maybe we'll have to cut our way through them.'

'Jesus,' Evelgold muttered.

'They want us to attack them, Sir John?' Magot asked.

'I would, if I were them!' Sir John turned to stare at the enemy. 'They don't want to cross this ground any more than we do, but they don't need to cross it. We do. We have to reach Calais or we die here of starvation. So if they don't attack us, we have to attack them.'

'Jesus,' Evelgold said again, and Hook tried to imagine the effort that would be needed to cross that half-mile of sucking, slippery, clinging mud. Let the French attack, he thought, and suddenly shivered violently. He was cold, he was hungry, he was tired. The fear came in waves and was turning his bowels to water. He was not the only one, lots of men were slipping into the woods to empty their bowels.

'I need to go to the woods,' he said.

'If you need to shit, do it here,' Sir John said harshly, then shouted at the massed archers. 'No one's to use the woods!' He feared that men, losing courage, would hide in the trees. 'You're to shit where you stand!'

'Shit and die,' Tom Evelgold said.

'And go to hell with fouled breeches,' Sir John snarled, 'who cares?' He looked at each of his sergeants in turn, then spoke with a quiet intensity. 'This battle's not lost. Remember, we have archers, they don't.'

'But we don't have enough arrows,' Evelgold said.

'Then make each one count,' Sir John said, impatient with his centenar's pessimism, then scowled at Hook. 'Jesus, man, can't you do that upwind of me?'

'Sorry, Sir John.'

Sir John grinned. 'At least you can take a shit. Try doing that in full armour. I tell you, we're not going to smell like lilies by the time we've finished our work today.' He gazed at the enemy, his bright eyes looking at the oriflamme. 'And one last thing,' he said forcefully, 'no one's to start taking prisoners until we give the order that it's safe to capture instead of kill.'

'You think we'll take prisoners?' Evelgold asked with astonished disbelief.

'If men try to take prisoners too soon they weaken the line,' Sir John said, ignoring the question. 'You have to fight and kill until the bastards can fight no more, and only then can you set about finding ransoms.' He clapped Evelgold on a mail-clad shoulder. 'Tell your lads we'll be feasting on captured French provisions tonight.'

Either that, Hook thought, or eating hell's rations. He struggled back to his men who each stood by a stake. Those stakes, over two thousand of them on this right flank of the English army, made a dense thicket of sharpened points. Men could move among them easily enough, but no warhorse could manoeuvre about them.

'What did Sir John want?' Will of the Dale asked.

'To tell you that we'll be eating French rations tonight.'

'He thinks they'll take us prisoner?' Will asked sceptically.

'No, he thinks we'll win.'

That prompted some bitter laughter. Hook ignored it and watched the enemy. The front rank of their dismounted men-at-arms stretched across the skyline, thick with the metal points of shortened lances. Still they did not move and still the English waited. French horsemen went on exercising their destriers and, because the horses disliked the thick furrows, many of the knights went to the grassy pastures beyond the woods. The sun climbed higher behind the thinning clouds. The king's emissaries, sent to make an offer of peace, had met with a similar group of Frenchmen and now rode back across the ploughland and, moments later, a rumour spread that the French had agreed to let the English pass, then the rumour was denied. 'If they don't want to fight,' Tom Scarlet said, 'then perhaps they'll just stand there all day!'

'We have to get past them, Tom.'

'Jesus, we could sneak off tonight! Go back to Harfleur.'

'The king won't do that.'

'Why not for God's sake? He wants to die?'

'He's got God on his side,' Hook said.

Tom shivered. 'God might have sent us a decent breakfast.'

Women brought what little food they had hoarded against this day. Melisande gave Hook an oatcake. 'We share it,' Hook said.

'It's for you,' she insisted. There was mould on the oats, but Hook ate half anyway and gave Melisande the other half. There was no ale, just water from a stream that Melisande brought in an old leather wine bottle. The water tasted rank. Melisande stood beside him and stared at the French. 'So many,' she said quietly.

'They're not moving,' Hook said.

'So what will happen?'

'We'll have to attack them.'

She shivered. 'You think my father's there?'

'I'm sure of it.'

She said nothing. They waited. Waited. The trumpets and drums still sounded, but the musicians were tiring and the music was less exuberant. Hook could hear robins singing fitfully among the trees, some of which had already lost their leaves so that their branches were gaunt as scaffolds against the grey sky. The glistening wet ploughland between the waiting armies was flitting with fieldfares and redwings that sought worms in the furrows. Hook thought of home, of the cows being milked, the sound of rutting stags in the woods, the shortening evenings and firelight in the cottages.

Then there was a stir and Hook, startled back to reality, saw that the king, mounted once again on the small white horse and accompanied only by his standard-bearer, had ridden out ahead of the army. He was coming towards the archers on the right flank and his horse, troubled by the uncertain footing, was lifting its hooves high. The king had taken off his crowned helm and the small wind tousled his short brown hair, making him look younger than his twenty-eight years. He curbed the horse a few paces in front of the foremost stakes and the centenars shouted at their men to take off their helmets and kneel. This time the king accepted the obeisance, waiting until all two and a half thousand archers were on their knees.

'Bowmen of England!' the king called, then was silent as the men shuffled closer to hear him. Cased bows and pole-axes were slung on their shoulders. Some men were armed with foresters' axes or lead-weighted mallets. Most had a sword, though some carried nothing except a bow and a knife. Those with helmets had taken off their bascinets and others clawed back their mail hoods as they stared at their bareheaded king.

'Bowmen of England!' Henry called again, and there was a catch in his voice, so that he paused again. The wind stirred the mane of his horse. 'We fight today because of my quarrel!' the king shouted, his voice clear and confident now. 'Our enemy deny me the crown that God has granted me! Today they believe they will humble us! Today they believe they will drag me as a prisoner before the crowds in Paris!' He paused as a murmur of protest went through the hundreds of bowmen. 'Our enemy,' the king went on, 'have threatened to cut off the fingers of every Englishman who draws a bow!' The murmur was louder now, a growl of indignation, and Hook remembered the square in Soissons where the cutting off of fingers had just been the start of the horror. 'Of every Welshman who draws a bow!' the king added, and a ripple of cheers sounded from among the archers' ranks.

'All that they believe,' the king called, 'yet they have forgotten God's will. They are blind to Saint George and to Saint Edward who watch over us, and it is not just those saints who offer us their protection! This day is the feast of Saint Crispin and Saint Crispinian, and those saints want vengeance for the evils done to them at Soissons.' He paused again, but no murmur sounded. To most of the archers Soissons was a name that meant nothing, but they were still listening intently. 'It has fallen to us,' the king said, 'to wreak that vengeance and you must know, as certainly as I know, that we are God's instruments this day! God is in your bows, God is in your arrows, God is in your weapons, God is in your hearts and God is in your souls. God will preserve us and God will destroy our enemies!' He paused again as another low murmur sounded among the archers. 'With your help!' the king shouted loud now, 'with your strength! We will win today!' There was a heartbeat of silence, then the

363

archers cheered. The king waited for the sound to die away. 'I have offered peace to our foe! Grant me my rights, I said to them, and we shall have peace, but there is neither peace in their hearts nor mercy in their souls, and so we have come to this place of judgement!' Here, for the first time, the king took his eyes from the throng of kneeling archers and turned to look at the clay furrows that lay between the armies.

He looked back to his audience. 'I have brought you to this place,' he said, his voice lower now, but intense, 'to this field in France, but I will not leave you here! I am, by the grace of God, your king,' his voice rose, 'but this day I am no more than you and I am no less than you. This day I fight for you and I pledge you my life!' The king had to pause because the bowmen were cheering him again. He raised a gauntleted hand and waited for silence. 'If you die here, I die here! I will not be taken captive!' Again the archers cheered, and again the king raised a hand and waited till the sound stopped. He smiled then, a confiding smile. 'But I do not expect to be taken captive nor will I be killed, because all that I ask is that you fight for me this day as I will fight for you!' He thrust his right hand towards the archers, sweeping his fingers around to encompass them all. His horse capered sideways in the mud and the king calmed it expertly. 'Today I fight for your homes, for your wives, for your sweethearts, for your mothers, for your fathers, for your children, for your lives, for your England!' The cheer that greeted those words must have been heard at the field's far end where the French still waited beneath their bright banners. 'Today we are brothers! We were born in England, we were born in Wales, and I swear on the lance of Saint George and on the dove of Saint David that I shall take you home to England, home to Wales, with new glories to our name! Fight as Englishmen! That is all I ask of you! And I promise that I will fight beside you and for you! I am your king, but this day I am your brother, and I swear on my immortal soul that I will not forsake my brothers! God save you, my brothers!' And with those words the king wheeled his horse and rode to give the same speech to the men-at-arms, leaving the archers on the right flank cheering him.

'By God,' Will of the Dale said, 'but he really thinks we'll win!'

And at the field's far end the gusting wind lifted the red silk of the oriflamme so that it rippled above the enemy's lance points. No prisoners.

And still the French did not move. The archers were sitting now, despite the damp ground. Some even slept, snoring in the mud. The priests still offered absolution. Father Christopher used his stub of charcoal to write the talismanic name of Jesus on Melisande's forehead. 'You will stay with the baggage train,' he told her.

'I will, father.'

'And keep your horse saddled,' the priest advised.

'To run away?' she asked.

'To run away,' he agreed.

'And wear your father's jupon,' Hook added.

'I will,' she promised. She had the surcoat in a sack that held her worldly possessions, and now she took out the fine linen and unfolded it. 'Give me your knife, Nick.'

He gave her his archer's dagger and she used it to cut a sliver of material from the bottom hem of the jupon. She gave it to him. 'There,' she said.

'I wear it?' Hook asked.

'Of course you do,' Father Christopher said. 'That's what a soldier does. He wears his lady's colours.' He gestured towards the English men-at-arms, most of whom wore a silken handkerchief or favour around their necks. Hook looped his own strip about his neck, then took Melisande into his arms.

'You heard the king,' he told her, 'God is on our side.'

'I hope God knows that,' she said.

'I pray so too,' Father Christopher said.

Then, suddenly, there was movement. Not from the French who showed no sign of wanting to attack, but from a group of English men-at-arms who had mounted horses and now rode along the army's front. 'We're to advance!' the man who came to the right wing shouted. 'Pick up your stakes! We're to advance!'

'Fellows!' It was the king himself who had gone a few paces ahead of the line and now stood in his stirrups and waved his arms to encompass all his countrymen. 'Fellows! Let's go!'

'Oh, my God, my God,' Melisande said.

'Go back to the baggage,' Hook told her, then began wrestling his thick stake out of the clinging earth. 'Go on, love,' he said, 'I'll be all right. There's not a Frenchman who can kill me.' He did not believe that, but he forced a smile for her sake. He felt his stomach lurch. Fear was making him cold. He felt fragile, weak, shaking, but somehow he dragged the stake free and laid it over his shoulder.

He did not look back at Melisande. He started walking, struggling in the thick mud, and all along the English line men were doing the same. They moved pitifully slowly, dragging their feet out of the wet, clinging soil, and going pace by difficult pace towards the French.

And the French watched them. Just watched. 'If the bastards had any sense they'd attack us now,' Evelgold said.

'Maybe they will,' Hook said. He watched the distant enemy. Some horsemen who had been exercising their destriers were walking them back towards the flanks of the army, but there appeared to be no urgency in their actions.

The trumpets did not change their tune. The French seemed content to let the English march the length of the plough-land, and Hook felt his mind skittering like a hare in the spring grass. Had it really been the king who came to the archers in the night? He had forgotten to whip the centre of one of his spare bowstrings where the cord engaged an arrow's nock. Would the king really pray for Michael? Would death be quick? Piers Candeler suddenly loosed a string of oaths and kicked off both boots to negotiate the plough barefoot. Hook remembered the archer he had hanged in London and wondered if that man had felt just this same fear when he watched the Scottish army come to fight on Homildon's green hill, and then he thought of all the other Englishmen who had carried a war bow for their king. They had fought the Scots, the Welsh, each other, and always, always, they had fought the French, and still these French did not move. Their immobility was scaring Hook. They seemed content to wait, knowing that the small English army must throw itself on their blades.

Hook's left foot was trapped in the soil's suction so he did what other archers were doing, let the boot go. He pulled off the other boot and went barefoot, finding it easier. 'If they move,' Evelgold shouted in warning, 'we stop, string bows and plant stakes.'

Yet the French did not move. Hook could see still more men joining their army, most coming from the east. The mounted men-at-arms on either flank were watching the English, but not spurring the big warhorses, which had armoured faces and padded cloths over their chests and rumps. The riders' long lances were held upright. Some of the steel-tipped, ash-shafted lances had pennons attached. The horsemen had their helmets' visors open and Hook could see steel-framed faces. He was cold even though he was sweating. He wore a padded haubergeon over his leather-lined mail coat, and that armour might stop a sword swing, but it would easily be pierced by a lance. He tried to imagine dodging a spear's thrust in this thick mud and knew it would be impossible.

'Slow down!' a voice ordered. The archers were getting too far ahead of the English men-at-arms who, encumbered by their armour, were making hard work of the waterlogged ploughland. Yet, step by step, they advanced steadily, and the woods on either side drew closer so that the English line now filled the space between the trees. The bright group of heralds, French, English and Burgundian, were walking their horses closer to the French, holding a position halfway between the two armies.

'Christ on His goddam cross,' Evelgold grumbled, 'but how close does he want us?'

Then a voice bellowed at the archers to replant their stakes. The enemy was close now, only a little more than two hundred paces away, and that was no further than the most distant marks at an archery contest, and Hook remembered those summer days with jugglers and dancing bears and free ale and the crowds cheering as the archers drew and loosed. 'Stakes!' a man shouted, 'plant them firm!'

Hook's stake slid easily enough into the soft ground. He glanced at the enemy, saw that they were still not moving, and so unslung his poleaxe and gave the stake's sharpened tip three hard blows that blunted the wood even as it drove the stake deeper into the ground. He used his knife to shave away the crushed wood and thus sharpen the replanted stake, and then, at last, he uncased the bow from its horsehide sheath. All around him archers were fixing stakes or stringing bows. Hook braced his bow against the stake's lower end and bent the yew to slip the cord's noose over the upper nock. He took both arrow bags from his shoulder. He pulled the arrows free and pushed them point down into the soil, bodkins to the left and the half-dozen broadheads to the right. He kissed the bow's belly, where the dark wood met the light. Dear God, he prayed, and then he prayed to Saint Crispinian, and his heart felt like a trapped bird and his mouth was dry and his right leg shivered, and still the French were motionless and Saint Crispinian made no answer to Hook's prayer.

The archers were spread out. Their stakes did not make a solid line facing the French, but instead were sunk in scattered lines, filling a space as wide and deep as the marketplace where Henry had burned and hanged the Lollards. There were a couple of paces between stakes, space enough for a man to move, but too tight for any horse to manoeuvre freely. The archers' crude ranks stretched back so that the men in the rear could not see the enemy because of the archers in front of them, but that did not matter yet because at two hundred paces they would need to shoot high in the air if their arrows were to reach the French. Hook was in the foremost rank and he turned to see Thomas Perrill hammering in his stake some paces behind and to his right. There was no sign of Sir Martin and Hook wondered if the priest had gone back to the camp. That thought made him shiver for Melisande's safety, but there was no time to worry about that because Tom Evelgold was shouting at his men to face front.

Hook thought the enemy was at last advancing, but the French were not stirring. Their centre was a long thick line of dismounted men-at-arms in bright surcoats and polished armour, while their flanks were two masses of horsemen armed with lances. The flags were silken-bright against the grey sky and, in the very centre of the French line, where the banners were thickest, the oriflamme was a red streak of wind-driven ripples telling the English that the enemy would show them no mercy.

Hook tried to find the Sire de Lanferelle in the enemy ranks, but could not see him. Instead he saw the weapons.

He saw swords, lances, poleaxes, falcon-beaks, mauls, battle-axes and maces. Some of the maces had spiked heads. He laid a broadhead across the bow's thick-bellied stave and suddenly wanted to empty his bowels again. He closed his eyes for an instant and said another fervent prayer to Saint Crispinian, then planted his bare feet in the slimy earth. He braced himself.

'Sweet Jesus Christ,' Thomas Scarlet said.

'Oh God, oh God,' Will of the Dale muttered.

Sir Thomas Erpingham, grey-haired and bareheaded, had mounted his small horse and ridden a few paces ahead of the English line. The horse picked its feet high, unhappy with the sticky soil. Behind Sir Thomas the English men-at-arms waited. The nine hundred were arrayed four deep, with the king, resplendent in shining armour and with a jewelled crown of gold ringing his battle-helm, standing in their centre. Sir Thomas, in a green surcoat blazoned with the red cross of Saint George, turned the horse so that his back was towards the French. He waited a few heartbeats.

'Be with me now,' Hook prayed aloud to Saint Crispinian.

He wished the saint would talk to him, but Crispinian was still silent.

'Draw!' Thomas Evelgold ordered in a low voice.

Hook lifted the bow. He drew the hemp-string all the way to his ear and felt the savage power in the bent wood. He aimed at a horse directly ahead of him, but knew it would be luck if the arrow struck where he aimed. If the French had been fifty paces closer he would have picked his targets and been sure of hitting each one, but at extreme bowshot he would be lucky to land the arrow within four or five feet of his target. He held the string back and his right arm quivered.

Five thousand archers had drawn their bows. Five thousand arrows were held on five thousand strings.

A flock of starlings flew up beyond the Tramecourt woods, their wingbeats sudden and loud. They resembled a swirl of dark smoke above the trees and then, as suddenly as they had appeared, they went. All along the French line the visors were being dropped. Hook had seen faces, but now could see only faceless steel.

'God be with us,' an archer muttered as Sir Thomas stood in his saddle.

Sir Thomas Erpingham threw the green baton high so that it circled in the damp air. There was silence above the field of Azincourt, a silence in which the green baton flew, its golden finials bright against the dull sky. 'Now,' Sir Thomas shouted, 'strike!'

The baton fell.

Hook released.

The arrows flew.

The first sound was the bowstrings, the snap of five thousand hemp cords being tightened by stressed yew, and that sound was like the devil's harpstrings being plucked. Then there was the arrow sound, the sigh of air over feathers, but multiplied, so that it was like the rushing of a wind. That sound diminished as two clouds of arrows, thick as any flock of starlings, climbed into the grey sky. Hook, reaching for another broadhead, marvelled at the sight of five thousand arrows in two sky-shadowing groups. The two storms seemed to hover for a heart's beat at the height of their trajectory, and then the missiles fell.

It was Saint Crispin's Day in Picardy.

For an instant there was silence.

Then the arrows struck.

It was the sound of steel on steel. A clatter, like Satan's hailstorm.

And the day's noise of pain began. It was a scream from

a horse that reared with a broadhead deep in its rump. The horse bolted forward, jerking its steel-clad rider in his high saddle, and the motion of the wounded horse served as a signal so that more horses followed, then all the riders spurred and the whole French line gave a great shout as their cavalry began their charge. *'Saint Denis! Montjoie!'*

'Saint George!' someone shouted in the English line, and the shout was taken up by the small army. 'Saint George!' The men-at-arms taunted the French with hunting calls, and the noise grew to a clamour as the trumpets screamed at the sky.

Where Hook's second broadhead was on its way.

Ghillebert, Seigneur de Lanferelle, was in the front rank of the French army. He was one of over eight thousand dismounted men-at-arms who formed the first of the three French battles. He wore polished plate armour beneath his surcoat of the sun and falcon, though the armour's leg pieces were now spattered with mud. At his side hung a long battle-sword, across his shoulder was a lead-weighted mace studded with spikes, while in his hands was an ash-shafted lance shortened to seven feet and tipped with a steel spike. His head was enclosed in a leather hood that was laced beneath his chin and beneath which his long hair was coiled. Over the hood he wore a chain-mail aventail that covered his head and shoulders, and above the aventail, completely encasing his skull, was an Italian battle-helm. The helm's visor was pushed up so he could see the English and see, too, that their army was risibly small.

The French were ebullient. Henry of England had dared to march his pathetic army from Normandy to Picardy, thinking he could shame his enemy by parading his insolent banners across French territory, and now he was trapped. Lanferelle, watching the enemy since dawn, had reckoned

372

that there were only a thousand men-at-arms in their line, and that figure had seemed so ridiculously small that he had checked again and again by dividing the line into quarters, counting heads and multiplying by four, and each time he arrived at the same total. Maybe one thousand men-at-arms who were faced by three successive French battles, each with at least eight thousand men-at-arms, but there were also the two wings of the English.

Archers.

Thousands of archers, too many to count, though the French scouts had reported figures as various as four thousand to eight thousand. And those archers, Lanferelle knew, carried the long yew bows and had bags of steel-tipped arrows that, at close range, could slash through the best armour in Christendom. That was why all Lanferelle's armour was shaped and curved so that the arrows would be deflected, yet even so he knew an unlucky hit could find lodgment. And so Ghillebert, the Lord of Hell, Sire of Lanferelle, did not share his compatriots' ebullience. He did not doubt for a second that the French men-at-arms could slaughter the English men-at-arms, but to reach that paltry battle-line they would have to endure the arrows.

In the night, as other men drank, the Sire of Lanferelle had gone to an astrologer, a famous man from Paris who was reputed to see the future, and Lanferelle had joined the long line waiting to consult the seer. The man, bearded, grave, and swathed in a fur-edged black cloak, had taken Lanferelle's gold and then, after much groaning and sighing, had declared he saw nothing but glory in the future. 'You will kill, my lord,' the astrologer had said, 'you will kill and kill, and gain both glory and riches.' Afterwards, standing outside the astrologer's tent in the seething rain, Lanferelle had felt hollow.

He would kill and kill, of that he was certain, but the

ambition was not to slaughter the English, but to capture them, and at the very centre of the enemy line, beneath the tallest banners, was the King of England. Take Henry captive and the English nation would spend years raising the ransom. Frenchmen were relishing that prospect. There were also royal dukes in the English line, and great lords, and any one of them could make a man rich beyond his wildest dream.

But between the dream and the reality were the archers.

And Ghillebert, Seigneur de Lanferelle, understood the power of the yew bow.

Which was why, when the English had begun their long, laborious advance across the plough-ruined field between Tramecourt and Azincourt, Lanferelle had called to the constable that it was time to attack. The English, as they struggled forward, had lost their cohesion. Instead of being an army in battle formation they were suddenly a mud-spattered rabble trudging across the treacherous furrows, and Lanferelle had seen the archers in disarray and had called again to Marshal Boucicault and to the constable, d'Albret. 'Let the horsemen go now!'

The horsemen were on either French wing, big men on big horses, the stallions with armoured faces and thick padding covering their chests, and their job was to charge into the archers on the wings and slaughter them mercilessly, but many of the horsemen had ridden away to exercise their destriers on the grassy meadows beyond the woods to keep the animals warm and the remaining horsemen merely watched the English.

'The decision isn't mine,' Marshal Boucicault answered Lanferelle.

'Then whose is it?'

'Not mine,' Boucicault said curtly and grimly, and Lanferelle understood that Boucicault shared his fear of the archers' abilities.

'For the love of Christ!' Lanferelle said when still no order was given for the horsemen to charge. Instead they stood their big destriers and watched as the English struggled ever closer.

'Who leads us? For Christ's sake, who leads us?' Lanferelle asked loudly. No one had given the French a rousing speech before the battle, though Lanferelle had seen the English king ride and pause along the enemy line and he had guessed Henry was rousing his men to slaughter.

Yet who spoke for France? Neither the constable nor the marshal commanded the vast army. That honour seemed to lie with the Duke of Brabant, or perhaps it was the young Duke of Orleans who had only just arrived on the field and was now watching the English advance and doubtless counting the ransoms to be made. The duke seemed content to let the enemy struggle towards their slaughter and so no order was given to the horsemen on either French wing.

Lanferelle watched, incredulous, as the English were allowed to come within long bowshot. The French had crossbowmen, they even had a handful of men who could shoot the yew bow, and they possessed some small cannons that were ready and loaded, but the waiting horsemen masked both the guns and the bowmen. The crossbow had a longer range than the yew bow, but the crossbowmen could not shoot and so the enemy archers pounded in their stakes unmolested. Dear God, Lanferelle thought, but this was madness. The archers should have been scattered and slaughtered by now, but instead they had been allowed to come within their bows' range and to pound their stakes into the soft ground as a deterrent to horsemen. He watched as they strung their bows, doing it all within crossbow range yet staying entirely undisturbed. 'Jesus,' he said to no one in particular, 'she comes in, takes off her clothes, lies on the bed, spreads her legs, and we do nothing.'

'Sire?' his squire asked.

Lanferelle ignored the question. 'Visors!' he shouted at his men. He led sixteen men-at-arms and he turned to make certain they had closed their visors before pulling down his own with a metallic thud.

He was instantly engulfed in darkness. A moment before he had been able to see the enemy clearly. He had even seen the glitter of gold circling Henry of England's helmet, but now there was a steel shutter in front of his eyes and the shutter was pierced by twenty small holes, none wide enough to admit even a bodkin arrow's narrow point, and to see anything through those holes Lanferelle had to move his head from side to side, and even then he could make out little of what happened.

Yet he did see the lone horseman ride from the centre of the English line.

And he saw the baton thrown into the air.

And he heard the words. 'Now, strike!'

He lowered his head as if he struggled into a fierce wind and he heard the rising rush of arrows and he flinched, flinched, teeth grinding together, and then the missiles struck.

There was a terrible noise as thousands of steel arrowheads plunged onto steel armour, and a man called out in sudden pain, and Lanferelle felt a thumping blow on his right shoulder, and even though the arrow was deflected it lurched him to one side with the sheer force of its blow. A second arrow quivered in his lance, though he could not see it. Some fool in the rear rank had left his visor open and was making a gargling noise around an arrow that had fallen from the sky to pierce his mouth and drive down into his windpipe. The man slowly sank to his knees and coughed a stream of thick blood. Other arrows plunged into the soil, or else glanced off armour. A horse whinnied and reared to Lanferelle's left.

'*Saint Denis! Montjoie!*' the French shouted and Lanferelle, jerking his head so that he could make some sense of what the small holes in his visor revealed, saw the horsemen at last start forward. Then another shout to advance came from the centre of the French line, where the oriflamme flew, and all the first battle lurched towards the enemy.

'*Montjoie!*' they shouted, the sound of their voices huge and deafening inside their helmets, and Lanferelle could hardly move because his armoured feet were stuck in the mud, but he jerked his right leg free and so began the advance. Men of mud and steel, no flesh in sight, lumbering towards the waiting English. And the English were howling hunting cries like rabid devils pursuing Christian souls.

And the second arrow-storm fell.

And the devil's hail rattled and more men screamed.

As the French, at last, attacked.

The horsemen came first. Hook saw one horse rearing, saw the rider topple backwards as his pennanted lance scraped a circle against the sky, and then that horse was swallowed by the charge. Knights rowelled back their spurs, lowered their lances and called their battle cry, and Hook saw great clods of earth being thrown up behind the monstrous hooves. The stallions tossed their armour-weighted heads, hating the uneven ground, and the spurs struck back again and the charge took shape as the horses gained speed.

The skill of a mounted charge was to start slow, the riders knee to knee, and to advance in that close formation so that the whole line of heavy horses struck the enemy together. Only at the last minute should a man kick his destrier into a gallop, but the ploughland was so soft and the arrow fall so sudden that men spurred impulsively forward to escape both. No one had ordered the charge, rather it was the sting of the first arrow-storm that prompted it, and now, on both flanks, the horsemen charged as fast as their big horses could carry them. Three hundred horsemen attacked the English right wing, and even fewer assaulted the left. There were supposed to be a thousand horsemen on either flank, but the other riders were missing, still exercising their destriers.

And the archers drew and loosed.

Hook used broadheads. They were useless against armour, but they could pierce the padded cloths protecting the horses' chests and, as the range shortened, so the arrows flew at a lower and lower trajectory, none wasting their force on the upper air, but searing straight into the charging animals, and for a moment Hook thought the arrows were having no effect, but then a horse stumbled and went down in a great flurry of mud, man, lance and harness. The horse screamed and its rider, trapped by the rolling body, screamed with it and the horse behind struck the rolling beast in front and Hook saw the second rider being pitched forward over his horse's head. He drew again, picking a big horse with shaggy fetlocks and drove an arrow into its side, just in front of the saddle's girth and the horse swerved away, colliding with another, and Hook's next arrow thumped into a padded chest to bury itself to the fledging and the world was hoofbeats and screams and the sound of bow cords and at least a dozen horses were on the ground, some struggling to get up, others splashing mud with frantic hooves as their lives drained away through sliced arteries. Will of the Dale put a bodkin into a rider's throat and the man jerked back under the arrow's strike, then rebounded forward from his saddle's high cantle and his lance buried its point in a furrow and so lifted the man out of his saddle as his horse galloped on, eyes white and visible through the holes in its face armour, and the man was dragged along by the stirrup as the horse took an arrow in the eye and veered to one side and so brought down two more horses.

The archers were shooting fast. The horsemen did not have far to charge, but the ground slowed them and in the minute it took the three hundred to reach the archers on the English right they were the target of over four thousand arrows. Only the bowmen in the front two ranks were shooting at the horses, the other archers, their view of the charge obscured by those front ranks, were still hoisting arrows high so that they fell among the dismounted French.

A maddened horse, blood spurting from a ripped belly, twisted away and charged at the French men-at-arms in the field's centre. Others followed it. Some horsemen, baulked by the corpses and by the dying horses to their front, pulled up, and then they were easy targets and the arrows whipped into them, each one striking a horse with the sound of a butcher's cleaver, and the horses were screaming and men were trying to control them.

Yet still some horses reached the English line.

'Back!' centenars shouted, 'back!'

The front ranks of archers stepped backwards to leave their stakes facing the enemy. They still shot. Hook had taken a handful of bodkin arrows and he let one fly at less than twenty paces and saw the heavy, oak-weighted point glance off a man-at-arm's armour. He drew again, this time plunging the arrow into the horse's chest.

Then the charge struck home.

But the riders had their visors down and could see nothing through the small slits or holes, while the horses, wearing their steel chamfrons, were almost as blinkered as the men. The charge struck home, but struck onto the stakes and a horse whimpered pitifully, a stake deep in its rib-shattered chest and blood bubbling from its open mouth. The stallion's rider flailed his lance at empty air. Arrows drove into him and both man and horse were twisting and screaming. Another destrier made it past the first stakes and somehow saw the second row and veered aside to lose its footing in the slick mud. Horse and rider fell in a crash of steel and ash lance. 'Mine!' Thomas Evelgold shouted and ran the few paces forward with his poleaxe. He swung it once, thumping the lead-weighted hammer onto the man-at-arms's helmet, then he knelt, hauled up the stunned man's visor and ran a knife through an exposed eye. The man-at-arms quivered and was still. The horse tried to struggle to its feet, but Evelgold stunned it with his poleaxe, then struck again with the axe blade that pierced the chamfron and cracked open the beast's skull.

'See them off!' Evelgold shouted.

The charge had ended at the stakes and the first French attack had ended in failure. The horsemen had been supposed to scatter the archers, but the arrows had done their wicked work and the stakes had stopped the survivors from getting among the bowmen. Some men-at-arms were already riding away, pursued by arrows, while riderless horses, crazed with pain, charged back at their own lines. One man, braver than brave, had dropped his lance to draw his sword and now tried to steer his destrier between the stakes, but the arrows whipped into his horse, which went to its knees, and a bodkin, shot at less than ten paces, drove through the rider's breastplate, killing him, and he sat there, a head-drooping corpse on a dying horse, and the English archers jeered him.

It was strange, Hook thought, that the fear had gone. Now, instead, an excitement sang in his veins and a thin shrill voice keened in his head. He went back to his stake and plucked up a bodkin. The horsemen were gone, defeated by arrows, but the main French attack still advanced. They came on foot, because armoured men on foot were less vulnerable to arrows than horses, and they came beneath bright banners, but their ranks had been churned to chaos by the wounded, riderless horses that had fled in blind panic to charge through the advancing French. Men went down under the heavy hooves, and other men tried to straighten the ragged line that stumbled across the deep furrows towards the English king and his men-at-arms. Hook picked his targets. He drew, the cord flowing back with deceptive ease, and he loosed arrow after arrow. Other archers crowded him, all jostling forward to pour their shafts at the French.

Who still came on. Their ranks had been broken by the panicked horses, and men were falling as arrows found their marks, but still they advanced. All France's high aristocracy was in the leading battle and they came beneath proud banners. Eight thousand dismounted men-at-arms attacking nine hundred.

Then a French gun fired.

Melisande was praying. It was not a conscious prayer, more a desperate and silent and unending cry for help aimed at a grey sky, which offered her no comfort.

The baggage had been supposed to follow the army up onto the plateau, but most had stayed around the village of Maisoncelles where the king had spent much of the night. The royal baggage wagons were parked there, guarded by ten men-at-arms and twenty archers, all of them reckoned too sick or lame to stand in the main line of battle. Father Christopher had led Melisande there, saying she would be safer than with the few packhorses that had been led up onto the high ploughland where the two armies met. The priest had written his mysterious letters on her forehead. IHC Nazar. 'It will preserve your life,' he had promised her.

'Write it on your own face,' Melisande had told him.

Father Christopher had smiled. 'God has me in the palm of His hand, my dear,' he said, then made the sign of the cross, 'and He will preserve you. But you must stay here. You will be safer here.' He had placed her with the other archers' wives between two empty wagons that had brought arrows to Azincourt, made sure that her horse was nearby and that the mare was saddled, and then Father Christopher had taken one of Sir John's horses and ridden up the slope towards the place where the armies waited. Melisande had watched him until he vanished over the crest of the hill, and that was when she had begun to pray. The other wives of Sir John's archers prayed too.

Melisande's prayer took shape slowly. It had begun as an incoherent cry for help, but she forced herself to choose her words carefully as she prayed to the Virgin. Nick is a good man, she told the Mother of Christ, and a strong one, but he can be angry and sour, so help him now to be strong and alive. Let him live. That was the prayer, to let her man live.

'What do we do if the French come?' Matilda Cobbold asked.

'Run,' one of the other women said, and just then there was a roar from the hidden high ground beyond the skyline. They had heard the war-shout of Saint George, but the women were too far away to hear the saint's name, only the great bellow of sound that told them something must be happening beyond the skyline.

'God help us,' Matilda said.

Melisande opened the sack that contained her worldly belongings. She wanted the jupon her father had sent her, but the sack also contained the ivory-stocked crossbow that Nick had given her almost three months before. She pulled it out.

'You'll fight them on your own?' Matilda asked.

Melisande smiled, but found it hard to speak. She was so nervous, so frightened, knowing that what happened beyond the high horizon would decide her life's course and that it was all beyond her control. She could only pray.

'Go up there, love,' Nell Candeler said, 'and shoot some of the bastards.'

'It's still cocked,' Melisande said in wonderment.

'What is?' Matilda asked.

'The bow,' Melisande said. 'I never released it.' She stared at the crossbow, remembering the day Matt Scarlet had died, the day she had pointed the crossbow at her father. Ever since that day the bow had been cocked, its steel-shanked stave under the thick cord's strain, and she had never noticed. She almost pulled the trigger, then impulsively thrust the bow back into her sack and pulled out the folded jupon. She stared at the bright cloth, half tempted to pull it over her head, but she suddenly knew she could not wear an enemy's badge while Nick was fighting, and then another certainty overtook her, the knowledge that she would never see Nick again so long as she was tempted to wear her father's jupon. It had to be thrown away. 'I'm going to the river,' she said.

'You can piss here,' Nell Candeler said.

'I want to walk,' Melisande said, and she picked up her heavy sack and went south, away from the armies on the plateau and away from the baggage. She walked through the army's sumpters that cropped the autumn grass, her feet soaked by the damp. She had an idea to throw the jupon into the Ternoise and watch it float downstream, but the River of Swords was too far away and so she settled for a stream that ran high and fast from the night's rain. The stream flowed through the tangle of small fields and woods that lay just south of the village and she crouched on its bank where the leaves of the alders and willows had turned yellow and gold and there she dropped the sack, closed her eyes and held the jupon in both hands as if it were an offering.

'Look after Nick,' she prayed, 'let him live,' and with those words she threw her father's jupon into the stream and watched it being carried fast away. The further it went, she thought, the safer Nick would be.

Then the French gun fired, and that sound was loud

383

enough to reverberate all through the valley behind the battlefield, loud enough to make Melisande turn and stare north.

To see Sir Martin, grinning and lanky, his grey hair slicked close against his narrow skull.

'Hello, little lady,' he said hungrily.

And there was no one for Melisande to ask for help.

She was alone.

A cloud of smoke rose above the horizon, marking the distant place where the gun had fired.

'All a-lonely,' Sir Martin said, 'just you and me.' He made a gurgling sound that might have been laughter, hitched up his robes, and came for her.

The gun fired, belching smoke above the left flank of the French army.

Hook saw the gun-stone and did not recognise what it was, but for an instant there was a dark object rising and falling above the ploughland and it seemed as if the thing, it was just a dark flicker, was coming straight for him and then the gun's noise splintered the sky and birds rose screeching from the trees as the gun-stone struck an archer's head a few paces from Hook.

The man's skull was obliterated in an instant spray of blood and shattered skull. The stone kept flying, leaving a feathered trail of misted blood until it slapped into the mud two hundred paces behind the English line. It narrowly missed the destriers of the men-at-arms that were empty-saddled and under the guard of pageboys.

'Jesus,' Tom Scarlet said in disgust. There were jellied scraps of brain trickling down his bow's shaft.

'Just keep shooting,' Hook said.

'Did you see that?' Scarlet asked in indignant amazement.

What Hook saw was dead and dying horses, dead riders, and beyond them a mass of dismounted men-at-arms advancing towards him. Crossbow bolts whirred close, but there were very few enemy bowmen who had a clear sight of the English. The French crossbowmen were aligned with the rearmost battle, too far to be sure of their aim, and most could not even see their enemy. Then, as the first French battle advanced to fill the space between the woodlands of Tramecourt and Azincourt, the French bowmen lost sight of the English altogether and the missiles stopped flying.

The first French battle was spread across the wide ploughed field between the trees, but, because those woods funnelled ever closer together, the line of armoured men was being squeezed inwards. Their ranks were already ragged, torn apart by the panicked horses that had bolted through them, but now they were jostling for space as the field contracted and all the while the arrows drove into them.

Hook was shooting steadily. He had already gone through one sheaf of arrows and had shouted for more. Boys were dumping fresh bundles among the archers, but hundreds of thousands were needed. Five thousand archers could easily shoot sixty thousand arrows in a minute and, when the cavalry had charged, they had shot even faster. Some men were still drawing and releasing as quickly as they could, but Hook slowed down. The closer the enemy came, the more lethal each arrow would be, so for now he was content to use broadheads against the advancing French.

The broadheads could never hope to pierce plate armour, but the blow of their strike was sufficient to knock a man backwards, and each man Hook knocked back caused a ripple of chaos, slowing the French, and the enemy were struggling, not just with mud, but with the incessant arrow strikes. He could hear the arrows cracking against steel, a weird noise, never-ending, and the French men-at-arms, who were still a hundred and fifty paces away, looked as though they bent into the face of a gale, but a gale that was bringing steel hail.

Thomas Brutte cursed when his bow cord snapped to send an arrow spinning crazily into the air. He took a spare string from his pouch and restrung the bow. Hook saw how each of the enemy banners had a dozen or more arrows caught in their weave. He aimed at a man in a bright yellow surcoat, loosed, and his arrow threw the man backwards. A horse lay on its side in front of the advancing French. The stallion's death throes made it thrash its head and beat its hooves and the French line became even more disordered as men tried to avoid the animal. Bowstrings made their dull quick noise all around Hook. The sky was dark with arrows. Most archers were shooting at the men-at-arms who directly threatened them and, to avoid that arrow-storm, the foremost ranks of the French crowded still further inwards, and that shrinking of the French line became more marked as the rearmost English archers, their aim frustrated by the men to their front, went into the thick briar underbrush of the Tramecourt woods and lined the edge of the trees from where they poured bodkins into the French flank.

The bravest of the French struggled to reach the English quickly, while the more prudent fell behind to gain the protection of the bolder men in front, and Hook saw how the French men-at-arms, who had begun their advance in a long straight line, were now coalescing into three crude wedges that were aimed at the flags waving in the centre of each of the three English battles. It would be man-at-arms against man-at-arms, and the French, Hook supposed, were hoping to punch three bloody holes through the English line. And once that line of nine hundred men broke there would be chaos and death. He spared a glance north, worried that the narrowing of the French battle would give their cross-bowmen a chance to shoot past the attackers' flank, but those French archers seemed to have gone backwards, almost as though they had lost interest in the fighting.

He picked up a bodkin and found the man in the yellow surcoat again. He drew, released, and was plucking up another arrow when he saw the yellow-clad man fall to his knees. So the bodkins were piercing, and Hook shot again and again, punching arrows into the slow-moving mass of men. He aimed at the leading rank and not all his arrows pierced their armour, but some struck plumb and tore their way through. Frenchmen were falling, tripping the ranks behind, yet still the great armoured crowd struggled on.

'I need arrows!' a man shouted.

'Bring us goddamned arrows!' another shouted.

Hook still had a dozen. The enemy was close now, less than a hundred paces from the English line, but the arrow-storm was weakening as archers ran out of shafts. Hook drew long, picked a victim in a black surcoat, released and saw his arrow slap through the side of the pot-helm and the man seemed to totter in a circle, the arrow protruding from his brain as his lance knocked over another knight before the dying man dropped to his knees and fell full length in the mud. The next arrow glanced off a breastplate. Hook shot again, close enough now to see the details of his target's livery. He saw a man in blue and green who had what appeared to be a gilded coronet around his helmet and Hook shot at him, then cursed himself because such a man could afford the finest armour and sure enough the arrow was deflected by the plate, though the man did stagger and was only rescued by his standard-bearer who pushed him back upright. Hook loosed again, shooting his arrow in a low trajectory that ended in a Frenchman's thigh, and then there was only one arrow left. He held it on the stave, watching. It seemed to Hook that all the thousands of arrows had done surprisingly little damage to the enemy. Many Frenchmen were down and their bodies impeded the rest, but still the ploughland seemed filled with living, mud-plastered, armoured Frenchmen carrying their lances, swords, maces and axes to the thin English line. They lumbered closer, each step an effort in the cloying earth, and Hook selected a man who seemed more eager than the rest and he sent his final arrow into that tall man's chest. The bodkin point struck through steel plate and punctured a rib to pierce a lung and so fill the man's helmet with a rush of blood that bubbled from his mouth and spilled from his visor's holes.

'Arrows!' Hook bellowed, but there were none except the few remaining in the hands of the rearmost archers, and those men saved their missiles. The archers were spectators now. They stood among their stakes, a few yards from the nearest French wedge that was just paces from the English vanguard.

The archers had done their job. Now it was England's men-at-arms who would have to fight.

While the French, spared the arrows at last, gave a hoarse shout and lunged to the kill.

The Sire de Lanferelle could vault onto the back of his horse while wearing a full suit of plate armour, he even danced in armour sometimes, not just because women adored a man dressed for killing, but to demonstrate that he was more elegant and lithe in armour than most men were without. Yet now he could hardly move. Each step was a fight against the soil's suction. In places he sank to mid-calf and could find no purchase to drag his feet free, yet step by step he managed to keep going, sometimes leaning on his neighbour so he could wrench an armoured foot out of the clinging earth. He tried to step in the furrows where water lay, because those furrows had the firmest bottoms, but he could scarce see the ground through the tight holes of his closed visor.

Nor did he dare open the helmet, because the arrows were clattering and clashing and banging all around him. He was hit on the forehead by a bodkin that snapped his head back and almost toppled him, except that one of his men pushed him upright. Another arrow struck his breastplate, tearing a long rip in his jupon and scraping across the steel with a high-pitched squeal. His armour resisted both blows, though other men were not so fortunate. Every few heartbeats, in the middle of the metallic rain of arrows, a man would gasp or scream or call for help. Lanferelle did not see them fall, only hear them, and he was aware that the attack was losing its cohesion because men were crushing in from his left where most of the arrows came from, and those men squeezed the formation. Armour plate clanged against armour plate. Lanferelle himself was pushed so tight against his right-hand neighbour that he could not move his arm holding the lance and he bellowed a protest and made a huge effort to get a step ahead of the man. He was sweeping his head from side to side, trying to make sense of the blur of grey ahead. The English, he noticed, had their visors raised. They were not threatened by arrows and so could see to kill, but Lanferelle dared not lift his own visor because a handful of archers were posted between the English battles straight ahead and those men would thank God for the target of an unvisored French face.

His breathing was hoarse inside the helmet. He reckoned himself to be a strong man, yet he was gasping as he waded through the thick soil. Sweat streamed down his face. His left foot slipped in a patch of slick mud and he sank to his right knee, but managed to heave himself upright and stagger onwards. Then he tripped on something and sprawled again, this time falling beside the corpse of an unhorsed man-at-arms. Two of his men pulled him to his feet. He was sheeted in mud now. Some of the holes in his visor were blocked by mud and he pawed at them with his left hand, but the armoured gauntlet could not clear the thick wet earth. Just get close, he told himself, just get close and the killing could start and Lanferelle was confident of his ability to kill. He might not be a mud-wader, but he was a killer, and so he made another huge effort, trying to get ahead of the crush so he would have room to use his weapons. He turned his head again, scanning through the visor's remaining holes, and saw, straight ahead, a great banner showing the royal arms of England with their impudent appropriation of the French lily. The royal arms on the flag were defaced with three white bars, each bar with three red balls, and he recognised the badge as that of Edward, Duke of York. He would serve as a prisoner, Lanferelle thought. The ransom for an English royal duke would make Lanferelle rich, and that prospect seemed to give his tired legs a new strength. He was growling now, though quite unaware of it. The English line was close. 'Are you with me, Jean?' he shouted, and his squire shouted yes. Lanferelle intended to strike the English line with his lance and then, as the enemy recoiled from that blow, drop the cumbersome weapon and use the mace that was slung on his shoulder, and if the mace broke he would take one of the spare weapons carried by his squire. Lanferelle felt a sudden elation. He had lived this long, he had survived the arrow-storm and he was taking his lance to the enemy, but just then a bodkin point ripped from the flank and struck plumb in one of the visor's holes and sudden light flooded Lanferelle's eyes as the arrow peeled back the steel and sliced a savage cut in the bridge of his nose. His head was wrenched painfully to one side as the arrow missed his right eyeball by a hair's breadth and scored across his cheekbone to lodge in his helmet.

He could see suddenly. He could see through the ragged hole torn by the arrow that he wrenched free with his left hand. He could not see much, but a sudden noise to his left made him turn to see a tall man pitch forward with blood bubbling from his visor's holes, and then Lanferelle looked back to his front and the Duke of York was only a few paces away and so he dropped his left hand to brace the lance, took a deep breath, and shouted his war cry. He was still shouting as he charged, or rather as he churned his way through the last paces of muddy ploughland. The shout mingled anger and elation. Anger at this impudent enemy and elation that he had survived the archers.

And he had come to the killing place.

Sir John Cornewaille was also angry.

Since the day the army had landed in France he had been one of the commanders of the vanguard. He had led the short march to Harfleur, been in the first rank of the men who had assaulted that stubborn city, and he had led the march north from the Seine to this muddy field in Picardy, yet now the king's relative, the Duke of York, had been given command of the vanguard, and the pious duke, in Sir John's view, was an uninspiring leader.

Yet the duke commanded and Sir John, a few places to the duke's right, could only submit to the appointment, but that did not mean he could not tell the men of the right-hand battle what they should do when the French came. He was watching the enemy men-at-arms approach, and he was seeing how they struggled in the mud, and he was awed by the thickness of the arrow-storms that converged from left and right to pierce and wound and kill. Not one French visor was open, so they were half blinded by steel and almost crippled by the mud, and Sir John was waiting for them with lance, poleaxe and sword. 'Are you listening!' he shouted. Ostensibly he was calling to his own men-at-arms, but only a fool would not heed Sir John Cornewaille's words when it came to a fight. 'Listen!' he bellowed through his unvisored helmet. 'When they reach us they're going to rush the last few paces! They want to hit us hard! They want the fight over! When I give the word we all step back three paces. You hear me? We step back three paces!'

His own men, he knew, would obey him, as would Sir William Porter's men-at-arms. Sir John had trained his men in the brief manoeuvre. The enemy would come at a rush and expect to lunge their shortened lances straight at English groins or faces, and if the English were suddenly to step back then those first energetic blows would be wasted on air. That was the moment Sir John would counterattack, when the enemy was off balance. 'You wait for my command!' he shouted, and felt a brief moment of concern. Perhaps it was dangerous to step backwards in such treacherous ground, but he reckoned the enemy was more likely to slip and fall than his own men. Those men were arrayed in three crude ranks that swelled to six where the Duke of York's big company was arrayed around their lord. The duke, anxious face showing through his open helm, had not turned to look when Sir John shouted. Instead he had stared straight ahead while the tip of his sword, made of the best Bordeaux steel, rested lightly on the furrows. 'When they come to strike!' Sir John bellowed, watching to see if the duke showed any response. 'Cheat their blow! Step back! And when they falter, attack!' The duke did not acknowledge the advice, he still stared at the French horde that was losing its order. The flanks were crushing inwards to escape the arrows, and the leading men were skewing what was left of the French formation by deliberately advancing on those places in the English line where the banners proclaimed the position of high nobility who might expect to pay extravagant ransoms. Yet, disorganised though the French were, this first battle was still a horde. It outnumbered the English men-at-arms by eight to one; it was an armoured herd spiked with lances, thick with blades, a grinding wave of steel that seemed to shrug off the arrows as a bull might ignore the stings of swarming horseflies. Some Frenchmen fell, and whenever a man was put down by a bodkin point he would trip the men behind, and Sir John saw the crowding and jostling, the pushing and shoving. Some men were struggling to be in the front rank, wanting to win renown, others were reluctant to be the first to strike, yet all, he knew, were anticipating ransoms and riches and rejoicing.

'God be with you, John,' Sir William Porter said nervously. He had moved to be next to his friend.

'I think God will let us win,' Sir John said loudly.

'I wish God had sent us a thousand more English men-at-arms,' Sir William said.

'You heard what our king said,' Sir John shouted in response, 'don't wish for another man on our side! Why share the victory? We're English! If we were only half our number we would be enough to slaughter these turd-sucking sons of rancid whores!'

'God help us,' Sir William said softly.

'Do what I say, William,' Sir John said quietly. 'Let them come at you, step back, then strike. Once you have the first man down you've made an obstacle for the second. You understand me?'

Sir William nodded. The two sides were now close enough for men on either side to recognise each other by their jupons, except the surcoats of the French were so spattered with mud that some were hard to read and nearly every surcoat had two or more arrows caught in its folds.

'Then kill the second man,' Sir John went on. 'Don't use your sword. A sword's no good in this fight. Hammer the bastards down with a poleaxe. Stun them, break their legs, crack their skulls. Put the second man down, William,

394

and the third can't reach you without stumbling over two corpses.'

'I'd rather use a lance,' Sir William said diffidently.

'Then stab at their visors,' Sir John said. 'That's the weakest point in armour. Ram it home, William, and make the goddam bastards suffer.' The French were fewer than fifty paces away. The arrow strikes had almost stopped, though a few bodkins still streaked across the face of the advancing enemy to strike from the flank. The archers posted between the battles were readying to file back between the men-at-arms so that the English line of fully-armoured men would be continuous. Those archers still had a few arrows left and were shooting them fast before they were ordered to the rear. More Frenchmen went down. One, an arrow deep in his belly, knelt and then opened his visor to vomit a mix of puke and blood before the men behind trod him into the furrows.

'We're three ranks deep,' Sir John said, 'and they're at least twenty ranks deep. The men behind will push the men in front and so they're going to be forced onto our blades.' He grinned suddenly. 'And we're sober, William. We ran out of wine so we're fighting sober, but I'll wager half their army is soaked in wine. God is with us, William.'

'You believe that?'

'Believe it?' Sir John laughed, 'I know it! Now brace yourselves!'

The noise was rising as the enemy shouted their war cries. Off to Sir John's left where a thick crowd of Frenchmen was advancing on the king's banner, he could see the oriflamme, red and wicked, high on its pole, and then he forgot that symbol because the enemy in front had summoned a last great effort. They were shouting, they were even trying to run, they were coming to take their victory.

Their lances were poised to strike. They were screaming.

'*Saint Denis! Montjoie! Montjoie!*' and the English were howling like huntsmen closing on their prey.

'Now!' Sir John bellowed. 'Now!'

Sir Martin shoved Melisande down, planting his hand between her breasts and thrusting hard and quickly so that she fell back between the trees on the stream's bank. 'There,' he said, 'you just stay there like a good little girl. No!' he held up a hand as she tried to scramble away. There was a terrible threat in that raised hand and Melisande went still again, making Sir Martin smile. He had yellowed stumps for teeth. 'I've got a knife somewhere,' he told her, 'I know I do.' He fumbled in a pouch at his belt. 'A good knife, too. Oh! Here it is!' He smiled as he showed her the short blade. 'Put a knife to thy throat, the holy book says, if thou art a man of appetite, and I am, I am, but I don't want to cut your pretty throat, girl. It does spoil matters if you're scrambling about in blood. So just be good and lie there like a nice little girl and it'll soon be over.' He laughed at that, then knelt over her, his knees either side of her belly. 'But I do think we want you naked. Naked is blessed, girl. In nakedness lies truth. Those are the words of our Lord and Saviour.' He had invented the text, but in his mind it still had the ring of scriptural truth. He planted his left hand on her breasts, making her whimper. He was grinning, and in his deepset eyes Melisande saw the glints of madness. She hardly moved, she hardly dared move because the knife was coming towards her throat, but she groped to find the neck of her sack and slowly pulled it towards her.

'And what shall divide us from the love of Christ?' Sir Martin asked her in a hoarse voice, 'tell me that, eh?' He grinned still, reaching for the neck of her dress with his left hand. 'That's what the holy scriptures ask us, girl, they ask us what shall divide us from Christ's love! What shall divide you and me, eh? Not tribulation, the word of the Lord says, nor distress, nor persecution, nor hunger, are you listening to me?'

Melisande nodded. The sack inched towards her and she felt for its opening.

'The words of God, little girl,' Sir Martin said, this time relying on genuine words of scripture, 'written for our comfort by the blessed Saint Paul himself. Neither danger nor the sword shall keep us from Christ's love, and nor, the apostle says, will nakedness!' And with that he slashed at her dress with the short knife and, with a twitching grimace, ripped the cloth down so that her breasts were exposed.

'Oh my,' Sir Martin said reverently, 'oh my, oh my, oh my. Nakedness will not keep you from Christ's love, my child, that is the promise of the scripture. You should be glad of my coming. You should rejoice in it.' He no longer straddled her, but knelt beside her as he tore the linen dress down to its lower hem and then he stared with awed reverence at her pale body. Melisande lay still, her right hand inside the sack now, but not moving.

'We went naked, girl, before woman brought sin into the world,' Sir Martin said, 'and it is only meet and just that woman should be punished for that first sin. Don't you agree?' A vagary of the wind brought the sound of shouting from the high plateau and the priest turned and looked at the distant crest for an instant. Melisande thrust her hand deeper into the sack, fumbling for one of the short leather-fledged bolts. She went still again as Sir Martin looked back to her. 'They're having their games up there,' he said. 'They do like to fight, they do, but the Frenchies will win this one! There's thousands of the bastards! Your Nick will go down, girl. Down to a Frenchie's sword. Cos you're a Frenchie, aren't you? A pretty little Frenchie. I'm just sorry your Nick will never know I've punished you for your sins. Woman brought sin into the world and woman must be punished. I'd like your Nick to die knowing I'd punished you, but he won't, and so it is, so it falls out, so the good Lord disposes. My Thomas will probably die too, and that's a pity, cos I do like my Thomas, but I've other sons. Maybe you'll have one for me?' He smiled at that idea as he fumbled to hitch up his robe. 'I won't die. The Frenchies won't kill a priest cos they really don't want to go to hell. And if you're nice to me, little girl, you won't die either. You can live and have my little baby. Maybe we'll call him Thomas? Right! Get those pretty legs apart.'

Melisande did not move, but the priest kicked at her knees, then kicked harder and so forced his foot between her thighs. 'Our Henry has led his men into the devil's shit-pot, hasn't he?' he said. 'And now they're all going to be dead. They're all going to be dead and there'll just be you and me, little girl, just you and me, so you might as well be nice to me.' He pulled the black robe above his waist and grinned at her. 'Handsome, isn't he? Now, little one, make him welcome.'

He forced his knees between her legs.

'I've been wanting to do this,' he said, kneeling above her, 'for ever such a long time.' He gave a spasm, then leaned forward, propping himself on his left hand while still holding the knife to her throat with his right. A second pouch was about his neck, tied next to a wooden crucifix with a leather cord, and both cross and pouch swung free, annoying the priest. 'Don't need those, do we?' he asked. 'They just gets in the way, girl.' He used his knife hand to take the pouch and crucifix from his neck. The pouch clinked as he dropped it on the stream's bank and the sound made him grin. 'That's Frenchie gold, little girl, gold that I found in Harfleur, and if you're nice to me I'll give you a groat or two. You are going to be nice, aren't you? All quiet and nice like a good little girl?'

Melisande pushed her hand deeper into the sack and found what she wanted.

'I shall be nice,' she said in a frightened voice.

'Oh you will,' Sir Martin said hoarsely, putting the knife back to her throat, 'you surely will.'

Sir John stepped back. Two paces were sufficient. At first he thought he had called the command too soon, then feared it was too late because his feet were stuck in the mud, but he wrenched them free and stumbled back two paces and the opposing Frenchmen gave a shout, thinking the English were trying to run away, then their lances thrust into empty air and the momentum of the lunges unbalanced them, and that was when Sir John struck. 'Now!' he bellowed. 'Strike!' and he rammed his own lance forward, spearing the iron-tipped point into the groin of the closest enemy. The English lances, like the French, had been cut down, but the French had cut their shafts shorter and so did not have the reach of the English weapons. Sir John's lance slammed into metal and he leaned into the blow and saw the enemy fold over the point, and he pulled the lance back, watching the man fall, then struck it forward again.

The French, wasting their first blows on air, were stumbling. They were tired and could not pull their feet out of the sticky furrows and the force of the English lance blows was toppling them. To Sir John's left and right there were men on their knees, and he slammed the lance hard into the visored face of a man in the second rank to throw him backwards. Then he hurled the lance down and reached behind with his right hand. 'Poleaxe!'

His squire gave him the weapon.

And the killing could start.

A lance struck Sir John's head. His visor was missing and the Frenchman had tried to skewer Sir John's eyes, but the blow glanced off his helmet and Sir John pushed a step forward and swung the poleaxe in a short cut that smacked on the man's helmet, crushing it, and so another man was down in the mud. A whole rank of men had stumbled, and Sir John made certain they stayed down by cracking the lead-weighted hammer on their helmets. The man who had folded around Sir John's lance was trying to rise again and Sir John chopped the axe blade hard against his backplate, then shouted at his squire to finish the man off. 'Open his visor,' he shouted, 'kill him!' Then Sir John planted his feet and began picking his enemies.

Those enemies were already encumbered. The first rank of Frenchmen was mostly on the ground where they were bleeding in a tangle of bodies and discarded lances, and the following ranks had to stumble over those obstacles and as they tried so they were met with axe blades, mace heads and lance points. It might not have mattered if the French had been able to negotiate the obstacles in their own time, but they were pushed onto them by the press of men behind and so they stumbled haplessly into the English blades. 'Kill them!' Sir John bellowed. 'Kill them! Kill them! Kill them!' That was when the battle joy came to him, the pure joy of being a warlord, armoured and armed, dangerous and invincible. He used the poleaxe's hammerhead to beat down armoured enemies. The hammer did not need to pierce armour, few weapons could, but the weight alone could stun a man and one blow was usually sufficient to put a man down or cripple him.

The French, it seemed to Sir John, moved with a painful slowness, while he was endowed with a godlike speed. He was grinning and he was watching three or four enemies at once, picking which one to attack first and already knowing how the second and third would be destroyed. They came to him and he sensed their panic. The rearward ranks of the

French carried short weapons, maces or swords or axes, but they had no time to use them as they were forced onto the bodies of the fallen. They tripped into the blows of Sir John and his men, and so many were put down that Sir John had to negotiate the dead himself. Now the English were carrying the fight to the French. Nine hundred men were attacking eight thousand, but the nine hundred could take care where they stepped without fear of being pushed from behind.

A Frenchman in mud-spattered armour that had been scoured until it shone like silver, lunged a sword at Sir John who let the weapon waste its force against the cuisse protecting his left thigh. The man to Sir John's left battered the polished helmet with a poleaxe hammer, and the Frenchman collapsed like a felled ox as Sir John rammed his pole's spike into the face of a man wearing the livery of a wheatsheaf. The spike-mangled visor, teeth and palate, jerking the man's head back as his body was pushed forward. Sir John let his neighbour crack a hammer against the fallen man's helmet as he backswung his poleaxe into a pot-helm surmounted by a plume of feathers. 'Come on, you bastards! I want you!' Sir John shouted. He was laughing. At that moment it never once occurred to him that some Frenchmen were eager for the renown that would follow the death or capture of Sir John Cornewaille. They came and they fell, victims of the wet ground and of the obstacles they could not see through their closed visors, and they came to the short, hard blows of a poleaxe that made more obstacles.

'Stay tight, stay tight!' Sir John bellowed, making sure there was a man to his left and Sir William to his right. You fought shoulder to shoulder to give the enemy no room to pierce the line, and Sir John's men-at-arms were fighting as he had trained them to fight. They had stepped over the first fallen Frenchmen and the second line of English were lifting enemy visors and sliding knives into the eyes or mouths of

401

the wounded to stop them from striking up from the ground. Frenchmen screamed when they saw the blade coming, they twisted in the mud to escape the quick stabs, they died in spasms, and still more came to be hammered or chopped or crushed. Some Frenchmen, reckoning themselves safe from arrows, had lifted their visors and Sir John slammed the pole-axe's spike into a man's face, twisting it as it pierced the eye socket, dragging it back jellied and bloodied, watching as the man, in frantic dying pain, flailed and impeded more Frenchmen. Sir William Porter was stabbing his lance at men's faces. One blow was usually enough to unbalance an enemy and Sir William's other neighbour would finish the job with a hammer blow. Sir William, usually a quiet and studious man, was growling and snarling as he picked his victims. 'God's blood, William,' Sir John shouted, 'but this is joy!'

The noise was unending. Steel on steel, screams, war-shouts. Enough Frenchmen had fallen to stop the ponderous charge, and the men behind could not negotiate the piled bodies without stumbling into the English blades. There was blood in the furrows. Sir John stepped on a wounded Frenchman's helmet, unaware that he did so, but conscious that his right foot had found firm standing, and his weight drove the man's visor into the mud that seeped through the visor holes and slowly stifled him. He drowned in mud, choking for breath as Sir John taunted the French, begged them to come to him, then stepped forward again, hungry for more death. 'Kill them!' he screamed. 'Kill them!' He felt a burst of energy and used it to crash into the French line, opening it so his men could follow, stabbing and lunging with the speed of Christendom's most feared tournament fighter. He crippled men with the spike, driving it through the faulds covering their groins, and as they doubled in screaming pain he would crash the hammer or axe onto their helmets and leave it to the men behind to give the fallen enemy the mercy of death. Sir John took blows on his armour, but they were feeble until a Frenchman managed a hard swing with a poleaxe and Sir John was only saved because the enemy's shaft broke and Sir John screamed in challenge and swung his own axe at the man's legs, driving the blade through a roundel to chop into a knee. The man went down and lunged with his weapon's broken shaft, and Sir John smashed the hammerhead onto the enemy's helmet with such force that the steel collapsed and bloody ooze spurted from the visor. Sir John and his men-at-arms were hacking a deep hole in the crammed French ranks, killing again to make new corpses to trip the enemy.

To his left, unseen by Sir John, the Duke of York died.

The French attack had struck the English vanguard first. A hundred men were dead in that fight before the oriflamme reached King Henry's men, and in the front of the foremost men was Ghillebert, Seigneur de Lanferelle, and he was half aware that the English to his left had stepped back as the charge crashed home, but the Duke of York and his men had stayed put, thrusting with lances, and Lanferelle had twisted aside, letting a lance slide off his breastplate's flank, then ramming his own lance into an unvisored face. 'Lanferelle!' he shouted, 'Lanferelle!' He wanted the English to know whom they faced, and he fended off a lance with his own then unslung his mace and started to hack. This was no place for the subtle graces of a tournament field, no place to show a swordsman's skills, this was a place to hack and kill, chop and wound, to fill an enemy with fear, and Lanferelle drove the spiked mace down into a man wearing the duke's livery and wrenched the bloody spikes out of the split helmet and skull and thumped it forward into another man, hurling him back and he could see the duke clearly now, just to his right, but first he had to kill a man to his left, which he did with the heavy mace in a blow that rang up his arm. 'Yield!' he shouted at the duke who had dropped his visor, and the duke's response was to swing his sword that clanged on Lanferelle's plate and Lanferelle dropped the mace head over the duke's shoulder and pulled so that the tall man stumbled forward, lost his footing and fell full length. 'He's mine!' Lanferelle shouted, 'the bastard's mine,' and that was when the battle joy came to Lanferelle, the exultation of a fighter who dominated his foes.

He stood over the duke, one foot on the fallen man's spine, and killed any man who tried a rescue. Four of his own men-at-arms flanked him with poleaxes and they shouted insults at the English before killing them. 'I want the standard!' Lanferelle shouted. He thought the duke's great flag would be a welcome decoration in his manor hall where it could hang from the smoke-darkened beams beneath the musicians' gallery and the duke, a prisoner in Lanferelle's keeping, would be forced to see that standard every day. 'Come and die!' Lanferelle shouted at the standard-bearer, but English men-at-arms pushed the man back out of immediate danger and closed on Lanferelle and he parried their blows, thrusting back hard, depending on the weight of his mace to throw his opponents off balance, and all the while he shouted at his men in the second rank to defend his back. They had to keep the crush of Frenchmen from crowding him, and they did it by threatening their own ranks, giving Lanferelle room to slash the mace at any man who dared oppose him. His four men were using their pole-axes to hack at the English line that was so thin Lanferelle reckoned he could fight through it and lead a mass of Frenchmen to the rear of the English centre. Why not capture a king as well as a duke? 'Forward!' he bellowed. 'Forward!' but when he tried to go forward he half tripped on the bodies that had fallen across the Duke of York's legs. Lanferelle tried to kick the dead men out of his path, but a lance thrust from an Englishman hammered his breastplate and threw him back. 'Bastard!' Lanferelle shouted, driving the mace's bloody spikes towards the snarling face, then a shout of warning made him glance to his left and he saw that the English were driving into the French ranks and threatening to fight around to his rear. He reckoned there was still time to break the enemy line and he tried to go forward again and once more was checked by the dead men, and a sudden rush of Englishmen came to oppose him, their lances, poleaxes and maces battering his armour and he had no choice but to step back. His chance to cleave the line was gone for the moment.

He backed away, leaving the Duke of York face down in the mud. The duke, stunned and trampled, had drowned in a blood-drenched puddle and now the English advanced across his corpse, coming for Lanferelle and for his standard of the sun and falcon, and Lanferelle held them at bay with swift hard strokes. He did not know the duke was dead, only regretted that he had temporarily lost him, but then he saw another standard to his left, a standard deep in the French ranks that showed a rearing lion blazoned with a crown and he reckoned Sir John Cornewaille's ransom would make him rich enough. 'With me!' he bellowed, and he rammed and shoved and fought his way towards Sir John.

Away to Lanferelle's right a furious battle raged around the king's four standards. Scores of Frenchmen wanted the honour of capturing England's king, but they faced the same horrors that dogged the rest of the French attackers. Their front rank had gone down fast, its men exhausted by the mud and wounded by the arrow-storm, and the king's bodyguard had killed them with axes, maces and mauls. Now the attackers tripped on bodies and were met by axe strokes, yet still they pushed forward and a French lance pierced the faulds of Humphrey, Duke of Gloucester, the king's younger brother, and the blow to the groin drove him down into the furrows. Frenchmen surged to take the fallen man prisoner, but Henry stood over his injured brother and used his sword two-handed to hack at the enemy. He fought with a sword because he regarded that as a royal weapon, and if it put him at a disadvantage against men armed with poleaxes and maces, then Henry did not acknowledge it, because he knew God was with him. He could feel God in his heart, he sensed God giving him strength, and even when a French poleaxe rang on his crowned helmet with a sudden blinding force, God protected him. A golden fleuret was chopped from the crown and his helmet was dented, but the steel was not broken and the leather liner soaked some of the blow's force and Henry stayed conscious as he lunged the sword into the axeman's armpit and screamed his war cry. 'Saint George!'

Henry of England was filled by a God-given joy. Never, in all his life, had he felt closer to God, and he almost pitied the men who came to be killed for they were being killed by God. Henry's bodyguard flanked him and, one by one, they killed eighteen Frenchmen who, only the night before, had sworn a solemn oath to kill or capture the King of England. The eighteen had been bound together by their oath and they had advanced together and now they died together. Their bodies lay tangled and bloody to impede the men who still wanted the fame of capturing a king. A Frenchman bellowed his challenge, stumbling forward, spiked mace thrashing at the king, and the king slammed the sword hard forward to lodge the point in the slit of the Frenchman's visor, and the mace struck a man next to the king, who staggered, and another Englishman drove his poleaxe spike into the Frenchman's throat so that blood ran down the axe's iron-sheathed handle. The man sank to his knees, and the king rammed the blade into the visor's slit, butchering the man's lips and tongue. Blood welled at the slit, a poleaxe slammed onto the man's helmet, driving in the steel and opening the skull to spray the king with blood as he ripped his sword free and parried a lance thrust. 'Saint George!' he shouted and felt the divine power thrill through his veins. The Frenchman with the lance had an open visor and Henry saw fear in the man's eyes, then a mute appeal for mercy as his lance was wrenched from his hands, but God did not want mercy for Henry's enemies and so the king cut his sword across the man's face to slice open both his eyeballs. One of the royal bodyguard cracked the blinded man's helmet with a maul, and so another body was added to the heap of French dead that protected the English line.

And the English line held. In places it had been driven back by the weight of attacking men-at-arms, but the line did not break, and now it was protected by ramparts of dead and wounded Frenchmen, and in places the line bulged forward as the English counterattacked into the French formation. And the French, unable to march straight ahead, began to spread to their flanks.

Where the archers had no arrows.

'You can die, or you can fight.' The voice was distant and amused, as though the speaker did not care what Nicholas Hook's fate would be.

'God's holy shit, Nick, they're coming for us,' Tom Scarlet said nervously. The archers had pulled back behind the foremost stakes and then watched the French men-at-arms crash into the English line. There had been loud cheers from the archers when that perilously thin line stopped the enemy, but now that enemy was spreading towards the stakes.

'We can fight or die,' Hook said. He threw down his bow. It was useless without arrows, and there were no arrows.

'So fight,' the voice spoke again, and Hook knew it was Saint Crispin, the harsher saint, who was talking to him.

'You're here!' he said aloud in relief and wonderment.

'I'm here, Nick,' Scarlet said, 'don't want to be, but I am.'

'Of course we're here!' Saint Crispin said harshly. 'We're here to get revenge! So fight them, you bastard! What are you waiting for?'

Hook had paused to watch the French. He sensed they were not trying to outflank the English men-at-arms, but rather to escape the killing that was so loud to his left, but soon, he thought, some Frenchman would decide to attack the lightly-armoured archers and thus reach the rear of the king's line.

'What are you waiting for?' the saint again demanded angrily. 'Do God's work, for Christ's sake! Just kill the goddamned bastards!'

Hook felt a tremor of fear. A Frenchman staggered closer to the stakes. His left arm was hanging limply from his shoulder where an espalier was split and bloody.

'What do we do, Nick?' Scarlet asked.

Hook took the poleaxe from his shoulder. 'Kill them!' he roared. 'Kill the goddamned bastards! Saint Crispin! Kill!'

The shout released the archers, who suddenly gave a great shout of defiance and streamed between their stakes to attack the French flank. The bowmen were armed with poleaxes, swords or mallets. Most were barefoot, none had leg armour and few could afford a breastplate, but in the mud they could move much faster than the French. 'Kill them!' Evelgold bellowed, and still more archers took up the shout. There was a wildness in the grey air, a sudden and savage desire to kill the men who had promised to chop off archers' fingers, and so Welshmen and Englishmen, their arms hardened by years of archery, went to massacre the gentry of France.

Hook ignored the wounded man and instead attacked a giant in a bright red surcoat. His first blow was a wild swing that would have earned Sir John's scorn had he seen it, and the Frenchman swayed back to make it miss and then lunged with his shortened lance, but Hook's momentum had carried him past the man and, as the tall Frenchman turned to follow Hook, so Will of the Dale hammered the back of the man's helmet with a mallet and the enemy toppled into the mud. Geoffrey Horrocks knelt on him, lifted the visor and stabbed into an eye with a long, thin-bladed knife. Hook drove his poleaxe at a man in a black and white striped surcoat, thrusting him so hard in the breastplate that the enemy fell backwards, and then the hammerhead swung to crash into a man's sword arm, and another archer was there to swing a lead-weighted maul onto that man's helmet. The French, their feet trapped by the mud's suction, could not move to avoid the blows, and their own strokes and lunges were being wasted on air as the nimble archers dodged. The enemy, safe from arrows, was fighting with raised visors now and Hook discovered it was easy to stab the poleaxe's spike at their eyes, forcing them to twist aside when one of his companions would follow up with a hammer blow. It was the poleaxes, hammers and the mauls that were doing the damage, lead-weighted hammerheads wielded by archers' arms, and the hammers crushed helmets and shattered armour-encased bones. Archers without hammers picked up enemy poleaxes or maces. They were suddenly scenting easy pickings as still more bowmen came from the stakes to join the brawl.

It was a brawl. It was tavern fighting. It was like the Christmas football game when the men of two villages met to punch and trip and kick, only this game was played with lead, iron and steel. Two or three archers would attack one man, tripping him or striking him down with a hammer, then one would stoop to finish the enemy with a knife into the face. The quickest way was straight through an eye, and the Frenchmen screamed for mercy when they saw the blade approaching, then there was a slight, instantly released pressure as the knife tip pierced the eyeball before the screaming would fade as the blade slipped into the brain. Not much blood from such wounds, and all the time the English trumpets were braying and there was the steel on steel sound of men-at-arms fighting in the field's centre, and the shouts of archers who were slaughtering the enemy's flanks.

This was revenge. Hook fought with the memory of Soissons. He knew the two saints were with him. This was their feast day, and today they would repay France for what France had done to their town. Hook stabbed the axe point at men's faces and, when they twisted to evade the blow, he would hook the blade over a shoulder and tug until the enemy, his feet caught in the mire, stumbled forward and the hammerhead would crash into his helmet and another Frenchman was finished. Hundreds of archers were doing the same so that the deep-ploughed field, filling the space between the woods, had become one wide killing ground. The furrows, newly sown with winter wheat, were filling with blood.

There were so many dead and injured Frenchmen that Hook had to clamber over their bodies to reach the enemy. Tom Scarlet, big Will Sclate and Will of the Dale came with him, and other archers were doing the same, all yelling like demons. A sword slammed into Hook, but the blade's force was stopped by his haubergeon and mail, and Sclate, huge and glowering, hammered the swordsman down with his axe. Hook dropped another Frenchman with a lunge, and Will of the Dale drove his axe into the fallen man's thigh, splitting the cuisse so that thick blood welled out of the jagged rip. An archer was stoving in helmets with a maul, one blow sufficient to collapse steel, skull and life. A Frenchman with a hammer-broken leg was on his knees and shouting that he yielded, that he could pay ransom, but no one heard and he died when an archer slid a knife into an eye socket. Hook was screaming, unaware that he screamed, fighting with a desperate fury. The archers were mud-smeared, blood-spattered and bare-legged as they howled and killed. Their fear was all released into fury.

A French knight, glorious in a surcoat woven from cloth of gold, parried Tom Scarlet's swing and drew back his mace to crush the insolent archer's skull and Hook's axe head took the man in the back of his neck, powering through a steel bevor, and the man fell as Hook ripped the blade free and stabbed the spike into another man's waist. Sclate, the country-bred giant, swung a hammer between the man's legs and the resultant scream seared clear across Azincourt's blood-wet field.

Then a Frenchman in mud-spattered bright mail, with a blue silk ribbon about his neck and a silver lion crowning his helmet, dropped to one knee and took off his right gauntlet, which he held towards Hook. Hook was still four or five paces away and was planning to slam the hammer onto that glittering lion, but he suddenly understood what the Frenchman wanted. 'Prisoners!' he shouted. 'Prisoners!' He snatched the gauntlet from the Frenchman. 'Take your helmet off,' he ordered the man. No one had yet given the order to capture prisoners, and Sir John, before the fight, had stressed that none was to be taken until the king had deemed the battle won, but Hook did not care. The French were surrendering now.

More and more Frenchmen were holding out their gauntlets. Their helmets were left in the mud as their captors hauled them back from the fight. 'What do we do with the bastards?' Will of the Dale asked.

'Tie their hands,' Hook suggested. 'Use bow cords!'

The first French battle was retreating now. Too many had

411

died and the living had no stomach for a fight that had spilled so much blood into the furrows. Hook leaned on his poleaxe and watched an archer in a blue, blood-darkened surcoat cackling among the wounded enemy. The man had discovered a falcon-beak, a weapon that was half hammer and half claw, and he was killing the wounded by piercing their helmets with the curved beak, which was mounted on a long shaft. The wedge-shaped point easily drove through steel to shatter the skulls beneath. 'Like cracking eggs!' he called to no one in particular, and cracked another. 'Bastards,' he kept shouting, 'bastards!' He killed again and again. Injured men pleaded for mercy, but the beaked hammer would still fall. Hook had no energy to intervene. The man seemed oblivious of everything except the need to kill, and when he struck a wounded man he would do it repeatedly, long after the man was dead. A mastiff was standing over the body of its wounded master, barking at the English, and the archer killed the dog with the falcon-beak, then killed the dog's owner. 'You'd cut off my fingers!' he screamed at the man, swinging the beak to mangle the corpse's already crumpled helmet, 'I'll cut off your goddamned prick!' He suddenly raised his two string fingers at the corpses he had made and jerked the fingers up and down. 'Cut these off, would you? You bastards!'

'Sweet Jesus,' Tom Scarlet said. His face was covered in French blood, his haubergeon was red, his legs, bare beneath his short hose, were mud-covered. 'Sweet Jesus,' he said again.

The farthest point of the French advance was marked by a long heap of bodies, and the first battle had retreated from that horror and the English did not follow. Men were exhausted, slaked by the killing. Prisoners were being taken behind the line where Englishmen and Welshmen stared at each other as if astonished to be alive.

Then more trumpets called, and Hook looked northwards to see that the second French battle, every bit as large as the first, was coming.

So the battle must start again.

'They'll all be dying up there,' Sir Martin said, 'dying in their scores! You're probably a widow by now.' He grinned with yellow teeth. 'I heard you got married. Why, girl, why? Marriage is for the respectable folk, not for common pottage-eaters like Hook, but it doesn't matter now. You're a widow, girl! And oh my, but you are a beautiful widow! Now stay still, girl! Stay still! "The master of every woman is the man!" That's what the holy scripture, the blessed word of the Lord says, so you're to obey me!' He frowned suddenly. 'What's that mucky stuff on your forehead?'

'A blessing,' Melisande said. She had at last found a bolt and was fumbling to fit it in the crossbow's groove, but the crossbow was inside the sack and it was hard to feel its mechanism, let alone be certain the bolt was properly in place. Sir Martin was kneeling between her legs and leaning over her, propped on his left hand and using his right to grope between her thighs. A small stream of spittle swayed from his mouth.

'I don't like it,' Sir Martin said and took his right hand away from her groin to rub at the charcoal lettering. 'Don't like your blessing. You should look pretty for me! You're not staying still, girl! You want me to hit you?'

'I am still,' Melisande said, though in truth she was shifting desperately, heaving up as she tried to dislodge the awful weight that pressed on her. Sir Martin abandoned his attempt to clean her forehead and put his hand back between her legs. Melisande screamed at his touch and the sound made the priest grin.

'The woman is the glory of the man,' he said, 'which is

the holy word of Almighty God. So let's make a baby, shall we?'

She thought the bolt was in the groove, she was not sure, but nor could she wait to be sure, and so she wrenched the crossbow around, dragging the whole sack with it as Sir Martin raised himself, ready to plunge down. '*Ave Maria*,' he said, '*ave Maria*,' and Melisande thrust the sack into the space between her belly and his, then pulled the trigger.

Nothing happened.

The crossbow had been lying untended and fully-cocked in her sack and the trigger mechanism must have rusted. She screamed. Sir Martin's spittle fell and slapped across her face and she jerked her finger again and this time the pawl gave way to release the cord, the steel-shanked span made its vicious sound and the short, thick, iron bolt ripped through the sacking.

Sir Martin seemed to be lifted off her. He stared at her, wide-eyed, his mouth shaped into a horrified circle.

Then he bellowed like a boar being gelded. Blood spurted from his groin to pour warm and sudden on Melisande's thighs. The leather fledging of the bolt protruded from his bladder while the rusted point was protruding between his legs, and Melisande twisted away, scrambling desperately, and Sir Martin's clawing hands caught hold of her torn dress and held on. He was screaming now, clutching the linen as though it could save him, and Melisande tore herself away from him, abandoning the dress, and he curled up on the wet ground, whimpering and gasping, thrusting the torn linen into his ravaged groin.

'You'll die,' Melisande said. 'You will bleed to death.' She stooped beside him and his bloodshot eyes looked up at her desperately. 'And I shall laugh as you die,' she added.

Another scream sounded. It came from the village and Melisande saw strangers among the baggage. She saw more

414

people running towards the wagons and other folk coming along the stream's bank. They were local people, bringing hoes and axes and cleavers, peasants who wanted plunder. A man had spotted her and was heading towards her with the same hungry expression she had seen on Sir Martin's face.

Melisande was naked.

Then she remembered the jupon.

She took one last look at Sir Martin, who was dying in agony, snatched up her sack and his leather purse of coins, then jumped into the stream.

The Sire de Lanferelle spat curses. A man at his feet, his visor dented and sheeted with blood, moaned and gasped. The whole of the man's lower right leg had been lopped off and the blood pulsed slow and thick onto the corpse beneath him. 'A priest,' the man gasped, 'for the love of God, a priest.'

'There are no priests,' Lanferelle said angrily. He had thrown away his mace, deciding that a poleaxe would be a more vicious weapon, and viciousness was what he needed if he were to pull a victory from this apparent disaster. Lanferelle understood well enough what had happened. The French, exhausted by their slog through the mud and half blinded by their closed visors, had been easy victims for the English men-at-arms, but he also understood that those men-at-arms could not stretch their thin line to fill the whole space between the two woods. The ends of the line were manned by archers, and the archers, so far as he could tell, had no arrows. He snapped up his ripped visor, forcing the split metal over the rim of his helmet. 'We're going left,' he said.

None of his men answered him. The first French battle had pulled back a score of paces and the English, as if by agreement, had not followed. Both sides were tired. Men leaned on their weapons to draw breath. Between the two armies was a long heap of armour-encased bodies, some dead, some injured, many piled on top of others. The fallen men's plate, polished in the night to a bright sheen, was jagged with rips, plastered with mud and streaked with blood. Banners had fallen among the casualties, and a few Englishmen dragged those proud flags free and passed them back to where the French prisoners were being gathered. The oriflamme, which had proclaimed its merciless purpose above the French centre, had vanished.

The English were passing skins of water or wine from man to man and Lanferelle suddenly felt parched. 'Where's the wine?' he asked his squire.

'I don't have any, sire. You didn't tell me to bring any.'

'Do I have to order you to piss? Jesus, you stink like a midden. Did you shit yourself?'

The squire nodded miserably. He was not the only man whose bowels had loosened in terror, but he quailed under Lanferelle's scorn. 'We're going left!' Lanferelle called again. He had tried and failed to reach Sir John, so now he planned to lead his men to attack the lightly-armoured archers instead. He could see the bowmen were carrying maces and pole-axes, but that was better than having them armed with yew bows and ash arrows. He would cut the bastards down and lead Frenchmen through the stakes so they could turn the flank of the English men-at-arms. 'This battle isn't lost,' he told his followers, 'it hasn't even begun! They have no arrows left! So now we can kill the bastards! You hear me? We kill them!'

Trumpets sounded from the northern end of the field. The second French battle, its armour still gleaming and its banners untorn by arrows, was advancing on foot through the morass of ploughland churned deep by horses and by the eight thousand Frenchmen of the first attack. That second battle was passing the small group of heralds, English, French and Burgundian, who watched the battle together from the edge of the Tramecourt woods and the reinforcements, another eight thousand men-at-arms, would reach the killing place in another minute. Lanferelle, not wanting to be caught by the crush of the new arrivals, worked his way towards the flank of the French men-at-arms. He had eleven men with him now, and he reckoned they were enough to cut their way through the archers. And if the twelve led, other men would follow. 'Those goddam archers aren't trained to arms,' he told his men. 'They're tradesmen! They're nothing but tailors and basket-weavers! They're just hacking with those axes. So don't attack them first. Let them hack, then you parry and kill, you understand me?'

Men nodded. They understood, but the field reeked of blood, the oriflamme was gone and a dozen great lords of France were dead or missing, and Lanferelle knew that victory would only come when men began to believe in victory. So he would give that belief to them. He would fight his way through the English line and he would give France a triumph.

Englishmen saw the second attack closing and they straightened and hoisted weapons. The second French battle had reached the first and the newcomers gave a huge shout. '*Saint Denis! Montjoie! Montjoie!*'

'Saint George!' the English responded, and the hunting howls started again, the mocking sound of men inviting their quarry to come and die.

But the second battle could not reach the English because the survivors of the first were in their way, and they could only push those survivors forward, and so they churned through the mud, lances levelled, driving tired men onto the heaps of dead and onto the English blades beyond. The noise rose, the clash of steel and the screams of the dying and the

419

desperate blare of trumpets as eight thousand new French men-at-arms went to the killing ground.

And Lanferelle went for the archers.

The women and servants fled from the English baggage, running uphill towards the embattled army while behind them serfs and peasants scrambled over the English wagons in search of easy plunder.

Melisande was in the stream that ran fast, full, cold and muddy, fed by the torrential rain of the last few days. She floundered in the water, pushing past low growing branches until she saw the jupon snagged on a willow bough. She unhooked it, then forced her way through the briars and nettles that grew on the stream's bank. She pulled the jupon over her head. The wet linen clung cold and clammy, but it covered her and she crept slowly northwards through brambles and hazel scrub until she saw the horsemen.

There were fifty or sixty riders who were standing their horses to the west of the village and just watching the English encampment. They had no banner, and even if they had flown a flag Melisande doubted she would have recognised its badge, but she was certain that the small English army could never have spared so many horsemen to linger behind their line. That meant these riders were French, and Melisande, though she was French herself, now thought of the horsemen as her enemy and so she crouched in the bushes, hiding her bright surcoat behind a thornbush.

Then a new anxiety struck her. The surcoat covered her, but it also gnawed at her soul. 'Forgive me,' she prayed to the Virgin, 'for wearing the jupon. Let Nick live.'

She sensed no answer. There was just silence in her head.

She had sworn not to wear the jupon, believing that wearing her father's badge would doom Nick to death in the high ploughland, but now she was wearing the badge of the sun and the falcon, and the Virgin had given her no answer, and she knew she was breaking her bargain with heaven. She shivered, cold and wet, and suddenly trembled.

Nick would die, she was sure of it.

So she took the jupon off so that Nick might live.

And she crouched. She was praying, naked, cold and frightened. And from the north, beyond the horsemen and beyond the village and beyond the skyline, the sound of battle rose again.

'We killed them before,' Thomas Evelgold yelled, 'and we can kill them again! Kill for England!'

'For Wales!' a man shouted.

'For Saint George!' another man called.

'For Saint David!' the Welshman responded and on that battle cry the archers surged forward to attack the new enemy. They had already savaged the first French battle, and some men reckoned they would become rich from the prisoners they had taken. Those prisoners, without helmets and with their hands tied with spare bow cords, were behind the stakes, guarded there by a handful of wounded archers. Now the bowmen went to make new corpses and take new prisoners.

They went in a rush, and by now they knew how to take down men-at-arms who could not move in the thick mud, and so the archers crashed into the flank of the French and they hammered their enemy to make a new line of dead men, most stabbed through an eye by an archer's knife after they had been felled by a hammer blow. The screams were unending. The plateau seethed with mud-spattered steel-clad men who lumbered towards the archers, pushed onto them by the thick ranks of men behind, and the clumsy men tripped on bodies, were smashed on their helmets, were murdered with knives, and still they came. Some wore gold or silver chains around their necks, or wore armour that, by its magnificence, proclaimed the wearer's wealth or position, and those men the archers tried to capture. They would kill the rich man's companions and, like deerhounds about a bayed stag, would taunt and threaten the man until he pulled off his gauntlet.

'Come on, you bastard!' Tom Scarlet jeered at a man whose white surcoat bore the badge of a red swan. 'Come on!' The Frenchman was watching him, blue eyes visible through a raised visor. His helmet was chased with silver swirls and his red velvet sword belt was studded with golden lozenges. He picked his way among the corpses, lunged with his lance at Scarlet's belly, and Scarlet swatted the lance away with his poleaxe. A second Frenchman, wearing the same swan insignia, slashed a broad-bladed sword at the poleaxe, but the steel bounced off the iron-sheathed staff. Scarlet drove the axe hard forward, cracking its spike against the swan-badged belly armour and the man staggered back. The swordsman struck again and Scarlet just managed to block the cut with the axe shaft, then Will Sclate was beside him and grunted as he swung his poleaxe, which crushed the swordsman's helmet as though it were made of parchment. The helmet collapsed, bursting at its seams in a spray of blood and brains, and Sclate, huge and vicious, drew the hammerhead back.

'We want him, Will! Bastard's rich!' Tom Scarlet shouted and he slammed the poleaxe into the rich man again, and the lord, Scarlet was sure he opposed a nobleman, struck with his lance and this time Scarlet seized the lance one-handed and tugged hard. The man stumbled forward, tripping, and Scarlet gripped the bottom rim of the man's helmet and dragged him out of the killing line. Will Sclate was hammering down more men, helped by a dozen of Sir John's archers, as Scarlet turned his prisoner over. He crouched and grinned into the man's face. 'Rich, are you?'

The man stared back with hatred, so Scarlet drew his knife. He held the point just over the man's left eyeball. 'If you're rich,' he said, 'you live, and if you're poor, you die.'

'*Je suis le Comte de Pavilly*,' the man said, '*je me rends! Je me rends!*'

'Does that mean you're rich?' Scarlet asked.

'Behind you, Tom!' Hook's voice bellowed, and Tom Scarlet turned to see Frenchmen coming towards him, and at that moment the Count of Pavilly drove his own knife up into Tom Scarlet's groin. Scarlet screeched, the count heaved up from the mud, and stabbed again, this time into Tom Scarlet's belly, ripping and cutting, and then Will Sclate's poleaxe swung in a hay-cutting slash and the axe blade tore into the Count of Pavilly's face, breaking his remaining teeth and driving their fragments to the back of his skull. His blood mingled with Tom Scarlet's. The two bodies, rich man and poor man, were lying together as Sclate ripped his blade from the snagging tangle of steel and bone before being driven back by the sudden rush of Frenchmen.

And Hook was also being driven back.

A wedge of Frenchmen was crashing into the archers. So far the archers had been winning because they attacked and because they were more mobile than their enemy, but at last the French had found a way to carry the fight back to the bowmen. They came shoulder to shoulder and they let the archers waste their blows by parrying instead of cutting back, and if an archer slipped, or swung too hard and was slow to recover his balance, a blade would flicker and an Englishman would sink into the mud to be hammered with a mace. 'Just kill them!' the Sire de Lanferelle shouted as he led the wedge. 'One at a time! God will give us time to kill them all! *Saint Denis! Montjoie!*' He sensed victory now. Up to this moment the French had panicked and had allowed themselves to be driven like cattle to the winter slaughter, but Lanferelle was calm, he was deadly and he was confident, and more and more Frenchmen came to follow him, sensing at last that someone had taken command of their destiny.

Hook saw the falcon in its sunlit splendour.

'Behind you, Tom!' he had shouted at Scarlet, and then he had seen the Frenchman in the red and white jupon suddenly heave up, but he had no time to see more because Lanferelle was ahead of him, and Hook was forced to step back as Lanferelle's poleaxe stabbed at him. It was not meant as a killing thrust, but rather to unbalance Hook who had to step back a second time to avoid the spike and he might have tripped in the furrows except the small of his back struck one of the slanting stakes that held him upright. He swept his own poleaxe at Lanferelle's weapon, but the Frenchman somehow flicked Hook's cut aside and lunged again, and Hook had to twist around the stake, but the sharpened point caught in his haubergeon and he could not move. Panic blinded him. 'Get close,' Saint Crispin said, and Hook rammed his poleaxe hard forward, struggling in the mud to find good footing, and Lanferelle was so surprised at the sudden counterattack that he checked his next thrust. Hook's blade glanced off Lanferelle's armour, but the thrust had released the haubergeon and Hook could step back just before a blow from one of Lanferelle's men would have crushed his hand where it held the pole.

'I hoped we would meet,' Lanferelle said.

'You wanted to die?' Hook snarled. The panic still rippled in his body, but there was also a relief that he had survived, then he had to parry desperately as two blades darted towards his unarmoured legs. Tom Evelgold came to his help, as did Will of the Dale.

'Tom's dead,' Will said, then swept his big axe around to knock a lance aside.

'How's Melisande?' Lanferelle asked.

'So far as I know,' Hook said, 'she lives.' He thrust again and had the axe knocked aside again, but he had not put all his strength into the blow and recovered fast to sweep the lead-weighted head back to hit Lanferelle's arm, but still without sufficient force and the Frenchman scarce seemed to notice.

Lanferelle smiled. 'She lives,' he said, 'and you die.' He began stabbing his weapon in short, very controlled strokes that came fast, sometimes low, sometimes high, and Hook, unable to parry and without time to counter-strike, could only retreat. Lanferelle had crusted blood beside one eye, but his face was strangely calm, and that calmness scared Hook. The Frenchman watched Hook's eyes all the time, and Hook knew he would die unless he could somehow get past that flickering blade. Tom Evelgold had the same idea and he managed to shove a lance to one side and push past the blade so that he was on Lanferelle's right, and the centenar, holding his poleaxe two-handed like a levelled lance, screamed a curse as he rammed the blade forward with its spike aimed at the Frenchman's faulds. The spike would go through the plates, through the mail, through the leather to rip open Lanferelle's lower belly, except at the last moment Lanferelle raised the butt end of his pole to deflect the lunge and so take its huge force on his breastplate. The Milanese steel withstood the blow and threw it off, then Lanferelle jerked his head forward, smashing his raised visor hard into Tom Evelgold's face as another Frenchman skewered a sword into the Englishman's thigh and twisted it. Evelgold staggered, blood pouring down his leg and spreading from his crushed nose. He had been blinded by the head butt and so did not see the poleaxe spike that drove into his face. He made a high-pitched whining noise as he fell, and another axe chopped into his belly, cleaving haubergeon and mail,

425

opening his guts, and then the Frenchmen were past him, treading deliberately and carefully, driving deeper through the stakes and so ever closer to the English rear.

'Get close,' Saint Crispin shouted at Hook.

'I can't,' Hook said.

Tom Evelgold shuddered. A French man-at-arms slid a sword point into his gullet and there was a thick gush of blood and then the centenar was still. More and more Frenchmen were following Lanferelle, thickening his wedge, and though archers fought them, the enemy was at last driving forward. The stakes helped by giving them something firm to lean on in the treacherous ground and the archers were being outfought. Hook tried to rally them, but they did not have the armour to stand against trained men-at-arms and so they retreated. They had not broken, not yet, but they were being pushed further and further back.

Hook tried to stand. He traded blows with Lanferelle, but knew he could not beat the Frenchman. Lanferelle was too fast. He did not have Hook's strength, but he was much quicker with his weapons. 'I am sorry for Melisande,' Lanferelle said, 'because she will grieve for you.'

'Bastard,' Hook said, and rammed the poleaxe forward, had the lunge deflected, and he pulled the weapon back and this time the axe head caught on Lanferelle's axe head, and Hook hauled back hard and for the first time saw a look of surprise on the Frenchman's face, but Lanferelle simply let go of the shaft and Hook almost tumbled backwards.

'But women recover from grief,' Lanferelle said, 'by finding another man.' He stooped and picked up a fallen poleaxe, and did it so quickly that Hook had no chance to attack while he was down, and by the time Hook saw his chance it was too late. 'Or perhaps I will put her back in a nunnery,' Lanferelle said, 'and make her a proper bride of Christ.'

Lanferelle grinned at Hook, then the new poleaxe started its relentless stabbing.

'Get out of the way,' Saint Crispin snapped.

'I'll fight him,' Hook shouted back. He wanted to kill Lanferelle. He suddenly hated him. 'I'll kill him!' he shouted, and tried to step forward, but was checked by the Frenchman's whip-fast blade.

'Get out of the goddamned way!' the voice roared, but this was not Saint Crispin shouting, and Hook felt himself thrust unceremoniously away as Sir John Cornewaille threw him to one side. Sir John brought men-at-arms who crashed their lances into the French, steel points against plate armour, and Hook staggered to where Will Sclate was hacking at Lanferelle's followers. Lanferelle responded with a bellowed challenge and a charge at Sir John, and the other Frenchmen surged forward through the clay-thick mud. A poleaxe slammed onto Hook's helmet and, because he was already unbalanced, he fell. The axe blow had not been given with full force, but it still rang in Hook's head and the blade glanced off the helmet to cut through his haubergeon and almost slashed the mail on his shoulder open. He saw the Frenchman draw back the pole, ready to slide the spike into his belly or chest and Hook desperately slashed up with his own blade, a wild blow that drove the axe head into the man-at-arms's groin. Like the blow that had felled him, it was not given with full force, but it was hard enough to make the Frenchman double over in sudden, body-crippling pain, and then Will of the Dale hauled Hook upright and Hook found his feet and slammed his spike forward, shouting as he thrust, and the spike rammed into the enemy's upper chest, piercing the aventail and sliding over the breastplate's top edge. Hook rammed and shook the pole, grinding the blade deep into the enemy's ribcage, and he watched the lower part of the man's helmet fill with blood that spilt from the

427

visor opening. A sword smacked Hook from his right, but his mail stopped it, and he swept his weapon that way, dragging his victim with it to throw the swordsman off balance, and then Hook charged.

He used the dying man as a battering ram. He thrust him into the French ranks and Sclate and Will of the Dale followed, and both of them were shouting. 'Saint George!'

'Saint Crispin!' Hook bellowed. He was pushing the dying man into the French ranks, thrusting his body against other men. The wounded man splattered blood from his mouth as Hook tried to disengage the spike. Another man stabbed a pike at Hook, but Geoffrey Horrocks had followed Hook and hit the man's helmet with a mallet, and the strike of the lead-weighted iron thumped dully as the man's head snapped back. He dropped into the mud. The wounded man at last fell from the poleaxe and Hook, the weight released, began to scream wildly and swing the weapon from side to side as he thrust into the Frenchmen. 'Just kill the bastards, just kill the bastards!' he was shouting. Archers were following him, their anger released by the relief of Sir John's arrival.

Sir John was fighting Lanferelle, both men so fast with weapons that it was difficult to see thrust, cut or parry, while the other English men-at-arms attacked on either side with such sudden savagery that Lanferelle's followers instinctively stepped back, intent on defending themselves against the newly arrived men, and as they went back so some tripped on the bodies lying on the ground behind them. They fell and the English came at them, pole-spikes stabbing, axes splitting armour, faces grimacing with the effort of killing, and the sudden slaughter took the spirit from the remaining French who tried to back away and found archers on their flanks. Men began to shout that they yielded. They dragged off gauntlets and shouted their surrenders in desperate panic. 'Too late,' Will of the Dale sneered at one man and chopped down with his axe to split an espalier and slice the blade down through shoulder blade and upper ribs. Another Frenchman in a ripped surcoat crawled on hands and knees, blood drooling from his mouth, weeping from sightless eyes, blundering through mud till an archer kicked him down and casually killed him with a knife thrust in the mouth. Young Horrocks was beating a count to death, slamming a poleaxe again and again into the fallen man's backplate and screaming insults as the blade tore into steel and spine.

Lanferelle was left, still fighting Sir John, and by some unspoken agreement the other English men-at-arms did not intervene. Neither man spoke. They had their feet planted in the mud and they cut, lunged and feinted, yet both were so skilled and so quick that neither could find an advantage. They were the tournament champions of Christendom, one French, one English, and they were accustomed to the silken glories of the lists; the admiring women, the bright flags, the courtesy of chivalry, yet now they fought among corpses, amidst the moans and whimpers of the dying, on a field reeking of blood and shit.

The end came by accident. Lanferelle feinted a lunge to Sir John's left, recovered with astonishing speed, cut, and so forced Sir John to step to his right and his foot landed on the hoof of a dead destrier and the hoof rolled under the weight and Sir John slipped and fell onto one knee and Lanferelle, fast as a snake, whipped the poleaxe around and struck Sir John's helmet a ringing blow and Sir John fell full length onto the horse's bloody belly where he floundered, trying to find his balance and so get to his feet, and Lanferelle raised the poleaxe for the killing blow.

And thrust.

The French second battle had forced the survivors of the first back to the killing ground where the English waited behind a rampart of dead and dying Frenchmen. So many of the high nobility of France were already dead or bleeding; their bones shattered, their guts torn, their brains spilling from mangled helmets, their eyes gouged and bellies ripped. Men were weeping, some calling for God or for their wives or for their mothers, but neither God nor any woman was there to offer comfort.

The King of England was going forward now. He had pulled one corpse from atop two others to make a passage through the heaped dead and he carried his sword to an enemy who had dared defy God's choice for France's throne. His men-at-arms advanced with him, cutting their axes and grinding their maces and chopping their sharp-curved falcon-beaks into a demoralised and mud-wearied enemy. They made new piles of dead, new blood-laced corpses, and more cripples whose cries for help went unanswered. Henry led them, despite the shouts of men who wanted him to protect himself. His helmet was dented and scarred, a fleuret of gold had been severed from the bright crown, but England's king was replete with a righteous and holy joy because he saw in the enemy's suffering the proof of divine providence. Underfoot the ploughland's ridges and furrows had been trampled into a flat morass that was the colour of blood. Men waded in a slurry of mud, blood and shit, they struggled and died, and Henry's soul soared. God was with him and, in that assurance, he found new strength and went on killing.

Lanferelle thrust hard and vicious just as a poleaxe blade hooked about his left espalier and hauled him back hard and fast. The Frenchman's blow fell short of Sir John, but Lanferelle, miraculously keeping his footing, turned on his new enemy and then stopped.

The poleaxe had pulled him away from Sir John and denied him his kill, and now its spike was in his face, its

430

point mashing his lip against his teeth and Lanferelle found himself staring into Hook's face.

'When you fought him before,' Hook said, 'he let you stand up. You wouldn't do the same for him?'

'This is battle,' Lanferelle said, his voice distorted by the spike's pressure, 'and that was a tournament.'

'Then if this is battle,' Hook asked, 'why shouldn't I kill you?'

Sir John stood, but did not intervene. He just watched.

'Because Melisande would never forgive you,' Lanferelle said, and he saw the hesitation on Hook's face and he tensed, ready to bring up his own poleaxe, but then the steel spike ground into his mouth, ripping his upper gum.

'Go on,' Hook said, 'try.'

Sir John still watched.

'Just try,' Hook begged. He kept his eyes on Lanferelle's face. 'You want him, Sir John?'

'He's yours, Hook.'

'You're mine,' Hook said to Lanferelle.

'*Je me rends*,' Lanferelle said, and he released his poleaxe shaft so the weapon thumped into the mud.

'Take your helmet off,' Hook ordered, drawing back the blood-tipped poleaxe.

Lanferelle took off his helmet, then his aventail and the leather hood beneath, so releasing his long black hair. He gave Hook his right gauntlet and Hook, triumphant, took his prisoner back to where the other French captives were under guard. The Sire de Lanferelle looked tired suddenly, tired and distraught. 'Don't tie my hands,' he begged.

'Why not?'

'Because I have honour, Nicholas Hook. I have surrendered and I give you my word I will not try to fight again, nor will I try to escape.'

'Then wait here,' Hook said.

'I will wait,' Lanferelle promised.

Hook shouted at a pageboy to bring the Frenchman some water and then went back to the battle that was once again dying. The second French battle had done no better than the first. They had added more bodies to the heaps of the dead, and now the survivors struggled back through the mud, leaving corpses, injured men and prisoners behind. Hundreds of prisoners. Dukes and counts and lords and men-at-arms, all in surcoats streaked with mud and sodden with blood, all now standing behind the English line and watching, in disbelief, as the remnants of the two French battles limped away.

The third French battle remained. Its flags flew and all along that line men were climbing into saddles and calling on their squires to bring their long lances. 'Arrows,' Saint Crispinian spoke in Hook's head, 'you need arrows.'

The day's work was not over.

Melisande watched.

The English baggage was in the village of Maisoncelles and in the wet pastures around it, and some was halfway up the hill as pages and servants led packhorses towards the protection of the English army beyond the skyline, if indeed there was an English army any more. Melisande did not know. She had watched men spill over that horizon into the valley where Maisoncelles lay, but those men were few and, by their movements, she guessed they were wounded soldiers, and after a while other men had come, but slowly, not in panicked flight, and she had not understood that they were prisoners being taken towards the village. The lack of panic suggested the English army still held their line on the plateau, but she half expected and half feared to see it come spilling over the edge pursued by the vengeful French.

Instead the French horsemen had come from the west,

and now they spurred into the village and Melisande watched as they cut down pages and then dismounted to start pillaging the English baggage.

The horsemen drove away the peasants who had arrived first. A handful of English men-at-arms and wounded archers had been left to guard the encampment, but they only numbered thirty and they had spent their arrows on the serfs and those men now retreated uphill. The women of the army went with them as the horsemen found the English king's quarters. A priest and two pages had stayed with the king's treasures, and those three were quickly slaughtered and the plunder began.

Melisande watched. She saw a man parade in a fur-trimmed red robe and with a crown on his head, making his companions laugh. She did not understand what was happening. She could only pray that Nick lived, and so she shut her eyes, crouched low, and prayed.

Hook lived.

The two French battles had retreated, struggling back over the ploughland and leaving the space in front of the English thick with bodies in mud-smeared armour. The third French battle was mounted now. It was the smallest of the three French battles, yet it still outnumbered the English. The riders' lances were upright, some flaunted pennants. Trumpets sounded. The third battle could not charge yet for so many dismounted Frenchmen were in front of them, but they moved their horses a few paces forward before stopping again.

'Arrows!' Hook shouted at his men.

'We don't have any!' Will of the Dale called back.

'Yes we do,' Hook said. He found his bow, slung it on his shoulder and led his men out into the field where the French bodies lay, and all around those fallen men were spent arrows. Some, because they had struck good armour head on, were

433

now useless because their bodkin points had bent or crumpled, but many were in fine condition. Hook found some undamaged points on arrows that had splintered shafts and he pulled those bodkins free and married them to good shafts. He also pillaged the French bodies. He found a silver chain about one man's neck and he thrust that into his arrow bag. Men-at-arms were also searching among the heaped French casualties, hauling the corpses away from the living, killing men too injured to survive or too poor to be worth ransoming, and rescuing the wealthy. Hook picked up a grey-fledged arrow trapped in the surcoat of a man lying on his back, and the man suddenly moved. Hook had thought he was dead, but the man groaned and turned his visored face towards the archer. Hook lifted the visor and saw scared eyes. '*Aidez moi*,' the man said, half choking. Hook could see no wound, no puncture in the armour, but the man screamed when Hook tried to lift him. The Frenchman was in such pain that he lost consciousness and Hook let him fall again. He took the arrow and moved on. A dog barked at him. It was standing over a corpse in a blood-soaked surcoat. Hook left the dog alone, skirting it to pick up a dozen more arrows that he thrust into his arrow bag.

'Nick!' Will of the Dale called, and Hook looked up to see a lone French horseman had ridden through the retreating fugitives of the first two battles. The rider was short and slightly built, and the only weapon he carried was a scabbarded sword. He wore plate armour, but he was not mounted on an armoured destrier, instead he rode a small piebald mare. His white linen jupon was decorated with two red axes above which was the glimmer of gold from a heavy chain that hung around his neck. His helmet's visor was raised and he seemed to be searching among the bodies, but checked his horse when he realised the archers were staring at him.

'Bastard wants trouble,' Will said.

'No, he's just looking at us,' Hook said, 'and he's only a little fellow. Let him be.' He picked up a broadhead, then another bodkin and glanced again at the horseman who had suddenly drawn his sword and kicked his horse forward. 'Maybe he does want trouble,' Hook said and he took the bow off his shoulder, braced it on a corpse's breastplate and looped its string about the upper nock.

The horseman stopped again, this time to gaze down into a tangle of armour and bodies. The dead lay on top of each other and the man seemed fascinated by the sight. He stared for a long time, now no more than twenty paces from the archers and then, abruptly, he screamed a high-pitched challenge and kicked his piebald horse straight at Hook. The mare responded, flailing its hooves in the mud to throw up great clods of earth.

'Stupid bastard,' Hook said angrily. He laid a bodkin over the string and raised the bow, just as a dozen other archers did the same. Hook thought the man must swerve away, but instead the rider lowered his sword to spear the blade at Hook who drew the cord to his right ear and did not even think about what he did. It was all instinctive. The cord came back, he watched the horseman rise and fall with the piebald's motion, saw the open visor and the unnaturally bright eyes, and loosed.

His arrow went clean through the rider's right eye and the force of it snapped the man's head hard back. The sword dropped and the mare slowed and then, puzzled, stopped a short lance's length away from Hook. No other archer had loosed.

A cheer went up from the English line as the dead rider fell slowly from the saddle. He took a long time to fall, slipping gently sideways and then suddenly collapsing in a clatter of armour. 'Get his horse,' Hook told Horrocks.

Hook went to the corpse. He tugged the arrow free from the ruined eye so he could pull the thick golden chain over the dead man's head, and then his hand stopped because there was a pendant hanging from the chain. It was a thick pendant, carved from white ivory, and mounted on that silver-rimmed disc was an antelope cut from jet.

'You stupid little bastard,' Hook said, and he lifted off the boy's helmet that was too big for him and looked down into the ruined face of Sir Philippe de Rouelles.

'He's just a boy,' Horrocks said in surprise.

'A stupid little bastard is what he is,' Hook said.

'What was he doing?'

'He was being goddam brave,' Hook said. He pulled off the heavy golden chain and walked the few paces to where the boy had stared down at the heaped dead, and there, lying on top of two other men, was a corpse in a surcoat that was so soaked in blood that at first Hook had difficulty making out the badge, but then he saw the outline of two red axes in the redder cloth. The dead man's helmet had come off and his throat had been cut to the spine. 'He came to find his father,' Hook told Horrocks.

'How do you know that?'

'I just know,' Hook said, 'the poor little bastard. He was just looking for his father.' He thrust the pendant into the arrow bag, picked up another bodkin and turned towards the English line.

Where the king, wearing his scarred helmet and with his surcoat torn by enemy blades, had mounted his small white horse to see the enemy more clearly. He saw the survivors of the slaughter struggling north, and beyond them was the third battle with its raised lances and he knew his archers had few or no arrows.

Then a messenger arrived to say the French were in the baggage camp, and the king twisted in the saddle to see that hundreds of his men were now guarding French prisoners. God knows how many prisoners there were, but they far outnumbered his men-at-arms. He glanced left and right. He had started with nine hundred men-at-arms and now the line was much thinner because so many men had taken prisoners and were guarding them. The archers had done the same. A few were out in the field, collecting arrows, and the king approved of that, but knew they could never collect enough arrows to kill the horses of the third battle. He watched some foolish Frenchman charge the archers and grimaced when his men cheered the brave fool's death, then looked again at his army.

It was disordered. Henry knew that the line would form again when the final French battle charged, but now there were hundreds of prisoners behind that line and those captured men could still fight. They had no helmets and their weapons had been taken, but they could still assault the rear of his line. Most had their hands tied, but not all, and the unpinioned men could free the others to throw themselves on the perilously thin English line. Then there was the threat of the Frenchmen pillaging his baggage, but that could wait. The vital thing now was to hold off the third French charge, and to do that he needed every blade in his small army. The advancing horses would be hampered by the hundreds of corpses, yet they would eventually get past those bodies and then the long lances would stab into his line. He needed men.

And men stared up at the king. They saw him close his eyes and knew he was praying to his stern God, the God who had spared his army so far this day, and Henry prayed that God's mercy would continue and, as his lips moved in the prayer, so the answer came to him. The answer was so astonishing that for a moment he did nothing, then he told himself God had spoken to him and so he opened his eyes.

'Kill the prisoners,' he ordered.

One of his household men-at-arms stared up at him. He was not sure he had heard right. 'Sire?'

'Kill the prisoners!'

That way the prisoners could not fight again and the men guarding them would be forced back into the battle line.

'Kill them all!' Henry shouted. He pointed a gauntleted hand at the captives. One of his men-at-arms had made a swift count and reckoned over two thousand Frenchmen had been taken and Henry's gesture encompassed them all. 'Kill them!' Henry commanded.

The French had flaunted the oriflamme, promising no quarter, so now no quarter would be given.

The prisoners would die.

The Sire de Lanferelle wandered bleakly behind the English line. He saw the English king in a battle-scarred helmet sitting on horseback, then was shocked to see that the Duke of Orleans, the French king's nephew, was a prisoner. He was just a young man, charming and witty, yet now, in a blood-spattered surcoat and with his arm gripped by an archer in English royal livery, he looked dazed, stricken and ill. 'Sire,' Lanferelle said, dropping to one knee.

'What happened?' Orleans asked.

'Mud,' Lanferelle said, standing again.

'My God,' the duke said. He flinched, not from pain for he was hardly wounded, but out of shame. 'Alençon's dead,' he went on, 'and so are Bar and Brabant. Sens died too.'

'The archbishop?' Lanferelle asked, somehow more shocked that a prince of the church was dead than that three of France's noblest dukes should have been killed.

'They gutted him, Lanferelle,' the duke said, 'they just gutted him. And d'Albret's dead too.'

'The constable?'

'Dead,' Orleans said, 'and Bourbon's captured.'

'Dear sweet God,' Lanferelle said, not because the Constable of France was dead or because the Duke of Bourbon, the victor of Soissons, was a prisoner, but because Marshal Boucicault, reckoned the toughest man in France, was now being led to join the Duke of Orleans.

Boucicault stared at Lanferelle, then at the royal duke, then shook his grizzled head. 'It seems we're all doomed to English hospitality,' he growled.

'They treated me well enough when I was a prisoner,' Lanferelle said.

'Jesus Christ, you have to find a second ransom?' Boucicault asked. His white surcoat with its red badge of a two-headed eagle was ripped and bloodstained. His armour, that had been polished through the night to a dazzling sheen, was scarred by blades and streaked with mud. He turned a bitter gaze on the other prisoners. 'What's it like over there?' he asked.

'Sour wine and good ale,' Lanferelle said, 'and rain, of course.'

'Rain,' Boucicault said bitterly, 'that was our undoing. Rain and mud.' He had advised against fighting Henry's army at all, rain or no rain, fearing what the English archers could do. Better, he had said, to let them straggle dispiritedly into Calais and to concentrate France's forces on the recapture of Harfleur, but the hot-headed royal dukes, like young Orleans, had insisted that the battle be fought. Boucicault felt a surge of bile, a temptation to spit an accusation at the duke, but he resisted it. 'Damp England,' he said instead. 'Tell me the women are damp too?'

'Oh, they are,' Lanferelle said.

'I'll need women,' the Marshal of France said, staring up at the grey sky. 'I doubt France can raise our ransoms, which means we'll all probably die in England, and we'll need something to pass the time.'

439

Lanferelle wondered where Melisande was. He suddenly wanted to see her, to talk to her, but the only women in sight were a handful who brought water to wounded men. Priests were offering other men the final rites, while doctors knelt beside the injured. They cut armour buckles, pulled mangled steel from pulverised flesh and held men down as they thrashed in agony. Lanferelle saw one of his own men and, leaving Orleans and the marshal to their guards, went to crouch beside the man and flinched at the mangled ruin of his left leg that had been half severed by axe blows. Someone had tied a bow cord around the man's thigh, but blood still seeped in thick pulses from the ragged wound. 'I'm sorry, Jules,' Lanferelle said.

Jules could say nothing. He twisted his head from side to side. He had bitten his lower lip so hard that blood trickled down his chin.

'You'll live, Jules,' Lanferelle said, doubting he spoke the truth, and then he twisted as he heard a bellow of anger.

He stared, incredulous. English archers were murdering the prisoners. For a moment Lanferelle thought the archers must be mad, then he saw that a man-at-arms in royal livery commanded them. French prisoners, their hands tied, tried to run away, but the archers caught them, turned them and slashed long knives across their throats. Blood was spraying from the cuts to soak the grinning archers, and more bowmen were hurrying to the slaughter with drawn blades. Some English men-at-arms were dragging prisoners away, evidently intent on preserving their prospects of ransoms, while the noblest and most valuable captives, like Marshal Boucicault and the Dukes of Orleans and Bourbon, were being guarded against the massacre, but the rest were being ruthlessly killed. Lanferelle understood then. The King of England was frightened of the prisoners attacking the rear of his line when the last French battle made its assault and to prevent that he was killing the captives, and though that made sense it still astonished Lanferelle. Then he saw archers coming towards him and he patted Jules's shoulder. 'Pretend to be dead, Jules,' he said. He could think of no other way of preventing the man's killing for he could not defend him without weapons, and so he hurried away in search of Sir John. Sir John, he was sure, would protect him, and if he could not find Sir John he would try to reach the Tramecourt woods and hide in its briar thickets.

Some prisoners tried to fight back, but they were unarmed and the archers felled them with poleaxes. The bowmen moved deftly in the mud, killing with a horrible efficiency. The English destriers, almost a thousand saddled stallions, were at the southern end of the field and a handful of prisoners tried to reach them, but some of the pageboys who guarded the horses mounted and drove the fugitives back to where the archers killed. There was panic and blood and screams as men died and as others were herded towards the slaughtermen. More archers came to the killing, and the prisoners blundered through the thick plough in search of an escape that did not exist. It did not exist for Lanferelle either. He reached the right flank of the English line where a small forester's cottage stood at the treeline. It was burning, and he heard the screams of dying men coming from the flames and thick smoke. The archers who had set the cottage ablaze saw Lanferelle and headed towards him and he swerved northwards, but only to see more archers between him and the English line where Sir John's standard flew. Then, to his relief, he recognised the tall figure and dark face of Nicholas Hook.

'Hook!' he shouted, but Hook did not hear him. 'Melisande!' He called his daughter's name in hope that it would pierce the turmoil of screaming. Trumpets were playing again, summoning Englishmen to their standards. 'Hook!' he bellowed in desperation.

'What do you want with Hook?' a man asked, and Lanferelle turned to see four archers facing him. The man who had spoken was tall and gaunt with a lantern jaw and held a bloodied poleaxe. 'You know Hook?' the man asked.

Lanferelle backed away.

'I asked you a question,' the man said, following Lanferelle. He was grinning, enjoying the fear on the Frenchman's face. 'Rich, are you? Cos if you're rich then we might let you live. But you've got to be very rich.' He slashed the poleaxe at Lanferelle's legs, hoping to cut into a knee and topple the Frenchman, but Lanferelle managed to step back without tripping and so avoided the blow. He staggered for balance in the mud.

'I'm rich,' he said desperately, 'very rich.'

'He speaks English,' the archer said to his companions, 'he's rich and he speaks English.' He lunged with the poleaxe and the spike rammed against Lanferelle's left cuisse, but the armour held and the point slid off Lanferelle's thigh. 'So why were you shouting for Hook?' the man asked, drawing the poleaxe back for another thrust.

Lanferelle raised his hands in a placatory gesture. 'I am his prisoner,' he said.

The tall man laughed. 'Our Nick? Got a rich prisoner, has he? That will never do.' He lunged with the poleaxe, striking the point onto Lanferelle's breastplate and Lanferelle staggered backwards, but again was not tripped. He glanced around desperately, hoping to see a fallen weapon and the tall English archer grinned at the fear on the Frenchman's bloodied face. The archer was wearing a haubergeon over a mail coat, and the padded jacket had been slashed so that the wool stuffing hung in tattered blood-crusted clumps. His red cross of Saint George had run in the rain so that his short surcoat, patterned with moon and stars, looked blood red. 'We can't have Nick Hook being rich,' the man said, and

442

raised the poleaxe ready to bring it down on Lanferelle's unprotected head.

And just then Lanferelle saw the sword. It was a short and clumsy sword, a cheap sword, and it was turning in the air and for a heartbeat he thought it had been thrown at him, then realised it was being thrown to him. The blade circled, came over the tall archer's shoulder, and Lanferelle snatched at it and somehow caught the hilt, but the axe was already falling, driven with an archer's huge strength and Lanferelle had no time to parry, only to throw himself forward, inside the blade's swing, and he drove his armoured weight into the archer's chest to throw him backwards. The axe shaft struck his left arm and Lanferelle brought up the sword, but with no strength in the cut that wasted itself on the man's arrow bag. One of the other archers struck with a poleaxe, but Lanferelle had recovered now and threw the lunge off with his blade that he flicked back with his extraordinary speed to slash across the second man's face. That man reeled away, blood flowing from a shattered nose and split cheek as Lanferelle stepped back again, sword ready for the tall man.

Three archers faced Lanferelle now, but two had no stomach for the fight, which left the tall man alone. He glanced around to see Hook approaching. 'Bastard,' he spat at Hook, 'you gave him that sword!'

'He's my prisoner,' Hook said.

'And the king said to kill the prisoners!'

'Then kill him, Tom,' Hook said, amused. 'Kill him!'

Tom Perrill looked back to the Frenchman. He saw the feral look in Lanferelle's eyes, remembered the speed with which the man had evaded and parried and so he lowered the poleaxe. 'You kill him, Hook,' he sneered.

'My lord,' Hook spoke to Lanferelle now, 'this man was offered money to rape your daughter. He failed, but so long as he lives your Melisande is in danger.'

'Then kill him,' Lanferelle said.

'I promised God I wouldn't.'

'But I made no promise to God,' Lanferelle said and flicked the cheap sword at Tom Perrill's face, forcing the archer back. Perrill glanced wide-eyed at Hook, unable to hide his fear and astonishment, then turned back to Lanferelle, who was smiling. The Frenchman's weapon was puny and cheap, far outranged by the poleaxe, but Lanferelle showed a blithe confidence as he stepped forward.

'Kill him!' Perrill shouted at his companions, but neither of them moved, and Perrill thrust the axe forward in a desperate stab at Lanferelle's midriff and the Frenchman swept the blade aside with contemptuous ease, then simply raised the sword and gave one lunge.

The blade sliced into Perrill's gullet, starting a gush of blood. The archer stared at his killer, his tongue slowly pushed out and blood ran from it to pour thick and silent down the sword to soak Lanferelle's ungauntleted hand. For a heart-beat the two men were motionless, then Perrill dropped and Lanferelle wrenched the blade loose and tossed it to Hook.

'Enough! Enough!' A man-at-arms in royal livery was riding behind the line and shouting at the archers. 'Enough! Stop the killing! Hold! Enough!'

Hook walked back to the English line.

He saw grey clouds covering the ploughland of Azincourt.

And he saw, in front of the English army, a field of dead and dying men. More dead, Hook thought, than the number of men the king had led to this wet slaughteryard. They lay tangled and bloody, countless dead, sprawled and blood-stained, armoured corpses, ripped and stabbed and crushed. There were men and horses. There were abandoned weapons, fallen flags, and dead hopes. A field sown with winter wheat had yielded a harvest of blood.

And at the end of that field, beyond the dead, beyond the

dying and the weeping, the third French battle was turning away.

The might of France was turning away and men were heading north, leaving Azincourt, riding to escape the risibly small army that had turned their world to horror.

It was over.

Epilogue

It was a November day, sky-bright and cold, filled with the sounds of church bells, cheers and singing.

Hook had never seen such crowds. London was celebrating its king and his victory. The water towers had been filled with wine, mock castles erected at street corners, and choirs of boys costumed as angels, old men disguised as prophets and girls masquerading as virgins sang paeans of praise, and through it all the king rode in modest dress, without crown or sceptre. The noblest of the French and Burgundian prisoners followed the king; Charles, Duke of Orleans, the Duke of Bourbon, the Marshal of France, still more dukes and countless counts, all exposed to the crowd's good-natured jeers. Small boys ran alongside the horses of the mounted archers who guarded the prisoners and reached up to touch cased bows and scabbarded swords. 'Were you there?' they asked, 'were you there?'

'I was there,' Hook answered, though he had left the procession and the cheers and the singing and the white doves circling.

He had ridden with four companions into the little streets that lay north of Cheapside. Father Christopher led them, taking the group into smaller and smaller alleys, alleys so tight that they had to ride single-file and constantly duck so their heads would not strike the overhanging storeys of the timber-framed houses. Hook wore a mail coat, two pairs of breeches to keep out the cold, a padded haubergeon for warmth, boots taken from a dead count at Azincourt, and over it all a new surcoat blazoned with Sir John's proud lion. Around his neck was a chain of gold, the symbol of his rank; centenar to Sir John Cornewaille. His helmet, of Milanese steel and only slightly scarred from an axe strike, hung from his saddle's pommel. His sword had been made in Bordeaux and its hilt was decorated with a carved horse, the badge of the Frenchman who had once owned both sword and helmet. 'I was there,' he told a small ragged boy, 'we were all there,' he added, then he followed Father Christopher around a corner, ducked beneath a hanging bush, the sign of a wineshop, and entered a small square that stank of the sewage flowing through its open gutters. A church stood on the square's northern side. It was a miserable church, its walls made of wattle and daub and its sorry excuse for a tower built from wood. A single bell hung in the tower. The bell was being tolled so that its cracked note could join the cacophony of noise that rejoiced in England's victory. 'That's it,' Father Christopher said, gesturing at the little church.

Hook dismounted. He cuffed away another curious boy, then helped Melisande from her horse. She was in a dress of blue velvet, given to her in Calais by Lady Bardolf, the governor's wife. Over it she wore a cloak of white linen, padded with wool and hemmed with fox-fur. A beggar on wood-sheathed stumps lurched towards her and she dropped a coin into his outstretched hand before following Hook and Father Christopher into the church. 'Were you there?' a boy asked the last man to dismount.

'I was there,' Lanferelle said. The Frenchman paused before

entering the church to give a coin to Will of the Dale who stayed outside to guard the horses.

The church floor was rush-covered earth. Only the choir was paved. It was dark inside because the surrounding buildings stopped any light coming through the unglazed windows. A priest had been tolling the bell, but he stopped when he saw the three men and the richly dressed woman come into his tiny sanctuary. The priest was nervous of the strangers, but then recognised Father Christopher in his rich black robes. 'You've come again, father,' he said, sounding surprised.

'I told you I would,' Father Christopher said gently.

'Then you are all welcome,' the priest said.

The main altar was a wooden table covered with a shabby linen cloth on which stood a copper-gilt crucifix and two empty candlesticks. Behind the altar was a leather hanging on which a bad painter had depicted two angels kneeling to God. The four visitors all made a brief genuflection and the sign of the cross, then Father Christopher plucked Hook's elbow towards the southern side of the church where a second altar stood. This second shrine was even less impressive than the first, being nothing but a battered table without any covering, and with a wooden crucifix and no candlesticks. One of Christ's legs had broken off so He hung on His cross one-legged. Above Him was a painted leather picture of a woman in a white dress, though the white had peeled and faded, and her yellow halo had mostly flaked away.

Hook stared at the woman. Her face, what could be seen of it in the dim light and through the cracked paint, was long and sad. 'How did you know she was here?' he asked Father Christopher.

'I asked,' the priest said, smiling. 'There's always someone who knows about the oddities of London. I found that man and I asked him.'

'An oddity?' the Sire de Lanferelle asked.

'I'm assured this is the only shrine to Saint Sarah in the whole city,' Father Christopher said.

'It is,' the parish priest said. He was a ragged man, shivering in a threadbare robe. His face had been scarred by the pox.

Lanferelle gave a brief smile. 'Sarah? A French saint?'

'Perhaps,' Father Christopher said. 'Some say she was Mary Magdalene's servant, some say she gave refuge to the Magdalene in her house in France. I don't know.'

'She was a martyr,' Hook interrupted harshly. 'She died not far from here, murdered by an evil man. And I didn't save her life.' He nodded to Melisande who went to the altar, knelt there, and took a leather purse from beneath her cloak. She laid the purse on the altar.

'For Sarah, father,' she told the priest.

The priest took the purse and unlaced it. His eyes widened and he looked at Melisande almost in fear, as though he suspected she might have second thoughts and take back the gold.

'I took them,' she said, 'from the man who raped Sarah.'

The priest dropped to his knees and made the sign of the cross. He was called Roger and Father Christopher had spoken with him the day before and afterwards had assured Hook that Father Roger was a good man. 'A good man and a fool, of course,' Father Christopher had said.

'A fool?' Hook had asked.

'He believes the meek will inherit the earth. He believes the church's task is to comfort the sick, to feed the hungry and clothe the naked. You know I found your wife stark naked?'

'You always were a lucky man,' Hook had said. 'So what is the church's task?'

'To comfort the rich, feed the fat and clothe the bishops in finery, of course, but Father Roger still clings to a vision

452

of Christ the Redeemer. As I said, he is a fool,' he had spoken gently.

Hook now tapped the fool on the shoulder. 'Father Roger?'

'Lord?'

'I'm no lord, just an archer,' Hook said, 'and you will have this.' He held out the thick gold chain with its pendant badge of the antelope. 'And with the money you make from its sale,' Hook went on, 'you will make an altar to Saints Crispin and Crispinian.'

'Yes,' Father Roger said, then frowned because Hook had not let go of the fabulous chain.

'And every day,' Hook said, 'you will say a mass for the soul of Sarah, who died.'

'Yes,' the priest said, and still Hook did not let go of the chain.

'And a prayer for your brother?' Melisande suggested.

'A king is praying for Michael,' Hook said, 'and he needs no more. A daily mass for Sarah, father.'

'It will be done,' Father Roger said.

'She was a Lollard,' Hook said, testing the priest.

Father Roger gave a quick and secret smile. 'Then I shall recite a mass for her twice every day,' he promised, and so Hook let go of the gold.

The bells rang. *Te Deums* were being sung in the city's abbeys, churches and cathedral. They gave thanks to God because England had sailed to Normandy and England had been harried into a corner of Picardy and there England had been faced with the almost certain death of its king and of his army.

But then the arrows flew.

Hook and Melisande took the westward road. They were going home.

BEHIND THE BATTLE

EXCLUSIVE BONUS SECTION

- Historical note by Bernard Cornwell

- Bernard Cornwell on the importance of the longbow

- Extract of *1356*, Bernard Cornwell's new standalone novel on another great battle of The Hundred Years War, the Battle of Poitiers

Historical Note

The battle of Agincourt (Azincourt was and remains the French spelling) was one of the most remarkable events of medieval Europe, a battle whose reputation far outranked its importance. In the long history of Anglo-French rivalry only Hastings, Waterloo, Trafalgar and Crécy share Agincourt's renown. It is arguable that Poitiers was a more significant battle and an even more complete victory, or that Verneuil was just as astonishing a triumph, and it's certain that Hastings, Blenheim, Victoria, Trafalgar and Waterloo were more influential on the course of history, yet Agincourt still holds its extraordinary place in English legend. Something quite remarkable happened on 25 October 1415 (Agincourt was fought long before Christendom's conversion to the new-style calendar, so the modern anniversary should be on 4 November). It was something so remarkable that its fame persists almost seven hundred years later.

Agincourt's fame could just be an accident, a quirk of history reinforced by Shakespeare's genius, but the evidence suggests it really was a battle that sent a shock wave through Europe. For years afterwards the French called 25 October 1415 *la malheureuse journée* (the unfortunate day). Even after they had expelled the English from France they remembered *la malheureuse journée* with sadness. It had been a disaster.

Yet it was so nearly a disaster for Henry V and his small, but well-equipped army. That army had sailed from Southampton Water with high hopes, the chief of which was the swift capture of Harfleur, which would be followed by a foray into the French heartland in hope, presumably, of bringing the French to battle. A victory in that battle would demonstrate, at least in the pious Henry's mind, God's support of his claim to the French throne, and might even propel him onto that throne. Such hopes were not vain when his army was intact, but the siege of Harfleur took much longer than expected and Henry's army was almost ruined by dysentery.

The tale of the siege in the novel is, by and large, accurate, though I did take one great liberty, which was to sink a mineshaft opposite the Leure Gate. There was no such shaft, the ground would not allow it, and all the real mines were dug by the Duke of Clarence's forces that were assailing the eastern side of Harfleur. The French counter-mines defeated those diggings, but I wanted to give a flavour, however inadequately, of the horrors men faced in fighting beneath the earth. The defence of Harfleur was magnificent, for which much of the praise must go to Raoul de Gaucourt, one of the garrison's leaders. His defiance, and the long days of the siege, gave the French a chance to raise a much larger army than any they might have fielded against Henry if the siege had ended, say, in early September.

Harfleur did finally surrender and was spared the sack and the horrors that had followed the fall of Soissons in 1414. This was another event that shocked Europe, though in the case of Soissons it was the barbaric behaviour of the French army towards its own citizens that provoked the shock. There is a rumour that English mercenaries took money to betray the city, which explains the actions of the fictional Sir Roger Pallaire, but in the context of the

Agincourt campaign the significance of Soissons was its patron saints, Crispin and Crispinian, whose feast day was, indeed, 25 October. For many in Europe the events of Saint Crispin's Day in 1415 demonstrated a heavenly revenge for the horrors of the sack of Soissons in 1414.

Common sense suggests that Henry should have abandoned any thoughts of further campaigning after Harfleur's surrender. He could have just garrisoned the newly captured port and sailed home for England, but such a course would have amounted to a virtual defeat. To have spent all that money and, in return, gained nothing more than a Norman harbour would have looked like a paltry achievement and, damaged as French interests were by the loss of Harfleur, the possession of the city gave Henry very little bargaining power. True it was now English (and would remain so for another twenty years), but its capture had wasted precious time and the necessity of garrisoning the damaged city took still more men from Henry's army so that, by the time the English launched their foray into France, only about half of their army was able to march. Yet Henry did decide to march. He rejected the good advice to abandon the campaign and instead set his small, sickly army the task of marching from Harfleur to Calais.

This was not, on the face of it, an enormous challenge. The distance is about 120 miles and the army, all of it mounted on horseback, might expect to make that journey in about eight days. The march was not undertaken for plunder, Henry had neither the equipment nor the time to lay siege to the walled towns and castles (into which anything valuable would have been taken as the English approached) that lay on the route, nor was it a classic *chevauchée*, one of those destructive progresses through France whereby English armies laid waste to everything in their path in hope of provoking the French to battle. I doubt that Henry did hope to provoke the French to battle because, despite his fervent belief in God's support, he must have realised the weakness of his army. If he had wanted battle it would have made more sense to march directly inland, but instead he skirted the coastline. It seems to me he was 'cocking a snook'. At the end of an unsatisfactory siege, and facing the humiliation of returning to England with no great achievement, he merely wished to humiliate the French by demonstrating that he could march through their country with impunity.

That demonstration would have worked well if the fords at Blanchetaque had not been guarded. To reach Calais in eight days he needed to cross the Somme quickly, but the French had blocked the fords and so Henry was driven inland in search of another crossing, and the days stretched from eight to eighteen (or sixteen, the chroniclers are maddeningly vague about which day the army left Harfleur) and the food ran out, and the French at last concentrated their army and moved to trap the hapless English.

And so Henry's risibly small army met its enemy on the plateau of Agincourt on Crispin's Day, 1415. Without knowing it, that army had just marched into legend.

In 1976, when Sir John Keegan wrote his magnificent book, *The Face of Battle*, he was able to write of Agincourt 'the events of the Agincourt campaign are, for the military historian, gratifyingly straightforward . . . there is less than the usual wild uncertainty over the numbers engaged on either side.'

Alas, that confidence has vanished, if not for the

events, at least for the numbers engaged. In 2005 Professor Anne Curry, who is among the most respected authorities on the Hundred Years War, published her book *Agincourt, A New History,* in which, after detailed argument, she proposed that the numbers engaged on either side were much closer than history has ever allowed. The usual consensus is that about 6,000 English faced around 30,000 French and Dr Curry amended those figures to 9,000 English and 12,000 French. If true, then the battle is an imposter, for its fame surely rests on the gross imbalance between the two sides. Shakespeare could hardly be justified in writing 'we few, we happy few' if the French were very nearly as few.

Now Sir John Keegan was right in describing any attempt to assess numbers engaged in a medieval battle as beset by 'wild uncertainty'. We are fortunate that a number of eyewitnesses wrote descriptions of the battle, and we have other sources from writers who left accounts shortly after, but their estimates of the numbers vary enormously. English chroniclers assess the French forces as anything from 60,000 to 150,000, while French and Burgundian sources offer anything from 8,000 to 50,000. The best eyewitnesses cite French numbers as 30,000, 36,000 and 50,000, all contributing to the wild uncertainty that Dr Curry made even wilder. In the end I decided that the generally accepted figure was correct, and that around 6,000 English faced approximately 30,000 French. This was not, I must stress, the result of close academic study on my part, but rather a gut instinct that the contemporary reaction to the battle reflected that something astonishing had taken place, and what is most astonishing about the various accounts of Agincourt is that disparity of numbers. An English chaplain, present at the battle, estimated that disparity as thirty Frenchmen for every Englishman, an obvious exaggeration, yet strong support for the traditional view that it was the sheer numerical inequality of the engaged forces that persuaded folk that Agincourt was truly extraordinary. Still, I am no scholar, and rejecting Dr Curry's conclusions seemed foolhardy.

Then, in the same year that Dr Curry's history appeared, Juliet Barker's book, *Agincourt*, was published and proved to be a vivid, comprehensive and compelling account of the campaign and the battle. Juliet Barker acknowledges Dr Curry's conclusions, yet courteously and firmly disagrees with them, and as Juliet Barker is as fine a scholar as she is a writer, and as, like Dr Curry, she had done her research among the French and English archives, I felt more than justified in following my instinct. Any reader who wishes to know more about the campaign and battle would do well to read all three of the books I have mentioned; *The Face of Battle* by John Keegan, *Agincourt, A New History* by Anne Curry and *Agincourt* by Juliet Barker. I should also acknowledge that, although I used many many sources to write this novel, the one book to which I turned again and again, and always with pleasure, was Juliet Barker's *Agincourt*.

What is beyond contention is the disparity within the English army. It was primarily an army of archers who, when they left England, outnumbered the men-at-arms by about three to one, but by St Crispin's Day had a preponderance of nearly six to one. You can find still more argument, endless argument, about how those archers were deployed, whether they were all on the flanks of the English army, or were arrayed between or in front of the men-at-arms. I cannot believe archers were placed in front, simply because of the difficulty of extricating them through the ranks before the hand-to-hand fighting began, and believe that the vast majority were indeed on the left and right of the main line of battle. A good discussion of archery in battle can be found in Robert Hardy's terrific book, *Longbow, a Social and Military History*.

I have tried, as far as possible, to follow the real events that took place on that damp Saint Crispin's Day in France. In brief it seems certain that the English advanced first (and it seems Henry really did say 'let's go, fellows!') and re-established their line within extreme bowshot of the French army, and that the French, foolishly, left that manoeuvre uncontested. The archers then provoked the first French attack with a volley of arrows. That first assault was by mounted men-at-arms who were supposed to scatter and so defeat the feared archers, but those attacks failed, partly because horses, even wearing armour, were fatally vulnerable to arrows, and because of the stakes that formed enough of an obstacle to take any impetus out of the charge. Some of the retreating French horses, maddened by arrows, appear to have galloped into the first advancing French battle, causing chaos in its close-packed ranks.

That first battle, probably consisting of about 8,000 men-at-arms, already had severe problems. The fields of Agincourt had recently been ploughed for winter wheat and it is true, as Nicholas Hook says, that you plough deeper for winter wheat than for spring wheat. It had also rained torrentially the previous night, and so the French were trudging through sticky clay soil. It must have been a nightmare. No one could hurry, and all the while the arrows were striking and, the closer the French came to the English line, the more lethal those arrow strikes were. There is more argument about the effect of arrows, with some scholars claiming that even the heaviest bodkin, shot from the strongest yew bow, could not pierce plate armour. Yet why else would Henry have so many archers? The arrows could pierce plate, though the strike had to be plumb, and undoubtedly the best plate, such as that made by the Milanese, was better able to resist. If nothing else the arrow-storm forced the French to advance with closed visors, severely restricting their vision.

A good archer could shoot fifteen accurate arrows in a minute. (I've seen it done with a bow that had a draw-weight of 110 pounds, some twenty to thirty pounds lighter than the bows carried at Agincourt, but far heavier than any modern competition bow). Assume that the archers at Agincourt averaged a mere twelve a minute and that there were 5,000 bowmen; that means in one minute 60,000 arrows struck the French, a thousand arrows a second. It also means that in ten minutes the archers would have shot 600,000 arrows and the conclusion is that they must have run out of arrows fairly quickly. Yet what that storm of arrows achieved was to drive the flanks of the disordered French advance inwards, onto the waiting English men-at-arms. That shrinking of the French line must have exposed the flanks of the English army, both composed of archers, to the French crossbowmen, but there is no evidence that the French seized the opportunity. Apart from a few volleys at the very beginning of the battle the French archers appear to have taken no part, a fatal error that must be ascribed to the abysmal lack of leadership on the French side.

The battle lasted between three and four hours,

yet it was probably as good as over in the very first minutes when the leading French battle struck home. The French men-at-arms were weary, half blinded, disordered and mud-crippled. What seems to have happened is that their leading ranks went down quickly and so formed a barrier to the men behind who, in turn, were being pushed onto that barrier by the rearmost men. So the French stumbled into the English weapons and the English (with some Welsh and a few Gascons) had more freedom to fight and to kill. That first French battle had contained most of France's high nobility, and so it went to the slaughter and the great names fell; the Duke of Alençon, the Duke of Bar, the Duke of Brabant, the Archbishop of Sens, the Constable of France and at least eight counts. Others, like the Duke of Orleans, the Duke of Bourbon, and the Marshal of France, were captured. The English did not have it all their own way; the Duke of York was killed, as was the Earl of Suffolk (his father had died of dysentery at Harfleur), but English casualties seem to have been remarkably slight. Henry undoubtedly fought in the front rank of the English and all eighteen Frenchmen who had sworn an oath of brotherhood to kill him were killed instead. Henry's brother Humphrey, Duke of Gloucester, was badly wounded in the fight and it is said that Henry stood over him and fought off the Frenchmen trying to drag the injured duke away.

The second French battle went to reinforce the first, but by now the French were trying to fight across a barrier of dead and dying men, and they were also fighting the English archers who had abandoned their bows and were now wielding pole-axes, swords and mallets. The advantage the English archers possessed was manoeuvrability; unencumbered by sixty pounds of mud-weighted armour they must have been lethal in their attacks. I cannot confirm that the British two-fingered salute began at Agincourt as a taunt to the defeated French, demonstrating that the archers still possessed their string fingers despite French threats to sever them, but it seems a likely tale.

Sometime after the advance of the second French battle a small force of horsemen, led by the Sire of Azincourt, attacked the English baggage. This event, and the apparent readiness of the remaining Frenchmen to attack, persuaded Henry to issue his order to kill the prisoners. That order appals us today, yet the contemporary chroniclers do not condemn it. By that stage there were around two thousand French prisoners close behind the English line that was half expecting an attack by another eight thousand, so far unengaged, Frenchmen. Those prisoners could well have swung the battle by assailing Henry's rear, and so the order was given to the evident displeasure of many English men-at-arms (who were losing valuable ransoms). Henry sent a squire and two hundred archers to do the killing instead, though it was evidently stopped fairly quickly when it became apparent that the raid on the baggage did not presage an attack from the rear, and that the threat of the third French battle had evaporated. The French had taken enough, their survivors began to leave the battlefield and Henry had won the extraordinary victory of Agincourt. Wild uncertainty surrounds the casualties, but undoubtedly the French suffered dreadful losses. An English eyewitness, a priest, recorded ninety-eight dead from the French nobility, around 1,500 French knights killed and between four and five thousand men-at-arms. French losses were in the thousands, and might well have been as high as 5,000, while English losses were most likely as small as 200 (including one archer, Roger Hunt, killed by a gun). The battle was a slaughter that, like the sack of Soissons, shocked Christendom. It was an age inured to violence. Henry did burn and hang the Lollards in London, and he executed an archer for stealing the copper-gilt pyx during the march to Agincourt, but those events were commonplace. Soissons and Agincourt, uncannily linked by Saints Crispin and Crispinian, were thought extraordinary.

Except for Thomas Perrill, I took all the names of the archers at Agincourt from the muster rolls of Henry's army, which still exist in the National Archives (readers wanting a more accessible source can find the names printed in Anne Curry's appendices). There really was a Nicholas Hook at Agincourt, though he did not serve Sir John Cornewaille, who was indeed the tournament champion of Europe. His name is often spelt Cornwell, a slight embarrassment, as he is no relation.

The field of Agincourt is remarkably unchanged, though the flanking woods have shrunk somewhat and the small castle that gave the battle its name has long disappeared. There is a splendid little museum in the village, and a memorial and battle-map at nearby Maisoncelles, which was where the English baggage was raided (much of Henry's lost treasure was later recovered). A Calvary on the battlefield marks the supposed spot of one of the grave-pits where the French buried their dead. Harfleur has vanished, subsumed into the greater city of Le Havre, though traces of the medieval town do still exist. Petrochemical works now stretch where the English fleet landed.

Henry V's leadership was an undoubted contribution to the unlikely victory. He went on fighting in France and eventually forced the French to yield to his demands that he was the rightful king, and it was agreed that he would be crowned on the death of the mad King Charles, but Henry was to die first. His son was crowned King of France instead, but the French would recover to expel the English from their territory. Marshal Boucicault, a great soldier, was to die in English captivity, while Charles, Duke of Orleans, was to spend twenty-five years as a prisoner, not being released until 1440. He wrote much poetry during those years and Juliet Barker, in *Agincourt*, translates a verse he wrote during his time in England, a verse that can bring an end to this story of a battle long ago:

Peace is a treasure which one cannot praise too highly.
I hate war. It should never be prized;
For a long time it has prevented me, rightly or wrongly,
From seeing France which my heart must love.

The Longbow

The longbow is an ancient weapon. A pair of yew longbows was found in a Neolithic grave in Yorkshire, proving that the weapon stretches back at least four thousand years, yet it only became a common weapon in the fourteenth and fifteenth centuries, and only in certain parts of the British Isles.

Archery, of course, was a very old skill, but the usual bow used for both hunting and war was the short bow. The arrow that famously went through Harold's eye at the Battle of Hastings was almost certainly shot from a short bow. A short bow was, perhaps, four feet long and it was an adequate weapon, as Harold learned. It was the bow used to hunt game, and an accurate arrow from a short bow would kill a deer or a man. The short bow was much easier to shoot than a longbow. The archer drew the cord to his eye, which meant he could aim down the shaft of the arrow like a rifleman looking along a barrel. So long as the aim was good and the arrow flew true the archer would probably strike his target. So why was the longbow preferred? As a weapon it was much more difficult to aim because, to use the full power of the long yew stave, the cord had to be drawn back to the archer's ear and that broke the relationship of the eye and the arrow-shaft. When a longbow is full-drawn by a right-handed archer the arrow is pointing to his left and it was necessary to learn how to compensate for that offset. So shooting a longbow becomes an instinctive process in which the brain makes a calculation about range and offset, and that calculation only came with a lot of experience.

The reason the longbow was preferred was, of course, its power. The short bow, though it could kill a man, did not have the power to drive an arrow through most armour. Even a coat of mail was probably sufficient to stop a short bow arrow, but the longbow was far more powerful and could even drive an arrow through plate mail. To gain that power, the bows were extremely stiff. A modern competition bow requires a draw-weight of around forty pounds, but a war bow, in the hands of an archer at Agincourt, needed a draw-weight of at least 120 pounds and sometimes much more. To pull the string just once needed huge strength, while to shoot arrow after arrow needed an immensely strong man, and the necessary muscles took years to develop. The skeletons of mediaeval English archers show distorted upper bones because the normal bone structure did not provide sufficient attachments for the muscles. A longbowman had almost grotesquely over-developed arms, chest and back muscles. No man could simply pick up a longbow and shoot it. He needed maybe ten years of training, starting as a child, to develop his muscles, increase his bone-mass and acquire the skill of calculating the arrow's flight.

So the longbow is an extraordinarily difficult weapon to master, which probably explains why, before the fourteenth century, very few men (and probably even fewer women) ever used it. We know they did use it, those two bows from Yorkshire are witness to that, but almost certainly such men were the most specialised of hunters. Yet suddenly, for no apparent reason, thousands of men became proficient with the longbow just in time to make England's army the most feared in Christendom. Why?

One suggestion is that a period of turmoil on

the frontiers of England, Wales and Scotland provoked a need by common folk to possess a weapon
of extraordinary power. Perhaps that is true, except
that those frontiers had always been turbulent and
centuries of raids had not previously produced a
mass of longbowmen. Another suggestion is simply
that shooting a longbow became a sudden enthusiasm, a craze even, and well-rewarded competi-
tions between villages and counties encouraged that
enthusiasm. Whatever the cause, the result was
that suddenly certain counties of England, Wales
and lowland Scotland began to produce hundreds,
indeed thousands, of men capable of drawing the
long war bow. It did not take long for the nobility
to notice this new weapon or for the government to
harness it. In 1252 a law required that every man
between the ages of fifteen and sixty should equip
himself with a bow. Training sessions were ordered
by law, usually on a Sunday, and in many villages
there is still a street called The Butts which marks
the place where archers shot at targets - the butts.

A good war bow was made from yew, but not any
yew. The best came from the sunny climates of
southern Europe, and soon there was a huge trade
importing staves from Italy and southern France.
English yew could be used, as could ash or elm,
but no native tree produced a bow as powerful as a
stave cut from the trunk of a Mediterranean grown
yew. The raw stave looked bi-coloured, for it was
cut where the dark heartwood met the lighter sapwood, and both were used in the finished bow. The
heartwood was stiff and resisted bending, while the
sapwood was springy. A bow made of heartwood
alone would be too stiff to draw, while a bow made
only of sapwood would quickly 'follow the string',
i.e. become permanently bent and so lose its force.

But together they were lethal. When the cord was released the sapwood served to accentuate the heartwood's natural tendency to straighten, and the longbow was capable of shooting an arrow around 250 yards, the same distance, say, that a good club golfer can drive a ball. The bows were at least the height of a man and their tips were reinforced by notched horn caps which provided lodgement for the waxed hemp strings. Bowyers soon became a powerful craft guild in England.

Arrows were made on an industrial scale. Foresters discovered the shafts, usually of ash, fletchers or fledgers applied the feathers, which on any one arrow all had to be from the same wing of a goose, and blacksmiths made the heads. Millions of arrows were needed and there was an impressive organisation which collected finished arrows from the countryside and stored them in county capitals, eventually passing them onto the Tower of London which was the main armoury for English forces travelling abroad. The 5,000 English archers at Agincourt could shoot 75,000 arrows in one minute, 750,000 in just ten minutes. What made the arrows so effective was not just their power, but their quantity. This was a volley weapon, swamping the enemy with missiles. Arrowmakers developed different arrowheads for different purposes, of which the most important was the bodkin. The bodkin (the word means needle) was the armour-piercing arrow and, like many modern armour-piercing missiles, depended on the shock of a slender, heavy bolt punching its concentrated mass through the target. By the time of Agincourt, though, the armourers of Europe had learned to beef-up their product so that the finest plate could either deflect or resist a bodkin strike. The age of the longbow was ending, though even during the reign of the Tudors it was still reckoned a formidable weapon against lightly armoured opponents. The Duke of Wellington, well aware of the longbow's power, enquired whether a corps of archers could not be raised for service in the Peninsular War, but the answer came back that there were no longer enough men strong or skilled enough to use the weapon. The Duke's idea was right, of course. Two hundred archers from Agincourt would easily have defeated ten times their number of musket-armed opponents. The smoothbore musket was horribly inaccurate compared to a longbow and had a pitifully slow rate of fire, yet a musketeer could be trained to proficiency in a week, while it took ten years of dedication to make a longbowman.

The French were not fools. They deployed crossbows which, though they had greater range than longbows, took so long to reload that longbowmen could advance into killing range between the first and second bolts. The French tried to train their own longbowmen, but the laws they enacted were ineffective and failed. They attempted to import bowyers and fletchers and archers from Britain, but very few succumbed to the temptations. And so, for at least a hundred years, a bow made of yew, the war bow (it was never called the longbow), was king of the battlefield. At Crécy, at Poitiers, at Agincourt, and on a thousand other forgotten fields, the archers of England became the most feared warriors of Europe.

Read the opening extract of Bernard Cornwell's new novel

1356

PROLOGUE

Carcassonne

He was late.

Now it was dark and he had no lantern, but the city's flames gave a lurid glow that reached deep into the church and gave just enough light to show the stone slabs in the deep crypt where the man struck at the floor with an iron crow.

He was attacking a stone incised with a crest that showed a goblet wreathed by a buckled belt on which was written *Calix Meus Inebrians*. Sun rays carved into the granite gave the impression of light radiating from the cup. The carving and inscription were worn smooth by time, and the man had taken little notice of them, though he did notice the cries from the alleyways around the small church. It was a night of fire and suffering, so much screaming that it smothered the noise as he struck the stone flags at the edge of the slab to chip a small space into which he could thrust the long crow. He rammed the iron bar down, then froze as he heard laughter and footsteps in the church above. He shrank behind an archway just before two men came down into the crypt. They carried a flaming torch that lit the long, arched space and showed that there was no easy plunder in sight. The crypt's altar was plain stone with nothing but a wooden cross for decoration, not even a candlestick, and one of the men said something in a strange language, the other laughed, and both climbed back to the nave where the flames from the streets lit the painted walls and the desecrated altars.

The man with the iron crow was cloaked and hooded in black. Beneath the heavy cloak he wore a white robe that was smeared with dirt, and the robe was girdled with a three-knotted cord. He was a Black Friar, a Dominican, though on this night that promised no protection from the army that ravaged Carcassonne. He was tall and strong, and before he had taken his vows he had been a man-at-arms. He had known how to thrust a lance, cut with a sword, or kill with an axe. He had been called Sire Ferdinand de Rodez, but now he was simply Fra Ferdinand. Once he had worn mail and plate, he had ridden in tournaments and slaughtered in battle, but for fifteen years he had been a friar and had prayed each day for his sins to be forgiven. He was old now, almost sixty, though still broad in the shoulders. He had walked to reach this city, but the rains had slowed his journey by flooding the rivers and making fords impassable and that was why he was late. Late and tired. He rammed the crow beneath the carved slab and heaved again, fearing that the iron would bend before the stone yielded, then suddenly there was a coarse grating sound and the granite lifted and then slid sideways to offer a small gap into the space beneath.

The space was dark because the devil's flamelight from the burning city could not reach into the grave, and so the friar knelt by the dark hole and groped. He discovered wood and so he thrust the crow down again. One blow, two blows, and the wood splintered, and he prayed there was no lead coffin inside the timber casket. He thrust the crow a last time, then reached down and pulled pieces of splintered wood out of the hole.

There was no lead coffin. His fingers, reaching far down into the tomb, found cloth that crumbled when he touched it. Then he felt bones. His fingers explored a dry eye-hole, loose teeth, and discovered the curve of a rib. He lay down so he could stretch his arm deeper and he groped in the grave's blackness and found something solid that was not bone. But it was not what he sought; it was the wrong shape. It was a crucifix. Voices were suddenly loud in the church above. A man laughed and a woman sobbed. The friar lay motionless, listening and praying. For a moment he despaired, thinking that the object he sought was not in the tomb, but then he reached as far as he could and his fingers touched something wrapped in a fine cloth that did not crumble. He fumbled in the dark, caught hold of the cloth, and tugged. Some object was wrapped inside the fine cloth, something heavy, and he inched it towards him, then caught proper hold of it and drew the object free of the bone hands that had been clutching it. He pulled the thing from the tomb and stood. He did not need to unwrap it. He knew he had found *la Malice*, and in thanks he turned to the simple altar at the crypt's eastern end and made the sign of the cross. 'Thank you, Lord,' he said in a murmur, 'and thank you, Saint Peter, and thank you Saint Junien. Now keep me safe.'

The friar would need heavenly help to be safe. For a moment he considered hiding in the crypt till the invading army left Carcassonne, but that might take days and, besides, once the soldiers had plundered everything easy they would open the crypt's tombs to search for rings, crucifixes, or anything else that might fetch a coin. The crypt had sheltered *la Malice* for a century and a half, but the friar knew it would offer him no safety beyond a few hours.

Fra Ferdinand abandoned the crow and climbed the stairs. *La Malice* was as long as his arm and surprisingly heavy. She had been equipped with a handle once, but only the thin metal tang remained and he held her by that crude grip. She was still wrapped in what he thought was silk.

The church nave was lit by the houses that burned in the small square outside. There were three men inside the church, and one called a challenge to the dark-cloaked figure who appeared from the crypt steps. The three were archers, their long bow staves were propped against the altar, but despite the challenge they were not really interested in the stranger, only in the woman they had spreadeagled on the altar steps. For a heartbeat Fra Ferdinand was tempted to rescue the woman, but then four or five new men came through a side door and whooped when they saw the naked body stretched on the steps.

They had brought another girl with them, a girl who screamed and struggled, and the friar shuddered at the sound of her distress. He heard her clothes tearing, heard her wail, and he remembered all his own sins. He made the sign of the cross, 'Forgive me, Christ Jesus,' he whispered and, unable to help the girls, he stepped through the church door and into the small square outside. Flames were consuming thatched roofs that flared bright, spewing wild sparks into the night wind. Smoke writhed above the city. A soldier wearing the red cross of Saint George was being sick on the church steps and a dog ran to lap up the vomit. The friar turned towards the river, hoping to cross the bridge and climb to the Cité. He thought that Carcassonne's double walls, towers and crenellations would protect him because he doubted that this rampaging army would have the patience to conduct a siege. They had captured the *bourg*, the commercial district that lay west of the river, but that had never been defensible. Most of the town's businesses were in the *bourg*, the leather shops and silversmiths and armourers and poulterers and cloth merchants, yet only an earth wall had surrounded those riches, and the army had swarmed over that puny barrier like a flood. Carcassonne's Cité, though, was a fortress, one of the greatest in France, a bastion ringed by vast stone turrets and towering walls. He would be safe there. He would find a place to hide *la Malice* and wait until he could return it to its owner.

He edged into a street that had not been fired. Men were breaking into houses, using hammers or axes to splinter doors. Most of the citizens had fled to the Cité, but a few foolish souls had remained, perhaps hoping to protect their properties. The army had arrived so swiftly that there had been no time to take every valuable across the bridge and up to the monstrous gates that protected the hilltop citadel. Two bodies lay in the central gutter. They wore the four lions of Armagnac, crossbowmen killed in the hopeless defence of the *bourg*.

Fra Ferdinand did not know the city. Now he tried to find a hidden way to the river, using shadowed alleys and narrow passages. God, he thought, was with him, for he met no enemies as he hurried eastwards, but then he came to a wider street, lit bright by flames, and he saw the long bridge, and beyond it, high on the hill, the fire-reflecting walls of the Cité. The stones of the wall were reddened by the fires blazing in the *bourg*. The walls of hell, the friar thought, and then a gust of the night wind swirled a great mask of smoke down to shroud his view of the walls, but not the bridge, and on the bridge, guarding its western end, were archers. English archers with their red-crossed tunics and their long deadly bows. Two horsemen, mailed and helmeted, were with the archers.

No way to cross, he thought. No way to reach the safety of the Cité. He crouched, thinking, then headed back into the alleys. He would go north.

He had to cross a major street lit by newly set fires. A chain, one of the many that had been strung across the roadway to hold up the invaders, lay in the gutter where a cat lapped at blood. Fra Ferdinand ran through the firelight, dodged into another alley, and kept running. God was still with him. The stars were obscured by smoke in which sparks flew. He crossed a square, was baulked by a dead-end alley, retraced his steps, and headed north again. A cow bellowed in a burning building, a dog ran across his path with something black and dripping in its teeth. He passed a tanner's shop, jumping over the hides that were strewn on the cobbles, and there ahead was the risible earth bank that was the *bourg*'s only defence, and he climbed it, then heard a shout and glanced behind to see three men pursuing him.

'Who are you?' one shouted.

'Stop!' another bellowed.

The friar ignored them. He ran down the slope, heading towards the dark countryside that lay beyond the huddle of cottages built outside the earthen bank, as an arrow hissed past him, missing him by the grace of God and the width of a finger, and he twisted aside into a passage between two of the small houses. A steaming manure heap stank there. He ran past the dung and saw the passage ended in a wall, and turned back to see the three men barring his path. They were grinning.

'What have you got?' one of them asked.

'*Je suis Gascon*,' Fra Ferdinand said. He knew the city's invaders were both Gascons and English, and he spoke no English. '*Je suis Gascon!*' he said again, walking towards them.

'He's a Black Friar,' one of the men said.

'But why did the goddamned bastard run?' another of the

Englishmen asked. 'Got something to hide, have you?'

'Give it here,' the third man said, holding out his hand. He was the only one with a strung bow; the other two had their bows slung on their backs and were holding swords. 'Come on, arseface, give it me.' The man reached for *la Malice*.

The three men were half the friar's age, and, because they were archers, probably twice as strong, but Fra Ferdinand had been a great man-at-arms and the skills of the sword had never deserted him. And he was angry. Angry because of the suffering he had seen and the cruelties he had heard, and that anger made him savage. 'In the name of God,' he said, and whipped *la Malice* upwards. She was still wrapped in silk, but her blade cut hard into the archer's outstretched wrist, severing the tendons and breaking bone. Fra Ferdinand was holding her by the tang, which offered a perilous grip, but she seemed alive to him. The wounded man recoiled, bleeding, as his companions roared with anger and stabbed their blades forward, and the friar parried both with one cut and lunged forward, and *la Malice*, though she had been in a tomb for over a hundred and fifty years, proved as sharp as a newly honed blade and her fore-edge skewered through the padded haubergeon of the nearest man and opened his ribs and ripped into a lung, and before the man even knew he had been wounded Fra Ferdinand had swept the blade sideways to take the third man's eyes and blood brightened the alleyway and all three men were retreating now, but the Black Friar gave them no chance to escape. The blinded man tripped backwards onto the manure pile, his companion hacked his blade in desperation, and *la Malice* met it and the English sword broke in two and the friar flicked the silk-wrapped blade to cut that man's gullet and felt the blood splash on his face. So warm, he thought, and God forgive me. A bird shrieked in the darkness, and the flames roared up from the *bourg*.

He killed all three archers, then used the silk wrapping to clean *la Malice*'s blade. He thought of saying a brief prayer for the men he had just killed, then decided he did not want to share heaven with such brutes. Instead he kissed *la Malice*, then searched the three bodies and found some coins, a lump of cheese, four bowstrings, and a knife.

The city of Carcassonne burned and filled the winter night with smoke.

And the Black Friar walked north. He was going home, home to the tower.

He carried *la Malice* and the fate of Christendom.

And he vanished into darkness.

The men came to the tower four days after Carcassonne had been sacked.

There were sixteen of them, all cloaked in fine, thick wool and all mounted on good horses. Fifteen of the men wore mail and had swords at their waists, while the remaining rider was a priest who carried a hooded hawk on his wrist.

The wind came harsh down the mountain pass, ruffling the hawk's feathers, rattling the pines and whipping the smoke from the small cottages of the village that lay beneath the tower. It was cold. This part of France rarely saw snow, but the priest, glancing from beneath the black hood of his cloak, thought there might be flakes in the wind.

There were ruined walls about the tower, evidence that this had once been a stronghold, but all that was left of the old castle was the tower itself and a low thatched building where perhaps servants lived. Chickens scratched in the dust, a tethered goat stared at the horses, while a cat ignored the newcomers. What had once been a fine small fortress, guarding the road into the mountains, was now a farmstead, though the priest noticed that the tower was still in good repair, and the small village in the hollow beneath the old fortress looked prosperous enough.

A man scurried from the thatched hut and bowed low to the horsemen. He did not bow because he recognised them, but because men with swords command respect. 'Lords?' the man asked anxiously.

'Shelter the horses,' the priest demanded.

'Walk them first,' one of the mailed men added, 'walk them, rub them down, don't let them eat too much.'

'Lord,' the man said, bowing again.

'This is Mouthoumet?' the priest asked as he dismounted.

'Yes, father.'

'And you serve the Sire of Mouthoumet?' the priest asked.

'The Count of Mouthoumet, yes, lord.'

'He lives?'

'Praise be to God, father, he lives.'

'Praise be to God indeed,' the priest said carelessly, then strode to the tower door, which stood at the top of a brief flight of stone steps. He called for two of the mailed men to accompany him and ordered the rest to wait in the yard, then he pushed open the door to find himself in a wide, round room used to store firewood. Hams and bunches of herbs hung from the beams. A stair led around one half of the wall, and the priest, not bothering to announce himself or wait for an attendant to greet him, took the stairs to the upper floor where a hearth was built into the wall. A fire burned there, though much of its smoke swirled about the circular room, driven back through the vent by the cold wind. The ancient wooden floorboards were covered in threadbare rugs; there were two wooden chests on which candles burned because, though it was daylight outside, the room's two windows had been hung with blankets to block the draughts. There was a table on which lay two books, some parchments, an ink bottle, a sheaf of quills, a knife, and an old rusted breastplate that served as a bowl for three wrinkled apples. A chair stood by the table while the Count of Mouthoumet, lord of this lonely tower, lay in a bed close to the smouldering fire. A grey-haired priest sat beside him, and two elderly women knelt at the bed's foot. 'Leave,' the newly arrived priest ordered the three. The two mailed men came up the stairs behind him and seemed to fill the room with their baleful presence.

'Who are you?' the grey-haired priest asked nervously.

'I said leave, so leave.'

'He's dying!'

'Go!'

The old priest, a scapular about his neck, abandoned the sacraments and followed the two women down the stairs. The dying man watched the newcomers, but said nothing. His hair was long and white, his beard untrimmed, and his eyes sunken. He saw the priest place the hawk on the table, where the bird's talons made scratching noises. 'She is *une calade*,' the priest explained.

'*Une calade*?' the count asked, his voice very low. He stared at the bird's slate-grey feathers and pale streaked breast. 'It is too late for a *calade*.'

'You must have faith,' the priest said.

'I have lived over eighty years,' the count said, 'and I have more faith than I have time.'

'You have enough time for this,' the priest said grimly. The two mailed men stood at the stairhead and said nothing. The *calade* made a mewing noise, but when the priest snapped his fingers the hooded bird went still and quiet. 'You were given the sacrament?' the priest asked.

'Father Jacques was about to give it to me,' the dying man said.

'I will do it,' the priest said.

'Who are you?'

'I come from Avignon.'

'From the Pope?'

'Who else?' the priest asked. He walked about the room, examining it, and the old man watched him. He saw a tall, hard-faced man, his priest's robes finely tailored. When the visitor lifted a hand to touch the crucifix hanging on the wall his sleeve fell open to reveal a lining of red silk. The old man knew this kind of priest, hard and ambitious, rich and clever, the kind who did not minister to the poor, but climbed the ladder of clerical power into the company of the rich and privileged. The priest turned and gazed at the old man with hard green eyes. 'Tell me,' he said, 'where is *la Malice*?'

The old man hesitated a second too long. '*La Malice*?'

'Tell me where she is,' the priest demanded and, when the old man said nothing, added, 'I come from the Holy Father. I order you to tell me.'

'I don't know the answer,' the old man whispered, 'so how can I tell you?'

A log crackled in the fire, spewing sparks. 'The Black Friars,' the priest said, 'have been spreading heresies.'

'God forbid,' the old man said.

'You have heard them?'

The count shook his head. 'I hear little these days, father.'

The priest reached into a pouch that hung at his waist and brought out a scrap of parchment. 'The Seven Dark Lords possessed it,' he read aloud, 'and they are cursed. He who must rule us will find it, and he shall be blessed.'

'Is that heresy?' the count asked.

'It is a verse the Black Friars are telling all over France. All over Europe! There is only one man to rule us, and that is the Holy Father. If *la Malice* exists then it is your Christian duty to tell me what you know. She must be given to the church! A man who thinks otherwise is a heretic.'

'I am no heretic,' the old man said.

'Your father was a Dark Lord.'

The count shuddered. 'The sins of the father are not mine.'

'And the Dark Lords possessed *la Malice*.'

'They say many things about the Dark Lords,' the count said.

'They protected the treasures of the Cathar heretics,' the priest said, 'and when, by the grace of God, those heretics were burned from the land, the Dark Lords took their treasures and hid them.'

'I have heard that.' The count's voice was scarce above a whisper.

The priest reached out and stroked the hawk's back. '*La Malice*,' he said, 'has been lost these many years, but the Black Friars say she can be found. And she must be found! She is a treasure of the church, a thing of power! A weapon to bring Christ's kingdom to earth, and you conceal it!'

'I do not!' the old man protested.

The priest sat on the bed and leaned close to the count. 'Where is *la Malice*?' he asked.

'I don't know.'

'You are very close to God's judgement, old man,' the priest said, 'so do not lie to me.'

'In the name of God,' the count said, 'I do not know.' And that was true. He had known where *la Malice* was hidden, and, fearing that the English would discover her, he had sent his friend, Fra Ferdinand, to retrieve the relic and the count assumed the friar had done that, and if Fra Ferdinand had succeeded then the count did not know where *la Malice* was. So he had not lied, but nor had he told the priest the whole truth, because some secrets should be carried to the grave.

The priest stared at the count for a long time, then reached out his left hand to take the jesses of the hawk. The bird, still hooded, stepped cautiously onto the priest's wrist. He lifted it down to the bed and coaxed the bird to stand on the dying man's chest, then gently undid the hood's laces and lifted the leather from the bird's head. 'This *calade*,' he said, 'is different. It does not betray whether you will live or die, but whether you will die in a state of grace and go to heaven.'

'I pray I shall,' the dying man said.

'Look at the bird,' the priest commanded.

The Count of Mouthoumet looked up at the hawk. He had heard of such birds, *calades*, which could foretell a man's death or life. If the bird looked directly into a sick person's eyes then that person would recover, but if not, they would die. 'A bird that knows eternity?' the count asked.

'Look at him,' the priest said, 'and tell me, do you know where *la Malice* is hidden?'

'No,' the old man whispered.

The hawk seemed to be gazing at the wall. It shuffled on the old man's breast, its talons gripping the threadbare blanket. No one spoke. The bird was very still, but then, suddenly, it darted its head down and the count screamed.

'Quiet,' the priest snarled.

The hawk had sliced its hooked beak into the dying man's left eye, pulping it, leaving a trail of bloodied jelly on his unshaven cheek. The count was whimpering. The hawk's beak made a clattering noise as the priest moved the bird back down the bed.

'The *calade* tells me you lied,' the priest said, 'and now, if you wish to keep your right eye, you will tell me the truth. Where is *la Malice*?'

'I don't know,' the old man sobbed.

The priest was silent for a while. The fire crackled and the wind blew smoke into the room. 'You lie,' he said. 'The *calade* tells me you lie. You spit in the face of God and of His angels.'

'No!' the old man protested.

'Where is *la Malice*?'

'I don't know!'

'Your family name is Planchard,' the priest said accusingly, 'and the Planchards were ever heretics.'

'No!' the count protested, and then, sounding weaker, 'Who are you?'

'You may call me Father Calade,' the priest said, 'and I am

the man who decides whether you go to hell or go to heaven.'

'Then shrive me,' the old man pleaded.

'I would rather suck on the devil's arse,' Father Calade said.

An hour later, when the count was blinded and weeping, the priest was at last convinced that the old man did not know where *la Malice* was hidden. He coaxed the hawk onto his wrist and placed the hood back on its head, then he nodded to one of the mailed men. 'Send this old fool to his master.'

'To his master?' the man-at-arms asked, puzzled.

'To Satan,' the priest said.

'For God's sake,' the Count of Mouthoumet pleaded, then jerked helplessly as the man-at-arms thrust a fleece-stuffed pillow over his face. The old man took a surprisingly long time to die.

'We three go back to Avignon,' the priest told his companions, 'but the rest stay here. Tell them to search this place. Pull it down! Stone by stone.'

The priest rode east towards Avignon. Later that day some snow fell, soft and thin, whitening the pale olive trees in the valley beneath the dead man's tower.

Next morning the snow had gone, and a week later the English came.

PART ONE

Avignon

One

The message arrived in the town after midnight, carried by a young monk who had travelled all the way from England. He had left Carlisle in August with two other brethren, all three ordered to the great Cistercian house at Montpellier where Brother Michael, the youngest, was to learn medicine and the others were to study at the famous school of theology. The three had walked the length of England, sailed from Southampton to Bordeaux and then walked inland, and, like any travellers committed to a long journey, they had been entrusted with messages. There was one for the abbot at Puys, where Brother Vincent had died of the flux, then Michael and his companion had walked on to Toulouse, where Brother Peter had fallen sick and been committed to the hospital where, as far as Michael knew, he still lay. So the young monk was alone now and he had just one message left, a battered scrap of parchment, and he had been told that he might miss the man to whom it was addressed if he did not travel that same night. 'Le Bâtard,' the abbot at Paville had told him, 'moves swiftly. He was here two days ago, now he is at Villon, but tomorrow?'

'Le Bâtard?'

'That is his name in these parts,' the abbot had said, making the sign of the cross, which somehow suggested that the young English monk would be lucky to survive his encounter with the man named le Bâtard.

Now, after a day's walking, Brother Michael stared across the valley at the town of Villon. It had been easy to find because, as night fell, the sky was lit with flames that served as a beacon. Fugitives passing him on the road told him that Villon was burning, and so Brother Michael merely walked towards the bright fire so that he could find *le Bâtard* and thus deliver his message. He crossed the valley nervously, seeing fire twist above the town walls to fill the night with a churning smoke that was touched livid red where it reflected the flames. The young monk thought this was what Satan's sky must look like. Fugitives were still escaping the town and they told Brother Michael to turn around and flee because the devils of hell were loose in Villon, and he was tempted, oh so tempted, but another part of his young soul was curious. He had never seen a battle. He had never seen what men did when they unleashed themselves to violence, and so he walked on, putting his faith in God and in the stout pilgrim's staff he had carried all the way from Carlisle.

The fires were concentrated around the western gate, and their flames lit the bulk of the castle that crowned the hill to the east. It was the Lord of Villon's castle, that was what the abbot at Paville had told him, and the Lord of Villon was being besieged by an army led by the Bishop of Lavence and by the Count of Labrouillade, who together had hired the band of mercenaries led by *le Bâtard*.

'Their quarrel?' Brother Michael had asked the abbot.

'They have two quarrels,' the abbot had answered, pausing to let a servant pour him wine. 'The Lord of Villon confiscated a wagon of hides belonging to the bishop. Or so the bishop says.' He grimaced, for the wine was new and raw. 'In truth Villon is a Godless rogue, and the bishop would like a new neighbour.' He shrugged, as if to admit that the cause of the fighting was trivial.

'And the second quarrel?'

The abbot had paused. 'Villon took the Count of Labrouillade's wife,' he finally admitted.

'Ah.' Brother Michael had not known what else to say.

'Men are quarrelsome,' the abbot had said, 'but women always make them worse. Look at Troy! All those men killed for one pretty face!' He looked sternly at the young English monk. 'Women brought sin into this world, brother, and they have never ceased to bring it. Be grateful that you are a monk and sworn to celibacy.'

'Thanks be to God,' Brother Michael had said, though without much conviction.

Now the town of Villon was filled with burning houses and dead people, all because of a woman, her lover, and a cartload of hides. Brother Michael approached the town along the valley road, crossed a stone bridge and so came to Villon's western entrance, where he paused because the gates had been torn from the arch's stonework by a force so massive that he could not imagine what might do such a thing. The hinges were forged from iron, and each had been attached to its gate by brackets longer than a bishop's crozier, broader than a man's hand and thick as a thumb, yet the two leaves of the gate now hung askew, their scorched timbers shattered and their massive hinges wrenched into grotesque curls. It was as though the devil himself had plunged his monstrous fist through the arch to rip a path into the city. Brother Michael made the sign of the cross.

He edged past the fire-blackened gate and stopped again because, just beyond the arch, a house was burning and in the door opposite was the body of a young woman, face down, quite naked, her pale skin laced with rivulets of blood that appeared black in the firelight. The monk gazed at her, frowning slightly, wondering why the shape of a woman's back was so arousing, and then he was ashamed that he had thought such a thing. He crossed himself again. The devil, he thought, was everywhere this night, but especially here in this burning city beneath the fire-touched clouds of hell.

Two men, one in a ragged mail coat and the other in a loose leather jerkin and both holding long knives, stepped over the dead woman. They were alarmed by the sight of the monk and turned fast, eyes wide, ready to strike, but then recognised the grubby white robe and saw the wooden cross about Brother Michael's neck and ran off in search of richer victims. A third soldier vomited into the gutter. A rafter collapsed in the burning house, venting a blast of hot air and whirling sparks.

Brother Michael climbed the street, keeping his distance from the corpses, then saw a man sitting by a rain barrel where he was trying to staunch the bleeding from a wound in his belly. The young monk had been an assistant in his monastery's infirmary, and so he approached the wounded soldier. 'I can bind that up,' he said, kneeling, but the wounded man snarled at him and lashed out with a knife, which Brother Michael only avoided by toppling sideways. He scrambled to his feet and backed away.

'Take off your robe,' the wounded man said, trying to follow the monk, but Brother Michael ran uphill. The man collapsed again, spitting curses.'Come back,' he shouted, 'come back!' Over his leather jerkin he wore a jupon that showed a golden merlin against a red field and Brother Michael, dazedly trying to make sense of the chaos about him, realised that the golden bird was the symbol of the town's defenders, and that the wounded man had wanted to escape by stealing his monk's robe and using it as a disguise, but instead the man was trapped by two soldiers in green and white colours who cut his throat.

Some men wore a badge showing a yellow bishop's staff surrounded by four black cross-crosslets, and Brother Michael decided they had to be the bishop's soldiers, while the troops who wore the green horse on the white field must serve the Count of Labrouillade. Most of the dead displayed the golden merlin, and the monk noted how many of those corpses were spitted by long English arrows that had blood-speckled white feathers. The fighting had passed through this part of the town, leaving it burning. Fire leaped from thatched roof to thatched roof, while in the places where the fire had not reached a horde of drunken, undisciplined soldiers plundered and raped amidst the smoke. A baby cried, a woman shrieked, then a blinded man, his eyes nothing but blood-weeping pits, staggered from an alley to collide with the monk. The man shrank away, whimpering, holding up his hands to ward off the expected blow.

'I won't hurt you,' Brother Michael said in French, a language he had learned as a novice so he would be fitted to finish his education at Montpellier, but the blinded man ignored him and stumbled down the street. Somewhere, incongruous in the blood and smoke and shouting, a choir sang, and the monk wondered if he was dreaming, yet the voices were real, as real as the screaming women and sobbing children and barking dogs.

He went cautiously now, for the alleys were dark and the soldiers wild. He passed a tanner's shop where a fire burned and he saw a man had been drowned in a vat of the urine used to cure the hides. He came into a small square, decorated with a stone cross, and there he was attacked from behind by a bearded brute wearing the bishop's livery. The monk was pushed to the ground and the man bent to cut away the pouch hanging from his rope belt. 'Get away! Get away!' Brother Michael, panicking, forgot where he was and shouted in English. The man grinned and moved the knife to threaten the monk's eyes, then he opened his own eyes wide, looked horrified and the flame-lit night went dark with a spray of blood as the man slowly toppled over. Brother Michael was spattered with the blood and saw that his assailant had an arrow through his neck. The man was choking, clawing at the arrow, then began to shudder as blood pulsed from his open mouth.

'You're English, brother?' an English voice asked, and Michael looked up to see a man wearing a black livery on which a white badge was slashed with the diagonal bar of bastardy. 'You're English?' the man asked again.

'I'm English,' Brother Michael managed to speak.

'You should have clouted him,' the man said, picking up Brother Michael's staff, then hauling the monk to his feet. 'Clouted him hard and he'd have toppled over. Bastards are all drunk.'

'I'm English,' Brother Michael said again. He was shaking. The fresh blood felt warm on his skin. He shivered.

'And you're a long bloody way from home, brother,' the man said. He had a great war bow strung across his muscled shoulders. He stooped to the monk's assailant, drew a knife and cut the arrow out of the man's throat, killing him in the process. 'Arrows are hard to come by,' he explained, 'so we try to rescue them. If you see any, pick them up.'

Michael brushed down his white robe, then looked at the brutal badge on his rescuer's jupon. It showed a strange animal holding a cup in its claws. 'You serve . . .' he began.

'The Bastard,' the man interrupted. 'We're the Hellequin, brother.'

'The Hellequin?'

'The devil's souls,' the man said with a grin, 'and what the hell are you doing here?'

'I've a message for your master, *le Bâtard*.'

'Then let's find him. My name's Sam.'

The name suited the archer, who had a boyish, cheerful face

and a quick grin. He led the monk past a church that he and two other Hellequin had been guarding because it was a refuge for some of the townsfolk. 'The Bastard doesn't approve of rape,' he explained.

'Nor should he,' Michael responded dutifully.

'He might as well disapprove of rain,' Sam said cheerfully, leading the way into a larger square where a half-dozen horsemen waited with drawn swords. They were in mail and helmets, and all wore the bishop's livery, and behind them was the choir, a score of boys chanting a psalm. '*Domine eduxisti,*' they sang, '*de inferno animam meam vivificasti me ne descenderem in lacum.*'

'He'd know what that meant,' Sam said, tapping his badge and evidently meaning *le Bâtard*.

'It means God has brought our souls out of hell,' Brother Michael said, 'and given us life and will keep us from the pit.'

'That's very nice of God,' Sam said. He gave a perfunctory bow to the horsemen and touched his hand to his helmet. 'That's the bishop,' he explained, and Brother Michael saw a tall man, his dark face framed by a steel helmet, sitting on his horse beneath a banner showing the crozier and the crosses. 'He's waiting,' Sam explained, 'for us to do the fighting. They all do that. Come and fight with us, they say, then they all get pissing drunk while we do all the killing. Still, it's what we're paid for. Careful here, brother, it gets dangerous.' He took the bow from his shoulder, led the monk down an alley, then checked at the corner. He peered around. 'Bloody dangerous,' he added.

Brother Michael, fascinated and repelled by the carnage all about him, leaned past Sam and discovered they had reached the top of the town and were at the edge of a big open space, a marketplace perhaps, and on its far side was a road cut through black rock to the castle gate. The gatehouse, lit by the flames in the lower town, was hung with great banners. Some enjoined the help of the saints, while others showed the badge of the golden merlin. A crossbow bolt struck the wall near the priest then skittered down the cobbled alley. 'If we capture the castle by sundown tomorrow,' Sam said, putting an arrow on his string, 'our money is doubled.'

'Doubled? Why?'

'Because tomorrow is Saint Bertille's day,' Sam said, 'and our employer's wife is called Bertille, so the fall of the castle will prove that God is on our side and not on hers.'

Brother Michael thought that was dubious theology, but he did not argue the point. 'She's the wife who ran away?'

'Can't blame her. He's a pig, the count, a bloody pig, but marriage is marriage, ain't it? And it'll be a chill day in hell that a woman can choose a husband. Still, I do feel sorry for her, married to that pig.' He half drew the bow, stepped around the corner, looked for a target, saw none and stepped back. 'So the poor girl's in there,' he went on, 'and the pig is paying us to fetch her out double fast.'

Brother Michael peered around the corner, then twitched back as a pair of crossbow bolts caught the firelight. The bolts banged into the wall close to him, then ricocheted on down the alley. 'Lucky, aren't you?' Sam said cheerfully. 'Bastards saw me, took aim, then you showed yourself. You could be in heaven by now if the bastards could shoot straight.'

'You'll never get the lady out of that place,' Brother Michael opined.

'We won't?'

'It's too strong!'

'We're the Hellequin,' Sam said, 'which means the poor lass has got about an hour left with her lover boy. I hope he's giving her a good one to remember him by.'

Michael, unseen, blushed. He was troubled by women. For most of his life that temptation had not mattered because, closed away in the Cistercian house, he rarely saw any women, but the journey from Carlisle had strewn a thousand devil's snares across his path. In Toulouse a whore had grabbed him from behind, fondled him, and he had torn himself free, shaking with embarrassment, and fallen to his knees. The memory of her laughter was like a whip on his soul, as were the memories of all the girls he had seen, stared at, and wondered about, and he remembered the white naked skin of the girl at the town gate and he knew the devil was tempting him again, and he was about to say a prayer for strength when he was distracted by a whirring sound and saw a shower of crossbow bolts slashing down to the marketplace. Some, striking the cobbles, gave off bright sparks, and Brother Michael wondered why the defenders were shooting, then became aware that dark-cloaked men were running from every alleyway to line the open space. They were archers, who began loosing arrows at the high battlements. Flights of arrows; not the short, leather-fledged, metal bolts of crossbowmen, but English arrows, white-feathered and long, speeding silently up to the wall's top, propelled by the great yew war bows with their hempen strings that gave a harp's sharp note for every missile shot. The arrows trembled as they left the string, then their feathers caught the air and they streaked up, white flashes in the dark, the firelight glistening from their steel points, and the monk noted how the defenders' bolts, so thick a moment ago, were suddenly sparse. The archers were drenching the castle's defenders with arrows, forcing the crossbowmen to duck behind the wall's parapet, while other bowmen shot at the slits in the flanking towers. The sound of the steel heads striking the castle walls was like hail on cobbles. One archer fell back, a bolt in his chest, but that was the only casualty the monk saw, and then he heard the wheels.

'Stand back,' Sam warned him, and the priest stepped into the alley as a cart thundered past him. It was a small cart, light enough for six men to push, but it had been made heavier because ten great pavises, man-sized shields designed to protect a crossbowman as he reloaded his clumsy weapon, had been nailed to the front and sides to protect the men who pushed the cart, which was loaded with small wooden barrels.

'Much less than an hour,' Sam said, stepping into the street when the cart had passed. He drew the big bow and sent an arrow towards the castle's gate.

It was all strangely silent. Bother Michael had expected battle to be noise, he had expected to hear men calling to God for the sake of their souls, to hear voices raised in fear or pain, but the only sounds were the shrieks of the women in the lower town, the crackle of the flames, the harp-notes of the bows, the sound of the cart's wheels on the cobbles, and the rattle of bolts and arrows clattering on stone. Michael stared in awe as Sam kept shooting, not seeming to aim, but just whipping shaft after shaft at the castle's battlements.

'Good thing we can see,' Sam said, releasing another arrow.

'The flames, you mean?'

'That's why we set fire to the houses,' Sam said, 'to light up the bastards.' He loosed another shaft, seemingly without effort; when Brother Michael had once tried to draw a yew bow he had not been able to pull the string more than a hand's breadth.

The cart had reached the castle's gate now. It stopped there, a black shadow inside the dark archway, and Brother Michael saw a flicker of light spring up in that darkness, fade, revive, then steady to a dull glow as the six men who had pushed the cart ran back towards the archers. One of them fell, evidently struck by a crossbow bolt. Two of the others snatched his arms and dragged him back, and it was then that the monk caught his first sight of *le Bâtard*.

'That's him,' Sam said fondly, 'our bloody bastard.' Brother Michael saw a tall man dressed in a belted haubergeon of chain mail that had been painted black. He had high boots, a black sword scabbard and his helmet was a simple bascinet that was black like his mail. His sword was drawn and he used it to wave a dozen men-at-arms forward, forming them in a line, shields overlapping, in the open space. He glanced towards Brother Michael, who saw *le Bâtard*'s nose was broken and his cheek scarred, but he also saw a force in the face, a savagery, and he understood why the abbot at Paville had spoken of this man with awe. Brother Michael had expected *le Bâtard* to be an older man, and was surprised that the black-armoured soldier looked so young. Then *le Bâtard* saw Sam. 'I thought you were guarding the church, Sam,' he said.

'Poxface and Johnny are still there,' Sam said, 'but I brought this fellow to see you.' He jerked his head towards Brother Michael.

The monk took a step forward and felt the full force of *le Bâtard*'s gaze. He was suddenly nervous and his mouth went dry with fear. 'I have a message for you,' he stammered, 'it's from . . .'

'Later,' *le Bâtard* interrupted. A servant had brought him a shield that he looped onto his left arm, then turned to look at the castle.

Which suddenly gouted flame and smoke. The smoke was black and red, shot through with stabbing flames, and filling the night with a bursting thunder that made Brother Michael crouch in fear. Scraps of flaming wreckage seared through the night as the heated air punched past the alley's mouth. Smoke shrouded the open space as the noise of the blast echoed and rolled back from the valley's far side. Birds that had been nesting in crevices of the castle wall flapped into the smoky air, while one of the great banners, calling on the help of Saint Joseph, caught the fire and blazed bright against the battlements. 'Gunpowder,' Sam explained laconically.

'Gunpowder?'

'He's a clever bastard, our bastard,' Sam said. 'Knocks down gates fast, don't it? Mind you, it's expensive. The wifeless pig had to pay double if he wanted us to use powder. He must want the bitch bad to pay that much! I hope she's bloody worth it.'

Brother Michael saw small flames flickering in the archway's thick smoke. He understood now why the town's entrance looked as though it had been torn, blackened and wrenched apart by the devil's fist. *Le Bâtard* had forced his way into the town with gunpowder, and he had repeated the trick to blow down the castle's great wooden gates. Now he led his twenty men-at-arms towards the wreckage.

'Archers!' another man called, and the bowmen, including Sam, followed the men-at-arms towards the gate. They advanced in silence, and that too was terrifying. These men in their black and white livery, Brother Michael thought, had learned to live calmly and fight ruthlessly in the dark valley of death. None of them appeared to be drunk. They were disciplined, efficient and frightening.

Le Bâtard vanished in the smoke. There were shouts from the castle, but the monk could not see what was happening there, though it was plain the attackers were inside, for the archers were now streaming through the smoking gate-arch. More men were following, men wearing the badges of the bishop and the count, going to seek more plunder in the doomed fortress.

'It could be dangerous,' Sam warned the young monk.

'God is with us,' Brother Michael said, and wondered at the fierce excitement he felt, so fierce that he hefted the pilgrim's staff as though it were a weapon.

The castle had looked big from the alleyway, but as he jostled through the scorched gate Brother Michael saw it was much smaller than it had appeared. It had no bailey and no great keep, but merely the gatehouse and one tall tower, which were separated by a small courtyard where a dozen crossbowmen in the red and gold livery lay dying. One man had been eviscerated by the explosion at the gate and, though his intestines had spilt across the yard's stones, he still lived and moaned. The monk paused to offer the man some help, then sprang back as Sam, with an ease that was as casual as it seemed heartless, cut his throat. 'You killed him!' Brother Michael said in horror.

'Of course I bloody killed him,' Sam said cheerfully. 'What did you expect me to do? Kiss him? I hope someone does the same for me if I'm in that state.' He wiped the blood from his short knife. A defender screamed as he fell from the gatehouse parapet, while another man staggered down the tower steps to collapse at the foot.

There was a door at the top of the steps, but it had not been defended, or else the defenders' courage had evaporated when the main gate exploded inwards, and so le Bâtard's men were streaming into the tower. Brother Michael followed, then turned as a trumpet sounded. A cavalcade of horsemen, all in green and white, were forcing their way through the castle gate where they used swords to drive their own men from their path. At the centre of the horsemen, where he was protected by their weapons, was a monstrously fat man clad in mail and plate and mounted on a huge horse. The cavalcade stopped at the foot of the steps and it took four men to ease the fat one out of his saddle and steady him on his feet. 'His piggy lordship,' Sam said sardonically.

'The Count of Labrouillade?'

'One of our employers,' Sam said, 'and here's the other one.' The bishop and his men had followed the count through the gate, and Sam and Michael went onto their knees as the two leaders mounted the steps and went into the tower.

Sam and Brother Michael followed the bishop's men into the entrance chamber, up a flight of shallow stairs and into a great hall that was a high, pillared space lit by a dozen smoking torches and hung with tapestries showing the golden merlin on its red background. There were at least sixty men already in the hall and they now shuffled to the edges, allowing the Count of Labrouillade and the Bishop of Lavence to walk slowly towards the dais where two of le Bâtard's men were holding the defeated lord on his knees. Behind them, tall and black in his armour, was *le Bâtard* himself, his face expressionless, while beside him, unrestrained, was a young woman in a red dress. 'That's Bertille?' Brother Michael asked.

'Must be,' Sam said appreciatively. 'And a nice little mare she is too!'

Brother Michael held his breath, stared, and, for an heretical moment, he regretted ever taking holy orders. Bertille, the faithless Countess of Labrouillade, was more than a nice little mare, she was a beauty. She could not have been a day over twenty and had a sweet face, unmarked by scars or disease, with full lips and dark eyes. Her hair was black and curly, her eyes wide, and despite the obvious terror on her face she was so lovely that Brother Michael, who was only twenty-two himself, trembled. He thought he had never seen a creature so beautiful, and then he breathed again, made the sign of the cross, and uttered a silent prayer that the Virgin and Saint Michael would keep him from temptation. 'She's worth the price of the gunpowder, I'd say,' Sam commented cheerfully.

Brother Michael watched as Bertille's husband, who had taken off his helmet to reveal a head of greasy grey hair and a heavy, porcine face, waddled towards her. The count's breath was short because of the effort of walking in his heavy armour. He stopped a few paces from the dais and stared at the breast of his wife's dress, which was blazoned with the golden merlin, the symbol of her defeated lover. 'It seems to me, madame,' the count said, 'that you show poor taste in clothing.'

The countess dropped to her knees and held her clasped hands towards her husband. She wanted to speak, but the only sound she made was a whimpering sob. Tears on her cheeks reflected the flames of the torches. Brother Michael reminded himself that she was an adulteress, a sinner, a fornicator lost to grace, and Sam glanced at the young monk and thought that one day a woman would cause trouble in his life.

'Take that badge off her,' the count ordered two of his men-at-arms, gesturing at the golden merlin embroidered on his wife's dress, and the two men, their chain mail clinking and plated boots heavy on the flagstones, climbed the dais and seized the countess. She tried to resist them, shrieked once, but then surrendered as one man held her arms behind her back and the other drew a short knife from his belt.

Brother Michael instinctively moved as though to help her, but Sam checked him with his one hand. 'She's the count's wife, brother,' the archer said softly, 'which means she's his property. He can do with her whatever he wants, and if you interfere he'll slit your belly open.'

'I was not . . .' Brother Michael began, then fell silent rather than tell a lie, for he had been moved to intervene, or at least protest, but now he just watched as the man-at-arms slashed at the precious fabric, ripping the golden threads away from the scarlet, tearing the bodice down to the countess's waist and finally pulling the embroidered merlin free and throwing it at the feet of his master. The countess, released from the second man's grip, crouched and clutched the remnants of the dress to her breasts.

'Villon!' the count commanded. 'Look at me!'

The man held by *le Bâtard*'s two soldiers reluctantly looked up at his enemy. He was a young man, handsome as a hawk, and, till an hour before, he had been ruler of this place, lord of its lands and owner of its peasants, but now he was nothing. He was in mail, with a breastplate and leg plates, and a smear of blood in his dark hair showed that he had fought the besiegers, but now he was in their grasp and he was forced to watch as the fat count fumbled to drag up the skirt of his chain mail. No one in the hall moved or spoke, they just watched as the count wrenched leather and steel aside and then, with a smile on his face, pissed on the merlin torn from his wife's dress. He had the bladder of an ox and the urine splashed for a long time. Somewhere in the castle a man screamed and the scream went on and on, until at last, blessedly, it stopped.

The count finished at the same time, then held out a hand to his squire, who gave him a small knife with a wickedly curved blade. 'See this, Villon?' The count held the knife up so its blade caught the light. 'Know what it is?'

Villon, held by the two men-at-arms, said nothing.

'It's for you,' the count said. 'She,' he pointed the knife at his wife, 'will go back to Labrouillade, and so will you, but only after we've cut you.'

The men in green and white livery grinned, anticipating the pain and pleasure to come. The knife, its blade rusted and its handle a worn sliver of wood, was a castrator's knife, used to geld rams or calves or the small boys destined for the choirs of great churches. 'Strip him,' the count ordered his men.

'Oh, God,' Brother Michael murmured.

'No stomach for it, brother?' Sam asked.

'He fought well,' a new voice intervened, and the monk saw that *le Bâtard* had stepped to the edge of the dais. 'He fought bravely and he deserves to die like a man.'

Some of the count's men put their hands on their sword hilts, but the bishop waved them down. 'He has offended the laws of man and God,' the bishop told *le Bâtard*, 'and placed himself beyond the boundaries of chivalry.'

'The quarrel is mine,' the count snarled at *le Bâtard*, 'not yours.'

'He is my prisoner,' *le Bâtard* said.

'When we hired you,' the bishop said, 'it was agreed that all prisoners would belong to the count and myself, regardless of who captured them. Do you deny that?'

Le Bâtard hesitated, but it was clear the bishop had spoken the truth. The tall, black-armoured man glanced about the room, but his men were far outnumbered by the forces of the bishop and count. 'Then I appeal to you,' he said to the bishop, 'to let him go to his God like a man.'

'He is a fornicator and sinner,' the bishop said, 'and so I give him to the count to do with as he wishes. And I would remind you that your fee is contingent on obeying all our reasonable commands.'

'This is not reasonable,' *le Bâtard* insisted.

'The command for you to step aside is reasonable,' the bishop said, 'and I give it to you.'

The count's men-at-arms thumped their shields on the floor to show their agreement, and *le Bâtard*, knowing himself outnumbered and out-argued, shrugged and stepped away. Brother Michael saw a man-at-arms take the castrating knife and, unable to bear what was about to happen, he pushed his way out to the steps of the tower where he breathed the smoky night air. He wanted to get farther away, but some of the count's men had found an ox in the castle's stable and were torturing the beast, prodding it with spears and swords, skipping away when it lumbered around to face them, and he did not dare try to thread his way through the vicious game. Then the screaming began in the hall behind.

A hand touched his shoulder and he turned, raising the heavy staff, only to see it was a priest, an older man, who offered the monk a skin of wine. 'It seems,' the older man said, 'that you do not approve of what the count does?'

'You do?'

The priest shrugged. 'Villon took the count's wife, so what does he expect? And our church gave its blessing to the count's revenge, and with reason. Villon is a despicable man.'

'And the count is not?' Brother Michael decided he hated the fat count, with his greasy hair and heavy jowls.

'I am his chaplain and confessor,' the older priest said, 'so I know what he is.' He sounded bleak. 'And you,' he asked the monk, 'what brings you to this place?'

'I bring a message for *le Bâtard*,' Brother Michael said.

'What message?'

The English monk shook his head. 'I've not read it.'

'You should always read messages,' the older man said with a smile.

'It's sealed.'

'A hot knife will solve that.'

Brother Michael frowned. 'I was told not to read it.'

'By whom?'

'By the Earl of Northampton. He said it was urgent and private.'

'Urgent?'

Brother Michael crossed himself. 'It's said that the Prince of Wales is gathering another army. I think *le Bâtard* is ordered to join it.' He shrugged. 'That would make sense, anyway.'

'It would.'

The conversation had distracted Brother Michael from the terrible screams that sounded inside the hall. Those screams slowly subsided, became a pathetic whimpering, and only then did the count's chaplain lead the monk back to the flamelight in the pillared chamber. Brother Michael did not look at the naked thing on the bloody floor. He stayed at the back of the hall, hidden from the gelded man by the crowd of mailed soldiers.

'We are done,' the Count of Labrouillade said to *le Bâtard*.

'We are done, my lord,' *le Bâtard* agreed, 'except you owe us the money for capturing this place swiftly.'

'I owe you the money,' the count agreed, 'and it waits for you at Paville.'

'Then we shall go to Paville, my lord.' *Le Bâtard* offered the count a bow, then clapped his hands to get his men's attention. 'You know what to do! Do it!'

Le Bâtard's men had to collect their own wounded, pick up their dead, and retrieve the arrows shot in the fight, because English arrows were hard to find in Burgundy, Toulouse and Provence. It was dawn before *le Bâtard*'s men filed out of the city's ravaged gate, crossed the bridge in the valley and turned eastwards. The wounded were carried in carts, but every other man rode, and Brother Michael, who had snatched a few hours' sleep, could at last count *le Bâtard*'s company. He had learned that some of the Hellequin were still guarding the castle at Castillon that was their refuge, but *le Bâtard* still led a formidable force. There were just over sixty archers, all of them English or Welsh, and thirty-two men-at-arms, mostly from Gascony, but some from the Italian states, a handful from Burgundy, a dozen from England, and some from further away, all of them adventurers who sought money and had found it with *le Bâtard*. With their servants and squires, they formed a war band that could be hired by any lord who had the resources to afford the best, though any lord who wished to fight against the English or their Gascon allies had to look elsewhere because *le Bâtard* would not help. He liked to say that he helped England's enemies kill one another, and those enemies paid him for that help. They were mercenaries and they called themselves the Hellequin, the devil's beloved, and they boasted that they could not be defeated because their souls had already been sent to hell.

And Brother Michael, after witnessing his first fight, believed them.

COMING SOON

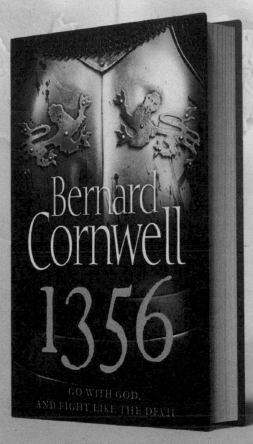

Bernard Cornwell

1356

GO WITH GOD,
AND FIGHT LIKE THE DEVIL

⊙ ebook • audio

'THE BEST BATTLE SCENES OF ANY
WRITER I'VE EVER READ, PAST
OR PRESENT. CORNWELL REALLY
MAKES HISTORY COME ALIVE'

GEORGE R.R. MARTIN

Keep up to date with the latest news on
Bernard Cornwell at his official website

bernardcornwell.net

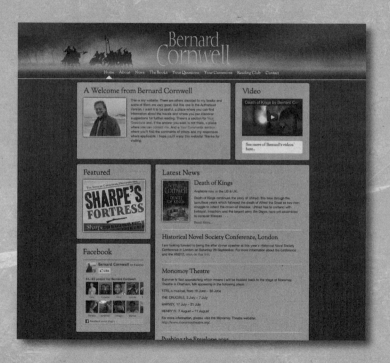

or follow him on Facebook at

facebook.com/bernard.cornwell